ILL WILL

Acclaim for J.M. Redmann's Micky Knight Series

Water Mark

Foreword Magazine Gold Medal Winner

Golden Crown Literary Award Winner

"*Water Mark* is a rich, deep novel filled with humor and pathos. Its exciting plot keeps the pages flying, while it shows that long after a front page story has ceased to exist, even in the back sections of the newspaper, it remains very real to those whose lives it touched. This is another great read from a fine author."—*Just About Write*

Death of a Dying Man

Lambda Literary Award Winner

"Like other books in the series, Redmann's pacing is sharp, her sense of place acute and her characters well crafted. The story has a definite edge, raising some discomfiting questions about the selfishly unsavory way some gay men and lesbians live their lives and what the consequences of that behavior can be. Redmann isn't all edge, however—she's got plenty of sass. Knight is funny, her relationship with Cordelia is believably long-term-lover sexy and little details of both the characters' lives and New Orleans give the atmosphere heft." —*Lambda Book Report*

"As the investigation continues and Mickey's personal dramas rage, a big storm is brewing. Redmann, whose day job is with NOAIDS, gets the Hurricane Katrina evacuation just right—at times she brought tears to my eyes. An unsettled Mickey searches for friends and does her work as she constantly grieves for her beloved city." —*New Orleans Times-Picayune*

The Intersection of Law and Desire

Lambda Literary Award Winner

San Francisco Chronicle Editor's Choice for the year

Profiled on *Fresh Air*, hosted by Terry Gross, and selected for book reviewer Maureen Corrigan's recommended holiday book list.

By the Author

The Micky Knight Mystery Series:

Death by the Riverside

Deaths of Jocasta

The Intersection of Law and Desire

Lost Daughters

Death of a Dying Man

Water Mark

Ill Will

Women of the Mean Streets: Lesbian Noir
edited with Greg Herren

Visit us at www.boldstrokesbooks.com

ILL WILL

by

J.M. Redmann

2012

ILL WILL

ISBN 13: 978-1-60282-657-1

This Trade Paperback Original Is Published By
Bold Strokes Books, Inc.
P.O. Box 249
Valley Falls, NY 12185

First Edition: April 2012

CREDITS
Editors: Greg Herren and Stacia Seaman
Production Design: Stacia Seaman
Cover Design by Sheri (graphicartist2020@hotmail.com)

Acknowledgments

A book is written alone. But the encouragement, the information, the knowledge, the editing, and the myriad of other background activities require other people before any author can sit alone in a room and write a book. This was an especially difficult book to write as I found that I didn't know—let's be honest, didn't have a clue—about certain elements of this book and had to consult various people more knowledgeable than I am, most particularly on the medical aspects of the book. My friends and consultants are competent and educated professionals; any mistakes are mine and mine alone. I'd like to thank Linda and Mary Ellen for setting me on the right path (and sushi), Jody for making connections, and Georgia for patiently answering what must have seemed like bizarre questions. Also the CDC and NIH websites for useful information. Plus various staff members at NO/AIDS who also assisted.

A big thank you to Greg Herren for his editorial insight and calmness in the midst of my rewrite storm. Also a big thanks to Cherry, my Web goddess, for keeping me in the digital age and her partner, Beth, for the delightful dinners. Charbroiled oysters are a thing of wonder and beauty. Of course I can't forget Mr. Squeaky, because if there ever was a cat smart enough to read and notice he was left out, it's him. Arnold, his furry companion, also deserves a mention just to not leave him out, although he has yet to figure out where the treats are kept—reading is way beyond him. Needless to say, I need to thank my partner, Gillian, who is the one who puts up with me disappearing all day at the day job and then taking up the evenings with writing (and rewriting and editing and promoting and everything else that goes with a writing career).

There are many people at my day job who keep me sane and are greatly encouraging and understanding about the writing career. Noel, our CEO and my boss, for his tireless leadership and letting me run off to do book things. My staff are great and make my job easy enough that I have time to write—Josh, Mark, Narquis, Robin, Melanie, Lauren, and all the members of the Prevention Department. I would love to be able to write full-time, but since I have to have a real job, I've very lucky to have one of the best ones I possibly could have.

Also big thanks to Rad for making Bold Strokes what it is. Ruth, Connie, Shelley, Sandy, Stacia, and Cindy for all their hard work behind the scenes, and everyone at BSB for being such a great and supportive publishing house.

CHAPTER ONE

He slammed the plastic container onto my desk. "Murder, I tell you, death in a chewable pill."

It was the end of the day—a long day. I still had to make the lengthy trek Uptown to buy groceries. I knew Cordelia wasn't going to do it. No matter how long my days were, hers always seemed to be longer.

"What are you going to do about it?" he demanded.

I was about to ask him a very similar question—"What do you expect me to do about it?"—with great effort to keep the extreme annoyance out of my voice.

Mr. Charles Williams had called about an hour ago, told me he had to see me today, that it was urgent. I told him if he was here by 5:00 p.m. I would see him. He showed up just after 5:20 as I was packing to leave. He was a tall, heavyset man, with a scraggly beard as if he didn't have time to shave. Or else he wanted the chin hair to counterbalance the hair that had receded to almost the exact top of his head. Or to hide the jowls that gave him a hound-dog look. There were muscles under the flab. I suspected Mr. Williams was used to intimidating people with his size and brawn. The onset of middle age and accumulation of too many pieces of fried chicken made that hard to do, and now he had to match his volume to his paunch.

My day had started at 7:00 this morning, with a drive to and back from Lafayette. Yesterday I had not gotten in until 10:00 after an evening of fruitless surveillance. Right after Katrina, I'd thought, what the hell does a destroyed city like New Orleans need a private investigator for? I learned quickly that chaos brings a need for order. My cases ranged from tracking down missing people—one to a grave in Iowa, another to a new life with a different name in Las Vegas, and the rest to just about every physical and psychic location in between—to insurance fraud, both on the part of people whose only visit to the area was to file a claim and insurance companies doing all they could to avoid paying after gobbling up premiums for decades.

Mr. Williams hadn't said what he wanted, just that it was urgent. Just not urgent enough for him to actually be on time for our appointment, I noted.

Someday I'll learn, I thought, as he stared at me. People who won't divulge what they want on the phone are hiding something. Some are paranoid, unwilling to use a thing that can be tapped or traced—in itself not a good sign. But most of them know they're likely to be turned down over the phone and are hoping once they become a real live person in my office I'll see it their way.

This rarely happens.

It wasn't happening today.

"I think the FDA handles cases like that," I finally said.

"You tell me where the fuckin' FDA office is. I couldn't find it before Katrina—"

I resisted the urge to stand up as he loomed over the desk. I knew the tricks and didn't intend to fall for his amateur versions.

"Mr. Williams, I understand that you're upset, but this isn't the kind of case I can help you with—"

"You don't get it!" he thundered, rattling the pill bottle under my nose. "People are dying. This stuff is poison they sell as nectar. No doctors, no hospitals, people are desperate. Some medical pirate promises a cure and they buy it. But the cancer doesn't get cured, AIDS doesn't go away. People are dying and something has to be done!"

As discreetly as I could, I glanced at my watch. Six o'clock was gone and would not return. I had a life to live and I couldn't solve Mr. Williams's problem. He'd given me the last speech two previous times, as if repetition would get me to change my answer.

He finally took a breath and I jumped in. "My standard rate is a hundred dollars an hour. If you want me to look into this, we can sign a contract, you pay an advance, and I'll see what I can do." At least that was the rate I quoted to people I wanted to get rid of.

"A hundred an hour?! I can't afford that!"

I was tired of this man and his exclamation point sentences. "I'm a private investigator, not a public service."

"You want to make money off people dying?" he demanded.

It's much harder to bully people over the phone—that was why he insisted on coming in person.

"I'm a private investigator, not a charity," I repeated. In an attempt to end this, I suggested, "You can do this on your own, you don't need to pay anyone. You can do most of the research on the Internet. Wait outside the office, talk to the people that go in and out and—"

"I don't have time for that. I work full-time and I'm rebuilding two houses."

"You want someone to do it for free, it's going to have to be you." I stood up. "I cannot do anything for you. This is not the kind of case I handle. You need to get someone with authority to solve this. I am not that person." I snapped off my computer without even bothering to shut it down. We've had so many unexpected power outages here, one more wouldn't make a difference. "You need to leave." He started to say something and I pulled out an exclamation point of my own. "Now!"

He reluctantly turned to go, moving as slowly as he could to be defiant. At my door he turned and said, "If my nephew dies, it'll be on your hands because you refused to help me!"

I had been on the verge of losing my temper for the last half hour; the struggle ended. "If your nephew dies, it'll be your fault because you made one feeble attempt to dump the problem on someone else rather than bothering to…"

He was already down the stairs, finally moving quickly to ensure that whatever I said he wouldn't hear.

What a fucking day, I thought as I threw my stuff into my briefcase. I'd been out in Lafayette to give a grieving presumed widow the not-so-cheery news that her husband was alive and well—and had changed his name, acquired a new Social Security number, and was living with a new wife in Vegas. I understood her throwing the lamp was more at him than me, but it still required the kind of fancy evasive footwork I try very hard to avoid. Even more annoying, she was having far too great an emotional storm for me to discuss my bill. People surprised me; sometimes the bad news ones paid promptly and the ones I gave good news to were chiselers. However, given that Ms. Left-for-Vegas now had neither a husband to support her nor his death insurance money, this one wasn't looking promising.

I gave Mr. Williams enough time to be well away from my doorstep before heading out.

As I locked the outer lock I heard footsteps coming up the stairs. I was alone in the building at this hour. The only possible other tenant was the space-cadet artist on the first floor, but he could barely find his way out the door; dialing 911 would take two days of detox.

Violence, like ducking thrown objects, is something I try very, very hard to shun. Mostly I succeed. But today didn't seem like it wanted to cooperate.

"Fuck," I muttered, dropping my briefcase and pulling out my gun. Cordelia hates that I carry one. But post-Katrina New Orleans has aspects of the Wild West to it. Construction work has brought in an influx of men with a deficit of women to keep them in line. Plus, the crooks had come back. They couldn't get a FEMA loan to cover the cost of lost cocaine; the dealers who had sold it to them weren't happy about not getting paid, and with fewer people in the city there were fewer addicts to sell to. Turf wars had sprung up. Plus, the criminals were as messed up about losing their homes as the rest of us, and a punk with a gun and post-traumatic stress syndrome is not a pleasant person to deal with.

I was hoping it was Mr. Charles Williams coming back for one last speech and the sight of me in a don't-fuck-with-me stance and the black barrel of a pistol pointed down the stairs would cause him to rethink.

I eased the safety off as the footsteps rounded the landing below me.

My stair climber was not a criminal, but a police officer.

One not very happy police officer. "Put that down right now," she told me.

I did. It is so impolite to point guns at friends. Especially friends who are cops and can point a gun back at you. My stair climber was Joanne Ranson, NOPD.

Something told me this was not a "hey, let's go out for beer" type visit.

I didn't even ask. I turned around and unlocked my office door. I muttered, "I meant to be gone an hour ago."

"Just my luck that you're not."

I noticed she didn't call it good luck.

"What do you know about Carl Prejean?" she asked as she followed me in.

"Who?" I said, sitting at my desk.

Joanne ignored the visitor's chair and perched on the near corner, forcing me to look up at her. I was getting a stiff neck from all these looming people.

"Like why would someone torch his house and car and why would he claim you sent them?"

"What?" I almost asked how and why, just to get all the interrogatives out of the way.

"He had your card, said you had hunted him down and threatened him."

Now it was coming back to me. "Wait, that's not quite what happened."

"So, tell me what did happen." She crossed her arms. This was official police business.

"Carl Prejean aka Karl Pearlman aka Cal Parker aka who knows who else, claims to be a contractor. A group of homeowners hired me to track him down after he absconded with their money."

"You know that for sure?"

"I'm not an amateur. They showed me cashed checks. I toured the properties. His only work on any of them was to show up, fake an estimate—I saw those, too—then disappear with the money. They wanted to find him to sue him."

"Well, one hothead decided not to wait for our courts to get back in gear. I'll need your client list."

I crossed my arms. "Not without more proof that one of them had something to do with it. He's a scumbag, and scumbags treat everyone to their pond slime. It could be an ex-girlfriend who didn't like him not paying child support, or workers he didn't pay, or other clients he ripped off."

"Except that you tracked him down and told them where he lived."

"I didn't suggest that they burn down his place, nor would I have given them the information if I thought they would do anything like this." I get pompous when I get defensive.

"I'm not accusing you. But your group knew which house to burn. I have no proof those other people exist or that they knew how to find him."

"Joanne, these are all honest, law-abiding people. The oldest was an eighty-two-year-old woman. He ripped her off for forty thousand dollars. She can't afford to rebuild now and she's going to probably have to spend the rest of her life in a rental apartment in Houston because of this crook. I'm not giving you their names without a subpoena."

"You think he deserved it?"

"You think he didn't?"

We stared at each other for a moment. I continued, "I told him the homeowners wanted either the repairs or their money back, with a strong preference on the latter. He blew me off, told me they could go fuck themselves and the next time I came near him, he'd greet me with a shotgun. He chose to rip them off, to make money off desperate people. He should go to jail and be sued for every penny he owns."

"But he wasn't. He had his house burned down instead."

"So now he has what he left them with—a ruined house. At least he'll get his insurance money and not have it stolen by a fake contractor."

We again stared at each other.

"I'm not giving you their names."

She sighed, and said, "I know." Then added, just because she's a cop, "You didn't do it for them, did you?"

"No, I didn't. Although I don't think I would've pissed on him to put the fire out. Plus every one of their homes was stripped of anything valuable—copper wire, upstairs carpet, toilets. After they signed contracts with him."

"Hard to prove. Those thieves are everywhere."

"He's not the innocent victim in all this. It wouldn't be bad if he decided to relocate."

She sighed again. "You need to watch your back. He said if he ever saw that girl private eye, she'd regret it."

"I don't plan on seeing him again."

"He might have other ideas. He knows where your office is. Watch your back."

"Why I carry a gun. I'm tired, I want to go home. Do I get a police escort to my car?"

"If you escort me to mine." She slid off the desk, indicating this interview was over. She'd done her job. We all made those calculations—how much time, how much effort, and finally, was it worth it. She knew I had a point, if he'd ripped off my ten clients it was likely that he'd cheated multiple others. If I could find him—and it hadn't been that hard, he wasn't as clever as he thought he was—others could as well. Would my list of clients bring her closer to the person whose breaking point was breaking the law? Or would it just subject innocent people to an undeserved hell on top of the hell they already lived in?

"You probably don't want to do this," she said as she waited for me to lock the door, "but you might try to get your clients to come to the police. If there is evidence that he stole from them, he should pay for it."

"I'll talk to them," I said following her down the stairs. In our silence we understood each other. Talking to them meant a call that could go unanswered for days because they were working on destroyed houses where there was no cell service. Or driving out to that desolate area hoping to find them there. The case should have been closed. I'd done what they asked. They'd paid me—not much, far less than it should have cost, but I couldn't add to their money woes. This was a half a day, a day, of extra time and work.

"Why the hell do we always have to do the right thing," I muttered as she held the downstairs door for me. It was still daylight, an orange glimmer of sun off to the west. At least the days were getting longer. Sunlight made a difference in a city with so many places without power.

"Because in the end it costs less," she answered.

"You sure about that?"

"How's Cordelia?"

"Busy. There aren't enough doctors in this town."

Joanne let the silence hang. I didn't fill it. Finally she spoke, "Must be hard on you, not seeing her all the time."

"I didn't say that."

"Yeah, you did."

"I'm supposed to be at the grocery store now. She's working near Touro Hospital. Half the city closer to the grocery store than I am. But I'm the only one who has time to go grocery shopping."

"Sucks to have a partner who saves people's lives."

"Especially when the cupboard is bare." I didn't want to talk about this. "How's Alex?"

"Loves the job. Hates the commute."

After Katrina, Alex, Joanne's partner, had been laid off, like many other city workers. No residents means no tax revenue means nothing to pay people with. She'd worked with me for a while. I was beyond busy and she was smart and good with computers. But she didn't want to rebuild a career as a private investigator, so when a job in arts and culture had opened in the lieutenant governor's office, she'd taken it. It just meant driving to Baton Rouge every day, a trip of about ninety miles each way. She'd talked about taking an apartment up there, but there were none to be had in anything resembling her price range. Baton Rouge, as well as the rest of the state, was bloated full with the dispossessed of New Orleans.

I repeated to Joanne, "Must be hard on you, not seeing her all the time."

"Sucks to have a partner who has to bring dance companies to Louisiana." Somehow she packed even more sarcasm into it than I had. With a glance at her watch, she said, "She won't be home for another hour or two. Want to go play pool or something?"

"You're welcome to come with me to the grocery store."

"Went yesterday. I'm way over my quota for long lines and Uptown ladies who don't like the little people shopping in their grocery store."

"I could so use a beer right about now," I said.

"Couldn't we all?" She looked at me. "Sometimes I almost feel like I'm single."

"Sometimes I almost wish I were." Both our statements hung in the air. Then I blurted out, "You were about to arrest me and now you're suggesting adultery?"

"I was not about to arrest you." She turned and walked to her car, which was parked just in front of mine.

I followed her. I had to get to my car, after all.

She turned just as she got to my front fender. "If you forget what I said, I'll forget what you said. It's been almost two years, you'd think we'd stop going crazy by now."

"You saying sex with me is crazy?" I said with a smile, trying to throw some humor on this.

"Come on, you know I'm not saying that. What I am saying— attempting to and doing it badly—is that I want what I can't have—my life before Katrina. A partner who works here in the city, who I can meet for lunch instead of a late dinner. A partner who doesn't just break down and cry for no reason. I got through the flood waters, but I'm not sure I can get through this."

I didn't know what to say. I knew what I wanted to say, to tell her no, she couldn't fall apart, because if my friends couldn't hold it together I wasn't sure I could. It was the so-called little things, the day after day after day, long lines and longer lines, starting to drive some place and realizing it's not there anymore, another person who came back but decided not to stay, all those lost pieces of the life we used to have. Katrina was over; the news cycle had moved on. The flood waters had gone away; what they had left was still here—those of us who couldn't forget because every day in some way, we had to remember.

"So there are dangerous moments when I long for...I don't even know what. Not to be here. Part of the most despised police force in the country. Having to take a report on the crooks who stole a new a/c compressor a block from where we're rebuilding our house. Frozen dinner after frozen dinner because who knows when Alex will get home and I can't be bothered to cook for myself."

"Hey, you get the groceries, I'll cook for you."

"Did I mention the kind, sensitive friends who are always there for you?"

"We are. As long as you don't try to arrest us."

"I wasn't trying to arrest you." She added, "You'd be in handcuffs now if I had been."

She needed something from me I wasn't sure I had to give. I simply said, "Joanne, you'll be okay." I put my arms around her and hugged her.

We held it for a moment. Too long. Then broke away.

"Gotta make groceries," I mumbled.

"Yeah. I hear a microwave calling my name." She took a step away, then said, "I mean it. Forget what I said. I think something and it sounds like an escape, then I say it and realize it's just another trap."

I watched her get in her car, then didn't want to watch her anymore. I knew too well what she meant about dangerous thoughts. For one horrific moment, Katrina had unmoored all of us, thrown us helter-skelter, a terrifying freedom. If we couldn't come back to New Orleans, where could we go? But some of us had fallen to earth here, on the flooded ground. Much as we tried to reclaim our old lives—or build new ones—we weren't sure the ground would hold us. Everything had changed, and maybe it had changed so far and in ways we couldn't even see that we'd never find our way back.

As she pulled away, I took out my cell phone. There would be no grocery run tonight. I was at the point that I'd shoot myself before I'd cross Canal Street today. A small grocery store in the French Quarter had opened, but parking was impossible. I occasionally made forays there on my bike, but it was near dark and I knew myself well enough to know I would not go home and leave again. I called a place on Frenchmen Street and ordered two shrimp po-boys. If Cordelia didn't like it, she could go to the grocery store.

That was part of what we'd lost and were yet to come to terms with. Before Katrina, there were two grocery stores within about ten blocks of our house. It was no problem for me to swing by them, even on busy days. That was our pattern. I'd get the food and do most of the cooking, since my hours were more flexible than hers, and she'd take the major part of the cleanup.

With her clinic destroyed and rebuilding still up in the air, she'd taken work where she could find it. There was a need for doctors, so great it was part of the problem. Cordelia worked longer hours than she had before the storm. So from her point of view, it probably still seemed like I should continue to do what we'd always done. It just wasn't working for me.

She was tired more often—or so she claimed. But her tiredness had stretched since before the holidays, now months past. I'd suggested depression, but she'd blown that off.

Just one more fucking thing to deal with in a fucked-up city. Cold shrimp po-boys wouldn't make anything any better. I started my car and drove away.

CHAPTER TWO

I thought you were going to the grocery store," Cordelia asked as she entered the kitchen and saw me unwrapping po-boys. She had been home long enough to have changed into sweatpants and a T-shirt, opened a beer, and finished a third of it.

"I work downtown. The only open grocery store is way uptown," I said.

"Oh, okay. Are you going to make it tomorrow? We're running low on toilet paper," she said, taking another swig of her beer.

"Do you have some grocery store disability?" I snapped. "Is there a reason I'm the only one to go even though your work is half a city closer than mine is?"

"You're angry," she ever-so-perceptively noticed.

"I'm tired," I said tersely. "I guess you haven't noticed I'm working a lot of hours, sometimes more than you. And that I'm the only one who goes to the grocery store. And that—"

"I've noticed," she cut in.

I got a beer out of the refrigerator and opened it.

"I don't guess you noticed when I took our car out to be serviced," she said.

"That was your car."

"That you were driving more than I was."

"It was two weeks ago," I pointed out.

"I had to drive out there in the morning, get Kathy to pick me up on her way to work and drop me back again in the evening to pick it up and I had blood on my clothes when I went back out there because I didn't have time to change and—"

"I was working that day. And I hate Metairie."

"It's not my favorite place in the world." In a softer tone she added, "I know. That's why I went there." For a moment we were both silent, "Please, Micky, let's not fight." And then very quietly added, as if to herself, "I can't do this if we're fighting."

Oh, no you don't, I started to say. But didn't—even I'm not that much of an asshole. This was her usual way out of the argument, to be too tired, too overwhelmed, too bruised and battered by what she'd been through in Katrina and what she faced afterward. I couldn't call her on it because it was true. But it was true for me as well, just not as ragged and messy. I hadn't been trapped in Charity Hospital for almost a week, waiting for rescue, helpless in the festering heat as patients who should have lived died. I had evacuated, watching my city and every part of my life torn apart on a TV screen. That was what we struggled with—we were all battered and no one was left whole to lean on.

"We need to find a better balance," I finally said. "I can't do everything I did before."

"Let's eat. Someone told me there's a new store up on Carrollton, that it just opened. I'll go after we're done."

"And stick me with the dishes?" That got a wan smile from her. I was trying to be funny. "Let's eat and then we can both go. A new grocery store on this side of Canal Street—even if it is up by City Park—is a good excuse for an outing."

"Thank you." She didn't move for a moment, the beer motionless in one hand, the other hand reaching for the sandwich wrapper, but still. "I'm sorry this is so hard. Please know that I love you."

I put down my beer, cupped her face in my hands. Something had happened today. I needed to find my better angel. "I know that. I'm sorry it's hard, too." I leaned in and gently kissed her. It was soft, a brief touch of comfort and love. Then I let go. "Should I microwave these? They're better hot than cold."

She nodded and I did. We talked as we ate, small talk, the weather, who'd told her about the newly open store—"he said he screamed like a girl when he heard the news"—what to put on the grocery list—talking as if we needed to avoid silence.

She let me drive.

As we waited for the light at Claiborne and Esplanade, she said, "I had an appointment with Jennifer today."

"Jennifer?" I asked, trying to place the name.

"A...specialist."

"Why?" I asked as the light changed and I shifted into first gear.

"Probably nothing. But I've been so tired lately. Plus losing weight."

"Which you've wanted to do."

"I'm not trying. Thought it might be thyroid, but we did those tests and everything came back negative."

I briefly glanced at her. Cordelia has struggled with her weight more than I have. I seem to have one of those obnoxious metabolisms that allows beer and brownies with no bulge. She'd lost weight after her ordeal in Charity and as far as I could tell hadn't regained it. The hollowness in her cheeks was still there. Had she lost more?

"What are you being checked for?" I asked.

"The usual, any swelling or mass."

"Cancer?" The word hung in the air.

"That'd be the worst-case scenario. It's most likely a low-grade infection causing the swollen lymph glands. I'm probably also going to find out that I'm borderline anemic and need to eat more protein."

"What are the possibilities?" I tried to keep my tone neutral. She brought it up because she was worried about it.

"The doctor side of me knows that most of the time it's nothing, a few tests, some anxious moments and that'll be it. We did the needle aspiration of the lymph nodes today. It'll be about a week before we get those results back."

"What about the patient side of you?"

"I'm not used to being the patient." She was silent. Finally she said, "It'll be okay. I'm probably only trying to find a physical reason for my mental malaise. Tell me about your day. Anything interesting?"

I let her avoid the subject. They'd run a few tests, we'd know then. There was no point in worrying about it now.

"It seems that someone is selling Lake Pontchartrain swamp water as the cure-all for everything. And it somehow became my job to solve the case."

"Lake Pontchartrain swamp water? Really?"

"Probably not," I amended. "But one of those 'natural miracle drugs' that the government doesn't want anyone to know about because it's so good. I was supposed to prove that it didn't work, convince the nephew he was throwing money away, all for a nominal fee that I'd waive in the end because this is such a do-gooder case."

"Did you take it?"

"No, of course not. I'm busy enough and have no experience in medical fraud even if he was willing to actually pay me anything. I told him to go to the FDA. If people are stupid enough to fall for swamp water as a cure for cancer, there's not much I can do about it."

"Desperate," she said softly.

"What?" I asked as I stopped for the light at Broad.

"Desperate," she repeated. "Most of them are desperate. Clinging to a fragile hope that the answers they've gotten so far—that there is no cure—aren't the only answers."

For a brief second a haunted look crossed her face, as if she could feel that desperation, then it was gone and the Cordelia I knew returned. I didn't know if she was talking about herself or remembering someone else's desperation.

"So desperate they'd try something insane?" I asked.

But the fear I had glimpsed was gone. Or hidden. The perilous week in Charity Hospital would haunt her to the grave. Maybe some vestige of that would always be hidden behind her eyes. Her answer was calm. "Snake oil salesmen have been with us since there were snakes. Until around a hundred years ago, it was a free-for-all, totally unregulated so-called patent medicines whose main ingredient was either alcohol or opium. We only started regulating these things in 1906." She was comfortable with information; sometimes she hid behind it. "The first law here was introduced then and it only required that ostensible medicines disclose ingredients like alcohol or opium. Quite a number of temperance ladies were distressed to discover that Mrs. Pinkham's potion was more alcoholic than their husband's gin."

I interrupted the lecture. "But that was then. Now we have better regulations, right?"

"Better regulations, yes, but also a much more complicated medical system. Drugs approved by the FDA have to go through a series of clinical trials to prove that they're safe—at least safer than the disease they're treating, all drugs have side effects—and actually work better than a placebo. If it says it reduces high blood pressure, then it has to reduce high blood pressure. But there is a whole unregulated side, the nutritional supplements."

"They don't have to work?"

"They can't claim to treat disease, they can't say 'reduces blood pressure,' but they can be vague and say things like 'promotes heart health.' They're considered safe until proven otherwise."

"So people can still sell snake oil?" I asked, making the left at City Park to get onto Carrolton.

"Essentially. They can't claim on the labeling that it cures cancer or HIV. The latest trick is to have one website extolling the virtues of snake oil with a link to another website that makes no health claims but actually sells the stuff."

"Is that legal?"

"Freedom of speech."

"So you can claim Lake Pontchartrain water cures every disease known to man—and woman, and I can sell it and it's all legal?"

"Pretty much."

"What if it kills someone?"

"If it's harmful, it can be pulled from the market."

"Cold comfort if you're already dead."

"Very cold. It took years for ephedra to be banned despite mounting evidence that it killed people. The deaths of several prominent athletes were required to get Congress to outlaw it. The supplement makers took it all the way to the Supreme Court to get the FDA ban overruled."

"They lost?"

"Yes, but they have a powerful lobby—the money to buy influence."

"So is all that stuff crap?"

"No, some of it is clearly worthless, some actually helpful, and most is in the don't-know category. It's expensive to do research, and there is no incentive to spend money when you're already making money without spending it."

The welcoming glow of lights appeared ahead of us. A grocery store had indeed opened below Canal Street. That burst of normality cheered me considerably. It still wasn't close to our house; before Katrina this had been the far grocery store, one I went to if I had something to do up here. Now it was the near one.

"It's true; they did reopen," Cordelia said. She reached over and took my hand. "I hate going to the grocery store because I always forget something and you get upset."

Peeved perhaps, I started to argue, but not really upset. But I have gotten old and wise enough to know that sometimes right and wrong isn't the issue. I kept my mouth shut.

She continued, "There are things that I just don't think about—like garlic—and if it's not on the list, I overlook it."

She had a point. Things like garlic, onions, and lemon are staples; they're always on the list, even if they aren't written down. But just because I know that in my head doesn't mean she does.

"Okay, how about I make the list and if it's not on the list, it's on me." I turned into the parking lot. Either not many people knew this store had opened, or it was late enough that it wasn't very crowded.

"Okay, fair enough," she said. "Thank you."

We went and made groceries, as they say down here.

CHAPTER THREE

As I was drinking my coffee after having just arrived at my office, I remembered how nice it was to have someone to share the daily chores with. In our grocery run last night we had flirted over the avocados. I'd found out that Cordelia liked a variety of apples, not just Red Delicious. We splurged on a really nice piece of salmon and a decent bottle of wine. If it had just been me, I would have gotten the usual apples, passed by the salmon and wine. And been prosaic over the avocados.

We held hands on the way home.

More importantly, we agreed that we had to find more ways to do this, to capture the small moments and be together. We had gotten too practical, dividing things so we ended up doing them alone to save time. But how you spend time can be more important than saving time.

The avocado flirting had led us to the bedroom and we'd made love, slowly, gently, not a hard passion, instead a tender connection.

"You devil, you," I said aloud to my coffee cup. "You're always in a better mood after sex." *Good sex*, I amended in my head.

I needed that good mood to get me through the morning. As Joanne had requested, I tried calling my former clients who had been scammed by Carl Prejean. As I had expected, I wasn't able to reach half of them and the other half were skeptical of reporting it to the police.

"Now, why would I want to waste my time going down there, waiting for someone to see me, waiting for someone to take a report, waiting to fill out some paperwork to be told that they'll get to it when they can. That's a day's worth of time, and I don't have any days to spare," was the typical response.

I mentioned his burned house to several of them just to see what their reaction would be. The only person who said, "Well, damn, wish the match had been in my hand," was eighty-two-year-old Dolores Murphy in Houston. If her spirit was guilty, her flesh certainly wasn't. The rest muttered appropriate responses along the lines of "Good karma to bad people," but there was no one who struck me as hiding something or guilty.

By lunchtime I'd done my duty. I could report to Joanne that I'd done—mostly, I wasn't going to call again those I hadn't reached—as she had asked and no one had confessed to arson.

As I was rooting in the small refrigerator for my sandwich, I was interrupted by a brief knock on the door. It opened to reveal my cousin Torbin.

"A sandwich? A mere sandwich?" he said, looking at the two slices of bread in my hand.

"Smoked turkey with sliced avocado," I defended. Torbin could be a food snob.

"Only if you made your own mayonnaise." He knew I hadn't. He knew I preferred mustard to mayo. Too much knowledge is a dangerous thing in a cousin like Torbin.

I put the sandwich back in the refrigerator, admitting defeat. "You treating?"

"You can't afford a burger and onion rings?"

"I take it treat is off the table."

"It is so totally a comfort food day. Look at the gray skies outside. We're not talking McBurger Thing. Bywater Bar-B-Que. Onion rings, pulled pork, big juicy burgers."

He was right, there were a few clouds in the sky; it might rain this week. I ignored the rational voice that reminded me that just about every week in New Orleans brought rain and let Torbin drag me out of my office and off to a comfort food lunch. The sandwich would keep until tomorrow. I could even sleep in five minutes later in the morning rather than slathering mustard on bread.

He waited until we were ensconced at our table and had ordered our food before getting down to his real reason for this lunch. He understood me well enough to know once the food was ordered, I'd have to stay.

"I need a favor. A big favor," he said.

"So you are treating?"

"Well," he said with a sigh, "I'm not bankrupt yet."

I caught the serious undertone to his voice. "What's going on?"

"I love Andy dearly, but he does computers well, not slicing and dicing. Last night he lost focus for a moment and opened what I'm sure is an artery on his thumb."

"Ouch." I didn't correct Tobin about the location of arteries. When it's your kitchen absorbing the blood, you get to engage in hyperbole.

"Yeah, ouch. We took a trip to the ER and used every old T-shirt we had to sop up the blood on the way there. It turns out neither Andy nor I do especially well at the sight of blood."

"Had to channel your inner lesbian?"

"Inner and outer. Our actual outer lesbians were not answering their phone."

He was referring to me, well, me and Cordelia, since I think he was more interested in her expertise in the situation. "Ah, sorry. We were otherwise occupied." I had turned the phone down for important bedroom activities.

"Still? Aren't you two well into the lesbian bed death era? The funeral should be a distant memory by now."

"Still. Lesbian bed death is a vicious rumor started by straight men who can't stand the competition." I took a sip of my iced tea. "However, we have slowed down a bit, only a couple of times a week now instead of every day."

"No wonder you don't have time to answer phone calls from desperate friends," he grumbled.

"How's Andy?" It was time to get away from my sex life and onto the reason for this lunch.

"It was not a fun experience. I was sure he was going to bleed to death before he was seen. His folly with a kitchen knife was regrettable, as it seemed every drug dealer in the city chose last night to get into a gun battle. Shotgun wounds trumped paring knives."

"Damn, you picked the wrong emergency room."

The serious look on Torbin's face was one I rarely saw. One of the reasons I loved my cousin was his ability to find the humor in just about everything. "We didn't have much choice," he said softly.

"Andy doesn't have insurance," I said.

He nodded.

Our appetizers were served. A heaping plate of onion rings seemed the only comfort available.

He took a bite out of one, chewed, swallowed, then said, "That's the favor I need to ask for. Andy's okay, but the cut looked kind of red and swollen this morning and he's in pain. Do you think Cordelia would be willing to take a look at it? We tried a regular doctor, but the earliest available appointment is sometime next week. And I think Andy would cut off his hand before going back to the ER."

Cordelia—and I—didn't want to be the local on-call doctor, so we had tried to discourage friends from cadging medical help from her. When she had her own clinic she was pretty good about working people in, but that clinic had been washed away in the floods and there didn't seem to be enough returned people to justify the cost—financial and emotional—of rebuilding it. Now that she was just a "doc for hire," she had far less leeway in who she saw. Torbin knew he was asking a big favor.

"Let me call her," I said. "Don't eat all the onion rings."

I walked outside before dialing. Just to be safe, I didn't want Torbin overhearing our conversation. Not because he would hear her saying no, but to avoid him hearing me tell her she could say no.

Luck—of some sort—was with me, as she answered the phone. When she's working it can be hard for her to take a call. I quickly explained the situation. "You don't have to do this. I know how tired you are and—"

She cut me off. "It's okay. Tell them it'll have to be after I'm home this evening. If they can wait until then. Tell Torbin if it gets worse, if Andy has a fever or something, then he needs to go to the ER."

"Andy doesn't have insurance."

"Damn," she swore softly. "He still needs to go. It's probably cheaper and easier than having his arm cut off. And I'll give him the lecture tonight about taking this as a wake-up call. He can get away with a knife wound; it'll heal. If it's cancer or a car accident, no insurance might kill him." Then she had to go.

Torbin had been good about the onion rings. No more than one had disappeared in the time I'd been gone.

"Come by the house tonight. If he has fever or things get worse, drag him back to the ER. You want your boyfriend to be hard, not stiff."

Torbin smiled his relief. And ate another onion ring.

Our main dish arrived, a burger for me and ribs for him. Major comfort food.

"What about you?" I asked. "What happens if you get hit by a Mack truck?"

He put down the rib he had been eating. "We used to be good. Before Katrina, Andy worked enough time with a computer company to have benefits and we eked out enough to cover an individual policy for me. But that company went underwater—literally, of course, so Andy lost his job and the insurance. He does okay for work freelance, but that doesn't have benefits.

"You know how the mail is, even now. My renewal notice came back when everything was delayed weeks and weeks, and we had to go Uptown to the post office to get it. I'd gotten nothing from two trips, so didn't get back, and when I finally did there was a big stack of mail for me to go through and I didn't want to go through it, so left it sitting for another week..."

"They didn't give you any leeway for being in New Orleans?"

"Maybe if I'd written enough letters and begged hard enough. But at that time Andy wasn't making much, I wasn't making much, and it felt like something we could hold off for a little while until things got better."

"It's been two years, haven't things got better?" I wanted to tell him, *You can't live so close to the edge because I can't bear to see you fall.*

He ate another rib before replying. "I reapplied a couple of months ago and they turned me down."

"Why?"

"They didn't really say, basically being a gay man in New Orleans. They probably assume that if I'm not HIV infected, I soon will be."

"Oh, Torbin, honey, I'm sorry."

"Yeah, me, too. So I applied for a big-boy job."

"Doing what?" Torbin had previously survived by being the best drag queen on the block and always being in demand for shows.

"That place on Frenchmen Street, an office of NO/AIDS? They need someone who knows the gay community to do outreach and testing."

"But you don't know anything about public health." I put half my burger on his place and grabbed a couple of ribs.

"But I do know the gay community and I'm used to working odd hours and I know just about everything there is to know about sex. Well, gay sex. Don't ask me how to do it during her period."

"Dildos, no. Tampons, *sí*."

"Please, I don't need that image while eating barbeque sauce."

I grabbed another rib to save him from menstrual barbeque sauce. "I'll leave you the rest of the onion rings."

I let him have the rest of the mac and cheese as well. I even treated him. A trip to the ER doesn't come cheap. He didn't argue, which told me he was worried. I rarely ever saw my buoyant cousin show strain.

We're getting older, I thought as I waved him away after he dropped me back at my office. We were both beyond forty—that seemed so impossibly old back when we were in our twenties and all the years stretched before us—the gray in our hair no longer an anomaly. It was sobering to think of Torbin in a regular job—well, as regular as handing out condoms in a bar could be.

I had insurance, but I paid a high—and increasingly higher—price for it. While I occasionally hire people to help out, especially when I'm doing surveillance, I'm essentially a solo operation. I do what most solo practitioners do, join professional associations and use their buying power to get group rates. It wasn't something I thought about much, other than every year to pay my dues, pay for the insurance, liability, health, shove the policy in a file, and hope that I never needed to use it. So far I've been pretty lucky. And my luck has been helped enormously by having a live-in doctor in the house. Being able to whine, "Honey, I think I'm getting a cold," and get actual doctor advice instead of tea and sympathy, has saved me from the usual run-of-the-mill medical visits.

I can still make it up three flights of stairs, I thought, as I climbed them, not too out of breath. Just one gasp and I was good to go. Okay, two.

I opened my door to the ringing of the phone. It was a little unnerving, as if someone was aware of me walking in the door.

"Knight Detective Agency," I answered, reminding myself I'd already had my one wheeze.

"You fucking bitch." My caller was not a happy person.

"I'm sorry, you have the wrong number; there are only celibate bitches here." I started to hang up the phone.

"I'm going to get you, Knight," was the kind of phrase that caught my attention, so I kept the phone close enough to my ear that I could hear, and far enough away that his voice was reduced to tiny insignificance. It made the threat easier to take.

"Who is this?" I asked, not exactly expecting a reply.

"The guy whose house you burned down, bitch!"

"I didn't burn anyone's house down."

"Lying bitch!" His vocabulary was limited; "bitch" seemed to be the only epithet he could come up with.

"I don't break the law, unlike lying contractors who cheat—"

"You shut the fuck up. I'm going to do to you what you did to me, you get that?"

"Good. As I've done nothing to you, you'll do nothing to me," I said in as obnoxiously cheery tone as I could muster.

"You burned my house and my car." My good cheer was not infectious.

"No, I didn't." Why am I arguing with this idiot? It was highly unlikely an appeal to reason would work here.

"Someone did. You led them there." Ah, some wavering.

"No, I didn't. It's illegal to burn houses or encourage people to do so."

"Then who the fuck burned my house down, bitch?"

"I the fuck don't know, bitch. But I do the fuck know that making threats is illegal, and when people break the law, I call the police. Got it, bitch?"

"I'm not a bitch," he said, and beat me hanging up by a millisecond.

Was he outside lighting a match right now? I hurried to the window but couldn't get a good view of the street. I had to run down half a flight of stairs to get to a window that gave me clear sight to the road below. A large black truck was turning the corner, but it was too far away to get a license plate or even the make of the vehicle.

I kept going down the stairs, wondering if I'd encounter flames and gasoline at my door step. Shoving through the security door at the ground floor, I didn't slow, my momentum carrying me halfway across the street.

And into the path of a puzzled bicyclist. I jerked to a halt, barely missing her front tire, forcing her to swerve to avoid rolling over my toes.

No flames, no gas, not even a spent match. Only a partly cloudy day and a bike rider who was muttering vague obscenities as she rounded the next corner.

Had he been watching me? Or was that just some random truck?

A threatening phone call, a big black truck right outside where I work. Was my fear causing me to see more than was here? Gigantic ugly trucks aren't a rare sight. If I stood here for ten minutes, I might see five of them. It didn't mean he was here, about to do something unpleasant. Why waste the gas when you can make a nasty call from the comfort of home?

I tried to picture him in bunny slippers calling me bitch.

The image didn't help. It only made him seem more psychotic and therefore more dangerous.

Okay, now I was panting. *It's not the stairs*, I told myself, *it's the fear that I might have been trapped in a building engulfed in flames*. However, the three flights of stairs back to my office convinced me that it wouldn't be a bad idea to have a look around down here.

The street was quiet, the bicyclist gone. No abandoned gas cans by the side of the road. The only thing flammable was a cigarette butt halfway down the block. Nothing to indicate someone had been watching my office—no tire marks by the side of the road or tossed-out drinks with ice still in them. The cigarette butt was at least a couple of days old and had been rained on. What happened to the good old days when the perps would leave a telltale pile of smoked butts? Had the crooks gotten as healthy as the rest of us?

There was nothing to do but trudge back up the stairs.

But once in my office—and after catching my breath—there were things to do. Like call Joanne.

After I gave her the rundown, she asked, "Are you sure?"

"What do you mean am I sure? Who else would be threatening me like that?"

"I don't know, you have a talent for pissing people off."

"Not many who have recently accused me of arson."

"Yeah, I know," she said quickly. "You met this guy once, talked to him for five minutes at most. A couple of weeks later someone you allege to be him calls you on the phone and threatens you. A bottom-of-the-class defense lawyer could rip that one apart."

"So what am I supposed to do, wait until he actually starts a fire?"

"Look, Micky, I agree, a fire threat does point to him. I can hunt him down and question him about it, but he's going to deny it and then it's your word against his."

"That's all you can do?"

"I'd take your word over his any day, but the legal system has to treat you both equally."

Maddening as it was, Joanne was right. He'd certainly implied that he was going to play with matches at my expense, but what proof did I really have? It was my word against his as to what he said. I didn't know his voice well enough to be certain it was his—it could be a bizarre coincidence, a wrong number and the caller was threatening a total stranger. Even in my weird world, that was stretching it. "Okay, I get you—and understand that sometimes the rule of law lets scum get away with things."

"If he really wanted to get you, he wouldn't have bothered with a phone call."

"Somehow that's not very reassuring."

"He's a con, not a fighter. He probably has to know you didn't set the actual fire, but he's angry and vents that anger with nasty phone calls. My bet is that he doesn't have the guts to start an actual fire."

"How much money are you putting on that bet?" I asked.

"If I lose the bet, you and CJ can hang out on our couch for as long as it takes to repair your place."

"Your couch isn't long enough for Cordelia, and it wouldn't fit both of us at the same time."

"We both hope this is a bet I don't win." She was gallant enough to hang up before I had to name what I'd wager if I lost.

My next less-than-pleasant task was to call and re-call all the clients who'd hired me to track down Mr. Prejean, or whatever his real name was. They needed to know he was an angry slime bag and threatening revenge arson against anyone who might have burned down his house.

"Can I shoot 'im if I see 'im?" was the first response. It was hard, but I put on my law-abiding hat and said that just seeing him wouldn't be sufficient cause for gunplay.

"You didn't give him my name, did you?" was the second one. I had to remind him he had hired Prejean to renovate his house and that usually involves the exchange of names. I tried to reassure him that as Prejean didn't intend to do any work, it was unlikely he kept the paperwork. Unless he was too lazy to throw it out, but I didn't mention that.

"You sure should have burned it down if that's his attitude," was number three. "Did you?" she ever-so-encouragingly asked. I explained that I had not and would not burn down anyone's house, no matter how far afoul of the law he was. I didn't like that she considered it possible I would commit arson.

Especially for the amount they'd paid me.

Number four told me, "You gotta call the police. Right now. Don't waste time with me." I made the mistake of telling him I did call the police and there wasn't much they could do. That got me the diatribe on how bad the New Orleans cops were, they were corrupt, never came when you called, had all been cowards during Katrina. I had to pretend I was losing my cell signal. On my landline.

And so it went. While their responses were different, there seemed an underlying theme: I was the professional, I knew how to deal with these things and so they were glad he'd come after me and not them. I could smell smoke; that was about all my professionalism afforded me.

Those calls took what was left of my afternoon. Those calls, and because I procrastinated as I didn't want to make the calls and it seemed that after every two, I had to check the weather online, which caused me to see a news story that I had to read, by which time I had to go to the bathroom and then make tea or get water depending on whether I was feeling cold or hot, which would ensure that I'd have to go to the bathroom again in time for another much-needed-and-well-deserved break.

Because every call wasn't just a brief "be on the lookout for" but a shared point of loss. This man had taken from them, their homes, their hopes of rebuilding, or at best the stealing of time and money that would take years to recover from. Now he had taken something from me as well. Every one of them told me to be careful and meant it. Even if Joanne was right—and I fervently hoped that she was—I'd have to be extra cautious, take extra time to make sure no vengeful man with a gas can was lurking about. A clear street at one moment didn't mean he couldn't arrive in the next minute or hour, the one time I wasn't watching because it's impossible to watch every second.

At least we have groceries, I thought as I packed to head home. We could make up for the unhealthy shrimp po-boys of last night.

CHAPTER FOUR

When I got home, the house was dark and the cats hungry. I had skimmed out sometime after four, but well before five. I can do that since I work for myself, so it made sense that Cordelia wasn't home yet.

My procrastinating side debated whether to start dinner now or to wait until after Andy and Torbin came and went.

Halos and horns. I started dinner and cracked open a beer to keep me company. There was a time in my life when I had a drinking problem—or what I considered a drinking solution to my problems. Not drinking at all had worked pretty well until I was hit with the double blast of Katrina washing away the New Orleans I'd known all my life, and my staid, sensible partner succumbing to the come-on of a famous lesbian doctor she was working with. I'd found out three days before the storm hit, when we all needed to be evacuating or writing wills. Katrina had thrown all our lives apart. And her affair had tossed me down a dark hole that I was still climbing out of.

Cordelia had stayed in the hellhole of Charity Hospital. It was a week—less, five days—but the person who went there on Sunday wasn't the person who came out on the following Friday. Whatever the affair had meant before the storm, the person afterward was too battered to build a new life with someone else, especially since that someone else didn't seem interested in a new girlfriend who was falling apart.

We had ended up back in New Orleans and ended up back together. On days like today, I had no regrets. I hadn't been perfect and she hadn't either. I mostly left it at that.

But I had started drinking again and wasn't able to quite stop. Now I just hoped I knew my limits, that I would keep it in the realm of social drinking, one beer while cooking dinner, that I had learned it could only blot out problems, not make them go away.

I knew Cordelia was concerned, but she didn't say anything. Maybe after she had fallen so far from grace she didn't feel she *could* say anything.

Garlic was chopped. As long as I didn't cut my finger off, the one beer would be okay. Tonight would be lemon/garlic chicken with a side of broccoli and some sliced fresh fruit for dessert. I made enough so we could feed Torbin and Andy if need be or have decent leftovers for the next day or so.

They live down the block from us, and must have been watching, because just as Cordelia parked her car, they were headed toward our house. Andy was cradling his hand and walking slowly.

I put the chicken in as they met on our front step and entered together.

"Smells good," she said, ushering them in.

Uncharacteristically Torbin did not comment on the food.

Cordelia picked up on it and said to Andy, "Let me look at your hand." She had brought what I thought of as her "doctor bag"—a roomy brown leather briefcase in which she stuck things as she needed them. She put the bag down on the kitchen table, grabbed a couple of clean dish towels, and created a makeshift hygienic space.

Andy sat down, with Torbin standing behind him, a hand on his shoulder. Andy gingerly laid his arm on the towels, then started to undo the bandages.

"Let me do that," Cordelia said. "It's easier with two hands." She smiled to reassure him.

People have different aspects of who they are. I'm used to Cordelia at home, as my partner, someone who has to be prompted to go through the stack of mail she's left by the door, who favors old jeans and a T-shirt sans bra at home. But she spent a good part of her day as a highly competent doctor who had to make important, at times life-or-death decisions. As I watched her gently unwrap Andy's bandage, she was skilled and professional.

It was a side of her I rarely saw.

Just as she rarely saw me as a capable and intuitive investigator. Or a freaked-out idiot madly dashing down stairs to startle innocent bicyclists in the street. There can be advantages to not knowing everything there is to know about each other.

"It hurts, doesn't it?" she said as she looked at his hand.

I glanced at it just long enough to convince myself that I needed to be careful with kitchen knives, then decidedly looked away. Unlike TV detectives, I try to stay as far away from gore and blood as possible. Especially my own, but other people's as well. He had a deeply red cut around the base of his thumb.

"How does it feel when you move your fingers?" Cordelia asked.

"I try not to do that," Andy said with a rueful smile. But he obliged her and wiggled his fingers. "Hurts some, but they feel okay."

"Is it infected?" Torbin asked.

Cordelia didn't answer immediately, picking up Andy's hand gently and examining it. "Maybe a little. There is some redness."

"It stings a lot," Andy said.

She brushed her finger lightly outside the wound. "The hand is a sensitive area, with copious blood vessels and nerves. The same cut elsewhere wouldn't hurt as much. There is just a little red around the wound opening. That could be your immune system at work rather than an actual infection. By tomorrow it should hurt less and the redness should be receding. If the inflammation spreads, the area around the wound gets tender—more than it is now, if there is pus or oozing blood or you run a fever, these are all signs of infection."

"What do we do if that happens?" Torbin asked. "The best we could get for a doctor's appointment was a week from today."

"If it's really bad, you need to go back to the ER. I can look at it tomorrow if you want," Cordelia offered. "But that shouldn't happen. Keep it clean, change the dressing often, and you should be good. Use soap and water, not anything abrasive like hydrogen peroxide."

"My mother used to swear by that," Andy said.

"It's okay initially when you need to clean the wound, but after that it can do more harm than good. Plain old soap and water work fine."

"What about those stitches?" Torbin asked. "They look like something out of a Frankenstein movie."

Cordelia again looked at Andy's hand. "It does look like you got someone with less-than-stellar sewing skills."

"It's going to scar, isn't it?" Torbin said.

"Probably," Cordelia admitted.

"Can't you do something?" he asked.

"It's okay," Andy cut in. "It'll remind me to always cut away from anything living."

"Like take out the stitches and do it again right?" Torbin said.

"The wound is healing. Undoing the stitches could open it up again."

"No blood in your kitchen," Torbin grumbled.

I started to say something, but Cordelia spoke first.

"Torbin, I can't do surgery on our table." Her voice was calm, reasonable, another professional side of her I rarely saw—she understood the pain and fear wasn't about her, but about the cancer or the cut, the control disease or harm rips from us. "Andy is lucky, no cut tendon, the knife seems to have hit the fatty pad below the thumb. There will be a scar; even the best stitches probably wouldn't prevent that."

"I guess this is what we get for medical care when we can't make someone money," Tobin complained.

"How much are we charging you?" I retorted. He seemed to forget that he was getting free medical care right now, from someone who had already put in a long day.

"It's okay, Micky," Cordelia said. "I know what he means. The system isn't perfect."

"It's designed to not be perfect," Andy said quietly. "I've been doing a lot of work for one company, so I asked about a real job. The guy I talked to told me that they're only using consultants now, independent contractors, to avoid the cost of benefits, like health insurance."

"This is crazy," Torbin said. "We make enough money to do okay, but we both have to look for full-time jobs we might not want just to have enough insurance not to be stuck in the gangland emergency room."

"What if we didn't know you?" Andy queried. "I'd be a home right now dousing my hand with hydrogen peroxide, hoping it would heal and I wouldn't need any more medical care."

"People die, don't they?" Torbin asked Cordelia. "They die because they're too poor, unlucky, or just stupid. They get health care only when they're desperate and when it's too late."

"We try to have safety nets…" she started.

"Shredded here," he cut in. "Maybe better in other parts of the country, but I think Katrina washed ours away."

I could tell she was upset. Torbin had a point, a brutally sharp one. It was a flawed system, and Cordelia was a part of that system.

"Katrina did damage," she admitted. "It destroyed a lot of the infrastructure. Doctors left and didn't come back. We're short hospital beds, especially mental health ones. Plus the stress and upheaval have had tremendous health costs." She paused as if gathering her thoughts. "But as bad as this is, there are places where it's worse. At least New Orleans is still an urban center. You don't have to drive a hundred miles to get to a hospital, or forty for just a doctor's visit."

Before Torbin could add or argue, I cut in, "Medical care in America is screwed up, profit more important than health. But we can argue about that all night and I have slaved too hard over dinner to let the chicken burn while we wrestle about something that will take years of fighting on multiple levels to change. Now, dear cousin of mine, tell my girlfriend how much you appreciate her seeing Andy after her already long day. And you can thank me as well for arranging this free, personal health-care session for you—and for the time I've been deprived of her company."

"You have my humble apologies," he said. But he knew he needed more than just his usual Torbin banter to get through this one. He put his arms around Cordelia and hugged her. "Thank you," he said to her. "It's…it means a lot to have people like you in our lives."

"You're welcome." Cordelia returned his hug.

"And as I tell my dear cousin almost daily, she has the best girlfriend in the world," Torbin added. He can't be serious long.

I invited them to stay for dinner, but they declined. Cordelia wrote Andy a prescription for antibiotics, but cautioned him to use it only if he developed signs of infection. Good doctor to the end, she explained if he did start taking them, to take the entire course to avoid helping to contribute to resistant bacteria.

And then we were alone.

I took the chicken out of the oven. It could rest while I threw the broccoli on to steam.

Cordelia got a beer out of the refrigerator.

"I'm sorry," I said. "I didn't think Torbin would go ballistic on you about health care."

She took a deep pull of her beer, then said, "It's okay. He and Andy spent a long night in the ER; they got adequate health care but not great health care. And it's a warning sign. What happens next time? One of them could be in an auto accident tomorrow. It brings up a lot of complicated questions for them. Fear often comes out as anger." She put her beer down on the counter, grabbed some knives and forks, and put them on the table.

"Yeah, but it shouldn't come out as anger at you when you're doing them a major favor."

Cordelia came around behind me as I stood at the stove and put her arms around my waist. "It comes out at all times. It comes out when I'm about to stick a needle in their butt. You'd think that would make people play nice."

"Maybe they're into good doctor/bad patient."

"Yuck. I don't even want to think those kinds of thoughts."

"More likely they're just stupid."

"Better thought." She tightened her embrace. "I'm glad I could help. Damn, that sounds so Pollyanna, doesn't it?"

"It sounds like you."

"On my better days." She quickly continued to avoid the weight of that, "Especially in this city everything is such a mess. At least I can make it less messy for my friends. And try to do what I can to make it better for everyone. It just feels like I'm part of a broken system. I earn decent money. Some days I wonder if it's not literal blood money."

At the risk of overcooking the broccoli, I turned to her. "It's like racism and sexism and homophobia. We're all part of it and we can all just do a little bit, like water against stone. I will not let you beat up on yourself because you can't walk on water and fix a vastly dysfunctional medical system."

"I am so lucky to have you." She put her head on my shoulder.

And started crying as if the weight of the world was on her back and she could no longer carry it.

I discreetly turned off the water under the broccoli and just held her.

"I'm sorry," she finally said. "Must be tired and hungry. So feed me."

I did. We flopped in front of the TV, both had another beer, and mentioned nothing more serious than picking up cat food the rest of the night.

CHAPTER FIVE

In the morning I remembered I'd meant to tell Cordelia to be on the lookout for gas can–wielding maniacs. By the time I'd remembered, she was already at work.

It wasn't likely, I told myself as I got in my car. He might be able to find where my office was. The card I'd given him had only a P.O. box as the address—I have a variety of cards for a variety of situations. But I was listed in the phone book, so only the truly lazy and inept couldn't find me. However, it would be much more difficult to ferret out my home address. Besides, Carl Prejean was a con, not a fighter.

It was still more a relief than I wanted to admit when my office building came into view and was just as I'd left it last night, slightly shabby, paint starting to peel where the southern sun hit it the hardest, perfect in its New Orleans decadent glory.

My relief went away when I noticed the outer security door was open. *Probably the space-cadet artist who rents the first floor*, I told myself as I stuck my head in, sniffing the air for anything that might scream "light me with a match and I'll show you a hot time." But the air had a bouquet of stale beer, overlaid with hints of mold and gardenia, infused with traces of cayenne and crab boil. It said New Orleans more than fire trap.

Unless I know someone is coming I tend to lock the downstairs door, as do the other tenants in the building. For the obvious reasons, I didn't want just anyone—especially anyone with less-than-kind intent—to be able to easily find me. And for the not-so-obvious reason that about a week ago a flyer about a missing pet python had appeared on the street corner.

But the artist's inner door was shut and no light appeared in the crack. He had taken over the entire first floor on promises to the landlord he would paint the building. Completion of the painting would mean that he'd have to pay rent, so I didn't see that happening anytime soon.

Maybe someone was moving into the second floor, vacant since Katrina. But no one was around up there, all the doors closed, the floors still dusty at the end of the hall, indicating no footsteps had been there in months. Plus if they were moving in, there should have been something glaringly obvious like a huge van or at least a big truck near the open door.

You're spooked because someone threatened you, I told myself as I cautiously mounted the stairs to the third floor. Two days ago, I would have assumed it was the wind or humidity that had popped the door open—coupled with someone who forgot to securely lock it. Now I was about to pull my gun to start my workday.

The door to my office was closed. Everything was as it should be.

Okay, so I'm being paranoid, I told myself as I fumbled with my keys.

Just as I was about to insert the key in the lock, the door opened.

Someone had broken in.

Tomorrow, I would start my day with coffee and gun in hand.

I just had to get through today.

In the split second before I either fled down my stairs or starting throwing kicks and punches, I took in a scene of jarring normality.

Two people were sitting in the usual client chairs before my desk. Mr. Charles Williams had opened my door to me.

"What are you doing here?" I demanded. My adrenaline was still poised for flight or fight. Or both.

"I'm a locksmith. It was looking like rain, so we decided to wait up here for you."

"You decided to break into my office?" I was still standing out on the landing and he was holding open the door, as if welcoming me.

"Nothing harmed, nothing broken. We just wanted to be warm. We even made coffee."

Still not moving, I said, "I told you yesterday I couldn't help you. What made you think it was a smart idea to come back?"

"I brought a paying customer."

For some reason it brought to mind when my cat presents me with a palmetto bug as a present. The cat is very proud, but I don't want it.

"I have a phone. Calling first is always a good idea."

"This is important. It couldn't wait. Why don't you come in and we can talk about this?"

"Yeah, why don't I come into my own office," I muttered and brushed by him.

It was clear Mr. Williams had been sitting at my desk. I ignored the coffee cup there and claimed my space. I moved his cup as far away as I could.

For the first time, I looked at the two people in front of me. They seemed to be a couple. She had dull brown hair with split ends crying for attention, clothing of equally dull colors, a brown skirt and beige blouse that buttoned up to her neck. She was petite, maybe five-two or three at most, and her hunched shoulders made her seem even smaller. Her mouth was a little small, her nose too large, her chin a point. She had never been pretty, never the cheerleader or the homecoming queen, too plain and mousy for a starring role, even one on as small a stage as high school. He had on a loud Hawaiian shirt, trendy cargo shorts, and man sandals. His hair was a streaked blond that said either surf or dye, and given the paunch around his waist and how little muscle there seemed in his arms and legs, my money wasn't on the beach. He was tall, had once been good-looking, but those looks had faded as he got older, the chin no longer firm, the jowls starting to sag, the hair thinning and combed forward in an attempt to hide the elongating forehead.

If they were indeed a romantic couple of any kind, it proved that opposites attracted.

A friend of mine described situations like this by saying, "There is not enough vodka or aspirin in the world." I could feel the headache starting.

"You got an extra chair?" Mr. Williams asked.

I pointed to a folding chair in the corner. He had made himself at home, he could continue by finding his own chair.

The blond dude stuck out his hand. "I'm Fletcher McConkle."

I dutifully shook his hand. He was older than he first looked, harsh lines around his eyes and his skin a leathery tan.

"And you are?" I asked the woman.

She glanced up, but looked at me only briefly. It was hard to read the expression in her eyes, timidity or annoyance—or some combination of the two.

"I'm Mrs. McConkle. Mrs. Donna McConkle," she said. Her voice was high and soft with almost a lisp to it. She was younger than she had first looked, her conservative clothes aging her. I guessed a fifteen- to twenty-year age gap between the two of them.

"And you know who I am," Mr. Charles Williams added.

"Yes, I do," I said with no smile. To hurry this along, I asked, "Tell me why you might need the services of a private investigator."

It was Fletcher, of course, who answered. "My aunt is being swindled. I need to put a stop to it."

"Criminal acts are a matter for the police," I said. "If someone is taking advantage of her, you should report it to them."

"It's more complicated than that," he said.

Which usually meant that it wasn't complicated at all, just massively unpleasant. I supplied the expected prompt. "Complicated how?"

"My aunt is elderly, suffers from a variety of ills, and is always looking for something that will fix those ills. Sometimes she doesn't choose wisely. A young dude used his wiles to gain her confidence and sell her so-called natural remedies for which she is paying several hundred dollars a week."

"Perhaps you should call elderly services," I suggested. Fletcher spoke in an affected way, as if it made him smarter and more refined. In his Hawaiian shirt.

"Do you not want this case?" he asked. "This is the second time you've suggested I go elsewhere."

"I recognize what I can and can't do. If I feel there is a more appropriate place that can offer greater help, it's only ethical I provide that referral," I said calmly. However, maybe Fletcher had married Mrs. Fletch because she was an heiress and he had money to burn. I didn't want to close out my options either. I'd be ethical and polite.

My answer seemed to satisfy him. "My aunt has all her faculties intact, and, alas, can decide for herself what she wants to do with her money."

"If she's spending money she doesn't have on things she doesn't need, then that might be an argument to intervene. Bad decisions about finances can be an early sign of dementia," I said.

"She has the money," Fletcher said. "If he sticks with only swindling her out of a few hundred a week, then she'll be okay unless she lives to well over a hundred. My concern is it could escalate as he gains her confidence, and it's not right she's being taken advantage of even if she can afford it."

"Not to mention you being her only living relative," Mr. Williams chimed in.

Now his unease made sense. He might well have been worried about his aunt, but my read was that the real concern was his possible inheritance.

I pretended to ignore Mr. Williams's very pertinent comment. "What do you think a private investigator could do to help you?"

"Expose this charlatan. Get the evidence he's knowingly pushing useless pills and potions. Give me enough proof I can show her he's not some nice boy who's genuinely concerned about old ladies, but a con man. I need to know who this man is, who he works for, and most important, get proof he's selling worthless nostrums."

"There are no guarantees," I said. Remembering my conversation with Cordelia, I told him, "For many of these so-called natural remedies, there is no proof whether they work or not—only anecdotal claims that can be hard to counter. Even if I get what most people would consider evidence, your aunt may not believe it. If he is a true snake oil salesman, he may have protected himself with shell companies, false names, and other subterfuges. In short, if I take the case, I may not be able to give you the results that you want."

"I need to do something to help protect my aunt," he said. Then the first break in his confident tone. "Alas, I'm not a wealthy man, so my resources are limited. However, once my aunt is no longer with us, I could probably—"

I cut him off. "You want me to wait until your aunt dies to get paid? I'm afraid that's not possible. If I incur expenses now, I get paid now."

He chewed his lip.

His wife finally spoke. "We can afford one thousand dollars. If you can help us for that amount, we can proceed. We'll pay half up front and the other half at the end."

My estimate of Fletcher went up. He was at least smart enough—or experienced enough—to understand the value of a wife who could handle money and the logistics of life.

"We'll expect a report every day, of course," he added, his bluster back.

"It's an hourly expense, and daily reports can eat into that," I pointed out. "When I'm about halfway through, I'll give you a verbal report and you can see if what I'm finding is worth your while."

This really wasn't a very complicated case. People who sell things—legal things anyway—have to have a method of reaching the public. That meant they left a paper trail, or increasingly these days, an electronic one. It shouldn't be too hard to get the information they were looking for.

Mrs. McConkle and I went over the paperwork while Fletcher and Mr. Williams discussed sports scores. I liked her a lot better than I liked him. She was still shy, but had a practical and no-nonsense side to her. She probably needed it as it seemed unlikely that her husband had much common sense under the bluster. She gave me what info there was to give, the name and address of the aunt, what days I was likely to find Mr. Snake Oil there. She'd even been smart enough to grab one of the empties out of the trash. It was a generic plastic bottle (not recyclable, I noticed) with a printed label pasted on. The label had nice graphics, so money was put into marketing. It was a swirling cascade of green into yellow and blue, so it looked like an abstract green field under a bright sun. Nature's Beautiful Gift was the brand name.

It would be a fairly easy thousand—easy enough for me to take the case.

Fletcher and Mr. Williams seemed to have run out of sports scores just as we finished up.

I happily escorted them downstairs, noting that both men were breathing rather heavily by the time we reached the bottom.

Fletcher and his wife got in their car. Mr. Williams took another deep breath. I put my hand on his arm, letting them drive away.

"So," I said, "I threw you out on your ear. Why bring me a client?"

He shrugged. "You were the only person who actually listened to me. At least you were honest and didn't just treat me like I was a nobody. No scratch, no time."

It took me a moment to remember that "scratch" was slang for "money." "How'd you hook up with the McConkles?"

"Fate was good to us. I got the call to do a lock replacement at a house they were working on. They heard me talking."

I didn't point out that by now most of New Orleans had heard him talking.

"I was going on about my nephew and the crap he's taking. And he mentioned his aunt and what was going on with her. They're both taking that Nature's Beautiful Gift crap. So, I thought if you looked into it for them, maybe you could find out stuff I could use as well."

No scratch, no time, just good survival instincts. "What I find out is confidential, but they might be nice enough to share."

"That's what I'm hoping," he said as he sauntered off.

"Hey, Charles?" I called after him. "No more breaking and entering, okay? Next time I might not be so nice."

He waved an acknowledgment. I took it to mean he wouldn't pick the locks unless he thought it was important.

It was back up three flights of stairs for me. I made sure the outer door was shut and the lock caught, then trudged up the steps.

Just as I entered my door, my office phone rang. Like it had been when Prejean threatened me. Could he know when I entered?

I debated not answering it, then let it ring long enough for the answering machine to kick in. This was an "innocent" way of recording the phone conversation.

"Knight Agency," I said, easing down the message volume so I wasn't speaking over myself.

"Micky, I tried your cell but you didn't answer." Cordelia.

"I was just walking some clients out and left my cell up here," I explained. And reminded myself that I needed to have my cell phone with me at all times. What if I'd found Prejean downstairs about to light a match? "What's up?" She rarely calls me during the day.

"I need to hit you up for a detective favor."

"Okay," I said cautiously.

"If you can do it," she added.

I was relieved to hear that. Even sane and sensible people like Cordelia can have TV versions of private detectives.

"Tell me what it is and I'll let you know."

"Some patients have gone missing. Well, not really missing, but one in particular missed his last appointment and he needs to be closely monitored."

"Can you give me his name and address?"

"Can you come up here and meet with us?"

Other than not wanting to bother with driving there—and finding parking—there was no reason not to. I did owe her a big favor for foisting Andy—and Torbin's worry and anger—on her last night.

"Sure, where should I meet you?"

She gave me an office address on Prytania, up near Touro Infirmary. It was one of the few that hadn't flooded.

So, time to go down the stairs again. I double-locked my door and set the alarm. Mr. Charles Williams was less likely to stay for coffee with a high-pitched whine ringing in his ears.

It took me almost half an hour to get there, much of the time taken by red lights and idiot drivers. I had to go through the CBD, Central Business District, with its heavy traffic and skim by the French Quarter with its tourists, drunks, and worst of all, drunken tourists jaywalking off the sidewalk—yes, cars will drive down these historic streets. No, worst of all was drunken tourists at eleven in the morning. Although to be fair, more than a few tourists have been known to be merrily drinking the night away waiting for last call to send them stumbling home only to notice a new light and realize it's the sun coming up.

What, they don't have a twenty-four-hour bar in Oshkosh?

There is a pay lot, but I'd discovered there is free parking on the street a few blocks away for anyone willing to walk those blocks.

The address was one of the older office buildings in the area. It had a creaky elevator that took me to the fifth floor, where her office was. Technically it wasn't her office; she was on temporary assignment, covering for a doctor on maternity leave. That was a lot of what she did these days, floating from positions like this as if she was reluctant to obligate herself to something more permanent. At times I wondered what that said about her commitment to New Orleans, or being a doctor. Or to me. But I mostly let it be. It was her path to find.

I had to wander around two corners before finding the reception desk. It was in a cramped room with tall stacks of medical records against the walls.

I gave my name and asked for Cordelia. The phone rang and the receptionist pointed me to the waiting room.

You're making me wait to do you a favor, I groused silently. It had been at least three minutes. She finally arrived after five minutes had passed.

"Hi, Micky, thanks for coming," Cordelia said as she motioned me to get up and follow her.

She looked sexy in her white lab coat with a stethoscope slung around her neck. I have a thing for smart, competent women. She led me around another two corners and into a conference room, really a room with a table too big for it and chairs I had to squeeze by to get around the table.

"Let me get the other folks," she said.

I politely moved to the far side of the table so others could easily sit. It was hard enough to get by the chairs when they were shoved in.

It was another five minutes before she reentered the room with three other people, two men and a woman.

"This is my partner, Micky," Cordelia introduced me to them. "As I mentioned, she's a private eye." She edged around the chairs to the one next to me.

"You're a woman?" the younger of the two men asked. He took the most convenient chair, forcing the others to maneuver around him. The woman gave an extra little shove to get past his chair. He seemed not to notice. His thick brown hair had been recently cut. I suspected it was cut on a regular basis to keep it as neat and conservatively short as it was now. He had regular features, not handsome especially, but pleasant enough. Clearly he worked out, but he was barely average height, a little stocky. A few years, children, a heavy work schedule and the paunch would quickly build. His tie was a boring navy strip, his shirt white, his lab coat white and starched. It was easy to imagine him voting Republican. His eyes were small, a narrow slit, gray or light brown, I couldn't tell. The kind of guy who would assume that Micky/private eye had to equal male.

"What planet have you been on, Ron?" the woman asked him as she sat down. To me, she offered her hand and said, "Lydia Skrmetta. Thanks for meeting with us."

Lydia was older than Ron. She was heavy, but her weight was in the right places, with a bustline and hips that could serve as launching pads. Her hair was short, practical, a sedate light blond that was either good genes or a good dye. Her clothes echoed her hair, sensible, practical, but high-end cotton, no polyester sprawl-mart for her. Her eyes were an open brown. She wore no makeup.

"Sorry," Ron said in a totally un-sorry voice. "Can't pay attention to all the gossip."

"Ron Hackler," Cordelia said, "and Brandon Kellogg."

Brandon also shook my hand before sitting; Ron was too far away to bother.

Brandon was still handsome; he had kept middle age at bay, with wavy sandy hair, a little gray at the temples. It was just enough to make him distinguished, not yet old. He was tall, his face wide and rugged, but softened by dimples in both his cheeks and chin. His smile was easy, showing perfect white teeth. His tie was bold, good silk with a print of jazz trombones that indicated he either didn't wear the kinds of ties his mother-in-law gave him or she liked one-of-a-kind ties. The smile reached his eyes, a clear and steady gray.

"Two patients have dropped out of care," Lydia started.

Ron cut in. "First things first. Everything said in this room must be confidential."

"Of course," I said. "That's standard procedure."

"And I mean everything," he emphasized. "This is sensitive information."

He was pushing a little too hard. "Everything is confidential. Even private eyes have a code of ethics. I won't cover up criminal activity, but if you're cheating on your wife, I won't be the one to tell her."

They looked at each other for a moment, Lydia said, "Look, we didn't do anything criminal."

"Argue that in front of a jury," Ron said sourly.

"Oh, good Lord," Lydia said. "That's not going to happen."

"No, probably not, but all the more reason for us to do the right thing," Brandon said. Again, the glance around the table as if making a decision.

I let the silence stretch out.

Brandon spoke. "We were all part of other practices that fell apart after Katrina, so we've only recently started all working together and in a new space."

"Cut to the chase," Ron interrupted. "I have patients to see."

"We had to have some work done, a pipe burst, and we canceled a number of patients. We left messages saying we'd contact them to reschedule. Most people did. But we had a change of receptionists during this period—"

"Missing oxycodone," Lydia put in.

"So two patients we really needed to keep in care got lost," Brandon said.

"They have medical issues that need follow-up," Cordelia added.

"And you're concerned that they might sue you if you don't go out of your way to fix the scheduling snafu," I summed up.

"Our first concern is they need to be in medical care," Lydia said. "But avoiding a malpractice charge isn't bad either."

"That's not going to happen. We're not committing malpractice here," Brandon said firmly.

"What attempts have you made to contact them?" I asked.

"Phone calls and e-mail," Brandon said.

"That's it?"

"Three phone calls with messages, a reminder postcard, several e-mails, the last one which asked that they let us know if they're in care elsewhere," Lydia said. "That was a week ago. No word."

"So about six or seven attempts," Brandon defended. "I know it might not sound like much, but we have a patient list of several thousand people. And like I said, we're still struggling to get everything in place."

I nodded. For their resources, these were probably reasonable attempts. "No one has gone to their house or attempted to physically track them down?" I asked. "Any idea if the e-mail addresses are still valid?"

Brandon shook his head sadly as if guilty. "No, I don't guess we even thought to do that."

"It's not like we can hunt patients down," Ron answered. "Lord knows we have enough to do as it is."

"Yeah, Ron, you're so overworked," Lydia said.

"I pull my weight," he retorted.

"And leave every day by five, unlike me and Brandon."

"I'm here every day by six thirty a.m.," Ron said.

"Let's focus on these patients," Brandon said. "What can we do?"

"What outcome are you looking for?" I asked.

"To locate them, make sure they understand they need to be under medical care and that if they don't want to come to us, they are at least going somewhere," he said.

"Or if they're not in care, that they have been informed that they should be, so whatever happens is on them," Ron added.

"Okay, so someone needs to locate them and actually talk to them or somehow communicate in a way that gets a response," I said, trying not to get annoyed with Ron.

"That's pretty much it," Lydia agreed.

"Can you do that?" Brandon asked as if this might be difficult.

"Probably. It's possible that for some reason they don't want to be found; that makes it harder. It might also depend on how much information you'll let me have."

Again they looked at each other.

Cordelia spoke, "Micky can sign a HIPAA compliance form and confidentiality statement. Finding them might be part of their medical care."

"I don't want to set a precedent here," Ron said. "Micky is just doing a favor for her girlfriend, we're not hiring her and this is a one-time thing. We can't chase every patient who misses an appointment."

"I'm doing a favor for my partner," I answered, wondering if he'd notice my correcting him.

That seemed to satisfy them, as this time they nodded.

"Good thing I have the forms with me," Lydia said, sliding several sheets of paper in my direction.

Cordelia took a pen out of her pocket and handed it to me.

"Should I read these things or can I trust that I'm not signing away a kidney?"

"You can sign safely."

"Can I go now?" Ron inquired.

Both Brandon and Lydia waved him away. He left without pushing his seat back in.

"Lydia, do you have the files?" Brandon asked. "They're both Tamara's patients, right?"

"If you know me, you know I have the files. I think they're hers."

"I hate to run, but I've got patients waiting. Do you need me for anything else?" he asked.

"We're good," she assured him.

So the men left the women to finish up, I thought. Although to be fair, maybe it was just they had people waiting and Lydia and Cordelia didn't.

Lydia produced two folders from the pile of paper she'd brought with her. I wondered if she traveled with that huge stack all the time or just brought it to this meeting to make an impressive show.

She opened one, placing it between us. "Reginald Banks. He's twenty-four and has sickle cell anemia. It's gotten bad for him and he's on medication. The problem with that is the meds have some pretty serious side effects, including increasing the possibility of infections. He came in last time with a bacterial illness. We gave him antibiotics and made an appointment for a week later for follow-up, and to come in sooner if he didn't get better. That was about six weeks ago, and that was the last we saw of him." She left his file in front of me and opened the second file folder.

"The second patient is Eugenia Hopkins, thirty-six, formerly Eugene, but transitioning. She's infected with HIV, was struggling with side effects of the treatment and then tested positive for TB. We started her on TB meds, again an appointment a week later and it got lost in the shuffle. Again, six weeks ago."

I appreciated that Lydia used layman's terms; I don't think Cordelia could have explained it as clearly, and she usually remembers not everyone has had a medical school education.

"Can you make me copies of all the contact info?" I pointed to one of the sheets I wanted. "Don't worry, I'll keep it as confidential as you do and shred it once it's served my purpose."

"We can sic the DIS on Eugenia, but that'll probably make her distrust the system even more."

"The what?" I asked.

"Disease Intervention Specialist," Cordelia answered. "People who work for the Office of Public Health and do contact tracing and find people out of care. But with the budget cuts they're probably overwhelmed anyway."

"Let me make you copies," Lydia said, retrieving the file folders. "Do you want the whole thing or just those few pages?"

"Just the contact info." I didn't need and wasn't interested in their medical histories. With just what she was giving me, I'd hit a bonanza—not just address, but date of birth, Social Security number, emergency contact info, the things that I almost never get when I have to track people down. We hadn't mentioned a fee and we'd already said that I was doing this as a favor to Cordelia, so I wasn't going to bring it up. Given the info I had, it shouldn't be too hard to find these patients.

Assuming that they were alive. Sometimes that was why people went missing.

I didn't want to think about that.

"Do you get a lunch break here?" I asked Cordelia.

She totally missed my hint and answered, "Mostly we do. It depends on the patients, if there is something complicated that eats time, part of the time it eats is lunch."

"How about today?"

Light dawned. "Oh." She smiled. "Let me check." She got up and left.

Cordelia came back before Lydia did. Maybe they were still waiting on the good copy machine to be delivered.

"My eleven thirty canceled—and was kind enough to call and let us know—and my next scheduled patient is at one. So, yeah, if we can do it in that time frame."

We could probably manage lunch. Other "do its" would have to wait.

Lydia returned with a stack of papers—and mercifully took a much smaller slice off the top and handed it to me.

"Hey, Lyd," Cordelia said, "is it okay if I sneak out for lunch? I don't have anyone scheduled until one."

"Stay within beeper range—I mean cell phone—just in case something comes up. But it should be fine."

"Can we get you something?" Cordelia asked her as I secured the papers in an inside pocket in my briefcase.

"Nope, brought my lunch today, but thanks."

I followed Cordelia, first to her office, so she could shuck the lab coat and stethoscope and get her purse and sunglasses, then out the labyrinth of turns to the elevators.

"Thank you," she said as the elevator doors opened and we stepped in.

They shut and I took advantage of the privacy to lean in and kiss her.

She kissed back long enough to let me know she appreciated my being here. We broke off in time so we were blandly standing next to each other as the elevator doors opened to let other people in.

"Where would you like to go?" she asked as we exited the building.

"What's around here?" I asked. This area wasn't my stomping grounds.

She shrugged. "I mostly bring my lunch."

We settled on a bar/burger joint just down the block.

After we placed our orders—me a decadent blue cheese burger and her a virtuous salad—I asked, "So, who are Lydia, Brandon, and Ron?"

"I've tried to stay out of the politics and personalities," was her preamble.

"But you still know more about them than I do," I prompted her.

She smiled agreement. "Lydia is a nurse practitioner and probably the mainstay of the group, with the major planning and organizational skills. Ron and Brandon are both doctors. They and Tamara, the doctor on maternity leave, form one section of the group practice. There are two other sections with about four doctors each. I've only met them in passing."

"So about twelve doctors all together?" I asked.

"Yes. I think about four of them were here before Katrina; several of their colleagues left, so it's been pick-up sticks in personnel for the last few years. Newer doctors get stuck together, so the older doctors don't have to deal with constant change."

"So why have a group practice?"

"Sharing of resources. We have the same clerical staff, phone systems, file space, copy machines. That sort of stuff."

"Guess that makes sense."

"Brandon and Lydia have worked together for a while and I think they joined this group as a team. Ron used to work out in New Orleans East and none of his partners came back. I think he's a good doctor, but people skills isn't his strong point."

"You think?"

"It took me a while, but I finally noticed."

"Think he's not cool with gay folks? He seemed pretty taken aback that I turned out to have a vagina and not a penis."

"Hard to tell, his usual style would make most people think he hates them. But…he is a straight white man and he got his undergrad at Ole Miss before coming to LSU for medical school."

"Thank the cosmos for Mississippi," I said. "It keeps Louisiana from always being at the bottom of everything."

"It doesn't really matter, Tamara will be back from maternity leave in about a month and I'll be somewhere else."

"So how legit is this finding patients thing?" I asked.

"We can't make people keep their appointments, and a fair number do just not show up. Most of the time, it's on them to reschedule. But because this is sort of our fault—or at least we can't put it in the category of the patient deciding not to show up—we brought them both up at our last case conference meeting. I mentioned that my partner was a private detective and a lot of what she—I did say 'she'—did was find missing people and maybe she'd have some ideas."

"And ideas turned into me coming here and agreeing to find them?"

"I wasn't really expecting you to say, 'yeah, I can do that.' Just give us whatever the magic trick is that you know."

I laughed. "It's not that big a deal. The PI equivalent of what you did for Andy," I reassured her. "And there is no magic trick. Some experience, some knowledge, but it's mostly doing the things you could do if you have the time and resources. I'll go knock on their door. If they don't answer, I'll go knock on the neighbor's doors and see if they know when the person might be around."

"And people just tell you?"

"Mostly. If they say he's such a nice guy, I tell them I'm looking for him because an uncle left him a small bequest. If they bitch about him always parking right in front of their house, then I say he owes major parking fines."

"You lie," she said, in an appreciative tone.

"I consider part of it protecting client confidentiality, not revealing the real reason I'm looking for the person. I'm ethical enough to only use negative reasons for people who are scumbags anyway."

"What do you do if the neighbors don't tell you anything?"

"It depends on what other info I have. With your patients I have just about everything I could wish for. I can track them using various databases—the Internet has really made it much easier to find people. There are some pretty powerful ones that you pay to use—which I do. The magic is if one method doesn't get results, I try another and then another until I get the results. I probably know a few more ways to search for people, and it's my job, so I can put a big part of my day into searching, unlike most people."

Of course we talked about our days, what we did. But it had been a long time since Cordelia asked me these kinds of questions, wanted to learn more of what I did and how I did it. I was enjoying the chance to show off to her. She was the doctor, highly trained, well respected for what she did. Sometimes my career felt insignificant compared to that. She saved lives. I found husbands who had decided to ditch their wives and start over in Vegas. It felt good to see the admiration in her eyes as I talked. I was glad I said yes to this, welcoming the chance to use my skills to help her and prove that what I did could do more than just locate errant spouses.

"I guess it seems magical because you do it so well," she said. "It actually takes a pretty special skill to just knock on random doors, talk to people and get the information you want from them."

"You do it with your patients," I pointed out.

"Yes, and to my credit, I'm pretty good with that. But it's different. They've come to me with the structure in place and expectation that we're going to talk about their health. I'm their access to care, prescriptions, a diagnosis. That's different from being someone on the street. I can do what I do; I don't think I could do what you do."

Annoyingly, our food arrived and interrupted her singing my praises.

She sparingly poured the dressing on her salad. I covered my French fries with ketchup.

But before she took a bite, she covered my hand with hers and said, "Hey, I kind of like us working together. It's nice to see you this way." Then she stole a French fry.

"It is nice," I agreed. "Let me pay for this and I can call it a business expense."

Just to make sure it was a legitimate expense, I asked Cordelia questions about the patients. I got the expected lecture on sickle cell disease, HIV, and TB. She is actually good at explaining these things.

I suspected she'd dealt with enough patients who lacked formal education that she was well versed in breaking things down into easy-to-understand terms.

Once she had finished telling me more than I really wanted to know about TB—I'd spend the next six months wondering if everyone who coughed behind me in the grocery line might infect me—I asked, "Did you treat either of them?"

"No, not really. I briefly saw Eugenia when she came in for a blood draw. She had some bruises that appeared for no reason. I told her mixing alcohol and TB meds could cause bruising. She swore she hadn't been drinking, but I got the feeling she said it because it was what she thought she was supposed to say. I also got the impression giving up drinking wasn't something she was willing to do; not for bruises anyway."

"That was it?" I cut a quarter off my burger and put it on her plate. She was envying me my fat and grease too much.

"Yep," she said, not objecting to the burger.

I speared a tomato in exchange. "Did she give you the impression she might be someone who would just flake out on medical treatment?"

"Hard to say. She wasn't happy about all the meds she was supposed to be on, but her record indicated she was keeping her appointments. That's one of the reasons Lydia flagged her. It seemed she understood how important this was. I was a little surprised by the drinking, but maybe it hadn't been explained to her clearly."

"What about the other patient?"

"A name in a file. No contact with him." She finished my last French fry. "I should get back." She didn't immediately move. "This has been nice. Maybe we should do this more often?"

The hesitancy in her question told me she was unsure what my answer would be. I smiled, looking in her eyes. "Maybe we should. Lunch during the day, or maybe meet after work and go out. I'd like that."

Her sudden smile told me she had been worried I might not really want to create that kind of space for her.

The waitress chose this moment to give us our bill. Cordelia's cell phone rang. It was a text message from Lydia asking if she could get back ASAP, as both yesterday's and today's one p.m. patients had just shown up early.

"I'll get the bill," I told her.

"Thanks," she said as she stood up. She bent down and kissed me full on the lips before hurrying away.

I tend to be the one who's more likely to say, "Let's do it in the street and scare the horses," and Cordelia leans toward discretion, occasionally holding hands in the French Quarter or at Pride, but mostly no public displays of affection. Kissing me in public in the middle of the day near where she worked was a major departure for her.

I thoroughly enjoyed it.

The woman is a good kisser, I reminded myself as I walked to my car.

That very pleasant thought got me serenely through the traffic tangle of the CBD and past the drunken tourists of the Quarter to my office.

CHAPTER SIX

I needed to show the woman who kissed me in public that I was pretty damn good at my job. Time for some magic private detecting.

Which consisted of pulling up a map and entering their addresses.

Eugenia lived not that far from my office, a bit farther down in the Bywater on Rampart Street. Reginald lived in Mid-City, near Broad and Orleans.

If I was lucky I might have this case closed before the day was done—if these were still their addresses and if they were home and willing to answer the door and talk to me.

At the very least I could report progress this evening, I thought. I grabbed my things, securely locked the door, set the alarm, and headed first for Eugenia's.

Her house was ramshackle, in need of paint, a faded pink that hadn't been a trendy color in years, and probably then only in fashion and not in houses. She probably rented, so I couldn't hold her responsible for the paint job.

I parked down a little from her address and used my rearview mirror to scan the street. Telling someone they missed a doctor's appointment isn't the same threat level as telling someone their wife wants the child support to be paid, but this was habit. There weren't many cars around; probably most people were at work. If Eugenia was trans she might have a hard time finding a traditional nine-to-five job. People can be so irrational about bathrooms—"the person in the next stall has to have a natural born vagina just like me or I can't pee"—and that makes some places reluctant to hire trans people. Which often leaves the option of working in places like bars. Or the sex trade. If Eugenia was in those last two, midafternoon might be the time to find her.

A cloud covered the sun, dulling the pink to a more sedate color. Time to knock on the door.

There was no knocker or buzzer, so I rapped my knuckles on the screen door frame.

No answer, no movement inside.

But a lot of being a private dick is being a persistent dick. I knocked again. This time I heard footsteps.

This third time, my knuckles were starting to sting. I pulled out my PI license since it looked sort of official and would at least prove I wasn't trying to save her soul with my particular brand of religion.

The footsteps came closer, as if sidling up to a window to see who would be out here.

"I'm looking for Eugenia Hopkins," I called out, giving my hand a break.

"Who's lookin'?" came a voice from the other side of the door.

"My name is Michele Knight, I'm a private investigator. You're not in trouble and I'm not selling anything."

One lock and then another was thrown and then the door opened.

Except for the Adam's apple, that she was several inches taller than I am and had hands the size of catcher's mitts, no one would have guessed the Eugenia had once been Eugene. Life and genetics have an infinite sense of irony.

"What do you want?" she demanded. At least the voice was high and almost girlish.

"To make sure you're in medical care."

She cocked an eyebrow at me. "They send PIs to do that these days?"

"Not usually," I admitted. "But my partner is one of the doctors there and they felt with the scheduling screwup being their fault, they needed to go the extra mile."

"I feel fine, I don't need to see a doctor," she said. And coughed.

"That's the thing with both HIV and TB, you can feel fine, but they're doing their damage."

"I don't have TB," she said.

"True, you don't have it" (Yes, Cordelia, I was paying attention) "but you've been exposed and to make sure you don't get it, you have to stay on your meds long enough to fight it off."

"Naw, I don't have it. Not at all. So I don't need to be on those stupid meds."

"I'm not a doctor," I said, "but it probably wouldn't hurt to have it checked out just to make sure."

"Are you deaf?" The hand was now on the hip; any second she'd pull out a cigarette holder and blow smoke in my face. "I did that, I had it checked out. Those stupid meds I was on were making me sick; I couldn't even get an appointment to get changed to something else, so at one of our hormone sessions I asked if they knew anything about TB. They gave me some natural stuff that boosts the immune system and can get rid of it. The hormone folks tested me a week later and it was gone, nothing. I don't have it. They'd have to stop the hormones if I had TB."

Cordelia had said I was good at this. Right now I wasn't feeling so good. "I guess there was some confusion," was the best I could come up with. "What about HIV? Did you get retested for that as well?"

The hand left the hip and she crossed it over her chest. "Yeah, no change there. Didn't get a two-fer."

"Who's looking after you for that?"

"At the moment, me, myself, and I. I just don't want to deal with meds and doctors right now, 'kay? So, no nagging."

"No nagging. But I'm old enough to remember people getting sick and dying. I lost a lot of friends when I was young."

"I'm not your friend, doll."

"No, you're not, but you're someone who doesn't have to die like my friends did. Go ahead and take a break right now if you need to. But don't wait too long."

"I won't, don't worry. Once I get my tits taken care of, I can do more other doctor stuff." Then the hand was back on the hip. "Hey, you said your partner was one of the docs there? That mean you're queer?"

"My partner is a woman, yes."

"So you're a dyke dick?" She guffawed at her joke.

I'd heard it enough times that I couldn't join in her merriment. I merely smiled and said, "Some people do call me that."

"Hey, is she that big old dyke?"

I didn't think of Cordelia as big, old, or stereotypically dykey.

"She's got that blondie hair, tiny, barely there pearl studs for earrings. Big bazooms and hips. Bit of a stomach. This high." Eugenie held her hand just under her almost breasts.

She was describing Lydia.

"Nope, that's not her. My partner is the tall one with the auburn hair. You're not a patient of hers, but you did talk to her once."

She looked puzzled for a moment, then remembered. "Oh, yeah, her. She was pretty nice. Real cool about the transitioning, you know."

"She's a lesbian, she should be."

"Doesn't always go that way. Some people who are out are looking for someone to be further out so they can feel superior. If I go back, can I see her?"

"If you come back soon. She's temp, covering for a doctor on maternity leave."

"Doctors do temp work?"

"In post-K New Orleans, we all do what we have to do."

"Good golly, Miss Molly, ain't that the truth. You need anything more from me, or can I go back to my beauty rest?"

"Nope, just wanted to check up on you, make sure you're okay and that you know you should be seeing a doctor somewhere."

"Your job's done. You tell that gorgeous woman of yours she needs to be her own doctor. She could see a lot of trans folks."

"I'll pass that on."

Eugenia shut the door. I headed back to my car.

I didn't immediately pull away. Truth is usually some muddy ground between two people's versions of what happened. But Eugenia seemed worrisomely further away from the middle. She claimed she didn't have TB, but her doctors were treating her for TB. I remembered Cordelia's explanation—exposure vs. infection. Maybe Eugenia was confused. But she still needed to finish the treatment in either case. I probably should have quizzed her further about where she was getting her hormone treatment—conflicting and possibly inaccurate advice could be the cause of her confusion. Or at least it gave her an excuse to believe what she wanted to believe.

And she coughed on me when she opened the door. Only once, but how many coughs was too many?

Denial is a powerful thing. Don't want to take your drugs and don't want to deal with the disconcerting thought that you might be killing yourself by not taking them? Just come up with a way to rationalize it—get a bogus test that tells you don't have the disease. Claim you can't get an appointment when your records show that you've been coming in on a regular basis.

Maybe she would go in and see Cordelia and maybe my gorgeous girlfriend could talk some sense into her.

Mission—sort of—accomplished. I had seen Eugenia Hopkins, talked to her about seeking medical care, and she seemed in right enough of a mind that she could make her own decisions. Even if they were the wrong ones.

I could only hope that I'd have better luck with Reginald Banks.

CHAPTER SEVEN

Reginald Banks's house was even in more need of paint than Eugenia's. At least it was a sedate creamy beige instead of what-were-you-thinking pink. As I had at her place, I drove past it, parking near the corner. This area had flooded; several houses appeared abandoned, with green vines twining up the clapboard and onto the roof. One of them was almost more plant than house. But other houses were restored, one even with the tamed nature of potted plants lining the porch. This wasn't a bad neighborhood, but it wasn't a good one either. Down the block I could see a laced-together pair of old sneakers tossed over a power line, often the signal that you could get drugs here.

But on this sunny afternoon, few people were out. Maybe it was early enough that people weren't interested in going to the methamphetamine mall.

I got out of my car and walked back to Reginald's house.

The first knock got no response.

Neither did the second.

Three strikes and you're out. My third try was as unproductive as the first two.

The door to the house next door opened. A woman poked her head out. "You lookin' for Reginald?"

"Yeah, you have any idea when he might be back?"

"I don't know he left. Saw him coming in about a week ago— maybe two weeks, it was around my aunt's birthday 'cause she mentioned all the leaves on the roof and that was three weeks back— not sure—carrying some groceries. I occasionally have him do some work so I asked him about cleaning my gutters. He said he was not

feeling well and needed to eat and rest. Haven't seen him since then."
She pointed across the street. "That's his car over there. It's been sitting
there the entire time."

I glanced at his car. Early springtime (aka still winter elsewhere)
in New Orleans is high pollen season, and his car was covered with a
greenish tinge that indicated it probably hadn't moved recently.

"So you haven't seen him in at least a week? Have you called
anyone to check up on him?"

"Nope, don't know anyone to call."

Cordelia is right, I am good at this. Right now I wanted to ask this
woman why the fuck she hadn't called someone like the police if she
didn't know anyone else to call, but I didn't do that. I kept a pleasant
smile on my face, like, yes, of course, if someone tells you they're
feeling sick and then you don't see them for over a week, it makes
perfect sense to do nothing.

"You seen anyone go in or out? Or heard any noises from over
here?" I asked.

"Nope, haven't seen anyone or heard nothin'."

"Maybe we should call the authorities," I said. "He might be
sick."

"You want to go check on him? He gave me a spare key a while
back, just in case he lost his."

Somehow I managed to keep my pleasant smile on my face. She
had a key, she could have checked on him but hadn't, instead waited for
some random stranger to show up and do it for her.

"Let me see if he answers his phone," I said. I had his number
on the information sheet Lydia had given me. I hadn't called initially
because the doctors had already tried contacting him by the telephone.

I dialed his number.

After a beat or two I could hear it ringing inside. It rang three
times, then switched to his voice mail. I hung up, counted slowly to
ten, and dialed again. Three rings and voice mail. I got the same result
the third time I tried.

I put my phone away and banged loudly on the door. "Reginald?
Are you in there? Are you okay?"

"We call him Reggie," his neighbor ever so helpfully let me
know.

"Reggie, we're worried about you," I called. "I'm from your doctor's office and we need to make sure you're okay."

Nothing.

Very faintly, I thought I heard a thump, like something—or someone—falling. It was hard to hear if it came from the house or not. Or it I had been listening so hard I was imagining it.

I pounded on the door again. "Reggie? Are you in there? Make a noise, anything and I'll come in."

I listened. Cars blocks away, the remote call of a bird, the shush then cease of wind. The quiet stretched, only small sounds that never really went away in a city, tires on asphalt, distant voices, real and electric.

It was probably time to call the police.

But then it happened again, a faint thump. It could have been inside the house, or a block away behind it. Some noise, some movement.

Something human.

I put the key in the lock.

It turned slowly, as if it had been dry and dusty for a week.

I opened the door, not yet stepping in. "Reggie, are you in here? I need to check on you."

Again, I listened. Nothing. Too silent for a house that should have someone living in it.

I stepped over the threshold, into the dim stillness.

This is when smart detectives call the police, I told myself. But it could be hours before they arrived, this wasn't a murder or a break-in, just a man who hadn't been seen recently and an indistinct sound.

I took a step in, then stopped to listen again.

The room had no lights on, no TV or radio anywhere. The furniture was old and secondhand, a hodgepodge that seemed assembled more for function than style, an olive green stuffed chair clashing next to a turquoise sofa, an end table that was glass and a coffee table that was colonial. A glass sat on the coffee table, but it was empty, rings of evaporation that had dried long ago. In the far corner, on a rickety table, was the phone I'd heard, cheap and ice blue in color, another clash of hues. It was old enough to be plugged into the wall.

"Reggie," I called as I crossed the room.

No answer.

The kitchen was in shambles, dirty dishes in the sink, plates and soup cans left on the counter, the smell of rotting food that had gone past ripe. I opened the refrigerator, but that was a mistake. Rotted food was oozing down the shelves and the bearable smell turned into a putrid waft that sent me back into the living room.

His electricity had been turned off and had clearly been off for days, long enough for anything in the refrigerator to have rotted into green and gray. Only the phone still worked, and only because it wasn't cordless. In a day or two, it would probably be cut off as well.

I covered my nose with my hand. My instinct was to leave, barrel out of the house and the stench and dial a number that would bring someone else here, wash my hands of it. If he was here, he was dead, and it is not my job to discover the dead.

I turned to leave.

And heard the noise again. Somewhere in this house, something fell or pushed or moved, a small, faint sound. A cat or a dog?

It was a little house, two bedrooms at most. I just needed to do a quick search, find the animal left behind, then get out of here. At least I might save a furry life.

I covered my nose with my sleeve, bypassed the kitchen, and headed down the center hall. The house was dark, little light filtering in from outside, the cheap blinds all shut.

The first door I opened was a bathroom, like the kitchen a mess, stains on the toilet and sink I didn't want to think about. I hastily closed the door.

The next was a study with an old, heavy computer, a large monitor taking up most of the desk. Like the first room, it was dusty, as if no one had used it for a long time. I quickly looked inside the closet in this room, but it only contained stacks of books. A cat could hide anywhere and I didn't have a flashlight with me. I could only hope that if there was a cat or dog here, the animal would have enough sense—or be desperate enough—to come to me.

There was only one more door.

I opened it.

Like the kitchen and the bathroom, this place was rancid with use, a fetid smell of unclean, unwell. In the dim light it was hard to make out the shapes and lumps of the disorder.

Then I saw a body on the bed. Half-covered, half-out, an emaciated arm clutching the blanket, the other arm falling off the bed into a half light.

I pressed my sleeve harder against my nose to keep out the smell of death.

The hand moved and knocked a pill bottle off the nightstand onto the floor.

That was the noise I had heard. There were several objects scattered on the bare pine planks, a swath of the nightstand empty.

"Reggie?" I said softly, afraid to breathe.

He made a bare gurgle, someone trying to speak, but far beyond it.

I grabbed my cell phone, stepped back into the hallway, into air I could inhale and not retch. I choked out the words to the 911 operator— *someone very ill, needed help right away.*

Yes, I would stay, I told her.

I folded my phone and was left in the silence and the stench with a man about to die.

I came back to his doorway. "Reggie, help is on the way. They'll be here in a few minutes. You'll be okay."

I had to cover my nose with my sleeve again, afraid I might vomit. I tried to take a step into the room, but couldn't.

Some deaths are sudden, a flash from life into what's on the other side. His was not; it was a slow descent into illness, into a body giving up, the bowels letting go, sweat and urine on older sweat and urine, no dignity or grace, disease eating away everything save for a shallow breath and barely beating heart.

"They'll be here soon," I said. I didn't know whether I was talking to him or myself.

I thought to offer him water, to remind us both that he wasn't a dying animal. But he wasn't able to reply and I had no way of knowing whether he was capable of drinking.

They'd be here soon with IV fluids, medical people who had the knowledge to save this dying man.

I finally admitted my cowardice and left him. I tried to tell myself I would do him more good by being out front to wave the ambulance in, but I knew the truth. I was starting to gag, my lungs feeling invaded by the rancid smell, and I had to get air that was clean, baptized by sunshine, into my lungs.

Opening his front door, I put one foot out onto the top step, enough to get my head out into the fresh breeze. I could finally take my sleeve away from my face.

I could feel the neighbor who had given me the key looking in my direction, but I pointedly ignored her. If she wanted to know what had happened to him, she should have taken her key and checked. *You're lucky, lady*, I silently told her. *If I wasn't ignoring you, I'd be screaming at you.* All she'd know would be the arrival of the ambulance.

Time seemed to have stopped. The bright sunshine, the distant hiss of cars passing, a breeze picking up, then falling, nothing to distract me from knowing there was a man in there dying and I could do nothing for him except stand as far away as I could from him.

Then, finally, finally, the faint and growing siren, adding to it the engine, and the solid shape of the ambulance turning the corner, pulling in front. It was followed by a police car.

I quickly stepped into the street to meet them. Our talk was spare, a quick briefing for the EMTs, what I'd found, what they'd find.

Then I crossed the street, out of their way. I was a stranger here, not family, not friend, only here through a thin web of coincidence.

But the police had questions, and they had little to do other than question me.

I told them what had happened, why I was here.

The older one seemed content with my story, but the younger one asked, "Let me see your license."

I pulled out my wallet and showed it to him. The older woman gave it a quick look, the younger one examined it closely.

"So you came here as a favor to a friend?" he queried after he finally gave me the license back.

I had called Cordelia a friend because this didn't seem the place to have to explain the homosexual agenda. "Yes, she did a favor for my cousin, so I felt I owed her one," I told them. I again went over the broken pipe, the rescheduling mess, being as redundant and boring as possible.

The older cop yawned.

The younger cop asked, "Any chance it was foul play?"

A young man doesn't get medical treatment, gets so sick he almost dies. I would call it foul, but I didn't think the law did.

But his line of questioning was interrupted by the clattering of the EMTs taking Reginald Banks out of the house.

In the dim light I had barely seen him, a limp shape covered in lumpy sheets and blankets, those emaciated arms. For the first time, I saw his face clearly. In health he would have been a handsome man, high cheekbones, a proud nose, thick, curly hair, an olive skin that put him between races. Even illness could not erase everything he might have been. But the face that flashed by me was hollow and gaunt, the eyes dull, unable or no longer interested in seeing what was around him.

Even the bright sunshine couldn't keep me from shuddering. He seemed so close to death that part of him was already a ghost.

The younger cop decided to investigate the house for signs of "foul play." His older—and wiser—partner was content to let him go in. I was even kind enough to give him the key. He could return it to the incurious neighbor.

The older cop and I looked at each other, then she glanced down at her watch. She said softly, "I'll buy you a beer if he manages to stay in there more than ten minutes."

He was back out in less than two, retching on the side of the stone steps.

"There was a lot of foul in there," I muttered.

The older cop retrieved a bottle of water from the squad car and tossed it to her partner. He washed his mouth out three times before swallowing anything.

"We might need to contact you to follow up," she said, but I could see she didn't believe that would happen. We exchanged business cards.

"Yeah, there are a few more things we might need to check out," the younger cop said, attempting to regain his swagger.

From behind his shoulder, the older cop gave me a sad smile.

Reginald Banks would go the hospital; maybe medicine had a miracle for him and he would come back here and that would be the end of it. Or there would be no miracles and his death would be ruled accidental. And that would be the end of it, unless some absent relative decided that they could make money from a malpractice suit.

I headed for my car, vaguely hearing someone call, "Hey, you." It sounded like the woman who had given me the key. I ignored her. She wasn't curious enough to call again, or follow me to my car.

I drove away not even knowing where I was going. Home? The office? Somewhere else? Nowhere? I found myself on Orleans Avenue and just stayed on it until I hit City Park, slowing to follow its twisting roads through the leafy trees. Life went on here, people playing tennis, picnicking in the shade, everything green and growing, the abundance of spring.

The opposite of a man dying alone.

I finally wound my way to Esplanade, taking that back almost to the river before finally deciding to head to my office. I took Dauphine down to the Bywater where my office is. I wanted more of the common, everyday exigencies to fill my time, to create distance from what I had witnessed.

As I was about to put the key in the downstairs door lock, I realized I had neglected to check my surroundings. As Joanne had said, Prejean wasn't likely to carry out his threat, but that didn't excuse my inattention. But the street was quiet and silent. I carefully locked the door behind me before heading up the stairs.

I started with cleaning the coffeepot, but that wasn't demanding enough to keep me from wondering if some of the smell lingered in my clothes. I rummaged in the assortment of clothes I kept here, some for the purpose of changing how I looked, others for times like this, when I could no longer wear what I started out the day in. I found a baggy pair of jeans and a very bright purple LSU sweatshirt.

Cleaning the closet seemed a logical next step. Or next distraction. I arranged the clothing from frothy pink costumes to the sensible jeans and T-shirts, grouping this into clothes that only cases could compel me to wear to sensible, normal clothes appropriate for a sensible, normal lesbian like myself.

After finishing the closet—even dusting the top shelf—I turned to e-mail, then reading news stories online. Distance.

The afternoon passed. I stayed beyond my usual quitting time, temporarily safe in a cocoon of these enclosed walls, the world compressed to the size of a computer screen. No one was threatening me here; the smells were pleasant, freshly brewed coffee, a hint of cleaning fluid. I could pretend the world was safe and what had happened to Reginald Banks could never happen to anyone close to me.

"You can't stay here all night," I told myself, speaking just to break the silence. I carefully shut down the computer, neatened my desk, even filed several folders.

Just as I could find nothing more to delay my leaving, the phone rang.

"Knight Detective Agency," I answered.

"Micky, I'm glad I caught you," Cordelia said. "You don't need to look for Reginald Banks. He's—"

"I know," I cut her off. "In the hospital." I hoped he was there and not the morgue.

"How did you—you found him." Cordelia knew me well enough to answer her question.

"I'm on my way home. We can talk about it then." I didn't mean to cut her off, but I didn't want to start the story on the phone only to start it again when I got home.

"Okay," she said slowly, as if trying to gauge my mood. "Should I start dinner?"

"No, not yet. I'm not really hungry." Then I added, "I'm okay, it just hasn't been a great day in the PI world."

"I'll see you soon, then."

I quickly locked up. The distance I had tried to get from Reginald Banks was gone, my vision clouded with his emaciated arms shoving pill bottles to the floor in the hopes that someone would hear them.

I could talk to Cordelia about it and she would understand. I hurried down the stairs.

"Damn it," I cursed under my breath as I tried to lock the outer door, the key not cooperating.

A rough hand grabbed my shoulder, spun me around, and slammed me against the building.

My bad day was about to get worse.

Chapter Eight

I was looking up at a tall—very tall—man with bulked-up shoulders and arms. His neck alone was about the size of my waist.

"I'm sorry," I said, "You seem to have mistaken me for someone else."

"Not possible," he said, his voice so low it sounded more like a rumble in his chest than a clear tone. "You're Michele Knight, a little girl private dick who's poking about where she shouldn't. This is a message to you in person, in a way to make sure you'll remember."

He had one big burly hand on my shoulder, using his weight and strength to pin me against the building. My unhappy guess was that he was keeping his other arm free to make the message memorable.

I wiggled against his grasp. I wasn't trying to get away, but he would expect me to resist and I needed to have some idea of what it would take to break free when I really tried.

A miracle was my conclusion.

"Trust me, I'll remember this message. I'm off the case and—"

"You fucking called the police." His hand tightened his grasp, his fingers painfully digging into my flesh.

"No, they called me." That was true, although I suspected that facts were of little use here. "I want nothing more to do with this. If they call again, I'm hanging up." Needless to say, I did not add I'd be going there in person as soon as I got away from him, fervently hoping that would indeed be possible.

"You need to go on a long vacation. Get out of the city for a while.

We don't want to see your face. Someplace with no phones, no Internet, none of that shit." Then he grinned. It wasn't a happy face, his graying teeth a sign of meth mouth. "Like a coma." The grin got bigger as he cocked his fist.

I was about to get the shit pounded out of me unless I managed somehow to hit him hard enough to immobilize him. He had me pinned tightly, but my arms and legs were still free. I no longer trained, but had studied karate long enough to get a brown belt. I would have one chance to hit him one time. Yeah, a gym giant amped up on meth. Another six months he'd lose the muscle, but that didn't do me much good now.

I squirmed under his barbell-sized fist, as if I could manage nothing more than a pathetic wiggle against his might. It only made him grin more. Add sadist to the list of adjectives.

He had my right shoulder pinned. I could move my right arm, but not more than to reach his elbow, not exactly a vulnerable location.

That meant my one perfect blow had to be left-handed. Did I mention I'm right-handed? I could kick, but he was so tall I'd have to bring my foot to my chest level to hit anything useful, leaving me off balance and making it too easy for him to grab my foot. And that is so not a good place to be, dancing on one foot with the hand of a sadistic thug wrapped around the ankle of your other foot.

"I'm gonna beat the crap out of you, bitch," he cheerfully informed me.

I suppose, under the circumstances, I should be glad that he was only threatening to knock me around just like the boy PIs.

"Then I'm gonna fuck you till your pussy splits open."

Why, why, do they always need to go there?

He was enjoying himself, licking his lips, perfectly willing to telegraph his moves as if there was nothing I could do to escape.

But as they always told us women, anatomy is destiny.

The first motion of his fist sent me into action. I violently twisted my body, ducking my head at the same time I stepped forward with my left foot, using that motion—and everything else I could pack into it—to bring a hammer fist hard up against his groin, then I opened my hand, grabbed whatever I could, and yanked it down, turning my arm at the same time.

"What the—" turning into a grunt of pain.

Enough pain for him to release my shoulder. Now free, I ducked under his arm and quickly kicked him in the back of the knee. That usually forces the knee to suddenly bend, taking someone down, but I had to kick him in the other knee to bring him down.

I kicked again, this time between his legs into a place I was hoping was really hurting by now.

He let out another roar of pain.

I sprinted as fast as I could for my car, praising the gods of technology for a key that could open the doors twenty feet away.

Jerking open the door, I literally jumped in, slammed the key in the ignition. I don't think I even had my door closed before my foot was jammed on the accelerator and I was roaring around the corner.

I had time for the barest glance back in the rearview mirror.

He was still on his knees but reaching into his jacket.

Then he was out of sight. And, more importantly, I was out of his sighting line. I had to assume that he was going for a gun and not his cell phone to tell Prejean that he had botched the job.

I sped through two stop signs, zigged and zagged onto different streets so I would be far from the one he'd seen me turn onto. I had to assume that he would attempt to follow me, just for revenge at being taken by a girl. I even played the race card, guessing that since he was white, he'd be less likely to think I'd disappear into the so-called black areas of town, but that's exactly what I did, crossing St. Claude into the Seventh Ward, up Florida Ave. to where the old Desire project used to be. It was now a desolate area, the projects first torn down to be replaced with something better, but Katrina flooded those new empty shells, leaving it a water-marked no-man's-land.

It was only there that I slowed enough to make sure my door was properly closed and even took the time to buckle my seat belt.

And then another panicked thought hit me. What if he knew my home address and was on his way there now?

I hastily grabbed my cell phone. Did I call the police or call Cordelia?

Cordelia. I loved her.

"Micky? I thought you'd be here by now," was her greeting.

"Do not open the door to anyone but me. Or Joanne. I'm on my way. If you see a very tall man with scraggly blond hair and enough muscles to be in a freak show, call nine-one-one immediately."

"Micky, what's going on—"

"I'm on my way. I'll be there as quick as I can. But don't open the door."

I didn't even give her time to reply before hanging up. Getting there was more important than being polite. And I couldn't handle being terrified out of my head, driving in New Orleans, and talking on a cell phone trying to calm her down all at the same time.

"Fucking turn green," I muttered at the first red light I encountered. I slid through the stop signs. And speed limit? What speed limit? Although the potholes and other idiot drivers rarely let me get into fourth gear, let alone fifth, the speed I wanted.

Finally, I pulled in front of my house. And this time had enough sense to leave the car running and carefully scan the block. Nothing seemed out of place.

I called Joanne. Not even giving her time to speak, I said, "Hey, Prejean just did more than make threats—I'm okay, but worried that he might have come to my house. I'm going in now."

"Stay out!" she yelled.

"Cordelia's in there." I hung up.

He wanted me, not her. And if I had to give him me to get him away from her, then that was the only choice I had.

Not giving him an easy target, I ran from my car to the front steps. I banged on the door. "Core, it's me." She hates all the ways people choose to shorten her name, so I rarely do it, but there was not enough time for four syllables.

Of course now I was standing on my front steps being a perfectly easy target. Just as I got my keys out, the door was flung open.

Cordelia.

No one else.

She was talking on the phone. "She just got here. Do you have any idea what this is about?" She mouthed "Joanne" to me as I brushed past her, quickly locking the door behind me.

Once safely bolted in, I took the phone from Cordelia.

I gave them both—Joanne over the phone and Cordelia listening in—the quick and dirty version of what had happened.

Just as I finished talking, a squad car pulled up, lights flashing, but mercifully no siren.

Not so mercifully, they pulled their guns as they approached.

Cordelia started to open the door, but I pulled her back.

I yelled at the cops—and into the phone, but Joanne could have mentioned she was sending a patrol car, "Hey, we're okay in here. Please put your guns down." Then I slowly and carefully opened the door, coming out with my hands clearly visible. "I'm talking to Detective Sergeant Joanne Ranson," I spelled out, so they would consider the possibility that the thing in my hand was a phone.

Mercifully, they did, putting their guns away.

A tinny voice—the phone two feet from my ear—said, "I'll be there in about five minutes." Replaced by a tinny buzzing. She'd hung up.

Just as I had finished explaining to the patrol cops that I was a private detective and that a swindler hadn't appreciated my locating him for the people he had swindled and that he blamed me for a fire at his house—which I emphasized I had nothing to do with, lest they think otherwise—and just about everything else I could explain, Joanne arrived.

And I had to do it all over again.

And a third time when Danny showed up.

"If we just had an executioner, we'd be set," I muttered.

"Naw, we just need a defense attorney," Danny cheerfully corrected me. "This isn't a capital offense."

"I'm capitally offended," I answered.

Joanne was kind enough to do the walk-through of the house, as if knowing that there had to be a bra or two hanging out of the laundry basket, letting the patrol cops check the outside, where we could argue that the dirty bras weren't ours.

No big man, no gas can, nothing suspicious.

Maybe Prejean had only paid him for a one-shot deal. Maybe it was about scaring me and not really doing harm—although I was more than sure that someone was going to get hurt, the only choice was who.

But if he wanted me off the case, I was off the case. It was over. What I'd found couldn't be unfound. Beating me into a coma wouldn't change anything. It made no sense. Crooks and criminals are usually not high intellects; as we say here, a few sandbags short of a levee. It didn't have to make sense to me.

As Joanne rejoined us, she said, "I don't think you should stay here tonight."

"One of you can stay with us," Danny said.

"One of us?" Cordelia asked.

"Redoing the guest bedroom, so only the couch is available. Bad timing on our part," Danny said with a rueful shrug as if she really did regret home improvement.

Joanne said, "One of you is welcome at our place. We've barely finished painting all the rooms; no extra beds as of yet. We can put an air bed on the floor." They had flooded, their house in eight feet of water.

She turned from us to speak to the cops to let them know they were free to go, but to give this block an extra pass by if possible.

Cordelia and I looked at each other. We hadn't even had a chance to talk about Reginald Banks.

"Or there are a few hotels around," Danny suggested, seeing our reluctance at the idea of separate sleepovers.

"What about our cats?" I asked, worried that Prejean might have revenge arson on his mind.

"We can leave them with Torbin and Andy," Cordelia said. We usually left the cats with them when we traveled.

The other cops left and Joanne turned her attention back to us.

"How long do we stay away?" I asked. The question wasn't directly at her, but she answered.

"Not long. From your description, this man is a distinctive character. He's probably in the mug shots, certainly easy to spot if he's seen on the streets. Spend the night away. Tomorrow look at some pictures. He might be in custody by midafternoon."

"What about Prejean?"

"Once we get his thug, he'll likely turn on Prejean and then we can arrest him."

"And if he doesn't?"

"He will," Danny interjected. "Addict thugs aren't paid well enough to protect their masters. They're just high enough to think they won't get caught. Once they are, they'll sell their mothers for a deal."

"So, call Torbin about the cats," Joanne said.

Cordelia nodded, and after a brief search, found where I'd left the phone. "Can you corral the cats while I get our stuff?"

Okay, I forgot to pack the underwear once; now the cats are my duty and the other packing Cordelia's. Joanne and Danny helped round up the beasts and get them into the carrier just as Torbin and Andy arrived to collect them.

By the time I had finished explaining—yet again—what had happened, Cordelia came downstairs with two overnight bags—the ugly burnt orange presumably for me and the deep purple for her.

She handed the purple one to me.

"Who goes where?" Danny, ever the logistician, inquired.

"We stay together. I'll sleep on the floor," I said.

Joanne started to argue, but Danny put a hand on her arm, clearly understanding the decision had been made.

We ended up going with Joanne. Her empty room had more floor sleeping space than Danny's living room couch.

By the time we got there it was almost ten p.m. Both Cordelia and Joanne work in professions that demand an early start, and Alex's long commute made the same demands on her. We had a quick sandwich for food, then bedded down in their empty spare room.

CHAPTER NINE

I insisted Cordelia take the air mattress. She needed her sleep—her patients needed her awake. If I didn't sleep well, I could snooze at my desk without major consequences.

We'd managed only a brief conversation before she nodded off. She had little information, only that Reginald Banks had been rushed to one of the hospitals—she didn't even know which one, LSU, she assumed, as that had replaced Charity. Tamara was his attending physician. As she wasn't around, Brandon had been notified and that was all she knew. I'd have to wait until the morning to find out if he was alive or dead.

Cordelia on the air mattress left me on the floor, not the most comfortable place to sleep. I was now tossing and turning over the events of the day.

I had wanted distance from finding Reginald Banks. I'd gotten it.

Sex, drugs, and rock 'n' roll would have been so much more preferable.

What the hell was Prejean hoping to accomplish? I wasn't actively investigating him. Revenge came to mind. His house had been torched—he assumed; it could have been his shoddy workmanship—and he wanted someone to pay for it. That would be me.

I can't take the vacation a meth-addict thug "recommended" I take because we had one already planned—plane tickets bought and all—in the near future. Once Cordelia finished with this job, she was going to take time off and we were going to New York City to visit my mother. But that was over a month away, not well timed for me to vamoose right now. My thoughts were jumbled. I wondered if I could get Cordelia to carry a gun.

I pretty much knew the answer to that, but I'd ask again anyway.

Somehow I managed to fall asleep, but was still slow and groggy in the morning.

Joanne and Alex had already gone by the time we came downstairs, leaving a note of where the coffee was, and a spare key on top of it.

I was kind enough to make coffee while Cordelia showered. She borrowed a travel mug, grabbed a granola bar, and was on her way.

After a quick cup of coffee of my own, I cleaned up, deflating the air mattress. We would be sleeping in our own bed tonight, I vowed. I headed downtown to my office. Joanne and Alex lived in Mid-City, so in less than fifteen minutes I was at my door. Instead of stopping I carefully drove around the block. But nothing appeared out of the ordinary.

Once I finally parked in front of my door, I waited for several minutes to see if there was any movement. Meth addicts are not patient people.

A butterfly flitted by. A car passed, driven by a woman twice my age. Then the street was empty, save for my fear and worries clouding this bright, sunny day.

I finally got out, carefully making my way to the outside door, doing a thorough look around before putting the key in. I turned it in the lock as quickly as possible, hurrying through the door and slamming it closed, then just as quickly locking it.

I slowly mounted the stairs, ready for someone lurking on the landings. As I got to the top, I thought, *I can't live like this, constantly in fear, wondering when the hand will grab me again.* But the only threat on the stairs was a big spider web in one corner. Bad for the flies, not so much a worry for me.

Once in my office, I locked the door behind me. I usually leave it open, trusting the downstairs door and three flights of stairs to give me adequate warning of anyone heading this way.

After having brewed a big, strong pot of coffee to compensate for my night on the floor, I called Joanne.

"Morning, sunshine," she answered. Caller ID can be so annoying. "Sleep well?"

"Lovely," I lied. "Took me back to my bucolic camping days of snoozing on oak roots."

"We put out a description of your attacker, but it would be helpful if you'd come in and look at some mug shots."

After a hasty gulp of coffee, I retraced my steps, carefully locking and unlocking, going slowly down the stairs as if there could be danger on every landing. I hesitated at the door, listening for any sounds on the other side. Hearing nothing, I threw it open and ran to my car, checking out everything and everyone. No black trucks, no looming man.

As before, the height of danger was the spider. No one on the street, no one in my building.

In fifteen minutes—five of them spent looking for parking—I was at the front desk asking for Joanne. I had to wait another fifteen minutes for her to come get me. Other than a quick hello, our only interaction was for her to dump me in front of a beat-up old computer to scroll through pictures of the scum of the earth.

So much scum, so little time. It was bad enough that after about half an hour, I went in search of the overbrewed swill they call coffee just to keep my eyes focused.

It took me over an hour and some major eyestrain, but I finally found him. Dudley Etherton III. A string of bad-boy arrests, joyriding, drug stuff, a barroom brawl. No jail time; it seemed that Daddy had good lawyers. His rap sheet screamed rich-boy rebellion, spoiled enough to think that Daddy's bucks would always get him off. But Dudley was an addict; I knew that much from my brief encounter with him. The addiction—and the poor choices his cravings caused— would take him places where Daddy couldn't help. Dudley the III was devolving, doing things even Daddy's best lawyers couldn't get him out of. His listed address was in Old Metairie, a place where the rich who didn't want to risk bumping into New Orleans riffraff lived.

Instead of making more sense, this was making even less sense. How did a two-bit, out-of-town swindler like Prejean connect with a local bad boy like Dudley? Which I was guessing was not the moniker he went by. Where do locals and not-locals meet up? A bar—there were plenty of them in this city. Daddy cut off Dudley. He needed to go to twink town to get his meth fix. A stranger in a bar offers up cash—and maybe his drug of choice—and, poof, just like that, Dear Dudley is at my door.

That was the how. It didn't answer the why. Why come after me?

Dudley's message hadn't been that this was revenge for burning down Prejean's place. It had been to warn me off a case I had closed. Maybe Dudley had taken two warning gigs and mixed them up. That was as good an explanation as any I could come up with.

I found Joanne and showed her the mug shot. She called it in, told me to be careful, that she'd call when they picked him up, and then she was pulled back into the usual criminal chaos of New Orleans.

When they caught him? *If they catch him*, I thought as I headed back to my car. Even knowing who to look for wasn't a guarantee that the cops would find him anytime soon. If he was smart—well, I knew the answer to that—but if he had a modicum of survival instinct, or was around someone who did, like Prejean, he'd be halfway to Houston by now. If he'd put me in a coma—or killed me, not a pleasant thought— he might get away with it. But given that he'd left me merely bruised but otherwise a hale and hearty witness, there was a jail cell with his name on it.

However, until he was in that cell, I had to assume he might try again to finish what he'd started, in the dim hope that if I was dead I'd be unable to testify against him. He didn't even need to be that thoughtful. He could also want revenge for the damage inflected on something very important to him.

So it was careful plus back to my office. Constantly checking my rearview mirror to see if anyone was following me, scanning the pedestrians just in case one of them might lunge at my car door.

I was almost there when I decided that the best defense was a good offense. Maybe it was time I had a talk with Carl Prejean to inform him of how misguided his actions were. And if that didn't work, kick him in the balls as well.

Perhaps a long shot, but I was guessing he might be rebuilding his burned house. I pulled to the side of the road—keeping my engine running, just in case—to rifle through the various notebooks in the backseat of my car. I was pretty sure I'd jotted his address there.

Of course he lived in one of the pretentious houses over by the lake. This is a newer section of New Orleans compared to the older enclaves of wealth like the Garden District. The area adjacent to the lake was land reclaimed in the early 1900s. Because of this, it was somewhat higher than the surrounding area, so a small swath closest to the lake did not flood. The houses date mostly from the mid-century or later. It never quite feels like New Orleans, instead some alien place that could exist in any city, bereft of the history of the French Quarter, Tremé, the Garden District, Uptown.

Prejean's address was at the end of a cul-de-sac, a large house, with one side a different and presumably unplanned color than the other. It dated from sometime in the sixties, a large, sprawling house painted a trendy brown, with modern windows that now seemed dated and a clearly added newer section on one side. The lawn was large, well tended. Its asking price was probably far out of my price range and even farther out of my taste range. Especially on the white trim, I could see evidence of smoke. However, unless there was damage not visible from the outside, the house seemed in decent condition and could be easily rehabbed.

A brand-new red truck was parked in the driveway.

I glanced at my notebook. Ah, yes, the license plate matched one registered to Karl Pearlman, one of Prejean's aliases.

I parked just far enough down the street to have a clear view of the house and the truck. If I was going to confront him, I intended to do so in as public a place as I could. I'd wait for him to come to his truck.

That didn't take long. Not even fifteen minutes. Evidently Prejean, or whatever his name actually was, didn't seem to be hard at work on repairing his house. His clothes were cleanly pressed, no sign of sweat or dirt.

I started my car and pulled in behind him, hoping that blocking him in would be a successful bluff and he wouldn't use his much newer truck to batter past my older car.

As I hoped, Carl did seem to be a swindler, not a fighter. He stood stock still, his mouth open, as if unable to comprehend what was happening.

I got out, making sure to brush my jacket open enough to reveal the gun.

He still didn't move, other than to close his mouth. Swindlers are actors. He either thought I'd be the last person he'd see here or he was doing a damn good acting job.

"Hey, Carl," I called. "A word with you."

"A word? Haven't you caused me enough trouble?"

"And you've caused me plenty of trouble back. That macho bruiser you sent to beat me senseless? I don't appreciate that kind of trouble."

"What are you talking about?"

Well, of course he wasn't going to admit to it. "I'm talking about the muscle man you sicced after me yesterday. Tall, blond, meth teeth. The one you met in a bar and hired to do your dirty work."

"I have no idea what you're talking about."

"You tried to send me a message. Perhaps the dude messed it up. Not wise to have drug addicts do your dirty work. He told me to get off the case. Which I can't do, since I'm already off the case."

"I didn't send anyone after you. I don't know what you're talking about." Prejean took a small step toward his truck.

I lunged and grabbed the keys out of his hand. Since my car was blocking the driveway, I'd be very unhappy if he tried to get away before I moved.

"You're the person who called up and threatened me. We both know that, so don't waste my time denying it. Next thing that happens, some muscle-bound idiot tries to beat the crap out of me. Bit of advice: bulked-up macho men are prone to lying about how big and tough they are, especially after a few drinks. For some reason, I connect your threat with his assault. Go figure."

"I'm telling the truth. I didn't send anyone after you."

"When you were a baby out of the womb, you were probably crying lies." I knew he wasn't going to admit guilt; he had too much swindler experience to fall into that trap. Prejean was an experienced con, and crocodile tears—and acts of innocence—were his specialty. "I wanted to give you a message in return. Your big boy messed it up. He didn't land a blow. The cops probably have him run down by now. I don't do illegal, but I have friends who do. Friends who owe me big-time. You leave me alone; I'll leave you alone. Mess with me again and I'll make you regret it in ways that you don't want to think about. Got it?"

"I still don't know what you're talking about," he claimed.

I tossed his truck keys halfway across his lawn. He started to turn to them, but wisely decided to keep his eyes on me.

As I kept mine on him. I backed to my car, keeping him in sight the entire way, my hand on my waist just below my gun. I even backed my car halfway down the block so I could keep him in view. He didn't move at first. Only when he realized I really was leaving did he retrieve his keys.

I did a hasty U-turn and was down the block before he got back to his truck.

What have I gained, I wondered as I drove back to my office. Of course he had played possum, but that was expected. He did seem surprised, and a bit shaken, to have me show up at his house. Most cons are smarter than Prejean appeared to be—he clearly hadn't bothered to consider how I'd react to his threat. Maybe he didn't expect me to seek him out, but he should have expected some reaction. Perhaps what had seemed a nice idea in a bar with Dudley Dude making promises didn't seem so smart now that the consequences boomeranged. Maybe Prejean would have the sense to back off and move on to more lucrative swindle victims. Perhaps not a nice wish on my part, but he was going to con people; he could at least do it without making a mess in my life.

My trip back to the office was convoluted. I wanted to make sure no one was trailing me or could easily guess where I was going. I was so busy checking my rearview mirror I came close to running a red light.

When I finally got back, my routine was the same—drive by, around the block, park outside and wait, then get into the building as quickly as I could, then slowly up the stairs. The spider still lurked, but nothing and no one else was about.

And it wasn't even noon yet.

Deciding that offense was still better than defense—or at least better than sitting around waiting to see if I got attacked again—I contacted the Grannies.

I didn't become a private eye because I wanted to sit and stare at a computer screen. But the Internet and its troves of information treasure were an important tool. I solved my screen-staring dilemma by hiring out.

Illegal grandmothers? Who better to skirt the law than little old ladies? Sarah Clavish used to share the floor with me. Her side was still unused. After retiring, she had found her vocation in computer sleuthing. "I get to sit all day in the air-conditioning," as she said. She turned out to be quite good at it. Over time she had recruited several of her friends and they became Grannies Online, Inc.

But her sister and brother-in-law had decided that they could ride out any hurricane; they always had before. Their house was high, they had a boat. They lived down the river. She had gone there the day before Katrina to convince them to leave—this one was different. But her brother-in-law wasn't willing to abandon his house, his wife wouldn't abandon him, and in the end, Sarah didn't abandon her sister. He was able to get in the boat, but the violent waves took the two sisters.

Her two cohorts continued the work and I continued to use them. I can do the computer stuff, but much of it is tedious reading of some of the most boring documents in the world over and over again before finding anything useful. I'm just as happy to send it out. Plus, I don't have the hacking skills the Grannies have.

"Hey, Alma, I need a favor."

"You going to bring cookies again, honey?"

Alma called everyone "honey" save for those she called "scalawags." "Any kind of cookies you want," I promised. Then I asked for my favor—anything and everything about Carl Prejean and his aliases, with special emphasis on his burned house and the insurance claims made on it.

"Oh, and if anything happens to me, assume he's behind it and you may let loose whatever computer evil you wish." And I had to explain—yet again—what had happened.

They promised to dig "to the center of the computer earth."

As I hung up I thought that if the clock weren't just striking noon, I'd be ready to go home.

The phone rang. Assuming it was Alma with additional questions, I answered, "Yeah, honey pie, what kind of cookies do you want?"

"Micky?" Cordelia.

Good thing for me that she knew about the Grannies and about my cookie baking payment to them (cold hard cash as well, I do not take advantage of charming little old ladies and their sweet tooth) so my explanation just squeaked into the bounds of possible.

After which I added, "I'm free for lunch if you'd like to get together." On saying it, I realized it was true. Yesterday felt like such a jumble that it seemed we'd barely seen each other.

"I'd like to," she said wistfully, "but it's crazy here. I'm afraid I'm going to ask you for another favor."

Just the tone of her voice told me it was something that I probably wasn't going to want to do, so I hedged, "I'll do it if I can."

"Reginald Banks is in a coma. I just got the news from Lydia. She went over his records and realized that he had made an appointment and come in for it. His insurance was billed and they paid and there are notes in his chart. He was Tamara's patient. Lydia even called her, but she couldn't remember, although she was distracted by a screaming baby. So we can't understand why he deteriorated so quickly."

"I can't see how I'll be much help there," I said. "Take two aspirin is about as far as I get in the medical department."

"One possibility is that he was taking something that interfered with his treatment."

Ah, light dawned. "You want me to go back to his house and see what he might have been taking."

"I hate to ask…"

"But you're going to anyway."

"It might be his only chance. Admittedly not a great one, but if he was on drugs or even taking something like St. John's wort, it might shed some light."

"Would you consider carrying a gun?" One obnoxious request deserved another.

"A gun? You know how I—"

"A very bad man might be stalking you. At least until he's caught."

"So if I agree to carry a gun, you'll check out Reginald Banks's residence?" she asked.

"Yes, I would do that." I couldn't believe that she'd agree.

"Would you do it if I don't agree?"

"I want to keep you safe," I argued.

"Micky, if I truly thought it would keep me safe, I might agree. But first, I don't know how to fire a gun, so it might be more danger than not. And second, I took an oath. 'First do no harm.' I take that seriously. I don't know if I could fire a gun at another person."

"Not even to save the orphans, widows, and puppies?"

"I might shoot one of them rather than save them. No, I can't carry a gun. Does that mean my request is off the table?"

"No," I conceded. "I'll call the cops I saw there yesterday and see if they're okay with letting me in. I won't do B and E. Will that suffice?"

"Thank you."

"And you have to do the laundry." I couldn't handle another set of stench-infused clothing.

"Deal. Thank you. I do mean that."

I knew she did, I could hear it in her voice.

"And sex, lots of sex." But she had already hung up. However, laundry was the challenge—she had never been shy in the lots-of-sex department.

I gave myself a bathroom break before digging through my desk to find the cards from the cops I'd spoken to yesterday. They had gone into my I'll-never-need-this-again pile. Which was why I found them so easily—it's only the stuff I think I'll need that I can't find. I glanced at the two cards. Mr. Foul Play got tossed back into the desk—same pile.

First ring was answered by the woman cop.

I told her my mission.

The stars were in alignment. Against me. She still had the key and was willing to meet me there. In half an hour.

There would be no lunch today. No time now, and I doubted that I'd feel like eating after being in that house again.

I grabbed a big flashlight and a bottle of scented moisturizer. Noxious toxic sites are places I avoid, so I wasn't exactly prepared to deal with unwanted odors. Sandalwood rose was my only option. Also several pairs of latex gloves. This wasn't a crime scene, not of the prosecutable kind; they were more for my protection against the rot and decay.

No wonder the bad guys win, I thought as I again headed downstairs. It's impossible to be ever vigilant, always prepared for something that might not happen as I caught myself sauntering down the stairs as if spiders were my only worry. I managed to perk up my wariness by the time I was on the bottom steps. The memory of what had happened when I'd walked out this door was too recent for my animal brain not to go on alert when I reached it.

But the only threat was a cloud covering the sun, a hint of rain later.

I made it to Reginald's house in twenty-five minutes.

The woman cop—Pam Ferguson—was there right at thirty minutes sans Mr. Foul Play.

"Fancy that," she said cheerfully. "He offered to do paperwork rather than come back here." She held out the key for me. "However, if it's all the same with you, I'll hang out here and let you do the inside work."

I gingerly took the key. Then rubbed the sandalwood rose under my nose.

"Good excuse to moisturize," she said as she watched me.

"Bad excuse," I said as I dabbed a bit more, giving myself a lotion mustache. "Lousy excuse."

There was nothing to do except put the key in the lock and open the door. At least here I had a cop with a big gun watching my back.

The house felt different, or maybe it was just that I knew now how empty it was. Even though there was enough daylight to see, I turned on the flashlight. Whatever had happened to Reginald Banks shouldn't have happened, and those tragedies can haunt a place.

Using the strong beam of light, I did a quick sweep of the living room, looking for anything like a pill bottle or a container that might hint that he was taking something that wasn't doing him any good. The obvious answer was illegal drugs. After donning latex gloves, I did a rapid search under the sofa and chair cushions, places where crack pipes or joint butts might fall. Only a few crumbs were there.

I started to bypass the kitchen, but decided that it was better to hit that while the lotion under my lip was still fresh.

It was the same chaos it had been yesterday, a few flies now buzzing around. I didn't bother opening the refrigerator; I decided that it would be too much of a rotted mess to find anything useful. I might give it a quick check on my way out, but only if nothing else turned up.

The beam of the flashlight revealed dirty dishes with rotting food on them, probably placed in the sink with hopes that tomorrow he would feel better and be able to clean up. The place wasn't a pig sty, as if he always lived in a mess. Cordelia and I both had the same miserable cold once and neither of us was up to doing chores, so the dishes had piled up for three days. We could manage to microwave soup and put the bowl somewhere in the kitchen, and that was about it. But we got better and cleaned everything up. It looked like something similar had happened to Reginald, only he was sicker longer and never recovered enough to wash the dishes and take the trash out.

If he was eating something weird like kelp/seaweed smoothies, there was no way to tell in this mess. From what I could see, there were several empty microwave boxes in the trash, soup cans, half a loaf of bread still open and now covered in green mold. Some of the plastic microwave containers were in the sink, half-eaten as if he only could manage to consume a little at a time.

Why hadn't he called someone? Anyone? Even 911? If he could push pill bottles to the floor, he should have been able punch buttons on a phone. There was a cordless receiver in the kitchen. I picked it up, then realized that without power, it wouldn't work. The plugged-in, working phone was about as far from his bed as it could be in this house. The phone close to him didn't work and the one that did was too far away. Maybe that's what had happened. Possibly he wasn't that good about bills, so had forgotten to pay Entergy. I'd once rented half of a double in which the other side was rented by an ER doctor who was continually forgetting to pay her power bill. Several times she had her power cut off. I knew because they'd messed up in the back shed with the laundry and my side was wired to hers, so when she didn't pay up, my washing machine didn't work. The next day the power was back on—no lights is a powerful reminder to pay your bill.

Maybe that was what happened to Reginald. But when the power went out, he was too sick to drive to a local office and pay his bill. His phones were out if they were all cordless. But didn't everyone have a cell phone these days?

This isn't your mystery to solve, I reminded myself. My sole duty was to do a brief search for illicit pills and vamoose back to the sunshine and fresh air.

Next stop was the bathroom. The flashlight came in handy here. There was only one, small window, blocked by curtains. The sink and counter tops revealed only what I'd expect to find. Shaving stuff, soap, toothpaste, hair gel, a few metrosexual grooming products like cologne.

A glance in the trash can showed a pile of used tissues, several cardboard toilet paper rolls.

And an empty bottle.

I couldn't read the label; it was canted almost upside down. Switching the flashlight to my left hand, I tentatively stuck my arm—thankfully gloved—into the trash can and retrieved the plastic bottle.

The label read *Nature's Beautiful Gift, potent immune system booster.* The bottle was empty. Hidden under it in the trash was another bottle. *Nature's Beautiful Gift, herbal aid to circulation and blood disorders.* Also empty.

I tried to read the ingredients, but the print was tiny and it was hard to juggle the flashlight and the two bottles. Even if it was important, it probably wouldn't mean anything to me. I took the two bottles out to the living room, placed them on the coffee table, reapplied the sandalwood rose, and went back to the bathroom.

The medicine cabinet was disappointing. It was mainly empty save for a bottle of aspirin that was almost empty and a razor and extra blades.

The smell was starting to get to me—and that this felt like ghoulish digging through someone else's life, one I had no business being involved in. I dashed back into the kitchen to grab a plastic grocery bag. I covered my nose with my hand, hoping to create a little sandalwood bubble, and went into his bedroom. I did a quick look around the room. The bed covers were flung back; the pillow still held the indentation of his head. Scattered on the floor were bright new pieces of packaging left by the EMTs. Mixed in with them was other debris, half a slice of bread, candy bar wrappers, drink cans. On the bedside table were a number of medicine bottles, several of them prescriptions; others bore the now familiar Nature's Beautiful Gift label. The ones on the floor—that Reginald had knocked over in a desperate attempt to let someone know he was here—were all Nature's Beautiful Gift. I wondered if that was coincidence or if there was a message in his choices.

I didn't dare take a deep breath, but sucked as much of the sandalwood scent into my lungs as I could before removing my hand. I gathered all the various bottles and loaded them into the plastic bag.

I stooped to retrieve the ones from the floor, then swept the ones off the nightstand into the bag. My oxygen was running out. I took a shallow breath, then regretted it as I started to gag. Quickly clamping a hand over my nose, I left the room, returning to the front room and its kinder atmosphere. After another application of the lotion—and a few deep breaths of sandalwood, I returned to the bedroom. As unpleasant as it was, I wanted to make sure I didn't overlook anything. It would be even more unpleasant to have to come back.

I gave the room another hasty sweep with the flashlight. Maybe he was so hungry he ate the moldy bread—but I wasn't going to take that with me. Gripping the flashlight between my thighs, I took out my cell phone and snapped several pictures of the state of the room. Perhaps they would find some medical clue in that. There was a drawer in the nightstand.

Please don't let me find his sex toys, I bargained as I opened it.

Fate was kind. No sex toys, not even a condom. On top was several pieces of paper, and one opened envelope with a letter inside, like he has shoved correspondence in the drawer. Hidden under the paper were more bottles. But these weren't Nature's Beautiful Gift; instead they were wrapped in a plain dark blue label with white lettering. Slightly larger letters said *The Cure*. Under that the label continued: *Suppressed by the government and powerful corporations, this is what they don't want you to have—a powerful, natural cure for many of life's most tragic curses—cancer, heart disease, AIDS, aging, lupus, multiple sclerosis, and many others.*

Fate hadn't been kind to Reginald Banks. It gave him a disease with no cure and people who promised him something he desperately wanted, to be free of that disease.

I scooped the bottles into the plastic bag. My work here was done. I quickly left the bedroom and went back to the living room and breathable air.

Then my curiosity stopped me. Why had Reginald put that letter in his nightstand? I hurried back to his bedroom and hastily snatched the letter out of the drawer, then back to the living room.

I glanced at the letter. It was a denial of service from his insurance company. A lot of the codes and jargon they used made no sense to me, so I had no clue as to what was denied, but something wasn't right. He was almost dead because he didn't get the medical care he needed.

You're already here; you might as well check out his office, I told myself. First I reapplied the lotion, did as quick a run as I could in the kitchen to snag another plastic bag, then went back to his office.

I promised the empty room that I would return whatever I took and, if Reginald wanted it, help him fight whatever fight he needed to battle with his insurance company. Rather than taking the time to sort through things, I loaded up the bag with all the piles of paper on his desk. He seemed to be a file-by-pile person, as his desk drawers were used for pens, paper, sticky notes, and other office supplies. There was no file cabinet and his bookshelves held only books, a long shelf of science fiction, another couple of shelves that seemed to be college books, then another shelf on self-help books, nutritional books, several about natural healing and herbal medicines. I took several of those as well, to see if I could get an idea of what he was doing—or let Cordelia sift through them; she'd probably understand them far better than I could.

Then it was truly time to get out. At this point even sandalwood was starting to make me gag. I'd probably never be able to use that scent again.

I hastened back to the living room, grabbed the bag of medications, and then was out to the fresh air.

Pam, the cop, was lounging on the front steps, texting on her cell phone.

I hadn't seen one in the house and wasn't going to go back and look for something as small as a cell phone. Most likely it had fallen under the bed, and there was no way I was going to get on the floor in that bedroom and look for anything. It was possible that Reginald didn't have a cell phone. Or his battery had run down and with the power off, he couldn't recharge it.

"Oh, hey," she looked up and greeted me. "Was beginning to think you were lost in there."

"Not likely. But I wanted to make sure I'd checked everything. The last thing I want to do is go back."

"Makes sense to me. It's fine out here on the steps enjoying the breeze, so no problem on my end. Plus the longer I'm here, the more paperwork gets done without me. Hope this helps the guy."

I handed her the key back. "Yeah, me, too. Thanks for agreeing to meet me."

"Slow time of day—as if there is one. They're just waking up now from sleeping off last night's buzz." She waved good-bye as she got in her patrol car.

I put the two plastic bags in my trunk and got in my car, opening all the windows. My nose felt blasted by the tang of decay overlaid with the sweetness of sandalwood rose. At the moment, diesel fumes would be a welcome change.

I was headed for home. At the last minute I made a course change to take a convoluted route there. I needed a memory jog to remind me I was in mortal danger and until Dudley Dude was caught, hypervigilant needed to be my middle name.

The cats were happy to see me, especially with such interesting-smelling clothes. I went straight to the laundry room and stripped. Even the underwear went in. I tossed yesterday's clothes in as well and started the washing machine. As agreed, Cordelia could finish it up.

Then upstairs for a brief shower and into clean clothes.

Only now did I begin to feel like I could breathe without smelling a lingering odor.

It was way past lunchtime, but I wasn't very hungry. However, I grabbed an apple and some string cheese. It was remotely possible that I'd be hungry later, and this way I could stay safely locked in my office and not have to forage for food.

I just got back in my car when the phone rang.

"Micky? Where are you?" It was Cordelia.

"Uh…in the car." I started the engine just in case I needed to speed off. And locked all the doors.

"You don't need to go to Reginald's house anymore."

"He's okay?"

But she didn't immediately answer, and I knew he wasn't okay.

"He's… No, I'm sorry, he's not okay. He passed away. I just found out."

"Oh." I couldn't think of anything else to say.

"I'm sorry. I hope I saved you from a useless trip."

I didn't immediately answer, and that gave her the answer.

"Oh, honey," she said. "You're not there now, are you?"

"No, I left a little while ago. Came home to change clothes. Even started the washer for you." I coughed to cover that my voice was about to crack. I only knew this man as a name and a disease. And an emaciated hand shoving pill bottles to the floor as a plea for me to enter his home and find him. Find him to save him, and I hadn't done that.

You did what you could, my rational voice reminded me.

But someone should have saved him, and I was his last chance.

Cordelia said gently, "You know if you had waited until tomorrow to do this, I would love you just as much. You don't need to prove anything to me. You have stood by me and…" Her voice broke.

We are not going to sob over cell phones, I told myself. "Hey, love,

I've stuck with you because no one else would have me, okay? And… and going to Reginald's house today just happened to work into my schedule. And I only started the first load, so you're stuck with drying and folding the clothes. I think the cat blankets need to be washed as well."

"Thank you, thank you, thank you," she said, half-laughing and half-crying.

"And the bathroom rug and shower curtain."

"I love you. I will always love you." She wasn't crying anymore. She wasn't laughing either.

"You're crazy." Then I added, "I love you, too."

I caught myself smiling as I was driving back to my office. And forgetting to obsessively check my rearview mirror. I was sad about Reginald—he was young and shouldn't be dead—but he wasn't someone in my life, not someone I'd expect to see and talk to again. This evening I would be with Cordelia, we would talk as we usually did, hang out in the kitchen together as I cooked dinner. In the moments when you realize how fragile life is, you recognize how vital holding someone's hand, talking to them, sharing food, and just laughing are.

When I got to my office a big man was waiting outside for me. Mr. Charles Williams.

Don't I ever get a break, I thought as I got out of my car as slowly as possible.

He waited for me to emerge and then called, "Hey, wanted to see what progress you were making on the case."

"It's not your case," I reminded him as I opened the street door just wide enough for me to slip in.

"Yeah, yeah, but Fletch is a busy man, and this way I can help move things along."

I didn't budge from the doorway. "Client confidentiality. Can't divulge any info without written consent from," I blanked on his last name, "the client."

"I can call him up right now and have him fax you something."

"You can do that. And then you can call me and set up an appointment to come in and talk about it. That will not happen right now, as I have other clients I need to deal with." And for emphasis I added, "Ones who are paying me significantly more than Fletch."

"Not even five minutes? I drove all the way here."

"Not even a minute. You can save yourself a drive if you call first. I'm not responsible for your choice not to do that."

He stuck his foot in the door.

I opened the door a few inches, then slammed it against his foot. He had steel toe boots on, so I couldn't really do damage.

Not that it stopped him from acting as if it had. "Ouch, damn it, that hurt."

"If I have to do it again, it'll hurt even more. Mr. Charles Williams, you are trespassing. If you don't leave now, you'll never get a chance to come back and hear anything about this case unless Fletch himself chooses to tell you."

He slowly removed his foot. "How about tomorrow around this time?"

"I don't have my schedule book with me. Call me later and I'll see if that works. And I have to have a signed consent from Fletcher." Not giving him a chance to say anything else or stick another body part in, I slammed the door shut.

Through the door he yelled, "I'll call in about five minutes, that should give you time to get your schedule."

I pretended I hadn't heard, hurrying up the steps.

Once I was safely locked in my office, I picked up my phone and dialed Joanne. For once, I was more than happy to be put on hold to wait for them to find her. Six minutes would be perfect timing as far as I was concerned. I doubted that she had any updates for me, but it couldn't hurt to ask, especially if it forced Mr. Williams to leave a message.

At just five minutes into the hold, Joanne came on the line.

"I've been out in the field," I said, "wanted to see if you had any news about Dudley Dude."

"Damn, pay a few dollars in taxes and everyone wants a miracle. I haven't heard anything, but we're looking for him. I know it's not much comfort, but he's probably hiding out. He screwed up big-time in not taking you out."

"His screwup is my benefit. Any way to link him to Prejean?"

"Nothing so far. Hutch and I had a little talk with Mr. Prejean. He swears he had nothing to do with it, didn't hire anyone to rough you up, doesn't know anyone named Dudley or anyone answering to his description."

As hoped for, my second line rang softly. I'd let the answering machine pick up.

"Of course he's going to say that. When did you see him?"

"Just a little while ago. A patrol car called in his license and we caught up with him at that big box store on Carrollton."

Interesting he hadn't mentioned my earlier visit. Maybe he was smart enough to know the cops wouldn't believe him over me. Or maybe he wanted out of the mess he'd created and was hoping the less he said, the sooner it was all behind him.

"Thanks for doing this, Joanne."

"'To serve and protest,' that's what your tax dollars buy."

"So what do I do now?"

"You know the drill. Pay attention to your surroundings. Vary your routes. Look for suspicious activity. Make sure doors are locked, alarms set. Don't take candy from strangers. Avoid eighties rock music. Pork rinds are not a food."

"Got it."

"You're welcome to camp at our house for as long as you want."

"It's hard to have sex on an air mattress."

"There is the Motel 6 in Slidell."

"Seriously, should we stay away?"

"To be truly safe, yes. But, honestly, I don't know. You're probably going to be okay. My gut tells me that Prejean doesn't want to play rough games anymore. Dudley Etherton may feel he has a beef with you, but if he shows up anywhere close to you and you see him before he bashes you to kingdom come—which you'd better do—then he'll be arrested in two seconds."

"Floor sleeping doesn't agree with me, but I can't risk Cordelia being hurt."

"Want me to spend the night with you?" She quickly added, "At your place, that is? We could take turns standing guard."

"Let me think about it."

"Okay, call later and let me know."

Of course, five minutes after I hung up with Joanne, the phone rang again.

On the off chance that it might be someone like Cordelia, I answered, "Knight Detective Agency."

"How come you don't answer your phone?" My first guess was right: Mr. Charles Williams.

"Can you believe it? Both secretaries are out sick, and I was on an important call with the police, so I couldn't pick up. If you'd left a message I would have called back." Tomorrow.

"Got a chance to look at your schedule yet?"

"As a matter of fact, I did. I'm pretty booked up, but I can see you the day after tomorrow, but only at 7:30 a.m."

There was silence on the other end. I seemed to have correctly guessed Mr. Williams was not a morning person.

"That's not a great time for me," he finally said.

"It's all I've got open. Plus I'll still have to have the signed consent from Fletcher."

"Can you do it late in the day?"

"No, I can't."

"You sure?"

"I'm sure. I'm booked today and out of town after that," I lied. "How about next week?"

He was silent for a moment. "Nothing earlier?"

"You do need the signed consent form. Might be better to give it more time."

"Can we do it around this time?"

I glanced at my watch. It was 3:30 p.m. "If you're here promptly at three, we can meet. Does that work?"

He agreed reluctantly, as if hoping that if he was slow a miracle time would open up today or tomorrow.

After I finally got him off the phone, I decided I truly deserved my apple and string cheese. My brain wasn't hungry, but my stomach was growling.

While eating, I remembered the plastic bags in my car. I'd left them there to bring to Cordelia. I wondered if it mattered now.

Then I pulled the file on Fletcher McConkle's case. I hadn't seen or heard of Nature's Beautiful Gift before—which didn't mean all that much. Boiled shrimp instead of fried oysters is about as close as I get to health food. Cordelia worries about what she eats, so salads and veggies are a big part of our diet since we mostly eat together.

Greedy people are a dime a dozen, and selling cures is a time-honored rip-off. Perhaps a new marketer was in town, aggressively pushing their magic pills, and in a weird coincidence had snagged both Fletcher's aunt and Reginald Banks. If Reginald had been denied service by his insurance and didn't have adequate access to medical care, he might have turned to someone promising a cure, or at least relief that only required taking some pills every day.

Mr. Charles Williams was going to get his wish—assuming Fletcher, and his more astute wife, let him have access to my investigation.

First I had to learn everything I could about Nature's Beautiful Gift. I'd dig up what I could, but would probably also call in the Grannies. Time to go to the Internet.

After an hour of searching what I had learned was the NBG, as I was now abbreviating Nature's Beautiful Gift (who the hell thought up that name?) seemed like the classic multilevel marketing scheme. The big push was to get "naturalists," as they called their salespeople, to buy into "promoting the health and well-being in your community." Which translated to selling them any number of NBG products. The rhetoric was heavy on how altruistic it was to sell this product, like no one was actually making any money, but instead doing community service by making this fantastic creation available. It was "pure" and "wholesome" and "all natural," using, and I quote, "Nature's Beautiful Gift to help people live life to the fullest." They had a variety of products from "promoting skin health" to "enhancing intimacy." As Cordelia had pointed out, nothing actually claimed to cure or relieve any real physical condition, so they kept their toes on the right side of the legal line. But the main website had numerous links to other sites that weren't selling NBG, and those did make claims on how wonderful the products were. There were vague mentions of studies, but most of the claims were anecdotal, heartfelt claims from people who were sure that NBG had been the one and only reason their hemorrhoids or arthritis or intimacy problems were now cured.

According to the company shtick, a doctor in rural Alabama working in the 1930s was the supposed discoverer of the herbs used in NBG. The folksy story claimed that because he was so isolated, he often had to make do with what was at hand. He learned from the people around him, especially the sharecroppers, who had to depend on traditional cures. In other words, he had been a wonderfully enlightened white doctor working in rural Alabama, paying no attention to the Jim Crow laws of the time. So enlightened that his white patients were willing to mingle with black patients. In Alabama in the 1930s.

Maybe it happened, maybe they were isolated enough that no one dared complain about seeing the one doctor available.

Anyway, this enlightened doctor wrote down many of the herbal medicines, but he passed away without telling anyone about them. Modern medicine took over with their machines and expensive pills and this knowledge was lost. Until by a major stroke of luck, a pharmacist was moved to investigate the attic of a house he had bought with the intention of tearing it down and building his dream house for his family. A dream McMansion was my guess. He found the doctor's notebooks and because of his background and training understood the importance of his discovery.

Realizing how significant this find was to the health and well-being of the people he served, he decided to put the money that would have built his house into recreating the herbal remedies that had been discovered so long ago and make them widely available.

NBG was only five years old, but its products were so remarkable that it rapidly spread from Mobile, Alabama, where the pharmacist now lived, throughout the South, to Florida, Georgia, Mississippi, and was now expanding to Louisiana, Texas, and the Carolinas.

NBG claimed to be very selective in who was chosen to be part of the naturalist sales force—I was betting that gullibility was a major trait—only those who truly wanted to help their family, friends, and community should even consider it.

I was rather glad I hadn't eaten much lunch, as all this goodness and wholesomeness was about to make me barf. Some herbal remedies probably were useful, but it was highly unlikely that multiple miracles were just waiting to be picked off a tree. Any company promising to cure everything—like NBG—was suspicious. I had no doubt that NBG was selling something like dried iceberg lettuce, and any relief obtained would be from the placebo effect.

People spend money all the time on things they don't need. Even prescription medicines aren't a promise. Most of the time they do some good; sometimes they don't, sometimes they do harm. How much worse was Nature's Beautiful Gift?

As I thought about it, I realized there were differences. Science isn't exact; it's just what we know now. Prescription drugs at least had to go through clinical trials that required they prove they have some beneficial effect, at least most of the time for most of the people. An FDA panel, people who were not supposed to have any vested interest in the drug, had to weigh the evidence of the trials and decide whether to approve it or not. Perfect? No. No human endeavor is. But there were checks and balances and more than just another person's word.

Maybe Reginald Banks decided to use unproven, untested nostrums instead of going through another fight with the maze of insurance denials and appointment bungles. Nature's Beautiful Gift itself may not have hurt him, but if it gave him a rationale to avoid conventional medical treatment, it might have killed him. And I had to fault conventional medical treatment for putting that maze in front of him.

I had assumed that The Cure, the blue-labeled bottles I'd found as well, probably were linked to NBG. Part of that was finding them together—how many shyster schemes could Reginald Banks have come in contact with? But so far, I'd found no link from the NBG site. It was possible that they had nothing to do with each other.

Fletcher McConkle had hired me to investigate whether his aunt was being fleeced by someone selling NBG. And possibly The Cure? Now I had reasons beyond his money to investigate this case.

I glanced at my watch. It was just after four o'clock. Not a lot of time to really get going unless I wanted to be here all night. I didn't want Cordelia home alone for even one second. Plus I had to decide whether the comfort of a decent mattress was worth the risk that Dudley Dude might return.

I called the Grannies and asked them to research Nature's Beautiful Gift and The Cure. I wasn't interested in the NBG sales spiel but wanted info on where they were located, who actually owned the company, and whether the profit margin indicated community service or avarice.

Wherever we ended up sleeping tonight, Cordelia and I could look over the stuff in my truck from Reginald Banks's house. I could even call it part of my billable hours to Fletcher McConkle.

As Joanne had advised, I would vary my hours and leave now. That would give me adequate time to take enough of a complicated route home that no one would be able to follow me.

Chapter Ten

It was only a little past 4:30 when I got home, but Cordelia was already there. Or at least her car was.

"Cordelia?" I called. At first there was no answer. "Cordelia? Are you here?"

Faintly from the back of the house, I heard her indistinct reply.

I found her sitting on the screened-in porch, holding Rook, her cat.

"Are you okay?" I asked.

She didn't look at me immediately, "We need to talk."

We've had our differences; what couple hasn't? I didn't know if I wanted to talk. But especially in the last few months, it felt like things were okay—no, not just okay, but good. Good like our talk earlier today, caring, connected. What could have happened?

She glanced up at me. I was still standing.

"Please sit," she asked.

I slowly let myself down on a chair opposite her. I realized her eyes were red.

"What's going on?" I asked. My mind churned as to what could be wrong. She'd gotten the cats from Torbin and Andy. Had they fought—continued their fight about medical care? Could it have something to do with Reginald Banks and me suddenly being a part of her world?

"I...saw Jennifer today. Some of the tests had come back."

It was all I could do to not scream, *No, there can't be anything wrong with you.* But I held myself calm and said, "Tell me. Whatever it is, tell me."

"Those times, when I woke up so hot—sweating—and thought it was perimenopause," she said, stroking Rook as if she might have to say good-bye too soon. "And the swollen lymph nodes? I thought it was a lingering cold—that's what I wanted it to be."

"Yes, I remember."

"My blood counts are way off. And my lymph nodes are still swollen both under my arm and in my groin. Classic signs of non-Hodgkin's lymphoma. That's what the preliminary pathologist report indicates. He's doing further stains—tests—to be sure."

I wanted to scream, to pray to any god listening. Somehow I said, "Couldn't it be something else?"

She answered slowly, "It could, but the horse is lymphoma, zebras are something else." She referenced the standard lore of medical students, "If you hear hoofbeats, look for horses, not zebras." She added, "And the zebras might be even worse. If you're going to get sick, it's better not to have something exotic that no one knows how to treat."

I got up to sat beside her, petting Rook so that our hands touched. "What do we do now?" I asked.

"You go on living your life. And I…get more tests. I'm sorry, that came out wrong. I want you to keep going, keep everything as normal as possible for as long as possible."

I wrapped my arms around her and held her close. Rook, uncharacteristically, allowed himself to be swallowed in my embrace, as if he knew he was needed.

"They have much better treatments these days," I said. "I know you're a doctor, but you're not a cancer doctor and what you learned in medical school has probably changed a lot. Gotten better."

She nodded against my sleeve as if wanting to catch my optimism.

She was silent. I just held her.

Finally, she lifted her head. "We'll run more tests. Some are so slow they don't require treatment for a long time. Caught in time, it's a very curable cancer. Right now I know just enough to worry. Maybe it'll all be okay. It seems you can't get over forty without having a cancer scare."

"How much should I worry?" I asked her, wanting her to be honest with me.

"Save it for when you have something to really worry about, and we're not there yet." She kissed me softly, then again, not so softly.

The kissing stuff was too much for Rook and he chose now to squirm out of her arms.

Much as I wanted to sit here and hold her forever, the rest of life intruded. "Go on living your life," she'd said—we didn't have much choice.

Rook and Hepplewhite, our cats, weren't good guard cats and wouldn't be much help if Dudley decided to come visit.

I allowed one more kiss before gently breaking off. "There is nothing more I'd rather do, but the police haven't caught the asshole who jumped me yesterday. I have to worry that he might try again. And I have to make sure you're—we're safe."

She nodded reluctantly. "So, Ms. Security Professional, what do you recommend?"

"Joanne offered to come over and we could take turns standing watch."

"Won't that put Joanne at risk?"

"She's a cop. She carries a big gun."

"Nothing like a gun fight at home. Other options?"

"We could camp out again in their spare bedroom."

"Only if you take the air mattress this time."

"Even if I prefer the floor?"

"You don't prefer the floor; I heard your groans this morning. How about going to a hotel?"

"We can do that. Should I take the cats back to Torbin and Andy?"

"You don't think it's safe to stay here?"

"Once they catch him it will be."

"What if they don't catch him?" she asked.

That was the pesky question I had been asking myself. "He's not after me for himself. He was hired by a swindler who's a bit of a hothead. Unless there is money to be made my attacker has no reason to come after me. He'll be on to other things in a few days." Perhaps a little optimistic, but that was my best guess. Prejean would move on to other swindles, Dudley would ingest some more meth, the world would spin a few times, and I would be history.

"Then let's do a hotel tonight and we'll deal with tomorrow when it arrives," she decided for us.

Bribing Rook and Hepplewhite with treats coaxed them into their carrier and I toted them back to Torbin and Andy's place. Torbin was not there, so I was able to avoid any sharply pointed questions about the quick cat turnaround. Andy was fine with the explanation that we'd hoped the cops would catch my assailant by now but they hadn't, so to be safe, we'd stay away another night.

When I got back Cordelia had booked us a hotel in the French Quarter—yes, not that far away, but a random enough location it wasn't likely that Dudley could find us there. It was the upper Quarter, near Canal Street, and we live near the lower Quarter off Esplanade. Ten blocks can make a world of difference.

"So we play tourist for the night?" I asked as we threw a few things into our respective small bags—I let her have the nice purple one this time.

"No, we play locals out enjoying our beautiful city."

It'll all be okay, I told myself as I loaded our bags in the trunk. *Dudley will disappear, into jail, rehab or meth overdose, and Cordelia's tests will come back negative. The fates are just making us pay attention to the important things.*

She let me drive—she hates driving on the interstate or in the Quarter for the same reason, too many idiot drivers per square inch. Cordelia is a more stable and sane driver than I am, and I suspect her theory is I'm crazy enough to deal with these drivers—like the one in front of us trying to pass a buggy on a one-lane street. He seemed to think that some hotel driveway would give him enough room on the right to squeeze by. I was rooting for the donkey to kick his headlights out.

But the donkey was smarter than that—or more a creature of habit. It pulled over to the right into a no parking zone as a way to let the cars behind the carriage pass. However, Mr. Idiot Driver was so close that he couldn't easily pull around. I zoomed by him on the legal left, as did every car behind me. As I turned down Bienville Street, he was still stuck behind the buggy.

One of the nice things about driving a stick shift is that the valet parking guys view you with greater respect—you may be a middle-aged woman, but you're a middle-aged woman who knows how to drive a manual.

I waved away the bell man. Our duffels were hardly worth his effort, especially considering there were several other elderly guests arriving as well. He could help the little old ladies. Almost as an afterthought I grabbed the two bags that I had taken from Reginald Banks's house.

I let Cordelia do the checking-in stuff—it was her credit card paying for this, after all. If I were hotel security I'd want to know that one of my guests was here for the reasons we were here. I knew what to look for, the man in a sober suit who was watching people, not smiling at them. I found him at the far side of the lobby.

He was an ex-cop and seemed almost happy to have something real to be secure about.

"Don't you worry, ma'am," he told me. "He sounds like the kind of guy we'd have three guards surround the minute he walked in here even without your warning."

Cordelia and I met at the elevator. The hotel had not batted an eye about two women sharing a king-size bed. Ah, New Orleans.

Once we were in the room, she pulled me into her arms, barely giving me time to drop the bags, and kissed me thoroughly. I returned her kiss, enjoying the heat of the moment, the novel surroundings. We were lovers in a hotel in the French Quarter of New Orleans. For the moment, we could pretend that we didn't live ten blocks away and it was just us behind closed doors in a room with a big bed.

She broke off our kiss, still holding me in a tight hug. "Will you think I'm terminally unromantic if I suggest we wait until after dinner to continue?"

I kissed her on the cheek. "I think it's been well established that you fall more on the practical side of things than the romantic side."

She sighed. "I need to remember to bring you flowers more often."

"No, you don't. Practical is not a bad thing. You've never forgotten my birthday or our anniversary. I'm not with you because of a constant barrage of bouquets, but because you remember things like we need to eat. We can have wild hot monkey sex now and then discover that the only places open are the 'you're drunk and you need grease' type of places. Or we can go out now—"

"Have a romantic dinner," she interjected.

"Have a very romantic dinner," I echoed. "And have enough sustenance to keep us through—"

"A long night of hot human sex," she again broke in.

"Yes, exactly. Practical can be a very romantic thing."

She kissed me one more time then let go. "Unpack, put on the decent clothes, and let's go to a nice place." She put her duffel on the bed then noticed the bags. "What are those?"

I explained it was what I'd taken from Reginald Banks's house earlier. Then lamely added, "I mean, we can't have sex every single minute. I just grabbed it because it was there. We don't need to do anything."

"No, it's okay. I wonder what happened to him as well. If we don't look at it tonight we can do it in the next day or so."

Cordelia called the concierge to get reservations. Unlike visitors, we can always go to the really good restaurants here, so in consequence, we rarely go unless there is some compelling reason like a birthday or someone visiting. The upper Quarter is full of first-rate restaurants, ones we had wanted to try and just never gotten around to. While Cordelia was sussing out the possibilities, I hung up the few clothes we'd brought and was setting out our bathroom stuff.

She came up behind me and put her arms around my waist. "Okay, dinner at eight. We have a little time. I only brought one extra pair of underwear, so perhaps we should spend it looking at the stuff you found." She cupped my breasts and left a row of kisses on my neck.

"Tease," I muttered as she let go. But I followed her out of the bathroom and then gently upended the bags on the bed.

She put on her reading glasses and examined the bottles, first looking at the ones from Nature's Beautiful Gift, then The Cure. She spent several minutes examining them all, even taking out the pills and sniffing them. Finally, she threw the bottle she was holding down in frustration.

She pulled off her glasses and said, "There is no way to tell what these really are. Some of them smell like they have some herbs or something in them. Nature's Beautiful Gift seems to be on the legal side of the line with its claims; The Cure certainly not. The only way to know what's really in them would be with lab tests."

"What if it was something that caused or contributed to Banks's death?" I asked.

"That might be hard to prove. I have a brief overview of forensics back in med school, so there's not much I can tell you. If there was some foreign substance in his body that was harmful and that substance could be traced to one of these pills, then maybe something could be done. I'm not even sure that would be criminal, though. Usually if there are enough harmful side effects reported, the worst that happens is that the pills get pulled."

"Banks didn't seem to be very well-off. Why spend money on these things?"

She thought for a moment, "He wanted to be cured. Desperate people believe in false hope. Sometimes it's all they have to believe in."

"So these might have hurt him," I said.

"Might have. Certainly in the pocketbook. It's unlikely they helped him."

"What if they do the things they claim, provide relief far beyond what conventional medicine offers?"

"Reginald Banks is dead. They didn't seem to help him much."

"Couldn't you say the same about conventional medicine?"

"He died of a massive infection. That shouldn't have happened. If he'd been treated properly—earlier, he would be okay."

"So they both failed him," I pointed out.

"Yes, but in different ways," she argued. "Reginald Banks was failed by medical care because he didn't receive it. There are tragic flaws in the system, but mostly with access and affordability. If he'd been in a hospital three days earlier, he'd be alive. But the other stuff," she picked up one of the bottles, "this promises a cure. It didn't deliver."

I looked at the stark white lettering on the bottle. The Cure. No, it hadn't cured Reginald Banks. "I'm also curious about a denial of service letter he got from his insurance company." I rifled through the papers until I found it.

She put the glasses back on and read it. "There has to be some mistake. Insurance agencies profit by making errors. The real scumbags automatically deny services or payment on the premise that a certain percentage of people won't or can't fight. But Reginald had a clear medical need for his treatment, and this seems to claim he was getting medical tests too closely together. That shouldn't be true if he skipped an appointment and had fallen out of care. Sounds like someone transposed an account number and sent him the wrong thing." She handed the piece of paper back to me.

Was a stupid mistake what caused Reginald Banks's death? His insurance company screws up, denies service they shouldn't have denied, so he misses a needed appointment. I shoved the pill bottles and pile of papers back into their plastic bags. Maybe his next of kin would want them. I stuffed the bags in the closet where we didn't need to see them.

Right now I wanted to live furiously in the moment, with no thinking about thugs chasing me, waiting for medical tests, or worrying about a man who could no longer be saved.

I reached out and took Cordelia's hand. "Would you care to join me in an intimate dinner?"

"I would be delighted."

We left the hotel room into the clean air of early spring, to vibrant, happy streets and an unhurried, romantic feast.

CHAPTER ELEVEN

I made the coffee while Cordelia showered. The world kept turning. Much as we had wanted to linger in last night, morning had come, a gray dawn of off-and-on drizzle. The lingering was over. We weren't tourists; there would be no beignets or café au lait. She had to go to work. I did, too, I just had more leeway in my hours.

We had done what New Orleanians do, gone out to a wonderful restaurant only to talk about other great places we'd eaten, banter over recipes, decide what we'd try when the weekend came and we could take more time to cook. We focused on good memories and I was relieved to notice that it didn't feel strained, that one led to another and another as if we could never run out. We stayed away from the bad recollections and the worries of today, an unspoken compact that those could wait until the morning. Perhaps in the morning, Joanne would call to say that Dudley was arrested and Prejean had moved to some other disaster. And Cordelia's tests would turn out to have been messed up, or more extensive testing would find nothing.

When the words ran out, the physical spoke for us. First with passion and intensity, then more slowly, romance overtaking raw need, creating more memories to add to the pile of good ones. Someday time would run out, our passion seemed to say, but until it was gone, this touching was vital, essential as breathing.

But the night was now a memory and the coffee was brewed and Cordelia was coming out of the shower.

I quickly washed off while she dressed and drank her coffee—the caffeine would be quite necessary today.

When I emerged from the shower, she said, "Some weekend we should do this again, so we don't need to rush to work like this."

"That would be nice," I agreed as I quickly dressed and took a final sip of coffee.

Then we grabbed our duffels and headed for the door. I just barely remembered to snatch the plastic bags from the closet and bring them with me.

Perhaps I should have just left them, I thought as we headed down the hall. Reginald Banks was gone; they were useless talismans of his passing.

I retrieved the car while Cordelia finished checking out.

"I can just drive you to work," I told her as we got in.

"Then how do I get home?"

"I'll come pick you up."

"I'm okay," she replied to my unspoken implication. "Be there when—and if—I really need you. But right now I can drive myself to work. Then I'll run Uptown to the grocery store after and come home."

"Okay, but why don't you come home and we can both go to the store up on Carrollton?"

"Why? Don't trust that I'll remember to get lemons?"

"How easily you see through me." But she agreed to meet me and we'd go together.

The morning traffic was less insane than the evening, at least in the French Quarter. The drunks were either still sleeping it off or nursing hangovers.

I drove back to our place. Cordelia got out of my car to get into hers. I waited until she was in, her doors locked and on her way. I followed her briefly until Rampart, where she headed uptown and I turned downtown.

She's okay, I told myself, glancing at her receding car in my rearview mirror. *If Dudley is after anyone, it's me, not her. And for the other, she's a doctor, always worrying about getting enough fruits and vegetables in her diet and making sure she exercises regularly. I'm the one who goes out for lunch and gets the burger and fries. She gets a salad. People like that don't get cancer in their forties.*

It was time to concentrate on idiots driving in the drizzle. A big-ass truck was driving like rain-slicked roads would have no effect whatsoever on his brakes. Either he didn't see the Mini Cooper in front of him, or else he liked to play chicken on his way to work. He managed to stop with about two inches between his bumper and a red, albeit small, car.

I stayed safely behind, turning down a side street to get to my office. As is typical in New Orleans, it wasn't raining two blocks away, and in another two blocks the sun came out.

Nothing had happened for two days, so I was starting to assume that nothing would happen. The sight of the massive man standing right in front of my door was unnerving. How could he be here now? He seemed to be messing with the lock.

It was earlier than I usually got here. Dropping off Cordelia in time for her to make doctor's hours had altered my morning schedule.

Just as I was reaching for my cell phone to call Joanne, he saw me.

Thank the fates for a meth-addled brain. He stared just long enough for me to hit the accelerator and peel out down the sleepy block.

I'll bet the gunshot woke everyone up. It certainly got my adrenaline going. After the shock at his plans going awry once again, Dudley Dude did what he did best—violence. Have gun, will shoot.

The Bywater, where my office is located, is an older neighborhood, well on its transition from working class to artist trendy. The houses are mostly shotguns, close to each other and the street. It's residential; if people work here, it's at the local coffee shop or restaurant, maybe some of the businesses on St. Claude.

So not the kind of place to engage in a gun battle and car chase.

Like I was now.

Dudley had only remained in his surprised stupor for a bare second. That had given me just enough time to stomp on the gas and roar past him. He had his gun out firing as I screeched around the corner. The blocks here were short. I started to turn another corner, but saw a big yellow school bus a few blocks farther down.

Must avoid school zones, I told myself, jerking my car back to straight.

But my altruism gave Dudley enough time to get in his big truck (of course, it would be a big black truck) and sight my car still heading away from him.

In my rearview mirror, I saw him stick his hand out, holding something that looked like a gun.

I was a good two blocks away from him, moving at an insane speed, and he was shooting left-handed, so somebody else's car now had a bullet hole.

That was his advantage. I could have sped around the school bus so it was between us, but I wasn't willing to put other people at risk if I could avoid it. Dudley, even without drugs, probably didn't give a damn about anyone or anything. Throw a little meth into the mix and he didn't give a damn and didn't think he could get hurt.

I took a hard right. Maybe if I wasn't in his sight line, he wouldn't shoot. It would be luck if he actually hit me—Dudley didn't seem like the type to spend much time at the firing range—but stray bullets flying around could easily hurt someone else.

I sped left around another corner, trying to zig and zag away from Dudley. That was challenging enough. Add to that trying to open and dial—yeah, speed-dial, but even that wasn't easy—my cell phone.

I got it open, looked down for half a split second, and almost ran over a dog.

Okay, driving and driving only from now on. I'd have to pin my hopes that someone somewhere would notice that a big black truck was speeding through the neighborhood and firing guns. Or maybe that was too common an occurrence for anyone to even pay attention to.

For my safety I should head into the more traveled parts, go uptown. But there would be more people there and more chance Dudley's stray bullets or reckless driving would injure someone.

My other choice was to drive to St. Claude and cross the Industrial Canal into the Lower Ninth Ward. It had been inundated during Katrina, one of the most destroyed neighborhoods in New Orleans. People were poor there, often uninsured. Even now there was block after block of overgrown lots, staircases to nowhere peering out of the weeds, the only mark that this had once been an inhabited area.

Fewer people meant less of them to be hurt.

Of course, it also made it less likely that anyone would be around to dial 911 for me. Hell, cell service might not have been restored down there yet.

I deliberately didn't turn at the next block, heading straight for St.

Claude Ave. It was the main artery through the area and a straight shot over the Canal. The bridge was an old one, originally for both car and rail, but the tracks had been long gone, with the lanes dividing inner and outer.

The tricky part would be getting onto St. Claude. No, the tricky part was everything—staying far enough away from Dudley so he couldn't shoot me, driving through these narrow streets at speeds they were never intended for, avoiding dogs, children or any other living thing, and somehow attracting enough attention soon enough that someone with bigger guns and faster cars could end this. Turning onto St. Claude without causing a wreck was just a subsection of the above.

People were going to work, but would be going uptown, not downtown. At least it was a right turn; I wouldn't have to scream across two lanes and a median. Oh, the fates were kind to me today.

Dudley was again in my rearview mirror and the idiot was again trying to take potshots at me. There were a couple of pedestrians in the next block. I laid on my horn. I'm not sure if its blare or the sound of a gun was the cause of their hightailing it over a fence, but at least they had some protection. And perhaps even now were dialing those magic numbers, 911.

I blew though an intersection, horn still blasting, trying to warn any oncoming cars. A truck was there. He let me through, then foolishly decided it was his turn, crossed, fishtailing to get out of the way of Dudley's speeding vehicle. The virtues of looking both ways.

St. Claude was next. I slowed minimally. If I got in a car wreck, Dudley would have an easy shot. But he was closing the gap and my choice was between risking a wreck or being shot. Nothing like having options.

Again blaring the horn as I hit the intersection, my car squealed into a right turn. I was lucky; traffic going this way was light and the closest car was a good half block away.

There is a stoplight at the last street before the bridge. Car chases in the movies are fun, in real life not so much, more like traumatic—at each turn I risked wrecking, hurting someone, and/or being caught by someone wanting to kill me.

Dudley was gaining on me. He seemed to think his truck was big enough to plow through any crash and he wasn't worried about stray dogs or school children. He careered around the turn barely half a block behind me, causing the oncoming car to brake sharply and veer left to avoid him.

He stuck his hand out and took another shot. I heard something skim across my roof.

I wondered if my insurance would cover this.

On this straightaway, he was gaining quickly on me.

I have a sensible car, a little Mazda, peppy enough but not designed to be a king of the road. Dudley's truck, on the other hand, was clearly a powerful puppy, meant for macho posturing and passing the peons.

The light was green.

Dudley stuck his hand out for another shot.

I veered into the left lane.

Another wild shot.

He was still gaining. He jerked into the left lane behind me, closing the distance. I could hear the roar of his engine.

I was rethinking my decision to head to the Lower Ninth Ward. Once there it would be impossible to shake him. He had speed and power over me. A more maneuverable car was my only advantage. Maybe I could let him get closer and do a quick turn at one of the side streets and he would overshoot. That might not slow him down much, and he still had a gun and there were still too many people around.

But whatever I did had to be mere seconds away. The bridge was a scant two blocks farther, and if I went over it, then I was committed.

Then I had an idea. A desperate, last-chance idea.

He was no more than twenty feet behind me.

I steered to the left, going into the left hand turn lane at the road immediately before the bridge.

Just as he started to follow me, I jerked back, veering all the way into the right lane.

And then at the last of the last seconds, went even farther right into a little side street that ran parallel with the bridge. It dead-ended at the bank of the Industrial Canal.

His heavy truck couldn't correct in time. He tried to follow me, but the momentum of the truck was too fast and he couldn't get over far enough. Then he desperately wrenched the steering wheel as he tried to avoid crashing directly into the guardrail. He managed to avoid a head-on collision, instead sideswiping it, the impact so hard I thought the truck would roll over the rail and crash onto the pavement below.

Metal screamed, a sickening screech that went on and on.

My little side street was empty, a cul-de-sac of a few houses before the canal. I braked as rapidly as I safely could.

I could no longer see much of the upper roadway. The embankment hid most of the street.

Just because he crashed didn't mean he was dead, or even really hurt. That big truck could protect him. I couldn't depend on him being too stupid to wear his seat belt.

I quickly started my car again, backing up a little to make a right turn onto a side street that would take me away from St. Claude and the wreck. I wasn't leaving, but getting out of shooting range. I did another turn, now out of sight of anyone on St. Claude, then pulled to the side of the road and found my cell phone.

By now 911 had to have been called. There were too many cars and people around to witness Dudley's spectacular crash.

I dialed Joanne, using her personal number so I wouldn't have to wait for her to be found at her office.

"What?" she answered. Caller ID, she knew it was me.

"Dudley reappeared. We just did a car chase through the Bywater that ended with him running into the guardrail on the St. Claude bridge."

"What?" she repeated, in a very different tone.

I slowed down and repeated the story, filling in the details.

"Was anyone hurt?" she asked when I finished.

"Not that I know of. He was firing wild. But I can't be sure. All I saw was some car damage."

I gave her my route, all the streets I'd taken so that someone could retrace them and make sure no one was injured.

"Are you okay?" she asked.

Finally, the important stuff.

"Shaken. I might have to remove a brown stain from my car seat. But okay. A bullet zinged across my car roof. That's it."

"Stay on the line," she told me. "I need to warn the responders that he's armed and dangerous."

Then her voice became distant, indistinct. I couldn't make out the words. But I wasn't even trying, I was shaking so hard.

I didn't even want to count the number of ways I could have been killed in the last... I looked at my watch. Less than forty-five minutes ago I had dropped off Cordelia at our house. The whole chase had taken ten, at most fifteen minutes. The ways I could have been killed in the last ten minutes. That I was safe and whole, maybe a minor scrape on my car, seemed an unlikely miracle.

I took a deep breath, then another one, reassured by the sound of air coming in and out of my lungs.

Alive. Still alive.

A tinny voice was calling my name.

Joanne had come back on the phone. I put it back to my ear.

"Micky? Micky?" she called.

"Here. Sorry, just trying to…" Remind myself that I was alive.

"Where are you?"

"Uh…I'm not sure. One of those little streets that run into the canal."

"I've got a map." Using her map we located me on North Rampart Street between Kentucky and Poland. Whoever named these streets either had a shaky grasp of geography or a strong sense of irony.

Joanne stayed on the phone with me until the patrol car arrived.

I'm not sure what I said to her and I'm not sure I want to know. Now I had time to think of how close I'd come to being killed. I even discreetly checked the seat for a brown spot.

When the cops arrived they took pictures of my car, especially the bullet scrape on the roof. I agreed to a breath test. I didn't think I could be much more stone-cold sober than I was at the moment.

Then they took me to the police station. They didn't even ask if I wanted to drive. One of them took the keys out of my still-shaking hand and the other led me to the patrol car. I most assuredly did not want to be behind the wheel of a car for at least a year.

At the police station I again repeated my story, which was backed up by my earlier complaint about Dudley. Then I wrote out and signed a statement. Finally enough time passed, enough people questioned me, and my hands stopping shaking enough that I was able to go.

Joanne caught up with me just as I was leaving.

"Lunch?" she said, her question not really a question.

"Food? My stomach might still be in my throat." But I followed her.

We went—in her car—to a decent pizza place that wasn't too far away. Cheese and dough is comfort food.

Once we were seated and had ordered, she said, "Dudley got banged up pretty badly. No, I don't expect you to waste any tears over him. He was stupid and dangerous and at least, so far as we know, he hurt himself more than anyone else. Good news for the responders, he was out by the time they got there, so they weren't at risk."

"Any chance to question him?"

"No, last I heard he was in surgery and he's not likely to be in any condition to talk for a day or two—should he be that lucky. Everything on your end checks out. There was a gun in his truck, spent cartridges. Guess he thought he'd be able to clean up later."

"I'm not sure he was thinking. I doubt he expected to see me that early, and when he did he went into both fight and flight. If he'd been thinking clearly he would be in Houston by now."

"Do you suspect it was Prejean?"

"Flip a coin. Was he doing it for his ego or for Prejean? When I talked to him—"

"You talked to him?" Joanne cut in.

While I didn't want her to know I'd run off half-cocked, she needed to know everything—even if it made me look stupid. I told her about my encounter with Prejean. She was kind enough not to create for me another body orifice. "I know, but in a way I was trying to reason with him. His case is closed; what's done can't be undone. If he leaves me alone, I leave him alone. Maybe a bit of a hothead, but he's not really a fighter. At least that was my feeling about him."

"Oddly, mine, too. Money fraud is one thing—and bad enough, but once you cross over into violence, the cops pay a lot more attention. I'd think just from a business perspective, the last thing he'd want was more cops visiting him."

"So Dudley didn't like being kicked in the balls by a girl and he decided to freelance?"

Our food arrived. I suddenly realized I was ravenous. The fear and adrenaline of the chase had probably burned off more calories than a heavy aerobic class. Or maybe my taste buds were just so happy that they were still around to taste.

"That's the problem with addicts like Dudley," Joanne said as she slid a slice onto her plate. "They don't live in the same rational world we live in. It could be the pink rat told him to go after you."

I swallowed. I was already two bites in. "That's the sure sign of a drug nut. Never listen to the pink rat; he didn't even make it through mouse school. Turquoise rat, now, that's the one who knows the lay of the land."

Joanne shook her head, took a bite, "Dudley won't be coming after you again, not for a long while. He's going to be lucky if he walks again."

"That's a comfort," I said between mouthfuls.

"Prejean hangs with scum, but as far as we can tell, it's more along the lines of check forgers, identity theft, not the violent kind."

"That warms the cockles of my heart." I took another slice.

"No link to Dudley, so we're guessing it's a one-off, some chance encounter in a bar, as you surmised. That might mean Prejean isn't into using brute force to settle his problems and he doesn't have a ready supply of muscle men at his disposal."

"So you're saying with Dudley Dude down for the count, I might not have to look over my shoulder at every turn."

"We'll talk to Prejean again. Maybe emphasize the message that if anything happens to you, we're all over him. He doesn't need a police spotlight on him. We dig enough we'll find something. Now that his temper has cooled, he might be anxious to avoid Angola."

She finished her first slice. I was on my third.

"It would be nice if this was over," I said. "Especially with me in one piece and him in the hospital."

"I'm glad you're okay." She was quiet for a moment. "We lost so much during Katrina. I think if I lose one more damn thing I'll fall apart."

No, no, no. Her real concern, voiced too plainly, not hidden behind a smart remark, was too much. I was about to cry or yell. I coughed through a bite, managed to swallow, took a long swig of tea. Then another gulp. "Hey, I'm glad I'm okay, too. Nice that right at the moment my biggest concern is whether my insurance will cover the ding on my roof or not."

She started to say something but I overrode her. "And whether to have another slice of pizza or not."

Joanne glanced away, took a drink of water. She looked at me and covered my hand with hers. "I'm glad you're okay. I thought I might lose you, too." She took a breath, then continued, "Alex and I had it out last night. I told her she needed to get her shit together or else find one of those social work lesbians who like to solve other people's problems."

"Damn. How'd she react?" I slowly chewed, suddenly no longer hungry.

"Cried, even more than usual. Locked herself in the spare room and only stopped crying long enough to tell me to fuck myself and to find some other macho cop to brag at how well I did during Katrina. She was gone when I got up this morning. I don't know whether she'll come home or not."

"Joanne, look, I know it's hard—"

"I know I'm the asshole here. The girlfriend who couldn't be perfect and understanding for more than two years. Know why our spare room is in such crap shape? She's not sure she wants to rebuild our house, or even stay here. So I either do it without her or it doesn't get done. I can't keep living my life in her limbo."

"Have you considered counseling?"

"Please don't give me any Band-Aid solutions. There's no time, no money. Or she'll go if I go because she doesn't want to be the only one with a problem."

"Okay, I don't have any solutions, even Band-Aid. Except I care for both of you and don't want either of you hurt. More than you've already been hurt. I don't know what to do, but I'll do anything to help."

"That's where I am, I'll do anything, but nothing I do seems to make a difference. Right now I don't know where she is or even if she's okay."

"Have you tried calling her?" I gave her a look.

She returned my stare. "Yeah, three times. My last message was she didn't need to talk to me, just to let me know she was okay." She glanced at her watch to let me know that the message had long gone unanswered.

I got out my phone. "I'll call her."

"No, don't. She'll know I asked you to. And…"

"So what if she knows?" I started to scroll through my contacts.

"And…if she doesn't love me enough to let me know she's okay, maybe she doesn't love me enough for us to be together."

I looked away from my phone, then put it down.

I didn't know what to say to that. I'd call Alex later, without telling Joanne. "I'm not disagreeing with you that Alex is stuck. Hard as what you went through was, I think it was harder for her. You were here, true, but at least you had the chance to do something to make it better. Get in a rowboat and pull people off roofs. She was cooped up with her asshole relatives in Baton Rouge, listening to them blaming New Orleans for what happened, and when they were done with that, going on diatribes about homosexual child molesters. A great place to be lesbian and pregnant."

"I think she blames herself for the miscarriage," Joanne said softly. They had been trying to have a child; this was the one that had looked like it might go to term. Alex had miscarried shortly after Katrina. "And maybe she blames me, too, for not being there with her."

"And maybe you blame yourself as well. You weren't there. You couldn't be there."

"Thanks for the therapy."

"Hey, you want sympathy, you talk to Cordelia. You want a bitch slap into reality, you talk to me."

She didn't let go of my hand as the waiter came by to refill our tea.

"Sometimes I think…maybe Alex would do better with Cordelia and you and…"

"What, put the macho lesbian turds together and pair up the nice girls? I like you, Joanne—no, I love you. But we both carry guns and that could be a dangerous combination." I didn't let go of her hand. I couldn't give her what she wanted, but I could at least give her that.

"Yeah, you're probably right. I was also thinking that…maybe Cordelia could talk to her. They've known each other forever. Maybe…I don't know…maybe the two nice girls can work it out."

Maybe it was my face, or maybe my hand jerked.

Joanne looked at me. "What is it?" she asked.

I didn't want to say the words; that made them too real. "Cordelia is—they have to do more tests. It might be just a scare. But she's been not doing well lately. Her blood work was off. It might be cancer. But we have to have more tests. She has to have more tests," I corrected.

"Oh, shit, Micky. If there is anything I can do…"

I wanted to say, *Work it out with Alex. I can't lose anything more either.* But the day was out of miracles. "I'll let you know. Right now, it's wait and worry. I'll ask her about talking to Alex. I think she'd like to focus on something other than waiting for test results and trying to go through the usual routine of the day."

"Yeah, thanks. I'll leave it up to your judgment. If it's not the right time, don't mention anything. We'll get through this. I'll work on being perfect again." She let go of my hand.

We paid our bill. Joanne let me take the leftover pizza.

She didn't repeat what she said about losing someone.

CHAPTER TWELVE

My car was at the police station. Joanne took me back there, even offered to drive me wherever I needed to go.

But it was time for me to get behind the wheel again and learn to deal with the usual insanity of New Orleans drivers. I debated calling Cordelia to tell her about my exciting day, but prudently decided that should wait until I could do it in person.

"It's a normal day, no one is chasing you," I told myself before starting the ignition.

Once my car was started I didn't immediately pull out. I needed a destination. Part of me suggested going home and flopping in front of the TV to watch cooking shows.

I pulled into traffic still not sure where I would go.

A look in the rearview mirror revealed a big truck behind me. Never mind it was red and hauling a refrigerator, the sight of its grill starting my hands shaking again.

My house—and cooking shows—seemed the only sensible destination. My head would not wrap around anything useful today. I could talk my boss—me—into a sick day.

Home welcomed and calmed me in a way the familiar and safe can. I could put my feet up, there was chocolate to eat, a recent *National Geographic* to read, inane TV in the background to fill the rooms with voices, and a cup of tea beside me.

I spent a couple of hours drinking tea, reading about coral reefs, and watching cupcakes shows, letting the adrenaline drain from my body and the fear from my mind.

Cordelia. I needed to let her know I was safe and no more maniacs might knock on our door.

Just as I picked up my phone to call her and tell her all was well, I heard a familiar car and looked out the window as she parked in front of the house.

To let her know that everything was okay, I opened the door, waiting for her to get out. This is something we usually can't do because the cats are sure the streets outside are paved with tuna and, if they were here, would be clawing past my legs to get out. I hadn't even had the energy to go down the block and retrieve them yet.

She moved slowly getting out of the car, as if she was tired.

I smiled at her.

She tried to smile back and I knew something was wrong.

She didn't say anything as she entered the house. After shutting the door, she dropped her briefcase on the floor. Then she took one of my hands and lifted it to her throat, guiding my fingers to a lump just above her collarbone.

I knew what she was telling me and I didn't want to know. "But people get swollen lymph nodes from…"

She shook her head. "Not like this. We did the needle aspiration when I saw Jennifer—the biopsy—and it came back…came back…it's not good news. I'm a patient, not a doctor." Then she collapsed into my arms as if it had taken all her strength to make it through the day and she hadn't any left to even stand.

I caught her and held her, trying desperately not to fall apart myself.

It seemed we stood that way forever, her leaning into me, me finally losing my battle not to cry, until she finally lifted her head, roughly wiped her hand across her face and nose, and said, "I can't breathe." She pulled away from me and went to the kitchen sink, washing her face with dishwashing liquid.

I followed her and handed her a dish towel, grabbing a tissue for myself and discreetly blowing my nose.

When she finished drying her face, I said, "You should have called me. I would have come."

"I didn't want to worry you." She put her hand on my arm to forestall my reply. "That's not really it. I couldn't tell you over the phone. They worked me in as a favor—their office is just across the street. Didn't think I'd get the biopsy results so quickly—but John, the pathologist, went to med school with me. Sometimes professional courtesy isn't a good thing." She smiled weakly. I let her ramble. She rarely does; at times, I think she's too controlled and keeps things in. Unlike me.

She continued, "I knew it was bad news when Jennifer—the oncologist—called me at the end of the day. We think we're good at hiding it in our voices, but we're not. I wanted to say, 'No, it can wait until tomorrow,' but I knew that tomorrow wouldn't change anything."

"Except I could have been there."

She took my hand and lifted it to her cheek. Her normally soft skin was rough from crying. "Be here now. That's what I need from you."

Given that I had chosen to wait to tell her about almost being killed until I saw her, I could hardly be upset that she'd made essentially the same choice. "I'll be here," I told her. "Anything you need, I'm here."

She turned her face, kissing the palm of my hand. Then she shook herself. "I'm okay. People deal with this all the time. A lot of cancers are curable; this is one of them. I'm much better off than most people since I know many of the people who'll be treating me. We'll get through this. Hell, it often causes weight loss, so this could be my chance to take off those pounds that have crept on."

"What happens now?" I asked.

"More tests to determine the stage and what sub-type it is. Then chemo and maybe radiation therapy."

I guess my face showed what I was thinking. She said, "It'll be okay. Not easy, but okay." She kissed my hand again.

"You're not just telling me that, are you?"

"No, I'm telling you the truth as best I know it. I'm fairly young, don't have other complicating factors like diabetes or heart disease. I can handle the kind of treatment needed to eradicate it. Plus I'm part of the medical field, I know the questions to ask and what to expect."

"Okay, I'll trust you on this. Just tell me what you need."

She let go of my hand and was quiet for a moment. "I've put you through so much. Maybe…too much. You don't have to stick around through this, too."

"If I got sick—cancer—would you dump me?"

"No, of course not, but…you never left me."

"You didn't leave me. You had a fling."

"Whatever it was, I hurt you terribly. And…I don't think I can ever make that up to you."

"Whatever it was, it's over. I know that things change and you can't un-write the past. If I didn't want to be with you, I should have left you then. I'm not leaving you now."

She started to cry again. "I never stopped loving you. That's what made it so wrong."

I put my arms around her. "Remember, she was a lying, manipulative bitch. An attractive, charismatic, lying, manipulative bitch who relentlessly pursued you, I might add, so just stop this. I'm not leaving you—unless you'd prefer not to have me around and take up with some nice nurse who has a better bedside manner—and let's just get out of soap opera–ville."

"You have a great bedside manner," she snuffled. "You don't hover and you make me laugh." To prove that she was on the way out of soap opera land, she asked, "Where are the cats?"

"Still at Torbin's."

Then she looked at me with an expression that said she just remembered I was in danger.

Which meant I had to tell her about my morning with Dudley. A somewhat light-on-the-details version, as I was of the firm opinion that she had enough to worry about without considering how close I'd come to being killed mere hours ago. I'd just have to make sure we didn't turn on the TV, as it seemed likely that this one would make the local news.

"So we can stay here tonight," I ended my tale. "Should I go get the cats?"

She went with me to the front door to retrieve her briefcase, stopping me before I put the key in the lock to give me a long kiss.

Maybe she was right, I thought as I crossed the street, *maybe this will be okay.* It was hard to think that she could be here, working, talking, kissing me, and be truly ill. Maybe scary ill, but not truly, won't be here tomorrow ill.

Torbin was home and greeted me at the door. "The TV cameras did not get your good side."

"There were no TV cameras. You are a lying dog."

"Old footage. I gather you had quite an adventure today," he said as he led me into the kitchen where both of our cats came to greet me as if I might save them from a world of living with two other cats. Since he'd already seen it on TV, I gave him the less censored version of my morning's adventure while corralling Rook and Hepplewhite and depositing them in their cat carrier.

"So all's well that ends well," he summed up, over the raucous chorus of cats who wanted to express their displeasure at being penned in for five minutes. "My payment is that you and your gorgeous girlfriend have to come out and play on a school night. I'm doing the drag extravaganza next Wednesday, and I expect you both front row center."

I had debated whether to tell Torbin or wait. This made the decision for me. "I'm sorry, Tor, I don't think we're going to be able to make it. Cordelia might have...lymphoma." I stumbled, couldn't say the C word. "She's been tired lately, they did some tests and this is what came back. So, next week...I don't know, we just can't plan much right now."

"Shit, Micky, that sucks."

"She says it'll be okay. There aren't any good cancers to have, but this isn't one of the worst ones."

"Well, at least she's got decent insurance," Torbin said, a little resentment oozing through his words.

Wrong thing to say. No, *beyond* the wrong thing to say, his worry about his own situation had turned him into a self-absorbed lout. After having almost been killed in the morning and finding out that my partner had cancer in the afternoon, this was not the kind of day when I was willing or even capable of having someone say the wrong thing to me.

I yanked up the cat carrier in such a fashion that even the cats shut up. "If that's all you can think about, then fuck you. Just fuck you!"

I spun out of the room and was on the street before he had a chance to respond.

"Hey, Micky," he called. "I'm sorry."

"Fuck your sorry. Don't bother, don't try. There is no way I can hear it right now." I stormed down the block. He had enough sense to know that whatever apology he made would have to wait until I was calm enough to hear it.

I stopped at our front door, catching my breath and composing myself. A soft meow reminded me I was carrying living creatures and they needed to be taken care of.

One more deep breath, then I put the key in the lock and let myself in. Once the door was safely closed and no escape possible, I busied myself letting the cats out. They, at least, seemed happy to be home. Especially as Cordelia almost immediately fed them.

She didn't ask, so I didn't tell her about my fight with Torbin. I'd give it a few days and see if he managed a suitable apology before bringing it up. We had enough other things to worry about.

I threw together a shrimp stir fry. Neither of us was all that hungry, so there was plenty left over for lunch tomorrow.

Then we tried to make the night as normal as possible, watched a little TV, then read, our usual routine. But if it worked for Cordelia, it didn't work for me. I needed to hold her hand, the comfort of her warmth. When she started to get up, I'd jump up, getting her a glass of water, then a cup of tea. The third time she told me to sit down, that I couldn't go to the bathroom for her.

When she came back she found me crying. The normal routine was gone. Cordelia sat beside me on the couch and pulled me into her arms, comforting me, because she might be sick and I might lose her.

CHAPTER THIRTEEN

A weekend came and went. I didn't even remember until I got up on Saturday as if to go to work and Cordelia reminded me we could sleep a little later. I fed the cats as a bribe for them to leave us alone and flopped back into bed.

But the weekend didn't last and Monday came.

Other than not getting killed, I hadn't checked anything off last week's to-do list. Not even the basics like go to my office and retrieve my messages.

Cordelia had insisted on going to work. I hadn't been able to manage it. The problems of Charles Williams, the McConkles, and their bottles of nostrums felt minor compared to cancer and bullets.

Cordelia needed the distraction of other people's illnesses to help her cope with her own. But my work—the cases before me at the moment—carried no such weight. They would be just fine sitting on the shelf for a few days. I filled the time with the necessities of life, an oil change, cats to the vet for their yearly checkup, all the things we struggled to cram in our busy days. The days and weeks ahead would be hard. I wanted all the other distractions out of the way.

But time didn't stop and I had to get back to what I did to pay the bills.

Go to my office, check voice mail and e-mail, act like I was a big, bad, tough private eye. Clean my gun; maybe go to the rifle range. Like the gun had offered one whit of protection against Dudley and his monster truck.

That decided, I cautiously pulled into traffic. And drove like a granny all the way to my office. Just to be on the safe side, I did my routine of driving around the block, checking out everything and everyone. Two neighbors sitting on their stoops drinking coffee was the only activity.

I parked in front of my office and slowly got out of my car, as if this morning's mayhem could repeat and I still needed to be vigilant. But the only threat was the weatherman's chance of drizzle. No one was around.

He's in the hospital, I told myself as I put my key in the lock. There were some new scratch marks on the cylinder. Maybe he was trying to pick it. I shuddered at that thought. As bad as that morning was, having Dudley inside and waiting for me probably would have been worse. From the looks of it, he either hadn't gotten very far or had no talent in lock-picking. There were a few scratches, but everything else looked okay. I had suggested to the building owner that he might consider a better lock for the street door, but he was loath to do any maintenance unless required by law. I did have a high-tech lock on my office door—which attested to Mr. Charles Williams's locksmith skills. From now on it was going to stay locked whenever I was there.

When I got to my office, evidence of Mr. Williams's industriousness was present in a fax from Fletcher McConkle agreeing that Mr. Williams could act as his proxy. He'd been prudent enough—or his wife had—to add that if I felt any information was sensitive, I should check with him first.

There were no voice messages and my e-mail ran the gamut of reasons why a client couldn't pay my bill to ads for erectile dysfunction drugs.

I could probably use the distraction of working on my one current paying case.

Perhaps it was time to visit Fletcher's fleeced aunt. I went to my closet. Sometimes being a private eye works just dandy. Others times something more subtle—some might say devious—is required.

Much as I hated it, it seemed like this might be a pink dress one. From what Fletcher said, it sounded like his aunt was lonely, and company, even company of a commercial sort, was better than being alone.

Pretending to be doing a survey about health care and vitamins might get me in to see his aunt and get her talking about the supplements. For that to work, I had to seem likable and non-threatening. The leather jacket just doesn't accomplish that. I rummaged through my stack of fake business cards—ah, yes, Deborah Perkins, Research Policy Group. I could remember that I was a Deborah for a day.

Pretty in pink. Well, not so much, but with the pantyhose—yes, one must sacrifice for one's work—matching shoes—flats, heels aren't good for running, or walking or standing, although my excuse was that heels made me too tall and therefore threatening—and a little makeup somewhere this side of Halloween, I was ready for my ruse.

Maybe she'd offer me tea and crumpets. That might have to pass for lunch.

The most annoying thing about the subterfuge—even more so than the pantyhose—I had to toss my gun into a big, pinkish purse, one that went with the character I was playing. Even if I had a suitably pink jacket, a shoulder holster wasn't the fashion statement I was trying to make.

So, next stop, Marion McConkle's house. She lived in a nice Uptown neighborhood, not far from Audubon Park. Her house didn't scream money, but it wasn't talking poverty, either. If you were into clapboard turrets, it even had its quirky charm, with an octagonal room at three of the four corners. It was painted a nice sedate eggshell white with sunflower yellow trim. There was a short wrought iron fence surrounding the property. The money came out in the details. Both the house and the fence had been painted in the not-too-distant past. The yard had multiple flower beds, all neatly tended. The grass was perfectly mowed. Aunt Marion kept the place up.

I parked a little way down the block, with the house just barely in view. Maybe it was paranoia, but I called it observing the scene. I wanted to get an idea of the pace of this neighborhood. Fifteen minutes passed and I only glimpsed one dog walker going past on an adjoining street. The pace of this place seemed to be staying inside.

Time to play survey girl. I drove my car and parked in front of her house. As I got out of my car, I pulled a clipboard with a sheaf of paper and pretended to consult it. I was too old to do ingénue anymore, but I tried to channel a cheerleader who is now forty, divorced, and reduced to grunt work like door-to-door surveys.

I rang the doorbell. And waited. I'd be so disappointed if I'd put on pantyhose only to discover that this was the day Auntie played bridge.

I was debating whether to ring the doorbell a second time—could be considered pushy—or admit that cooking shows on TV would have been a better way to spend this day.

I heard footsteps, fairly spry ones, so maybe Nature's Beautiful Gift had some merit.

A voice called, "Who is it? I've gone to the Baptist church for the last fifty years and I'm not about to change."

"Hello, ma'am," I said. "I'm not selling anything, including religion. I'm part of a team doing surveys about health matters. I just need a few minutes of your time and it would greatly help our research." I proffered the fake business card, holding it up to the cut glass window in the door. "Your ideas and opinions would really help us."

That seemed to do the trick, although I was sincerely hoping the pink dress helped because I'd hate to think all that pink was wasted. The door opened.

I could see the resemblance to her nephew; more wrinkles, less height, no surfer attitude. Her hair, recently styled and cut, was a very real shade of brown, the dye job given away only by her age. Her clothes were Uptown casual, khaki pants smartly creased, a knit sweater that almost matched my pink dress, pearl earrings, several understated gold chains around her neck. And sensible shoes.

"Why don't you come in?" she asked.

"How do you do, ma'am?" I asked, furiously channeling aging cheerleader. "I'm Deborah Perkins, part of the Research Policy Group. We're conducting research on healthy living and lifestyle choices of a select group of people here in New Orleans."

"That sounds interesting," she said, standing aside so I could enter.

The house was beautifully furnished, Much of the furniture seemed old, perhaps passed down for generations. Clearly expensive and well cared for. She ushered me into a pleasant sitting room with several overstuffed chairs and a love seat arranged in front of a massive fireplace.

"Would you like some coffee or tea?" she asked.

"Thank you, ma'am. I don't want to be a bother."

"Oh, it's not a bother. I was about to get some for myself."

"That would be most kind. I'll have whatever you're having."

She smiled at me, the smile of someone who was lonely and bored and had just reeled in a person who clearly had to stay until the tea was finished.

"I'll be right back," she said and exited down the center hall.

I stood up and discreetly peered after her. She went to the back of the house. I would have some footsteps warning before she reentered. I quickly scanned the room. There were several built-in bookcases on one side and two massive windows on the other with window seats under both. But this room was clearly single purpose—sit and have tea. There was no desk or sign of anything that wouldn't be presentable for a stranger who happened on her doorstep. The books were old, classics or reference, and seemed to be arranged more by color than content. A pleasing picture, but it didn't invite reading. There were photographs on the mantel and bookshelves, but they were all posed like men with big prized fish. I did notice several of Fletcher, mostly younger ones, including one of him with a surfboard and a trophy.

I heard footsteps in the hallway and quickly scurried back to my seat. When Aunt Marion returned, I was sitting, making notations on my clipboard. She carried a tray with a small pot on it and a plate of an expensive brand of shortbread cookies.

"Help yourself," she said.

I did. It was the blackest, strongest, bitterest coffee I've ever tasted. So much for my herbal tea fantasy. I'm a black coffee drinker, even chicory black. That was probably the only thing that saved me from choking and spitting it out.

"Thank you so much. This will be a great perk-me-up." I wondered if I would sleep tonight. "Now, let's get started." I asked the usual demographic data, age, sex, race, did a delicate dance around income, "You don't need to answer this if you don't want to," but she had no qualms about putting herself in the "over $150,000" category.

"Now, I'm going to ask you some open-ended questions. Please answer them as honestly as you can. The first question is, what's your biggest health concern?"

That was either the absolute wrong question or the perfectly right question to ask. It certainly got her talking. From her bunions to her prolapsed uterus, head to toe.

I did try to direct the flow and broke in around flatulence, "But which of these would you say is your major one?"

"Oh, honey, they all bother me. Just let me give you the list and you tell me which one seems the most important." Because she'd been interrupted mid-fart, she started her bowel problems from the beginning. I didn't interrupt again, just scratched down random words so it looked like I was taking copious notes.

"So, which of these would you say is the big one?" she finally finished up.

"Well, ma'am, it seems to me that it would be the combination of everything you're dealing with. One problem is bad enough, but if you've got a whole bunch of them, that's a big challenge. How do you deal with all these problems? Do you see a number of doctors?"

"You know all that's a conspiracy? The drug companies don't want anyone cured. They want you hooked on pills all your life. They can cure just about everything known to man, but they won't because it would hurt their profits."

It was another five minutes of more of this before she took enough of a breath for me to ask, "So if you don't go to doctors, how do you manage? Do you take any herbal supplements or engage in natural healing?"

"Yes, that's what they don't want you to know about. There are cures out there, and some people are courageous enough to find them and bring them to us. The only reason I'm alive and as well as I am today is because I've done exhaustive research, found out the truth, and searched out what the drug companies and government don't want us to know."

"What kind of stuff do you take?"

"Ah, you just want to find out my secrets, don't you?"

"No, ma'am, not at all. This is for research purposes only."

"How do I know you're not part of them? Sent here to spy on me?"

When you wear a tinfoil hat, people tend not to flock around you. Perhaps that was part of Marion McConkle's loneliness.

"No, ma'am, I'm not a spy. Just a not very well-paid mother of two. My husband ran off after Katrina and I'm trying to make ends meet." I was being as pink as I possibly could be, hoping to fly below her paranoia. "And, ma'am, I have to admit that I have gas problems as well, so if you have any advice for me that you're willing to share, I'd sure appreciate it."

By the time she finished with her advice, I knew more than I wanted about Marion McConkle's colon, up to and including when she had her last enema—"weak coffee"—last bowel movement—"every morning regular as clockwork, except when my system is upset," and how often she had flatulence in public, especially the funerals, "they had just lifted the coffin up."

I was no longer a spy, instead had become a co-conspirator. I wasn't sure that was an improvement.

Then she said, "Wait, I've got something you should try. It's worked great for me."

She got up and left the room and I again peeked down the hall. She went to a different place than the kitchen, but returned much more quickly, barely giving me time to sit down again.

She handed me a bottle of Nature's Beautiful Gift that promised to help improve digestion and regularity.

I gave it my best wonderful-gift-that-I-never-would-have-given-myself look. "So, this is what you use? And it's really helped?"

"Oh, yes. Now I've always been pretty regular, but this really stepped it up. And there is still an occasional burp from the back end, if you know what I mean, but it is so much better. I'm not confined to home because I'm worried my gaseous outbreaks will embarrass me."

"Let me write this down," I said, peering at the label.

"Oh, you can have that. You've been so nice to me."

Right, my *nice* amounted to being trapped in her lair and asking the kinds of questions that allowed her to wax lyrical about farting at funerals.

Her doorbell rang.

"Oh, my," she said. "Time has gotten away from me. But you're in luck. That's Vincent. He's the one who told me about these miracle herbal supplements. He comes by about once a week to make sure I have everything I need. You can meet him and maybe he'll have some suggestions for you."

Oh, goody, not only was I in pink, but I'd get to discuss my faux flatulence problem with a stranger.

Marion hurried out of the room, not wanting to leave Vincent and his magic potions waiting.

I heard his voice from the hallway. "Hi, Marion, I've got some great new stuff for you if you're interested."

Great new stuff? These were supposedly old remedies discovered by a doctor in the 1930s. Maybe another serendipitous find in an attic? Just in time to add a new product line.

"Come into the sitting room, Vincent, dear. There is someone I'd like you to meet."

Vincent was in his late twenties, wearing a white polo shirt with a Nature's Beautiful Gift emblem on it. The shirt was tight, showing up his well-muscled arms. He was on the short side, although well within a normal range, probably around five-six. He looked like someone who spent a good part of his free time in a gym. His dark hair was a conservative cut and he had big, brown puppy-dog eyes. He'd do okay in a gay bar, but he wasn't a head turner. In short, just good-looking enough that an elderly woman like Marion McConkle would be flattered at his attention instead of knowing he was too good-looking to bother with her save for the money.

"Hi, Vincent, I'm Deborah Perkins of the Research Policy Groups." I hoped that was the right name. It wouldn't do to look at my business card. "I've been doing a sample of opinions about health and well-being and Mrs.—" Almost tripped. I wasn't supposed to know her name. She hadn't told me and I hadn't asked.

"Mrs. McConkle," she supplied, "but please call me Marion."

After what I knew about her colon, we *should* be on first name terms. "Ah, yes, Mrs., I mean, Marion, has told me how helpful your products have been." I acted appropriately embarrassed at the bottle in my hand, the one for "regularity."

Marion led us back to our seats—perhaps I was too close to the door and escape—before allowing Vincent to launch into his sales spiel. It was pretty much the same story I'd read on the website, but he told it in a sincere manner, making copious eye contact with his puppy-dog eyes. Even with all my years of cynicism, I began to wonder if maybe some of this stuff could help and maybe these were about bringing relief from suffering and not making money. Yeah, he was that good.

I didn't dare look at my watch. I had to keep a look of rapt fascination on my face, but I'd bet it was a good fifteen minutes before he finally got through the "basics."

"Wow, that all sounds so wonderful. You have a great job," I told him with as much pink as I could put into my voice.

He had a large sample case with him and he started aligning pill bottles on the coffee table, some the new stuff for Marion and some he thought I might be interested in.

Marion said yes to whatever he suggested—so much for exhaustive research—and didn't ask a single question. Once he had tallied up her purchases, he looked inquisitively at me.

"Thank you so much for this great information, but...uh, well, I don't get paid until next week and, uh...things are a little tight right now," I hemmed and hawed like someone who was embarrassed about her financial situation.

"How about some sample packs?" Vincent offered, taking several small foil packets out of his case.

"For me?" I said.

"Try 'em. We so back our product we think if you try them, you'll see such a difference that you'd be crazy not to buy them."

Marion enthusiastically sang his praises, well, praises for the product, but she was batting her eyelashes at Vincent the entire time.

"Thank you, that's so kind of you," I gushed. "Should I take them with food? Or on an empty stomach?"

"Either is okay," Vincent said smoothly. "When you first start out, you might want to take them with some food, especially if you're taking several at one time."

"All I need is a sip of coffee," Marion interjected as if taking the pills on an empty stomach was a mountain she had climbed. "Then I'm good to go for the rest of the day."

"Now, Marion, remember what I've told you. These pills are a miracle, but they don't replace nutrition taken through food. You need to promise me that you're eating three decent meals a day."

"Heavy on the veggies, light on the butter," she said, clearly repeating advice he had given her.

"Exactly," he answered. "When was the last time you had something fried?" he asked her.

She ducked her head, a move that would have been cute on a twenty-year-old. "Well, you know sometimes I don't have much of an appetite, and the one thing that always gets me going is the fried seafood platter at Salty Sally's."

"How many times this week?" he asked, but his tone was friendly, not a castigation. It was more like a friend trying to help someone.

"That really rainy day and just yesterday. I got a chill and needed something warm."

"You're doing better," he said cheerfully. "When we first met you were there every other day."

"Sometimes even twice a day, once for lunch and once for supper."

"So you are doing much better," he cheered her on. "Do you get any veggie sides with your meals?"

"I got the fried okra yesterday."

"Okay, well, how about get your fried seafood, but go for the steamed veggies next time?"

"You mean like the smothered green beans?"

Vincent shot me the barest look. We both clearly knew enough about Southern cooking to know that beans smothered with ham and bacon wasn't exactly the heath food he was aiming for. But neither of us said that.

"How about something really rad—steamed broccoli with lemon juice?"

Marion made a face that gave me a clue as to how hard Vincent was working to get her down to a massive plate of fried food twice a week. "But that's so chewy. I'll do vegetables but not chewy ones."

"Sweet potatoes are good," I chimed in.

"Oh, yes," she agreed. "With some brown sugar and melted butter. That's a good vegetable idea."

I didn't chime in again. She and Vincent continued for a few minutes more. I had to admire his patience with her. She'd shoot down most of his suggestions, but he remained cheerful and positive.

When they came to a break in their conversation, I said, "Marion, thank you so much for taking the time to talk to me. I've enjoyed meeting you, but I still have to get a few more surveys done today, so I'd better run." I stood up, but kept talking. "And, Vincent, I'm so glad I was here when you arrived." I patted the sample packets. "This might just be my lucky day."

He stood as well. "I've got to run along, too," he said. "But I'll be back next week."

"Same time, same place," Marion said, also clearly a long-running banter between them.

She also got up, moving slowly as if reluctant for us to leave. Of course, once we left, she'd be lonely again. Only her pill bottles as company.

Much as I wanted to get out of here, I patiently let her lead us to the door. It's what any woman in pink would do. I gave her a polite hand shake; Vincent gave her a hug and a final wink with those puppy-dog eyes. She remained at the door waving good-bye until we were almost at the street.

"Interested in a cup of coffee?" he asked. He gave me a lopsided grin and his best puppy dog stare, one that morphed into a slow trawl down my body.

OMG, Vincent, the pill-pusher man, thought he was in cougar town.

"That's very kind of you, but I do have to be going."

"Some other time? Can I have one of your cards?"

Clearly Vincent was so used to getting his way with old ladies that he was sure a woman in pink would be a pushover.

"Thanks, but I'm probably old enough to be your mother."

"Naw, I'm older than I look. Comes from good living. Plus I'm a modern guy; I don't think age differences should just go one way." He gave me an up-and-down look meant to be flattering.

I was supposed to be a divorced woman, out on her own in the big, bad world. Vincent obviously assumed that I had to be missing male company. Or he was missing female company and he was casting his line out at anything that swam by.

"You're tempting," I answered pinkly, "but I'm dating someone."

"Someone in as good shape as me?" He flexed a bicep to let me know what I was missing.

"Closer to my age. But, yeah, in pretty good shape." Lies work better when you stick close to what you know. "A doctor." I left out the female part.

"You're dating a doctor? Better hide those foil packs. I haven't met one yet who isn't bought into the whole for-profit medical model."

Oops, I had gotten a little too close to what I knew. I could lie and say it wasn't very serious, but that might give Vinnie the idea that I was available. Hell, I was already in pink; I might as well lie and lie again. "Not that kind of a doctor. A chiropractor. He's pretty open-minded. I once dated a surgeon and that was awful. If it hadn't been part of a peer-reviewed study, it didn't count."

"Yeah, I know the type. So, were you taking the samples to be polite or because you're really interested?"

Vincent seemed to have given up on bedding me and now was checking me out. If I rejected him, there had to be something hinky about me. I didn't want to end up in the hot pink zone—so eager that he'd think I was playing him or faking.

"I have to admit, I'm curious. But a little skeptical. I mean, Marion went through a long list of things wrong with her. Yet she's taking just about everything you have to offer. How come it's not doing more for her?"

"This is the first time you've met her, right?"

"Well, yes."

"She was shriveled-up old lady when I met her."

Which was how I'd describe her now. With money. "Okay…"

"Now she's much better, getting around more. Popping some pills can only help so much. Even as good as this stuff is, it can't totally make up for a lousy diet and no exercise. How old do you think I am?" he challenged.

"Uh,…around twenty-four." I deliberately guessed low. I'd really put him at around twenty-eight to thirty-two.

"I'm twenty-nine years old. But no one ever thinks I'm as old as I am. Because I do it right. I eat good food and get to the gym as often as I can. When I'm Marion's age, I'm going to look twenty years younger than I am."

"How do you know it's not just the healthy diet and exercise?"

"When I was younger," he said in a tone that no one less than fifty should use—and even then sparingly, "I tried to work out, but just couldn't get going. I ate the typical diet, hamburgers, fries at fast food joints five days a week. I was only able to really get in shape after I started on Nature's Beautiful Gift. I quit the burgers, turned to salads. And now I look ten years younger than I am."

Well, no, but I didn't say that. With his muscles and puppy-dog eyes, he probably did well with women—his easy come-on to me indicated he expected a yes—and he was used to getting the answer one usually gets from a brand-spanking-new love interest, an answer that rarely involves a cold, hard slap of realism.

He wasn't finished. "Plus my mom and dad take these every day and they've told me over and over again what a difference it makes. I have a college friend of mine who wasn't doing very well, childhood disease. I gave him the same sample packets I gave you and he was off the crutches in two days. It was amazing."

Vincent was a true believer. Maybe his intentions weren't evil like a scammer, but the result could be worse. True believers weren't lying, so there was no falsehood to detect. True believers invested not only their money, but their ego and honor. When they had that much at stake, it was hard for them to believe their grail was fool's gold.

I was skeptical—and educated enough to know about the placebo effect. (Well, and I was living with a doctor who liked explaining things to me.) Thirty percent of people get better—or feel like they have—with just a sugar pill. It's not fake; the mind is a powerful thing, and believing you will get better often makes it true. Clinical trials for new drugs have to do better than placebo effect, otherwise they're no more effective than the proverbial sugar pill. People like cause and effect—if they take a pill and get better, then the pill—or being outside, or resting in bed—made the difference. It couldn't just be random, because no one wants to live in a random world. But colds run their course; people recover, even if all they do is eat chicken soup. Some diseases, like multiple sclerosis—or sickle cell—often improve with only time as a remedy. But if you take a pill and get better, or exercise and take a pill, then life isn't random and you have control over your fate. It's a very seductive answer and Vincent had been seduced by it.

But he looked like a man very close to thirty, and Marion McConkle was a shriveled-up women, held together more by money and its access to good medical care and a comfortable lifestyle than the natural supplements she was gulping. Maybe they helped. Maybe Marion would be a little more shriveled and Vincent would look in his mid thirties instead of late twenties without them. There was nothing in the evidence that called for zeal either for or against.

I was willing to be skeptical both ways. Some of the herbal remedies might well help. Hell, I took fish oil pills. Joanne swore that glucosamine and chondroitin helped with joint pain. The medical establishment could be closed-minded as well.

But the true believers—on both sides—scared me. Nothing is perfect; nothing with benefit is without cost.

However, I wasn't here to have a debate with Vincent, I was here to get information for a case. And to get home and out of this pink dress as soon as possible.

"That sounds pretty convincing," I said. "But why not do more research, like what they do with regular drugs?"

"Those fake trials?" he replied. "They don't want people cured. They want people on their drugs for the rest of these lives. Their snake oil has to keep people just well enough so that they can keep on spending their money."

"So why is spending their money on your stuff better than spending it on medications that at least went through clinical trials?"

"Because our stuff is better and we're not in it just to make money. We charge as little as we can, just barely cover costs, so as many people as possible can afford these."

"I don't know, thirty-five dollars for a remedy for gas seems kind of expensive to me."

"Not for what you get. It's all natural, carefully processed so nothing is lost. And it really works."

"Drug companies do something called compassionate use. Do you do anything like that?" I asked.

"What's that?"

"If you can't afford their drugs but you need them, you can get them for free. Admittedly, your doctor has to fill out a bunch of paperwork and jump through some hoops, but at least it's a way for people to get needed medications."

"Please, they get a tax break, and given how much money they earn—they spend more on marketing than research—it's the least they can do."

That was hard to argue with—especially since I'd heard some quite knowledgeable people say pretty much the same thing.

"Yeah, you're probably right. I'm not saying the drug companies are great, their bottom line is making money, not saving lives. But there are some scams out there."

"This isn't one of them," he retorted. Just like a true believer.

"I'm not saying it is. You're much too nice and sincere to be doing that. I saw how caring you were with Marion, trying to get her to eat right and all that. It's just so hard to know."

"Come with me for a cup of coffee and I'll be glad to give you more details."

I suspected I'd get the facts only as pillow talk, and I just wasn't willing to go there for a case. "Can't. I really do need to be going. Is there any place I can learn more?"

"We're having a community event next week. If you give me your e-mail, I can get you the where and the when. Come to the session and then you'll get the facts."

He was persistent. "Damn, I'm all out of my cards. Give me your e-mail and I'll send you mine." He did and I scribbled it down.

And then it was adios to Vincent and his puppy-dog eyes.

He was parked in front of me, a new red truck. I fumbled with my seat belt long enough to let him drive away, keeping my license plate safely out of his sight. I noted his, quickly scribbling down the numbers as he pulled away. He might have been savvy enough to have gotten mine before he came in, but that wasn't likely save in my suspicious brain. He didn't know the car was connected to me then. I could have been a random stranger parking here. Plus, he was a cog in a multilevel marketing scheme, not a security expert. Noting license plates probably wasn't part of his everyday thinking, like it was mine.

I drove away slowly, wanting to let Vincent get blocks away. Maybe my recent brush with a raging muscle man make me wary of anyone with a bulging bicep, but I wasn't used to men coming on to me in such a sexually aggressive way. I wondered if he's really been okay with me turning him down or if he thought I was playing a game, one he'd eventually win.

I cut up to Freret Street, heading home through the 'hood, a poor area slowly coming back after the flooding of the levee failures. I didn't want to worry about Vincent, and this was his least likely route.

What I'd learned wasn't going to please my client—or Mr. Williams. From what I could see, Nature's Beautiful Gift was a legitimate company, selling a legal product. Marion McConkle was crazy, but not in a way that anyone would consider certifiable. She was a competent adult making her choices. I suspected those choices were swayed by Vincent and his puppy-dog eyes, but I didn't think he was deliberately trying to con her or get her to buy things she didn't need. He could have pushed anything and everything to her, but he confined his sales pitch to things that seemed to meet her complaints. He truly believed he was selling something that could help her. She believed the supplements were helping her. He was probably selling because of the time he spent with her. Clearly they talked about things like her eating habits that had nothing to do with a sales pitch and everything to do with him helping her live a healthier life.

If Fletcher McConkle wanted a larger slice of his aunt's money, he had to man up and visit regularly and fuss about her health. That would be his best line of defense against Vincent and Nature's Beautiful Gift.

Of course, I still had more work to do. I wanted to see what the Grannies had dug up. It would be interesting to see if NBG had any complaints against it, or reports of adverse reactions. Or financial malfeasance. Either—or both—of those could give me additional ammo to hand to Fletcher. I was reluctant to attend the "naturalist" session. I suspected it would be a high pressure, even if in a low-key "we're all just friends" way, sales sessions, with enough true believers there to exert enormous peer pressure. And perhaps a few not-so-true believers who understood that NBG was a pyramid scheme and that it was the people at the bottom who got screwed. Plus Vincent might be there and I'd have to wear a pink outfit–type costume again, as I'd have to go as Deborah Perkins. On the other hand, it might give me greater insight into their products and sales methods.

I hit the Central Business District just at the end of lunch. The only saving grace was that most of them were going in the opposite direction of where I was headed.

I had to return to my office if I wanted to shuck the pink dress there and get back in my regular clothes—which I did want to do. This was a PI costume, and it needed to stay with the PI costumes in my neatly arranged closet. Nor did I want to explain to Cordelia why I left in jeans and returned in pink.

When I got there I started to drive around the block again before realizing Dudley Dude was in the hospital. I didn't need to worry about him for a long time. I parked in front, a lightness in my step as I got out of my car. Of course, normal precautions were still needed, but it was much easier to deal with the random insanity of some mugger who happened to be on your block as you were getting out of your car than someone crazed meth user waiting for me specifically. Just as I got to the door I remembered the bags I'd taken from Reginald Banks's place.

I didn't want to leave them in my trunk, so I grabbed them. I could leave them in my office, not a much better solution.

I pushed open the downstairs door and almost ran into the first-floor tenant. He was an artist who had at some point in his life smoked or imbibed too much of something. He could wax on about his show in Paris, but that was a long time ago and he now mostly made his living by hanging out around Jackson Square and painting tourists. He looked like he had never seen me before. The only excuse I'd give him was he'd never seen me in pink before. I hurried past him with a mumbled hello lest I be again treated to the glories of his art show. Someday I'd have to ask him if it was Paris, France, or Paris, Texas—if I could ever actually be annoyed enough with him to be that snarky.

On the landing I called back to him, "Hey, remember to keep the downstairs door locked. We've had some muggings here lately." I kept going up the stairs, only hearing an indistinct reply what contained the word "Paris" at the end.

The first order of business was to get out of the pink dress. Annoyingly, the pantyhose had already developed a run and had to go in the trash. I already have about five pairs with runs in them in case I have to be the kind of person who would wear pantyhose with runs. Since some of these were from pre-Katrina, it's a role I mercifully don't have to often undertake.

Once safely changed into real clothes—jeans and a nice V-neck T-shirt—I did the usual routines of checking messages and e-mail. Two hang-ups and Mr. Charles Williams inquiring whether any time had opened in my schedule or if he'd have to wait until later in the week.

Oh, yes, indeed you will, I thought as I erased his message.

And then I was changed and comfortable and not sure what to do next. It was past three, almost time to go home. I was hoping I'd hear from the Grannies, but there was no message from them.

I glanced at the bags I'd taken from my trunk. His death nagged at me. It was probably only my irrational guilt—he was alive when I'd found him—that made me pick them up and empty them on my desk. The papers and the pills weren't likely to give me any insight into what had happened. But if I simply threw them in the trash because I assumed they were useless, then I'd never know for certain that they were.

First I turned my attention to the pills, taking one from each bottle, both NBG and The Cure. I placed that pill in front of each of the bottles, as if their size and shape might reveal secrets.

There were eleven bottles total, seven from Nature's Beautiful Gift and four from The Cure. Several of the NBG ones were the same ones I'd seen at Marion McConkle's place, including the one for "bowel regularity," making me glad that Cordelia insisted on a diet high in veggies and fiber. The other overlaps were for glowing skin and eye health. Reginald also had "virility enhancement"—he was a man after all. (Maybe that was Vincent's problem; he was taking too many of these.) Two of the bottles were the same, for promoting healthy blood production, and the last of the NBGs was for immune function.

The Cure dispensed with the properly legal wording on the NBG bottles and claimed, as its name suggested, that it cured "All Blood Disorders." He had two bottles of that one. The next one promised to cure all circulatory dysfunction, and the last promised a healthy and robust immune system: "Never get a cold or the flu again."

But Reginald hadn't been cured or saved. What had gone so wrong? Had he been even crazier than Marion McConkle and given up completely on the medical establishment?

I looked again at the pills; they varied in color from a cream white to a dusky hazel-green, and in size from small and round, to oblong horse pills that must have been a challenge to swallow. The NBG pills were all different in shape and color. The pills from The Cure looked very similar, large, dark greenish-yellow. I pulled out my magnifying glass, having to rummage in my bottom drawer to find it. Curiously, both the NBG "immune function" pill and all the pills from The Cure looked alike, same shape, close to the same color. On close examination, I could see some color differences. The Cure appeared to be slightly darker.

I didn't know enough about how supplements were made to know whether that meant anything or not. Maybe there were only so many pill sizes and colors, so there was bound to be overlap if you put enough of them out in a row. It was possible that the pill molds were standard, so only so much variation was possible unless someone wanted to shell out for a custom one.

I finally got tired of staring at the pills and playing with my magnifying glass—yellow-green is not a favorite color of mine. I put the supplements back in their appropriate bottles. Maybe the paperwork would be more revealing.

First I did a hasty organization, putting everything in order by date.

It was a big pile of medical and insurance paperwork. Most of the codes and jargon were beyond me. For about the first six months, things seemed to track. There was a receipt from the doctor—he saw several specialists—the insurance was billed, they paid except for his co-pay. What was interesting was that Reginald seemed to be an organized man, writing on the bills the number of the checks, the amount paid, the account number and the date.

Then he had a visit in late August of 2005, and after that nothing for four months. Many people, overwhelmed with evacuating and then suddenly scrambling to find a place to live while the city was being drained, never got past food and shelter to make it back into medical care. Reginald Banks seemed to be one of these people. In early December, he had an ER visit in Memphis. After that, two follow-up visits, one in Memphis, the second in Jackson, Mississippi.

Then shortly after the Jackson visit, about two years ago, he changed insurance companies and doctors, with the location shifting back to New Orleans. The number of visits increased. He had been out of care, had not had stable housing, I was guessing, from the multiple addresses of service right after Katrina, and his health had probably suffered. He started to get behind on his bills, making partial payments instead of full ones. After the initial increase, which lasted for about six months, then four months went by without any medical visits, only bills and his neat handing writing indicating how much he was paying.

I looked at his pharmacy bills. He was getting his prescriptions refilled about every five to six weeks, so it looked like he was stretching his monthly pills out to help decrease the cost.

Then a year ago, he switched doctors again, the address now of the group Cordelia was with. I found paperwork with Lydia's signature on it for compassionate use of one of his more expensive medications. He had several visits, mostly about a month apart, with the usual receipts matching the insurance bills.

Then there was an insurance form listing several visits, now mostly two weeks apart, and next to two of them, in Reginald's neat writing—

no visit, billing mistake. He noted that he had called the doctor's office about it.

Then another insurance form, with another list of visits of about every two weeks. Two of the visits had codes next to them that indicated they were beyond the usual and customary and would not be covered. They were what prompted the denial of services that Reginald had received about three months ago. Again, his neat handwriting: *billing mistake, called doctor, co-pays reversed.*

There was a copy of the letter he sent appealing the denial, claiming that there was a billing error and that he hadn't been seen by the doctor every two weeks, but only once a month.

A check for his most recent visit was sent back to him for insufficient funds in his account.

What had happened? A clerical error and his lack of money had kept him out of the doctor's office. He'd taken a turn for the worse, thought he could tough it out, and had been horribly wrong.

Then I remembered Eugenia, the other patient claiming that she hadn't been there when they said she had. Did it mean anything or was it just a coincidence? I'd have to tell Cordelia that she might suggest better training for the billing department.

All I knew was that I made my head hurt and seemed to have done little to answer why Reginald Banks, who shouldn't have died, was in a morgue.

It was almost five thirty. Time for me to stop thinking about this and go home.

CHAPTER FOURTEEN

We stumbled into the weekend, both of us exhausted. If I had to pick the worst week of my life the last one would be in the running. My answer to "how've you been" would be "Let's see, I almost got killed by a drug-addicted thug, my partner was diagnosed with cancer. If she survives it'll be because she's had to go through months of ugly chemo and being sick. And I had an epic fight with a cousin I was close with. I guess I won't be borrowing his saber saw anytime soon."

The free days passed in a blur; we didn't go out, hibernated in an attempt to heal from the blows fate had dealt us.

On Monday morning Cordelia insisted on going to work. "I want to—need to—keep everything as normal as possible," she told me.

I'd fallen apart last night, the free time finally let in the emotions I'd been holding at bay—I was going to blame it on the almost deadly car chase—so I wasn't allowed to again for a while. I kept to our routine—when I could remember what our routine was. I got up with her, unusual for us. I told her I couldn't sleep, which was true.

I made the coffee and breakfast—well, sliced bananas and strawberries for cereal. That wasn't so unusual, except for my being awake to do it.

Then she was out the door and I was left wondering how the fuck I'd keep to anything approaching normal today. My mind was blank on what would be typical right now. And then I realized that no way was normal going to apply, so I'd aim for abnormal but constructive.

I cleaned the house, oh, yes, even under the stove top. Not a slow cleaning either, but a whirling dervish cleaning, filling my nostrils with bleach and my hands covered with soapy water. That was done a little before noon. It had been a while since the place was this spick-and-span.

Maybe I was struggling against being Reginald, so ill that his normally clean house had turned to a cesspool. If I kept the place clean, then that would avert his fate.

I considered going to the grocery store, but decided we'd do it together. Cordelia seemed to want to and I knew I needed not to just take over as if she was already ill and incapable.

Which left going to work. That, at least, I could check off the normal category. So I took a quick shower to get rid of the worst of the bleach smell. Then I started a load of laundry. My cleaning clothes needed it, and the bleach in them would help the rest of the whites get oh-so sparkling fresh. After that there was nothing to do except get dressed—black jeans and a dark gray cotton sweater—colors seemed too much. I started to automatically put on my holster, but paused to wonder if I really needed it now. Cordelia didn't much like hugging me around the gun. I left it on; I could take it off at my office.

I realized I didn't want to go out in the world where people could see me and I had to pretend that everything was okay, when it so wasn't okay.

But the day was moving and I had to be aboard.

It was bright and sunny, as if the sun could shine through anything.

Maybe it would be okay.

At least I could enjoy the sunshine.

When I got to my office, there were two TV trucks parked in front. An amateur video of my car chase had surfaced and therefore Dudley's insane car chase was finally getting its fifteen minutes of fame. The DA, bless his political heart, had a press conference this morning to announce the arrest. He didn't want the story buried over the weekend. Given that Dudley was in the hospital and not talking, that left me as the only other principal capable of speech.

I kept driving, not changing speed to clue them into it being me in the car by speeding away. Nope, I was just another resident toolin' on by. The last thing I wanted to do was talk to the news media on a good day. And today was such not a good day. I turned the corner and parked near the next corner.

There is a back entrance to my building and it involves only minor trespassing. First I had to go through the little store on the corner, buying a newspaper, a couple of soft drinks and some chips—which I had no intention of eating—as a bribe to let me exit through the back. It was a good thing that I wasn't hankering for the chips. My next move was to toss the bag over a fence. It wasn't tall, so it was easy to step on an old wooden crate and hoist myself over. From there a quick cut through someone's backyard, over my building's tottering remains of a fence, and I was at the back door.

Without a key. But my landlord didn't think the back door was a security risk, so the lock could actually be opened with a credit card. I would have to talk to him about that, I thought, as I slipped inside. His one other nod to security back here was to pile a bunch of junk, making it an obstacle course to get to the stairs.

Oh, yeah, my normal routine.

When I got to my office, normal did await me. My answering machine light was blinking and the Grannies had a report for me. Hard choice, but I decided I could get my phone messages out of the way first, make a cup of coffee, then peruse what the Grannies had sent.

First one was Mr. Charles Williams calling about our meeting. I'd let him know we were meeting when we met.

Cordelia. "Hey, I just wanted you to know how much you mean to me. Love you. See you this evening. You don't need to call back. I just wanted to hear your voice. Even on an answering machine."

Yeah, normal. Although I was glad I wasn't the only one who couldn't perfectly keep to our usual routine.

The next message was from Joanne. "Hope you're still alive. Call me when you get a chance."

Danny. "I assume you're pressing charges. Call me so I can follow up on my boss's orders."

My good friend Carl Prejean. "Look, I didn't send any guy after you, okay? We're cool. I figured out who most likely torched my house. It wasn't you, okay? So call your cop friends off, okay?"

What a choice of messages.

I called Cordelia first. She didn't answer, which meant either she had turned her cell off or was with a patient. I left a message. "Hey, it's me. I got your message. You're going to be stuck hearing my voice for a long time. I love you. I'll see you tonight."

Joanne was next. She wasn't available. I just left the message that I had called.

Then Danny. She also wasn't around. Another message.

How to handle phone calls quickly and efficiently—just don't talk to anyone.

Time for the Grannies.

Nature's Beautiful Gift was privately owned. Only two complaints of adverse reactions had been reported to the FDA. One was for constipation—everything ends up at the colon—the other for headaches and fever. The complaints were for different supplements. No actions were taken. As the Grannies footnoted, usually action was only taken if there was a pattern of adverse events that could be traced to one particular product and if the problems were severe. The company was involved in a number of community projects, including donating to inner-city schools, and had underwritten playgrounds in poor neighborhoods. Its "naturalists" were independent salespeople, so it did operate as a multilevel marketing company. That meant that people like Vincent bought their supplies from the company, and it was up to them to sell enough of them to make a profit. Some of these were quite legit and offered people the chance to set their own hours and to work from home. There were some claims to the Better Business Bureau, but not as many as one might think. The Grannies had done some comparisons, and NBG had a fairly clean record compared to other companies with a similar setup. In fact the only company that had fewer complaints was one that sold sex toys. Guess people didn't want to admit that their dildos were defective.

More and more NBG was looking like a legitimate company. Maybe I should try the sample packs that Vincent had given me and see if my regularity improved.

I started skipping through the NBG stuff. Most of it seemed of little help or interest to my client. There was nothing he could use to convince his aunt she was being sold powdered Lake Pontchartrain slime. Plus it was boring. They'd found some reference to studies, although they tended to be small and funded by either NBG or some other similar firm. But they bolstered their claim that the products "helped improve" whatever they were supposed to. For the most part, though, they were in the usual limbo—nothing proved they did work, but nothing proved they didn't.

The Grannies had been less successful with The Cure. It had no website promoting its products. I was willing to bet that since they walked past the legal line, they had to be careful about to whom and where they promoted. They'd found references to it in several blogs, but some of it was secondhand—*My friend's aunt used something called the (sic) Cure and she was cancer free within weeks*—or part of a rant—*The government only lets the rich people have access to The Cure, the rest of us get to rot in their antiquated medieval medical system.* One claimed *The Cure will kill you*, but as they noted, the blog was old and hadn't had any entries in over six months.

They finished with saying that they'd keep searching for info on The Cure, but unless I wanted more on NBG, they'd stop there. As far as I was concerned, they could have stopped ten pages earlier on NBG than they had. The only advantage to the length of their report, I thought as I made a copy of it, was that I could hand this stack of paper to Mr. Charles Williams and then he could have as much fun as I did. Plus it would help Fletcher's wife feel like they'd gotten their money's worth.

My phone rang. Hoping it would be Cordelia, but knowing it wasn't likely, I picked it up.

Danny. "Hey, girlfriend. Need to follow up on the fun with one of my least favorite criminals."

"Fun? Then you and I disagree of the definition of fun."

"Naw, just the context." But this was business, so she continued, "Dudley's got a rich daddy. So in the past he's been able to get much better treatment than most common hoods. Promises of going into treatment instead of being sent to jail, probation, house arrest in the family manor in Old Metairie. If you're willing to press charges, we'll throw the book at him."

"Yeah? So what's in it for me?"

She was silent for a moment, as if not believing that I could be so venal.

"I mean, you should at least offer to cook those buttermilk blueberry pancakes."

I heard a discreet snort on her end. "I'll cook them for you as a friend, not as a bribe to have you testify. Got it?"

I got it. She was working and I needed to behave. Or at least deal with everything that was going on by not being an asshole to my friends.

J.M. REDMANN

"Okay, unless I'm likely to get killed I'll testify."

"You're probably safer with him in jail than with him out. I can't make absolute promises, but Daddy does his evil deeds with lawyers, not guns. Oh, and Mick? I'm glad you still have enough of your nine lives left to have made it through this one okay."

"Yeah, me, too. So what's next?"

"Nothing at the moment. Dudley is still unconscious. He has to be awake for us to charge him. Maybe the bump on his head will have made him a better person and he'll plead guilty."

"Yeah, wouldn't that be nice," I agreed. We both knew it was unlikely.

"Once he's awake, we'll have a better idea of how to proceed."

"Is it possible that you can give me a warning before he sets foot out of the hospital?"

"I'll do what I can. It may depend on how slick his father's lawyer is. But he should go from the hospital to the jail. Luck was on our side this time. Some concerned citizen with a decent cell phone camera got video of the chase down St. Claude. We might be able to turn Prejean to admit he hired Dudley for a little harassment that got out of hand."

I sighed. This wasn't bad news, but it meant I'd be entangled in the legal system—grand jury and court dates—and could only hope justice prevailed when it was finally finished. Luck—and evidence—were on my side, but money can trump even those. "So you basically called me to tell me to wait around?"

"That. And to make sure you're okay. And…" She hesitated.

I guessed what was coming next. Elly, Danny's partner, was a nurse who'd worked with Cordelia for a long time at her clinic.

"And," she continued, "Elly told me about Cordelia."

I didn't want to hear it, didn't want to talk about it. I could be normal only if I kept blinkers on, a fierce focus on the right now, the right in front of me. But those walls were fragile and Danny had just breached them.

"Yeah, I know," I cut in gruffly. "If there's anything you can do, yadda, yadda."

"I hope you know it's not just words. If there is anything we can do, we'll do it."

"How about miracles? You have any of those?"

• 160 •

"Those are hard to find. I'll see what I can do," she said gently. I guess Danny knew me well enough to know my rage was a defense and it wasn't aimed at her.

"I'm sorry, my other line is ringing," I lied. "Is there anything else we need to talk about right now?"

"No, I'll catch you later."

I put the handset down without saying anything else.

Then to make my lie the truth, my phone rang. I stared at it for a moment, hesitant to answer, but just before the answering machine kicked in, I grabbed it.

"Hello—Knight Detective Agency." I managed to make it close to professional.

My hasty decision did not go unpunished. "Hey, I know we didn't really set anything, but I was driving by, so is it okay if I come up now?" Mr. Charles Williams.

The one advantage of him coming now was that he would be leaving a little after now.

Again, I lied. "You're in luck. I had a cancellation, so I can fit you in."

The downstairs door was locked, so I had to climb down three flights of stairs to let him in. I didn't hurry, instead took my time trying to compose my thoughts and my expression to be a bland mask by the time I was at the door letting him in. Maybe I did, or maybe Mr. Charles Williams was not a man who easily read hidden emotions.

"Hey, was that you on the news?" he asked as he entered.

"I do everything I can to stay out of the news." I didn't add that I don't always succeed. Instead I headed back up the stairs at a quick enough pace that Mr. Williams had to choose between talking and breathing.

When we got to my office, I was determined to control the conversation. Barely giving him time to catch his breath, I said, "I got the fax from Mr. McConkle. As you should know, he did give you permission to hear about certain aspects of the case. However, he also gave me discretion as to what I can tell you. You argue, you get nothing, you understand?"

He flopped heavily down in the chair in front of my desk. It was a sturdy one, so it took his weight without even a groan.

I took the chair behind my desk and continued, "I did research on Nature's Beautiful Gift. As far as I can tell they're a legitimate company and they obey the laws regulating supplements."

"There are no laws," Mr. Williams cut in. "You know what I mean. If someone dies, they'll pull the stuff from the shelves. That's it."

"They can't make claims they can't back up with scientific evidence, like advertising that their products cure diseases."

"Yeah, they slime around that by things like 'promotes heart health,' 'aids in protection against cancer.'"

"Free speech," I reminded him. "The bottom line is that Nature's Beautiful Gift appears to have nothing illegal and untoward going on. You can argue that supplements are a waste of people's money because they're unproven or you can argue that there isn't enough money to do tests on pills that are made of plants and herbs because no one can afford it on something they can't patent and these companies are doing a service by making alternative remedies available. People get to make that choice, and you may have to live with people not making the right choice."

"My nephew is killing himself with this stuff," Mr. Williams burst out. "He's spending more money than he has because he's convinced they're making his problems go away."

"How old is your nephew?" I asked.

"In his late twenties. He should be old enough to know better, but he's not. He says he's sick and tired of going to doctors and having needles poked in him. He wants something that can give him a normal life."

"What's wrong with him?"

"He has sickle cell anemia. And, yeah, I get it. He has to go to the doctor as often as old men and get transfusions more times than I can count. He wants to have a regular life, play sports, date—he's a handsome devil when he's not sick-looking—go cheer at the Saints game and not worry he might get something from the public toilets."

I started to ask him when he had last seen his nephew, but stopped. I didn't want to know. There could certainly be many young men in the area with sickle cell anemia. But how many of them had put their faith in alternative medicine and turned their backs on standard treatment? If Reginald Banks was Charles Williams's nephew, I was not going to be the one to tell him what had happened.

"So how'd you get involved with being the one to pursue this? What about his parents?"

"They ended up in Milwaukee after the storm. My nephew didn't like the cold, so he came back down here. I'm the only family he has that's close."

It was time to change the subject. I didn't want to know any more. "I printed out all the stuff I found out about NBG and made a copy for you." I handed him the stack of paper.

He took it, giving it a dubious look.

"You can read, can't you?" I asked, not very politely.

"Not my favorite thing to do," he said, "but, yeah, I can read. I'm slow. Why don't you just give me that main stuff in this?"

I glanced pointedly at my watch. I realized I had assumed the Mr. Charles Williams was Reginald Banks's uncle and I was angry at him for not checking more regularly, for leaving me to find him too late. *You don't know that*, I told myself. And I was doing everything I could not to find out.

"The gist is pretty much what I said, that Nature's Beautiful Gift is a legitimate supplement company. It relies on multilevel marketing. Independent contractors buy the product and then turn around and sell it, doing things like house parties. Fletcher McConkle's aunt has a very nice young man who visits her regularly. Maybe your nephew has someone similar, a friend who spends time with him, cares about his health, and therefore he's likely to buy the pills from him. Maybe if you spent more time with your nephew you could get him to see your point of view."

He hung his head. "Yeah, well, I tried that. Went over almost every day. He finally got tired of me, told me to get out, that he could live his life without my interference. That he'd call me when he wanted to see me again. So far he hasn't called. When I call him, he doesn't answer."

This isn't my tragedy, I reminded myself. *I have one of my own.* "I'm sorry to hear that. If he's not willing to talk to you, then whatever I find out won't do much good."

"Yeah, I was hoping you'd find out they're a bunch of crooks and we could shut them down."

I said softly, "That's why we need movies and TV, so we clearly know what's right and wrong and most of the time the good guys win. Real life doesn't always give us that."

He stood up. Without me even prompting him. "No, it doesn't. At least you talked to me." He picked up the huge pile of paper I'd copied for him. "Would you be upset if I just burn this instead of reading it?"

"I made it for you. You get to do whatever you want to with it."

He nodded and started to head out.

I got up. "I have to let you out. Had some trouble lately, so we keep the bottom door locked."

He let me lead. I went down slowly, to let him keep pace. We talked about the weather, just words to fill the silence. Mr. Charles Williams was a man uncomfortable with silence. At the landing window I looked out to the street. From this angle the TV crews were gone.

I let him out the door, watching him as he crossed the street to his car. I couldn't protect him from much, but I could make sure he was safe crossing the street.

I was as slow going back up the stairs. There seemed no reason to rush to anything.

I spend fifteen minutes starting at my computer screen, trying to work, trying to do something—anything—to keep my mind consumed with some distracting task, but nothing worked.

The day had been long enough. I decided to go home.

CHAPTER FIFTEEN

We did need some groceries. Since I'd left early, I fit in a quick run to get the essential stuff, toilet paper and cat food, something to eat tonight. I decided on shrimp and cheese grits, one of Cordelia's favorites, but not something she often indulged in since it wasn't exactly hard-core healthy. And some salad stuff, so at least part of the menu would be virtuous.

Her car was already parked in front by the time I got home from the grocery run.

When I came into the house, I heard her on the phone.

"Micky just got home," she said. "We'll talk later, okay? And either you'll come over this weekend or we go out—I'll call tomorrow and work out the details."

Whoever she was talking to answered, as Cordelia was silent for several moments.

While she finished her conversation, I carried the groceries into the kitchen. It was just a couple of bags, so it was only one load.

"Who was that?" I asked as she joined me.

"You're spying on my phone calls?" she asked, her tone teasing.

"I think I distinctly heard you obligating us to either cook here or go out. Since that involves me, I have a right to know."

"That was Alex. I told her that I have cancer, so she has to get her shit together."

"You did not. Well, not like that."

"Yes, pretty much like that. She's gotten lost in her gloom and needs something to kick her out of it. If I have to have cancer, I might as well get as much mileage out of it as possible." She started unloading the second grocery bag. "Shrimp and grits? You must think I'm dying."

"No, not at all," I said too quickly. "But...but it's been a long day and it just seemed like a night for comfort food. So, how is Alex doing?"

"She spends about three hours a day driving back and forth from Baton Rouge, eight to ten hours at work, seven hours sleeping or trying to sleep, an hour in the morning getting up and ready to go, so that leaves, what, about three, maybe five hours a day for everything else, chores, eating dinner, catching up with people—we just spent forty-five minutes talking on the phone. Joanne was used to having a lot of Alex's attention, a good hour or two talking about her day. Put those all together and she has not only no time for herself, but is skimming the other things as well."

"I guess I hadn't thought about the day-to-day of her working ninety miles away."

"I'm not sure Joanne has either."

"You mean Joanne is being an insensitive brute," I said as I started to clean the shrimp.

"Not at all." Cordelia gave my hip a bump with hers for me to make room at the sink. "I'll peel, you devein." She picked up a big shrimp and started peeling. "What I mean is that we're all still struggling, with everything from a longer drive to the grocery store, a constantly changing city, to having to deal with people coming back and realizing they can't stay. Alex has had to train two new assistants in the last few months, you've had more work than you can handle and have often had to job in help or work with Chanse or Scotty."

"And I hate having to depend on other people's schedules."

"That's my point. Most of what we deal with isn't so big anymore, but the small things add up, they take an hour or two hours out of our days, sap energy. You and I, Joanne and Alex, we all have to keep adjusting to change, like driving at twilight."

"And who we are as we drive into the dark."

"Exactly. I think Alex is struggling because she's trying to deal with both what she went through and just day after day of having time sucked out of her life. That commute to Baton Rouge is killing her."

"It's certainly killing her relationship with Joanne," I said.

"Alex is thinking about getting a place up there," Cordelia said as she handed me a pile of shrimp.

"Joanne is not going to like that. She'll see Alex even less."

"Alex doesn't have any good choices. She needs a job. Her choice is between Baton Rouge or flipping burgers here. If she spends three hours a day in the car, she has no time for Joanne or herself."

I looked at her. "So you think they're going to break up."

"I think Alex needs to take care of herself or she can't be any good to anyone. She said herself that every hour she spends in traffic she falls apart a little more."

I rinsed my hands, getting the shrimp goop off as they were getting too sticky, then continued deveining. "And we're going to get together with them this weekend so we can watch them as they break up?"

"No, we're getting together with them because they're both good people, they're close friends of ours, and we want the best for them. And maybe some other solution will come up."

"Oh, yeah, that miracle tree. I keep meaning to visit it."

"There are worse things than breaking up, even a long-term relationship."

"Yeah, your partner could get cancer and die on you," I said bitterly.

Cordelia looked at me. "Oh, damn, I didn't mean…I was just…I don't even know."

"I know," I said. She was being general, but all I could see was my life. "I'm sorry. I'm not good at playing normal."

"Don't play at anything. If we can't be so-called normal, then we just can't. Please, Micky, I'm so sorry, I never wanted to put you through this."

"I think you're the one with cancer. The one who might…" But I couldn't say the word.

"Might die," she finished for me. "I'm going to try very hard not to. At least not for a long, long time, okay?"

"I know." I started to cry. I couldn't wipe my tears away because my hands were covered in shrimp slime. "Oh, fuck normal."

We both had to wash and dry our hands before we could embrace. I hated that I was falling apart, crying first and forcing Cordelia to comfort me.

"This isn't right," I said as she threw the towel she had dried her hands with onto the kitchen table and put her arms around me. "I should be taking care of you."

"Shh. Of course it's right. Let me take care of you while I can. The chemo is going to be messy. When I'm throwing up, you can take care of me. And fuck right or wrong. No one is judging."

So I fell apart. "What the hell am I going to do? If you're gone? I can't make it."

"Yes, you can," she said matter-of-factly. "Grief is hard and painful and I would certainly hope that you desperately miss me for a while. A year, maybe. But I want time to heal you, for you to go on, find someone else and love again."

"Yeah, right," I sobbed into her shoulder. It is hard to be sarcastic when you're crying. "Easy for you to say."

"If I die—I'm not planning to—and you don't start dating in two years, I'll come back and haunt you. I'll hide your coffee and your car keys."

"Damn it, you're not supposed to make jokes about this. Wait, hiding my coffee is not funny."

"If Alex and Joanne break up, that would at least mean there would be two eligible people to date."

"They're not breaking up; you're not dying. And you smell like shrimp."

And then we were both laughing.

I cooked the shrimp and cheese grits, made a big salad. We even opened a decent bottle of wine.

After a few more hand washings, the shrimp smell did fade.

CHAPTER SIXTEEN

The next day was a slap into reality. We were both up early. Cordelia was due for more tests and I insisted on going with her. She made a token protest, saying that I didn't need to, that if she didn't feel okay after, she could easily get someone else to drive her home, but I was adamant.

When we got to the clinic, the brave face she'd put on over the weekend was gone. She was pale and subdued. The light green walls, people in white coats, being the one to wait to be seen—the patient, not the doctor—made it real.

Then her name was called and all I could do was wait.

Hours passed, a book, a magazine; I flitted between the pile of reading material I'd brought. I tried not to wonder where she was and what was happening to her. The harder I tried, the less I succeeded. She'd explained what they were doing, taking some marrow from her hip to run more tests on it, going into medical detail that would have required me to ask her to explain every other word if I really wanted to understand. She needed to talk, to use information as a shield against what was happening to her. I knew enough—she would undergo a painful procedure so they could have more information about which type of lymphoma she had and therefore how to treat it.

How had our world changed so much? A few weeks ago life was normal; we didn't need to pretend otherwise. I had to cling to what she'd claimed—it would be hard, but it would be okay. She was young, relatively speaking; she had access to good medical care. We would get through this. It seemed a cruel irony that we were finally getting beyond what had happened in the past, finding a new level of trust and connection, only to slam into the hard wall of disease, illness, mortality.

She was moving slowly when she finally came back to the waiting area, but flashed me a wan smile. She seemed relieved to have it over. I joined her as she finished with paperwork and making the next appointment.

"I'm not used to this," she admitted to me as we left the building. "I usually just ask one of my coworkers, to see if my throat is red, or diagnose myself and get them to write me a prescription when we meet at the coffeepot."

"And now you're just a lowly patient like the rest of us," I said.

She gave me her small smile again. "But with a great girlfriend to take care of me."

And that was what I did. I drove her home, insisted that she plop in the comfortable chair, found something suitably mindless and entertaining on TV, fixed a lunch of soup and sandwiches. Left her in front of the small screen while I cleaned up after lunch.

After a while she was tired. I insisted she go ahead and take a nap, something she rarely does. But she fell asleep quickly, which told me how wearing the day had been.

I considering running by my office for an hour or two, just to catch up and make sure no fires were burning, but I didn't want her to wake and not find me here. The little things had become important now because all I could control were those little things. I did some cleaning although after my last frenzy, there was little that needed more than a quick dust. I played with the cats so they wouldn't go in and bother Cordelia. I turned to my standard fail-safe, cooking, making dough for a pizza, chopping several onions and caramelizing them. This was one of Cordelia's favorites, a white one with a layer of the onions topped with sun-dried tomatoes and artichoke hearts. I cried while I made the dough, I cried while she slept.

I wanted to be cried out by the time she woke.

The evening was slow, we ate, we talked. I listened as she told me about what she went through, my tears used up, so I heard it all calmly, holding her hand when she needed it. Sticking a needle in and extracting bone marrow is a painful procedure. She downplayed it, but she moved slowly and I knew it had to be hurting her.

The next day she went to work and insisted that I go, too.

It's how we get through the days, I thought as I drove to my office. *We pad them with the mundane, the activities that don't touch our hearts, so we can rest before the next break.*

But I did little, save what was required. I knew the test results would take days, maybe even a week to come back. Time felt too small to allow for anything more than waiting to hear from her, to hear her fate.

The mundane did indeed await me. Or maybe it just seemed mundane compared to my worry about Cordelia.

Prejean had left another message, again asking me to call off the cops. I deleted it.

Danny also left a message. It was a brief update—basically Dudley was still out of it although his doctors predicted that he'd be awake in a day or two and able to talk.

Mr. Charles Williams called asking for a favor. Maybe I could talk to his nephew. He might listen to me. He suspected it might be a long time before his nephew ever talked to him again. "Guess I can kind of come on strong," he admitted. *This isn't your heartbreak, it's someone else's*, I reminded myself. I couldn't help Mr. Williams. I suspected it might be forever before he'd talk to his nephew again.

The Grannies had done more digging for me. They'd even done some field work. Not surprising, it looked like Prejean was involved with insurance fraud. As I had noticed, his burned house didn't seem heavily damaged. According to his insurance claim, it had been almost destroyed. It wasn't just that house. He also had two more houses under different names, one had been vandalized and the third one also burned.

All through the same insurance agent.

With all the destruction that had taken place here, insurance companies were overwhelmed just as much as everyone else. They didn't always have time to investigate each claim as thoroughly as they might have otherwise. The claims were still rolling in, with destroyed houses now stripped of copper or new appliances stolen. Prejean had clearly found a crooked insurance agent and was taking advantage of him having little oversight. The Grannies had taken a ride and snapped pictures of each of his supposedly damaged properties. As I suspected, there wasn't much damage visible to the naked eye. As they noted, being an old lady was the perfect disguise. They could cruise with impunity.

I'd turn this over to Danny. This might be the pressure that would get Prejean to admit he'd hired Dudley and turn on him.

The randomness of life took me on a detour—two calls, several e-mails, mundane cases to work on—as mundane as finding a person gone missing can be, and tracing the tangled web of ownership for a property that was owned by the heirs of the heirs—every single second cousin had to be found and persuaded to sell. It was mostly tedious culling through dusty records, but I had to pay enough attention to make the hours—and the days—pass. The missing person was for another PI; he needed extra eyes and the money wasn't bad.

The hours added into days, the heirs located, the missing person traced to Atlanta and a drug habit that made him unwilling or unable to contact his parents. That it wasn't my case meant that I wasn't the one to deliver the news to the family. A final phone call to tie up the details of the case and then I was left staring at the neat piles on my desk. Everything had been sorted and filed, there was nothing to readily claim my time.

The hours became empty. I didn't know what to do next. I started to pick up the phone and ask Cordelia to meet for lunch, but I couldn't cling to her. It felt like Katrina again, Cordelia was trapped inside Charity and I was far away in a safe land and couldn't help her.

I had long ago given up believing in "God and His mysterious ways" as some catch-all explanation for bad things. Like God wanting to punish gay men with AIDS and mysteriously orphaning ten million children in Africa to get less than a million gay men in America and Europe.

Cordelia had cancer. I didn't. It was a small tragedy, one that happened every day to millions of people. Cancer or HIV or car wreck or any of the hundreds of ways life takes a sudden and jarring turn. It hit both those affected and those standing next to them.

Time changed. Would I hold her hand in the next springtime? Or visit a grave? I looked at a year that felt impossibly fleeting and as if it would take forever.

"She'll be okay," I said.

I was the one who had lived on the edge—alcohol, even cocaine and a few other things when I was young and could pretend nothing bad ever really happened. I'd stumbled over a few cases that had been dangerous, bullets instead of the usually moldy records.

It was a twist of fate too bizarre for her to be the one staring at her mortality and me still firmly left in the land of the healthy and well.

"Like life is ever fair," I said, my voice loud against the stillness of my thoughts.

I couldn't bear to be with those thoughts anymore.

I made a list of every possible office supply item I might need in the next year, drove out to the suburbs where the mega-office-type-crap stores are and distracted myself with avoiding the insane drivers—tiny blondes in big SUVs are the worst; the rude shoppers—why on earth would I be upset with you rolling your cart over my toes?; and clerks who had to use a calculator to understand that $120 minus $118.90 meant I got a buck and a dime in change.

By the time I got back to my office and put everything away, it was time to go home.

Even though it wasn't late, Cordelia had gotten there before me.

She was in the kitchen, doing the dishes.

She hates doing the dishes, usually approaching them with a glum determination that borders on the dourest Protestantism—that there was no possible joy because joy was an indication of sinning and eternal damnation. We often traded laundry and ironing for doing dishes. She was fair enough to feel that if I cooked—which I often did—that she should do the cleaning up afterward. But fairness didn't make her like sticking her hands in soapy water and dealing with grease, so her being alone in the house and deciding that the few dishes from breakfast were how she wanted to spend her evening was unusual.

Enough that it worried me.

"Hey, honey, I'm home," I called. She wasn't going to just blurt out what was going on. I needed to let her work her way to it.

"I was wondering when you'd get here." There was an edge to her tone that did nothing to ease my worry.

"Am I late?"

She put the bowl she had been washing back in the sink, abruptly turning off the tap. "No, no you're not. Sorry." She turned to me and managed a ghost of a smile.

I walked behind her and put my arms around her, just held her, saying nothing.

"It's…uh…it's not been a good day," she said softly.

"What's wrong?" I asked, tightening my embrace.

"Traffic was horrible coming home. Three people did a left turn from the right lane. Without signaling. The morning at the office was crazy. Brandon and Lydia got into a fight and Ron had to break it up—which is so not how things usually go."

"Mr. Abrasive as peacemaker?"

"Dr. Abrasive," she corrected. "None of the patients were routine—every one of them required extra time and extra paperwork. We had a mess with someone trying to use his brother's insurance—they only caught it as he paid, realizing that his card had a different name on it."

"Why would someone do that? Everyone checks IDs these days."

"Desperate. They were brothers, looked enough alike to use each other's IDs. The man that came in was laid off, lost his insurance, had gone fishing last weekend. The tip of a fishhook broke off in his hand and he wasn't able to get it out and had infected the wound. He needed to be seen, didn't want to pay an emergency room fee."

"What a mess! So what happened?"

"We let him slide by with paying out of pocket. Using a check that'll probably bounce. If it does, then he's going to be in even more trouble. The poverty spiral, how not having money for one thing affects everything you do. His brother is going to have to find another doctor. And I got to be the one to tell him."

"Ouch. That's not a good day," I agreed.

"That's not all," she said softly.

I wanted her not to talk, not to say anything. I could handle traffic, other people's tragedies, but not here, not now, not in these walls, the ones that had always kept me safe before.

I had to fight to get out the words, "Tell me."

"Chemo and radiation in the next few days. It's stage three, an aggressive form." She paused for a moment, picked up the bowl as if to continue washing, then put it down again. "It's what I expected—lymphoma is often only detected once it's progressed to several nodes. The advantage to the more aggressive form is that it can be eradicated; the less aggressive forms rarely clear, although they may move so slowly that they don't need immediate treatment."

I recognized the information dump for what it was—distance, control. For both of us. Letting her talk meant that I didn't need to respond. She ran down the various subtypes, how the tests worked, a list of chemo drugs, the advantages and disadvantages of each—a wash of medical jargon that I understood well enough to not ask for the definition of each word—she had cancer, it was serious, the treatment would be aggressive, and our lives would change.

My mind ran through a gamut of emotions, skimming past the most brutal of what-ifs and focusing on going to the grocery to get ingredients for chicken soup, stocking up on sports drinks. Chemo would probably cause nausea, and those were the small things that I could do to help with this big thing that had invaded our life.

Our lives. Suddenly we were very different people on very different journeys.

She abruptly said, "I'm sorry. I'm just spewing out facts. Like if I know enough about this, then I'm in charge and not these aberrant cells growing in my body."

"What do you need from me?" I asked.

She was silent. She tried to smile. Failed. Finally answered, "I don't know. I don't think I know anything at the moment. I don't know what I want, let alone what I need from you." She picked up the bowl again and washed it.

I let her go and fed the cats. They had been unusually patient, as if they knew that this was a time their begging would go ignored.

Cordelia finished the last few dishes in silence. Suddenly, she threw the dish towel she had been drying her hands on at me. "Let's have a good time. Let's do the things we've been promising ourselves we'd do—eat out at the restaurants we've been meaning to try. Do a swamp tour—I haven't done that in years. Drive over to the coast, maybe even go to a casino—I've never played a slot machine."

"All of that tonight, huh?" I echoed her mood.

"Perhaps not everything. How about going out to eat?"

I put my arms around her. "I think we can manage that. Where would you like to go?"

She managed a smile. "You know I hate making those kinds of decisions. This is what you can do for me, decide."

I kissed her, a sign that I would take care of it.

I first thought of calling Torbin—he was a restaurant maven and see what he suggested. But I hadn't heard from him since our last altercation and I wasn't willing to deal with him.

"To the computer," I pulled away from her. The Internet would have to substitute for my cousin. "How dressy?" I asked as I booted it up.

"All decisions are yours."

Cordelia did hate to make decisions—save for the ones she wanted to make—so was happy to defer to me. I usually didn't let her get away with that because I wasn't going to be stuck with the full responsibility if things screwed up.

I couldn't even complain that she was using cancer to get her way.

I choose fancy and dressy, one of the newer restaurants in the Warehouse District that some of our friends had been raving about.

We didn't talk about cancer, we enjoyed the food and drinks, made a list of where else we'd like to go—some were real, like the swamp tour, some more a wish list, like biking across the country. We'd have to brush the dust off our bikes and make it cross-town a few times first.

It was scary and exhilarating to live so fiercely in the moment. The daily details of work and laundry and picking up cat food, brushed aside to focus on doing what we'd always longed to do.

As if the future could contain only the next few days and we didn't dare to look beyond that.

CHAPTER SEVENTEEN

On Saturday night we went out with Alex and Joanne. We talked about Cordelia's diagnosis. She reassured them—and me—that this was a cancer that could be cured, that she'd be okay. Alex said that she was going to see if she could change her schedule to four long days and then most weeks have three days off. But we didn't dwell on the hard topics; instead we enjoyed the cool, clear evening and the food, let the good parts of life flow over us like a river that might never end.

Monday brought me back to work and my life.

Normal, Cordelia kept insisting. I would do my best to honor her wishes.

I needed to get back to my cases, to not leave them sitting on the shelf too long.

There were things I could do. If I could link The Cure to NBG, I could help extract Fletcher McConkle's aunt from the attentive grasp of Vincent. And perhaps find some justice for Reginald Banks, and someone who might be his uncle.

I quickly set up a fake e-mail for pink survey lady extraordinaire Deborah Perkins and e-mailed Vincent, asking for information about the meeting he had mentioned.

I also called up McConkle himself, although I actually talked to his wife. I said I wanted to give them an update on my progress on the case. Maybe they had some idea if his aunt had ever used The Cure and not just NBG. She seemed happy to hear from me, as if her being the one to sign on the dotted line made her responsible for my work. She asked if I could meet them at their workplace later in the day and I agreed.

Driving was distracting, and I was willing to do most anything not to stare at these walls. She gave me an address in the Gentilly area.

Then I packaged up everything the Grannies had found out about Prejean—well, the stuff that they could legally find out, I wasn't going to get them busted them for hacking—and e-mailed it off to Danny.

After that I completely dismantled and cleaned the coffeemaker. I wondered if it would taste as good without the sludge. A taste test was required, so I made a big pot. Caffeine can also be distracting. The caffeine was the motivator for me to file cases, catch up on billing, even to the woman whose dead husband was alive and newly married in Vegas—she might pay. The top of my desk slowly appeared.

Shortly after lunch, I got a reply from Vincent. Friendly, even a little sweet.

> *Dear Debbie,*
>
> *That's great! I'd love for you to learn more about NBG. We're having a prospective Naturalist meeting tomorrow night and I'm one of the people leading it. It would be great if you could come, although that might be a little soon. You've probably got a busy schedule. I think you'd be a great fit and NBG could be great for you.*
>
> *Looking forward to seeing you soon, Vincent.*

Would it be too much to say that Vinnie was not a great prose stylist? He gave me an address in Metairie, one of the suburbs of New Orleans. His e-mail had an automatic signature, giving contact info and repeating his name. Vincent Tranner. I had to leave to meet the McConkles, but once I was back, I could see what I could find out about Vinnie. I had not only his name, but his license plate number.

Getting to the address that Mrs. McConkle gave me was a straight shot up Elysian Fields, then squirreling around several turns into a residential area I'd never been in. Before Katrina this had been a tidy zone of G.I. Bill houses for the working class and lower middle class. It was slowly returning to a decent neighborhood, only a few houses empty and desolate as if no one had been there since August 29, 2005. Some of the houses were clearly repaired, newly painted, cars in the driveway. Others were on the way, a FEMA trailer parked out front, or the kinds of trucks that indicated carpenters and electricians.

The house I pulled in front of had a big blue pickup in the driveway, an indication that someone was actively working here.

The workers turned out to be the McConkles. He was a carpenter, she was an electrician. I found them inside the gutted house. He was framing walls and she was running conduit.

"Break time," she called when she saw me.

I suddenly liked them both a whole lot better. Fletcher had the sense to hook up with a woman who was both good with money and good with her hands. They seemed to be working together as a team. He was pulling his weight and had the sawdust in his hair to prove it.

"This your house?" I asked.

"Naw," he answered. "Donna's second cousin on her mother's side. Just close enough to get the family rate." He smiled a friendly tease at her.

"You offered," she rejoined. "They would have paid going rate to get it done right."

"They'd already been ripped off once. Thought they needed a break."

"Any chance their rip-off artist was named Prejean? Or Pearlman?

He looked at her and she shrugged her shoulders. "No, don't know the name," he made explicit. "Why?"

"Another case I'm working on. Bunch of folks ripped off by this lowlife," I explained.

"I can call Dad and get the info," she said.

"How are you doing about my aunt?" Fletcher asked.

Almost as an offering, I handed them the printout of what I'd found on NBG. Fletcher took it, then handed it to his wife. She paged through it.

He looked dubiously at the stack of papers. I gathered that reading wasn't his favorite activity. I did a verbal rundown of what I'd discovered, finishing with, "I think Vincent succeeds by giving your aunt attention. He's a true believer, not just in the pills but in living well, and is trying to get her to improve her eating habits and make other healthy lifestyle changes. Maybe you should visit her more often."

They gave each other a doubtful look.

Fletcher finally said, "The problem is that my aunt thinks us visiting means we're trying to get in her good graces and get her money. So she spends the entire time haranguing us about being greedy relatives."

His wife shot him a look and then said, "She's got her reasons. After the storm we were struggling, our house destroyed, not enough insurance. We knew we'd be working nonstop and would eventually make good."

He took over the narrative. "So we asked her for a loan. A loan. I made it clear this was a loan. She acted like we were walking on her grave and out to steal her blind. Instead we had to struggle for the last two years, six months bunking in a friend's living room, then a FEMA trailer, paying jobs during the day and working on our home whenever we could find time. After almost a year of not speaking she calls me up out of the blue and asks me to come clean her gutters. I know her well enough to know she'll never apologize, not outright, but maybe this is her way of healing the breach. Instead of working on our house or making money working on someone else's I take a morning to go clean her gutters. After I'm done, I wash up in her kitchen and she shows me all her herbal stuff and how great they make her feel even if they're costing her a pretty penny. A year of what she was paying was all the loan we were asking for. Then she thanks me and tells me her favorite program is coming on and she hates to be disturbed and shows me the door. Making it clear that the gutters were a favor from her nephew." He shook his head in disgust.

"We're all right," his wife said. "We've been working nonstop since the storm and making decent money. We've picked up some well-to-do clients. We finished our house about six months ago. But it would have made a big difference if…" She looked down at her hands, the calluses on them.

"So, it's hard to hear her perfectly willing to drop tons of money on dried plants, expect me to help when she needs it, and then get turned down flat when we ask for something. The last thing she yelled at us is that we'd get it when she's dead. I don't want that slimy bastard to take it all before then," he said.

"I don't know your aunt very well," I said carefully, "but she seems to have been alone for a long time, and like many lonely people, she's lost the habit of paying attention to other people."

"That's putting it mildly," he burst out. "If she didn't need me to do something around the house for her, I doubt she'd be aware of my existence."

"I can keep digging if you want, but I might not find much that can help you. From what you've said, you're doing well now and the struggle is behind you. Your aunt could have helped you when it would have meant a lot, but she didn't. It's a tough choice, but maybe you should let it go."

"What do you mean?" Fletcher asked.

"You're angry at her—justifiably so. She wouldn't help family after the disaster of the century, but spends freely on unproven herbs. Not fair. Your aunt is a capricious old woman who wants her control. If you let go of ever wanting something from her, she loses her control over you."

"It's not fair," he said. But he ignored the rest. "She said we'd get it when she's dead. I'd like her to keep her word at least once."

His wife gave me a look as if to say *I understand, but she's hurt him too often for him to let it go.*

I didn't push. Instead I asked, "Have you ever seen you aunt use something with a label that says 'The Cure' on it?"

Both of them shook their heads. Fletcher added he'd been there just that one time and only seen what his aunt had shown him.

"I'll keep digging," I said. "I can't promise I'll find anything."

"That's okay," his wife said. "Just do your best."

I turned to go, but Fletcher called after me, "Hey, I saw you on TV. That guy is a real asshole."

I spun back. "That guy? Dudley? How do you know him?"

"I don't," he made clear. "We're working on a fancy place out in Old Metairie, right across the street from where his parents live. Can't miss him when he roars up in the big, ugly truck of his, way over the speed limit, then screeching to a stop. He wants everyone to notice him. I'm pretty sure he's the asshole who broke our taillight, but I can't prove it."

"He'll be going to jail for a long time after this adventure," I assured them. "Your taillights will be safe from now on."

"Good thing," he agreed. "That fellow is doing major work, new pool, adding a home theater, billiards room and sauna and major upgrade on the kitchen. We'll be there for a while."

It was time for them to get back to work.

And for me to find some new way to make the time pass and keep my brain occupied.

I glanced at my watch. Only midafternoon, not nearly time to go home. If I knew Cordelia—and I did—she'd stay at work as if she had something to prove, that being a patient didn't mean she couldn't be a doctor.

I remembered that I needed to do a search on affable Vincent. If I was going to meet him tomorrow night as perky Debbie, the more info I had, the better armed I'd be.

So, back to the office and my friend, the Internet.

Vincent *was* a true believer, certainly enough of a one to use all the capitalist tools at his disposal to get the message out. He had an elaborate website, with his face front and center—his smile and puppy-dog eyes alone probably accounted for half of his sales. He was good at pitching himself. He had a grandfather who was shrimper and had lost everything in Hurricane Camille, but the family had struggled back after that. Camille had struck in 1969, so given Vincent's age, the struggle was well before he was born. His family was "hardworking, striving for the American dream"—a quick Internet search found an insurance agency with his last name that was founded around his father's time. *Insurance agent* just wasn't as romantic as shrimper on the high seas of the Gulf. He briefly mentioned studies, but listed no degree, so I guessed that hitting the books wasn't one of his favorite pastimes. He did prominently list various certificates testifying to him being a NBG "naturalist" of the first degree—whatever that signified, being a physical trainer, having gone through a "healthy living" seminar, a long list of the kind of things that might take a day, at most a week of training. He filled the space with a lot of pictures—an old one of a shrimp boat, putatively sailed by the paternal line. He had a number of himself—at the gym in a tight T-shirt that showed his muscles. And a big one that did ample justice to his puppy-dog eyes and big smile.

In big, bold print was a link to his selling page, with glowing descriptions of all the products offered by NBG. Vinnie listed all the ways you could get the products from him—in person (extra charge), pickup hours, delivery (and delivery charges), carrier pigeon, space wormhole. Okay, not quite, but he covered all the selling bases.

At the bottom was a links page. You had to click on that, and at the bottom of that page was a link at the actual official NBG site.

But the point of the website wasn't to impress people like me— skeptical and college educated. It was to impress his clients that Vincent was a healthy lifestyle expert and would only recommend products that could help them. Nothing as crass as making money here.

He pushed a long line of NBG products, but there was no mention of The Cure. He also sold himself as a lifestyle coach.

But this was the stuff he wanted people to know. It was time to search for the information he didn't want people to know. I did a quick and dirty search, using the databases available if you're willing to pay for them—tax deduction for me, so I was.

It seemed Vincent had led a wild youth. He'd racked up some DUIs, including one for possession of pot, but nothing in the last year or so. He'd moved to a number of different addresses, including back in twice with what I was guessing was his parents. He now lived in one of those young, single type apartment complexes out in Metairie. If I'd been straight and considered a dalliance with Vinnie, that would have nixed it in the bud—suburbs and pre-fab apartments with paper-thin walls were a major turn-off for Bachelorette Number One.

Ah, interesting. He liked to park his truck in the French Quarter on weekends, but he didn't like to pay to park and he hadn't wised up on how to avoid tickets, as he had a pack of them. He also had a bunch of unpaid ones from Houston, like that was far enough away he could blow the tickets off.

He had stopped breaking the laws with the worse consequences— drinking and driving—but there was still a little rebellious boy in there who was a scofflaw on traffic tickets.

His truck was new, only a year old. His apartment wasn't cheap; he had a two-bedroom and, as far as I could tell, no roommate. He had a membership in an expensive gym, and the money he was saving on parking (and paying later in tickets) was probably spent in the bars and eateries of the French Quarter. Assuming that he didn't get a ticket every time he was there, that still made him a regular party boy, and partying isn't cheap.

Aunt Marion and Nature's Beautiful Gift were very, very good to Vincent.

It was hard to see how working for himself as an herbal Avon lady could ring up the coins to keep Vinnie flush. It was possible that he had others working for him; they were the grunts and he raked in the bucks. It was possible that insurance Daddy didn't want his baby boy living in what insurance agents from Chalmette referred to as "not nice" neighborhoods, so he bankrolled junior. It was possible the Insurance Daddy had a bad heart and Vincent had inherited a bundle. Or that he was still dealing, just being smarter this time around.

Or one of the old ladies wanted more than pills in a bottle and he was a gigolo.

I turned off my computer.

Maybe I'm just cynical, always digging into what people want to keep hidden, seeing the sordid side of life. NBG could be only one of several jobs—although nothing else had surfaced. Two hours of Internet searching isn't going to reveal a complete person.

Nothing I'd found much changed my opinion of Vincent. He seemed to have been a lost little boy, searching for something besides a life selling insurance in Chalmette. Nature's Beautiful Gift gave him a cause—a profitable one, from the looks of it. He could truly believe that he was helping his community while making enough money to party hearty in the French Quarter.

Then the phone rang. It was one of the heirs from the property records case—one of the found people had been impolite enough to pass away (she was ninety-two) and now her heirs had to be tracked down. I was pulled away from true believers into musty records and their labyrinthine trail to ownership. NBG went to the back shelf for the next few days.

CHAPTER EIGHTEEN

Another morning, another day. Cordelia still insisted on working, but she was taking a break in the day to see a lawyer. She wanted to update her will, power of attorney and medical power of attorney.

Yes, it's necessary, but I hate this kind of paperwork drill, so she waved away my offer to accompany her.

When I got to my office there was a message from the police officer who'd let me into Reginald Banks's house. The tox screens had come back and they wanted to look at the stuff I had taken. She left a number to call her back.

Vincent had e-mailed me—well, pink Debbie, to say that he'd missed me at the meeting but there was so much interest that they had scheduled another one for this afternoon. This very afternoon—how could I resist? He hoped I could make it. I'd blown off the last meeting because it just seemed a whole lot more important to go out to dinner with my girlfriend.

I called Officer Ferguson. It was a brief conversation. She asked if I still had the stuff, and when I said I did, asked if I could meet her at the house, show where I'd taken it. I started to ask a question, but she cut me off, making it clear that she was at the station and couldn't—or wouldn't—talk.

After locating the bags, I headed back to my car. Not how I'd planned to spend my morning, but I was relieved to be rid of what I'd taken from Reginald Banks's house. It wasn't mine to worry about, and now these talismans would be taken from me.

The day was overcast, with an occasional spit of rain, a gloomy start to the week. The gray day wasn't kind to the neighborhood, leeching out the color of the faded coats of paint.

Officer Ferguson wasn't there when I arrived. I stayed in my car and waited. There was nothing I wanted to see here.

She arrived after about ten minutes. She seemed no more happy to be here than I was.

"So what's the deal?" I asked as I joined her on the porch. "Why the interest in his herbal junk?"

She handed me the key, indicating that I was the lucky one who got to lead.

"You didn't hear them from me, got it?"

I put the key in the lock. "Heard what from you?"

She waited until I had opened the door and we were in the living room. "They found ma huang—you know what that is?"

"Ephedra. It's a banned herbal stimulant."

"You should be on *Jeopardy*. That plus traces of amphetamine."

"Meth?"

"No, the old stuff, prescription kind. So the narco squad has some interest. They're wondering if maybe he was a drug dealer."

"More likely he was dealt drugs."

She gave me a look. I put the bags on his coffee table and pulled out one of the bottles labeled The Cure. The police had resources I didn't have. I would play straight with her.

"He had sickle cell anemia. It's lifelong, chronic, and can be pretty miserable, painful, and causes infections. My guess is that he fell out of treatment, thought he'd be okay in a day or two, but got worse instead. He may have thought he'd be okay because he was taking this shit." I tossed the pill bottle at her.

She easily caught it. Softball dyke, I guessed.

I continued, "Want to make people feel better? Like they're cured? Crank them up. Want to lay odds on whether those things contain some ma huang and speed from below the border?"

"Could be." She examined the bottle. "It's not going to make the narco boys happy."

"Why? Instead of one minor dealer, they have a major illegal drug running operation."

"Yeah, this stuff is illegal." She tossed the bottle in the air. "But it's a slap on the wrist. The company claims that they had no idea how this awful stuff ended up in their perfectly legal supplement. They might pay a fine. End of case."

"Even if someone died?"

"He took them voluntarily. Maybe if a relative has standing, he can sue the company. Still, it's all civil, not criminal." She shrugged. "You can report it to the FDA. They might do something."

I started to argue, but Officer Ferguson wasn't responsible. There was no point.

I sighed. "Let me show you where I found these."

Covering my nose, I hurriedly took her through the house, pointing out where I'd taken everything. As best I could, I tried to remember where each bottle was placed. She noted it down, but seemed to have lost interest. No drug deal, no black-and-white criminal case, just a messy gray area. She poked around in the kitchen and bathroom as if looking for a meth lab, even though she said they hadn't found meth.

She had no curiosity about the insurance paperwork, but took the pills. After debating for a moment, I left the documents in his office. If they were out of my hands, they were no longer my worry.

Then we were back on the doorstep on this gloomy day. She told me she'd let me know if she needed anything more from me. She kept the bottles and the key.

I slowly walked back to my car, watching her drive away. It shouldn't be like this. Maybe Reginald Banks had made the wrong choices and those choices had led to his death. But someone had influenced those choices, someone had promised him The Cure. All they gave him was some illegal speed.

A postman was making his way down the block. I watched him as he stopped at Reginald's place and put some mail in the box.

I started to call out, to tell him that no one was home. But it's not my tragedy. In a few days he would notice the piled-up mail. Or a relative—maybe an uncle—would come by and claim the letters.

I got back in my car. Then got out again. *Let it go*, I told myself, but after making sure the postman was around the corner, I headed back across the street to the mailbox. *It's probably junk, it never stops*, I told myself as I raised the lid. Three pieces of junk mail.

And something from his insurance company.

It is a federal crime to tamper with mail. Only if they catch you.

I carefully edged open the flap of the envelope, hoping that it would emerge in decent enough condition so it didn't clearly signal that someone had unfastened it. It was a standard form saying that an office visit had been paid for.

Two days before I'd found him on the verge of death.

I stared at the piece of paper. Another error? There was no way Reginald Banks had been well enough to go or do anything two days before I'd seen him. I carefully refolded the insurance form and placed it back in the envelope, smoothing over the flap, and put it back in the mailbox.

I slowly walked back to my car. This didn't add up.

Except it did, and not in a way I liked. Eugenia, the other patient, claimed she hadn't been to clinic visits as often as they'd listed in her charts. Now Reginald Banks's insurance had paid for a visit he hadn't made. Mistakes happen all the time. But when the mistakes benefit only one side and not the other, they get suspicious.

It brought up the very disturbing possibility that someone in Cordelia's current workplace was committing insurance fraud. She wasn't—couldn't be—involved. While she *might* do something like let the unlucky fisherman slide by on his brother's insurance—and she clearly hadn't done that—claiming patients had received care when they hadn't would be beyond wrong in her view.

My concern was she could be caught up in ugly ways. She had been placed there by an agency, so didn't technically work for the group, but I knew at some point there had been talk about her joining them, at least part-time. I have to confess I've perfected the art of looking interested while she talked about office politics when my brain was actually elsewhere. Even if she hadn't joined the practice formally, it might be tempting to forge the signature of the new and possibly temporary doctor on false claims.

The rain had changed from spitting to coming down with all the signs of an imminent downpour. If I drove in typical New Orleans fashion, I might make it back to my office before it was so heavy I'd be drenched going from my car to the door.

Why did I have to open his mail, I castigated myself as I turned onto Esplanade. *Curiosity has messed up better cats than you.*

As I got to the light at Claiborne, my brain veered back to it maybe being a mistake. I had one drag queen claiming she'd not been to appointments, maybe as a justification for her not following an unpleasant treatment. And an insurance form claiming Reginald Banks had been seen when he clearly could not have been.

Didn't Lydia mention they had recently fired an administrative worker for dipping into the prescriptions? Maybe she—or he, don't be sexist—had cooked the books to pay for a habit. But that person had been let go before I searched for Reginald. Maybe she/he was lazy, too and had set up some automatic payment system for patients, one she thought she could get away with. The new people hadn't caught it yet.

By the time I got to my office, I'd decided that it was probably either an honest mistake or one bad apple who'd already been pruned from the tree. At least I'd pretty much decided that. I just had to quiet the nagging voice in my head. I've done some fraud cases, but staring at piles of paper with numbers is my idea of one of the lesser circles of hell, so it wasn't something I did on anything like a regular basis.

Any decent accounting system should have layers of protection. The person who writes the checks, for example, shouldn't be the one who signs them. Many places require two signatures, which means at least three people have to be involved in and aware of money being spent.

I rushed through the rain to the door, my key hanging up just long enough to make sure I had a wet spot most places where water could reach. As I climbed the steps, the nagging voice got louder. Unless the accounting system is inexcusably sloppy, it's hard for fraud to be committed by just one person. How could one low-level receptionist commit insurance fraud and not be caught at it?

Except she had been fired, according to Lydia. Not for a money mess, but drugs. Maybe they didn't want to admit to the fraud and so just used drugs as an excuse.

But if they knew about the fraud, they'd have to assume that I might find out about it as I stumbled around looking for their patients, especially as the two I searched out had false bills sent in. It would be far better for them to clue me in than have me find out about it like I just had.

Which brought me back to them not being aware of it.

And that brought me back to it could still be going on.

Which led me to Cordelia being somehow caught in the middle of it.

Which all gave me a headache by the time I reached my office door.

This is not your case, I told myself as I put my key in the lock.

Except my girlfriend might be snared in it. I relocked the door, then flopped in the chair behind my desk.

The girlfriend, partner, lover, who was scheduled to start chemotherapy tomorrow.

Who had cancer that might kill her.

I felt like life had just taken a shotgun and blasted me with it.

No, she said it would be okay. Not easy, not kind. But if they poisoned her enough and irradiated her enough and if she lost enough hair and threw up over and over again, someday it would be over and she would be okay.

If I wanted to stay sane, I had to believe that.

And I also had to only look at the next few steps, the doable, the possible, the daily and mundane. That would get me through day after day until we reached okay.

So I forced myself to do the tedious stuff, returning phone calls that resulted in leaving another message, filing old cases, filling out reports for other things I was working on, sending them out. All the exigencies that pulled me through the day.

Lunch was a quick sandwich I ate because my stomach growled. I called Cordelia, but could only leave a message. She was either at the lawyer's or with a patient. I wondered how she did it—how she could be one of the sick yet have to put that all aside to take care of the sick?

I remembered Vincent's e-mail. The meeting was at two p.m.

That should prove distracting. However, I didn't have a vast wardrobe of pink. I had to settle for a somewhat tight pair of jeans with some rhinestones and a pink breast cancer T-shirt. That was as pink as I could get Debbie without wearing the same dress.

I printed out a copy of his e-mail. The address was out in Metairie. Of course so I had to map my way there. New Orleans proper I pretty much know, but the suburbs just didn't stick in my brain.

The drive out there wasn't helped by the now-pouring rain. I was tempted to turn back. It was miserable weather. But also because it was likely that few people would show up, and I didn't want to risk a tête-à-tête with Vincent.

When I finally found the location, it was in one of those

nondescript, sort of modern but made to look old without enough money to really look old buildings. There were a couple of barely-making-it storefronts anchored by a pizza place at one end and a beauty salon at the other. Sandwiched between were a title company, a payday loan place, a convenience store that seemed to do only lottery business, as everything else in the window appeared dusty, and an empty space where there once was a clothing store, as its faded sign proclaimed. Between the empty store and the pizza joint was a staircase. Vincent's e-mail indicated that the meeting was on the second floor.

I glanced around the parking lot before ascending the stairs. There seemed to be a decent enough allotment of other cars, far more than were in the pizza place. It was possible there would be a larger number of people than just I and Vinnie alone on the second floor. I did bring the big purse, stuffing my gun in the inside pocket. I also put my cell phone in my front jeans pocket. Nine-one-one might be more useful than a bullet.

But my fears were unfounded. Neither bullets nor bracelets would be needed. The room wasn't packed, but there were about a dozen people there.

I had deliberately—aided by the rain—timed my arrival to get here just as the meeting was supposed to start. Less time for Vincent to flirt. As I had hoped, he was already at the front of the room, adjusting a projector. He did see me and smiled a friendly smile, but was too far across the room to greet me.

I signed in using my fake name and found a seat near the back. I as Deborah would be interested, but a little skeptical, needing to be convinced. I as me wouldn't be here. And, I decided, she'd really be here for a relative who was ill, hoping for something—like The Cure—that could help.

As I worked through my fake story, I swallowed, then choked on something that went down wrong. The closer they are to the truth, the better lies work. But the truth—I did have a relative who had cancer—felt too intimate and painful to cheapen in a ruse. If I didn't use Cordelia and her cancer, I'd have to come up with another disease, another story, and one that I knew enough about to make it seem real. I made no decision, just veered between the two choices.

"Hi, everybody. Welcome. We're glad you could make it through the rain." The program—sales pitch—had started. I mentally tabled my illness search to pay attention to the show. Three men were at the front of the room, Vincent and two older men. They were all white and it was one of the older men who was speaking. As befitted selling a health product, all three of them were trim and handsome for their age, tanned, and obviously spent time doing physical exercise. The tans suggested golf for the older men.

The speaker explained what Nature's Beautiful Gift was, pretty much a repeat of what was on the web page. The slides kept him on track. He mostly parroted what was on them, rarely adding anything. He wasn't a great speaker, and after I'd already read what was on the screen it was hard to listen to him read it slowly.

I glanced around at the audience. It seemed more comprised of people who needed a job than true believers. About three-fourths of the people here were women, either middle-aged or young—newly divorced or just starting out. Two of the younger women seemed to be paying more attention to Vincent than to the speaker, so I gathered he was generous with his flirtations. I considered whether Deborah would be upset or relieved and finally went with my instincts that she was old enough to be mostly relieved. That also took into account my acting skills—I doubted I could be convincing at being jealous of young women who teased their hair. The few men—I counted four—were harder to peg. Needing a second job? Here with their wives/girlfriends? One was old enough that he probably needed to supplement his Social Security. Two were sitting next to women, so could be with them.

And one read as cop/private dick. He was sitting slumped on the far end of the row, in need of a shave, but not so scraggy as to say truly down on his luck. He had on a soft, old leather jacket that was an odd tan color. It was his eyes that gave him away. He was watching far too carefully, taking in not just the men at the front of the room, but also everyone in it—including me. I wondered if I could be as easily spotted.

I dropped my purse on the floor, catching it so the gun didn't clunk, then grabbed my cell phone out of my pocket like it was about to ring and I'd forgotten to turn it off. One advantage to being a female private eye is that we can play the bimbo, something the boys can't do. When I looked up again, he was looking elsewhere. Maybe I'd fooled him. Or maybe he was a caffeine junkie and his watchfulness was a result of the jitters.

The speakers switched roles, with Vincent now following the slides to discuss the products that NBG sold. He was a slightly better speaker than the first man, aided by his smile and his big, brown eyes. I tried to pay attention—well, look like I was paying attention. Between the web page and our meeting at Aunt Marion's, I was familiar with most of what Vincent was covering. I really did not need to think about colon health.

The first speaker, once finished, sat down in the front row. The other older man was scowling at him, as if anyone benefiting from NBG—as they presumably were—should be able to stand for the entire time. I guessed he was the alpha dog. He certainly didn't have puppy-dog eyes—cold steel gray from this distance.

Once Vincent had finished—he wisely chose to stand at the side of the room—the final man took over. This was the sell. He extolled how much benefit we could bring to our friends, family and neighbors if we introduced them to Nature's Beautiful Gift. He explained about sample packs, at a moderate but unspecified price. We could add to our arsenal, giving them out to convince those who weren't willing to purchase a full bottle until they'd tried them. He was the best salesman, rarely referring to the projected images, moving around, modulating his voice. He explained in a tone that contained almost real regret it was possible not all of us would make it as naturalists—it took drive and determination, of course, but also we had to want to bring this special gift—yes, those were his exact words—to the world. And to do that we had to be special.

He walked down the aisle as he said this, making eye contact with each of us. I put on my most "yes, I want to be special" expression—without going over the top. He gave me the barest smile and nod. I would have felt special if I hadn't noticed him doing the same thing with most of the other people in the room. He didn't look at the man I'd spotted as a pro—as if he knew that was someone who had no real interest in his spiel.

He walked back the aisle to stand in the brightest spot. On his way he briefly stopped in front of his sitting comrade. It was a just a step, then a quick one away, but the intention was clear; he was a little too close, his crotch bare inches from the other man's face. Oh, yes, he was the alpha dog and he was proving it.

The other pro noticed it, too. He was closely watching the speaker now. But the front man was now smiling, had moved away from the sitting man, continuing his speech in his warm, inviting voice.

Most people wouldn't have noticed. I told myself that he might be a good person. But clearly there had been a battle between him and the man in the front row. He had won and now was making his victory clear. It didn't make me like either of them, but I didn't want to rush to judgment. Maybe the sitter had gotten drunk at a company party and pawed his fourteen-year-old daughter. I didn't know. All I did know was this was not a happy family and Vincent had clearly chosen to side with the speaker.

He finished with a request that we all come forward and speak to him and the other naturalists—Vincent and the other man—to see if we were special enough to be let into the NBG family. There were three small tables at the side of the room. Vincent and the sitting man positioned themselves behind two of them—the sitter pulling up a chair. Vincent chose to remain standing until the end.

The two young women were immediately at Vincent's table. The speaker ushered Social Security Man and the heavier of the two older women to the sitter's table. He took the more attractive older woman for himself.

I was slow to get up, fumbling with my purse and cell phone. I didn't want to sign up to be a Nature's Beautiful Gift salesperson, but that might be the only way to get the keys to the kingdom.

The other pro—I wasn't sure if he was private, like me, or public, like an actual cop—stood, openly surveying the scene, but made no move to head to a table.

Shit or get off the pot. I chose shit and made my way to Vincent's table. The two young women were chatting up a storm. They weren't together, but neither was willing to be second in line—and possibly in Vincent's affection, so they were both standing at the table, each trying to crowd the other out. Alas for all of us, they were also young enough to think that parroting back in adoring tones the same stuff we'd just sat through was the key to Vincent's heart. I'd heard it just once and I was bored. Presumably Vincent did this once or twice a month. Even his puppy-dog eyes were struggling to feign interest. They insisted on laboring over each line on the order form, vying to out-order each other yet somehow not break their piggy banks.

For a brief moment when their heads were down, Vincent stole a look at me, gave a shrug and a brief smile as if imploring me to wait.

Good luck, Vincent, I said to myself. *These are the kinds of girls you'll have to explain where their clitoris is. And what it's for.*

I felt a hand on my shoulder.

"No one's in my line." The alpha dog. He gave me his warmest smile as if to promise he knew I'd be special. Too special to wait for his underling, Vincent.

It was an offer I couldn't refuse. I followed him to his table. It was set up a little apart from the others and was a little bigger. Perhaps alpha wolf would be a better descriptor.

"You are?" he asked.

Oh, hell, what was my name supposed to be? "Deborah…Perkins." Perkins was the surname for perky pink characters. "And I'm sorry, I know you introduced yourself in the beginning, but I've forgotten."

"Grant Walters. Pleased to meet you, Deborah. Or is it Debbie?" He again smiled.

"It can be either, Mr. Walters. My mother insists on Deborah. My friends call me Debbie."

"Please, Grant. And I hope we'll be friends, Debbie."

"I have to be honest, sir, I mean, Grant, I'm interested, but I'm on a tight budget at the moment, so I can't manage more than a small order right now."

"Small is okay. I started small." His face indicated he was pleased as punch to be spending his time taking a tiny order. Only the briefest sliding of his eyes to see who else was in the room betrayed him.

"Did you? That's encouraging. I wouldn't mind being where you are someday." It was time to throw a little ambition in with the pink. Grant wanted a woman who could make him money—there was no flirting here. He was trying to seduce me, of course, but with no sex involved. His seduction was about power. He had staked me as the most promising prospect in the room and gone after me.

"So, tell me about yourself. Why do you want to be where I am now?"

I spun Debbie's story. Recently divorced. Ex-husband was a lawyer, so she got just about nothing. Put him through law school, had planned to go herself, but they couldn't afford two tuitions, so as any woman who favored pink would, she let him go first and did administrative work, had worked her way up to assisting one of the top executives in the export firm, but it had been badly damaged by Katrina, the boss took the insurance money and decided not to rebuild. I (as Debbie) stayed in the area because my husband still had his job, only to find out a year ago that he was sleeping with his secretary and wanted a divorce. It was hard to find work after the storm, so I was struggling, yadda, yadda.

"Why this product?" he asked.

"I don't want to just make money. I'm getting old enough to worry about my health, my family's health. It would be nice to combine doing okay and making a difference. Vincent intrigued me—about Nature's Beautiful Gift," I made clear. "I still had my questions, but thought I should check it out. You don't strike me as the kind of man who would be part of a losing operation." Two could play the seduction game. "And it was your talk that made me decide maybe I could do this. I'd like to go back to college, so the flexible hours appeal to me. Plus I like that I get to decide how much I work. I can really push if I want and do well."

He nodded and grinned at me, friendly and conquering. My deception was to be the kind of acolyte he wanted. His smile told me I had succeeded.

"I think we can work something out," he said. "If you work hard you won't be small for long."

He was the boss. He let me start with half of what the usual minimum order would be.

"You'll be back soon, won't you?" he said as I counted out the money.

Luckily I had enough cash. I didn't have a credit card with Deborah Perkins name on it. "I have every intention of doing the best I can," I said. My best wouldn't have anything to do with selling Nature's Beautiful Gift, however. As I was signing the paperwork in Deborah Perkins's loopy handwriting, I asked softly, "What do you think might be best for someone who's really ill? Is there anything that might help?"

"Why do you ask?"

"I have a…relative, someone close to me…who has cancer. It's… not looking good." My words were slow because I still was ambivalent about using cancer, and therefore Cordelia, for something like this. But he took my hesitation for sorrow, not ambivalence.

"That's hard to say. There are some things that might help. Immune booster is always good. It also depends on where and how bad."

"Lymphoma," I said. "Stage three." That was it, my deal with the devil. But I couldn't come up with a good lie and the truth all too conveniently served my purpose.

"I'm sorry to hear that," he said. He really did look sorry. Then added quietly, "There might be something else. Something I've heard about. I'll have to check on it. Call me in a few days." He gave me his business card.

He was too important to call me; I had to call him. That worked for me. I could get a cheap cell phone with a number that had nothing to do with Micky Knight, private investigator.

I thanked him, we shook hands, and I walked away. I understood our interaction was over, that he had to move on to the next conquest, even if it was checking Vincent and the other man's paperwork.

Vincent had his two young girls following him around, so we all trooped down to the parking lot. There was still a damp drizzle, but at least the rain had slowed. Vincent, being the youngest and probably most eager disciple, was tasked with unloading the NBG truck and doling out to us the product we now had to sell. The two girls were vying to be the last one and therefore alone with Vincent. I was more than happy to assist by hurriedly backing my car up to the truck, popping the trunk and quickly hefting the boxes I had bought—ten bottles of eight of the most popular items, plus ten sample packs, which were priced at two dollars and fifty cents apiece. I'd purchased the bottles for ten dollars apiece and was supposed to sell them for nineteen-ninety-five each. Close to 100 percent mark-up.

I'd lost track of the private cop after getting in line and thought maybe I had been wrong about him. But then I spotted him in a nondescript car at the end of the parking lot watching us.

I managed to close my trunk and pull out just as the sky opened up again. Those poor girls. The rain was going to cause their makeup to run.

CHAPTER NINETEEN

I swung by my office long enough to change out of the pink shirt and the rhinestone jeans. So not my style. I wasn't sure what to do with the eighty pill bottles—plus ten sample packs—in my trunk, but carting them up three flights of stairs to my office didn't seem an appealing option.

I didn't even bother checking messages—they could hold until tomorrow. It would give me something to do while waiting for Cordelia.

She might be home by now, but I did a quick run by the grocery store. As quick as I could, given the distance. I planned to make a big pot of chicken soup tonight. I'd freeze some of it. That way she'd had something decent and quick to eat when she wasn't feeling well. Sports drinks—they're good if you're dehydrated. Plus a really good meal tonight, a decent bottle of red, filet mignon, some shrimp for an appetizer, spinach salad, and asparagus as the side. And some wickedly sinful ice cream for dessert.

She was indeed home. She even smiled as I unloaded the grocery bag.

"Thank you," she said as she put the ice cream away. "But you don't need to cook two big meals tonight. I can't eat after midnight and I doubt I'll want to eat much tomorrow. So the chicken soup can wait."

No it couldn't. Not for her, but for me. Cooking would keep me busy, keep me focusing on whether the chicken was tender or not and did it need more salt or more carrots? I dreaded tomorrow, didn't want it to come, and maybe if I kept myself distracted enough, it would get here without my agonizing over it. And once it was here, then I knew what I had to do. Go with her, stay with her, not let my worry become her burden.

I insisted she take it easy, sit and read. I poured the wine, gave her a glass while I chopped and diced for the soup. Once I had that on and simmering, I prepared our meal, grilling the shrimp, steak, and asparagus. It was a nice enough evening that we were able to eat outside. We didn't say much, held hands between cutting the steak, watched the last glimmer of the sun set. The days were getting longer, warmer.

Then we went back inside. She let me work as if knowing that I needed to—needed to do the little things like scrub out the shower because the big things were so out of my control.

I didn't sleep well and the morning came too early.

Cordelia usually does early mornings, or what I call early. It was odd to see her up but not dressed as she usually is, in something professional. Instead she was in baggy jeans and a T-shirt. She was the patient today.

She couldn't eat breakfast, I didn't want to.

We got in the car and drove to the doctor's office.

We were a little early; few other people were there.

"I put all my legal documents in the top drawer of my desk," she said. Today was the day to talk about the things we didn't want to talk about. "Updated will, medical and legal powers of attorney. The key to the safe deposit box is also there."

"Safe deposit box? What's in that?"

"Some jewelry from my grandmother and mother. Stuff I don't wear, but it has too much sentimental value to sell or give away. Copies of things like my birth certificate."

"You know this is like carrying an umbrella—it only rains when you don't have one," I said.

"That's my hope. It just makes sense to take care of everything anyway." In a change of subject, she said, "You don't need to come in with me if you don't want to. I'll just sit there and Jennifer will stick a needle in my arm."

"If you don't want me there, I'll stay here. Otherwise I'll go with you."

She nodded, seemingly relieved I'd chosen to stay with her. They called her name and we went down a long, pale blue hall to a small office. One chair like a dentist's was in the middle of the room. That was clearly the patient's seat. A wooden chair was crammed in the corner of the room. That would be mine.

The wait was short. First a nurse came in to check her vital signs. Then it was the nurse and the doctor, a woman who seemed too young to be doing this. Cordelia introduced me. They did what they needed to do, a needle in her arm, a fluid dripping into her veins.

It seemed small and anticlimactic, that her fate should be decided in a cramped office, outdated art on walls a beige color that would soon need to be repainted.

All I could do was sit and watch and keep out of the way.

After a while another doctor came in, another introduction. Cordelia was too young for this, so her friends were coming around. In a concession to space, I said I'd take a walk. One of the nurses pointed me to a little lounge just down the hallway. No one else was there.

I was there only a few minutes when Lydia came by. She didn't expect to see me and I didn't expect to see her. It was the same building where their office was, but a different floor.

"Hi," she said. "Is Cordelia here?"

"Yeah, down the hall. She's has a few visitors, so I vacated the space."

"Figures. I came by to see how she's doing. First time can be a bitch. I had thyroid cancer about ten years ago. Not a biggie. Small tumor, they cut it out. A little chemo and a thyroid pill every day for the rest of my life and I'm right as rain."

"Hard to be the patient when you're supposed to be the healer."

"That's the other bitch. Nothing like putting on those gowns to make you feel like a speck in the universe."

"You heard about Reginald, right?" I asked. The insurance mess was nagging at me. Maybe Lydia would be the best person to bring it up to. And I could only hope I wasn't so unlucky to choose the person responsible.

"Yeah, I did. I don't get it. Why didn't he come in for treatment?"

"Supposedly he did two days before he died."

"What?" She looked taken aback. "What are you talking about?"

She was either a top-notch actor—swindlers often are—or she truly had no idea what I was talking about. The money and training required to be a nurse practitioner would likely discourage a crook from picking this as a cover.

"Reginald had paperwork that indicated his insurance paid for a doctor's visit two days before he died."

"That can't be right. That's a bizarre mistake."

"When I searched his house I noticed a letter from his insurance company denying service because he was coming too often. They claimed there wasn't justification for his condition needing treatment that frequently."

"This is not making sense."

"When I spoke to Eugenia, the other patient, she also mentioned insurance claims for visits she said she never made. At first I blew it off."

"Wait," she cut in. "What are you getting at?"

"Went the same place you're going—has to be a mistake. But it's a huge stretch to think that I just happened to stumble over the only two patients with these kinds of mistakes. And a mistake that only goes one way."

"Where are you going with this?" Lydia still seemed puzzled. But she was a nurse, not a private detective.

"Anyone in your office doing really well? Claimed to have come into money recently?"

She stared at me. "Yes...but...no. It was an inheritance."

"A long illness or an uncle you'd never heard of before?"

No, she wasn't a good actress, because the look on her face gave me the answer she didn't want to offer me.

"No, nothing like that," she finally replied. "You're saying someone is deliberately submitting false insurance claims." Her tone was defiant, as if I couldn't possibly be really saying someone she knew was committing fraud.

"That is what I'm saying."

"Look, we just fired that receptionist," she said. "Maybe she did something stupid."

"You fired her for drugs, right?"

"Yes, but drug addicts will do anything."

"Did she work with your billing?"

Lydia was silent for a moment, before finally saying, "She wasn't supposed to, but she might have helped out on occasion."

"Enough to have learned your system well enough to have rigged it so she could steal money and no one would notice?"

She didn't answer. Instead she said, "This can't be right. Look, I'll figure it out in the next few days. Probably some computer error that's gotten lodged in the system. This can't be right," she repeated, shaking her head. "I need to get back. Let me just stick my head in and say hi to Cordelia." She started walking down the hall.

"Call me and let me know how wrong I am."

She turned back to look at me. "I will do that."

Then she disappeared through the door into Cordelia's room.

What she had told me without telling me was she was aware of someone having money that couldn't clearly be accounted for. They had a story, of course, one people would believe because they wanted to believe—we like to think we're smart and savvy and that we couldn't work day after day with a crook and not notice. But criminals are good at giving us the reality we want to believe in, especially the ones who stand beside you and steal when they think you're not watching.

Despite Lydia's claim that she needed to get back, it was a while before she came out. She passed me again with only a bare nod.

One of the other visitors had left at the same time, so I made my way back into the office, politely knocking at the door before I entered.

"Oh, it's you," Cordelia said as I came in. With, I was glad to note, relief in her voice. "They mean well, talking on the latest medical advances, letting me know I can get all the Oxycontin I might want," said with a wry grimace indicating that she really didn't want to think about major pain killers. "But...I'm not up for a social hour."

In the short time I'd been gone, she'd changed, looking tired now, bags under her eyes, the drip mostly empty, the poison in her. I pulled the wooden chair out of the corner, placing it close enough that I could hold her hand, the one without the needle in her arm. She closed her eyes and put her head back. But there was a downturn to her mouth and a tightness to her features that told me she was not resting.

She looked up at me, struggling for a smile as if to say, *See, this isn't so bad, I can do it.* But the smile faded and the tired look returned to her eyes.

I held her hand until they came back in and took the needle out.

Again, it was the profound and ordinary. The palpable change in our lives measured out with a bandage on her arm, some more paperwork, another appointment. And then we were back out in the parking lot and getting in the car.

Halfway home, she reached into her bag and took out a plastic sack, holding it as if she might need it. She swallowed hard and then again, resting her head against the window.

I sped up slightly, wanting to hurry home, but not make it a jarring ride. When I looked at her again, her eyes were closed, her jaw tight.

At home, I quickly parked and jumped out to open the front door, not wanting her to wait. But she moved slowly, as if any jostle would be uncomfortable.

I held the door open. She went straight to the bathroom.

I followed her there, asking from the doorway, "What can I do?"

She was sitting on the toilet, still fully clothed, resting her head between her knees.

"Make it go away," she murmured softly, as if not really speaking to me.

I stepped in, briefly touched her hand, then went back to the kitchen and found anti-nausea medication. Before I got back to the bathroom, I heard retching sounds.

Cordelia doesn't like an audience when she's sick. I've learned hovering behind her isn't helpful. I filled a plastic cup with water, wet a paper towel, and placed them next to her, and then withdrew to the kitchen.

I started to do the dishes, then decided I'd put away the ones in the dishwasher, then decided wiping the counters down was quieter so I could listen if she needed me. And finally gave up, leaning miserably against the counter, unable to do anything but listen to her throwing up.

She finally emerged, wiping her face with the paper towel. "I'm sorry, I messed up my clothes," she said, a euphemism meaning that her vomiting stomach had kicked her bladder into emptying. Two orifices and one toilet means something's going to get messy. She shook her head slowly as if ashamed.

"That's okay, we needed to do laundry anyway," I said. "Let's get you changed."

"I can do it in a little bit." But she moved slowly, as if empty of energy and afraid that any movement would start the nausea again. I helped her out of her clothes. Was about to wash her off when she took the wet rag out of my hand. "Let me do that," she said, hastily washing her face again, then between her legs down to her knees.

I took her soiled clothes directly out to the washing machine and returned to find her still standing naked in the kitchen.

"They say it gets better over time," she said and tried to smile, barely getting one edge of her lip to curl up. Then softly, talking to herself as much as to me, "This will pass. It'll get better."

"Yes, it will. Can you eat anything?" I asked.

She grimaced and shook her head. "Let me lie down for a while. I think just closing my eyes and resting will help." With that she went to the bedroom and got in bed, covering her eyes with her arms, taking shallow breaths as if to calm her stomach.

I refilled the glass of water and placed it and the anti-nausea meds beside her on the bedside table. She murmured a thanks, covered herself with the blanket as if she was cold. I left, leaving the door cracked open so I would hear her if she needed.

I busied myself with cleaning the bathroom, back to the kitchen, dishes washed, put away. All the little things that I could control.

Then I broke down crying, trying to do it softly so she wouldn't notice.

Chapter Twenty

She slept most of the afternoon, or at least rested. She did have another round of nausea in the midafternoon, but none after that and was even able to eat some of the chicken soup for supper. In the morning, she downed the anti-nausea stuff with coffee and some toast. Even with resting most of the day before and going to bed early last evening, she still looked tired and pale in the morning.

"Can't you take the day off?" I asked.

"I could, but..."

"But what? You have to prove you're tough?"

She sighed. "It's not tough, it's vulnerable. I'm working a temp position; if I can't work enough to make it worth their while, they can fire me. If I get fired, I lose my insurance. And right now..."

I finished for her, "You need your insurance."

"Yeah, so I have to push through as best I can. I never thought I'd have to worry about this."

"I could look into seeing if there is any way I can get you on mine," I offered. I had looked into it at one point, mostly out of curiosity. The answer was no. We had to be married and we couldn't be legally married in this state. It hadn't really mattered at the time; Cordelia had better insurance than I did. But that had been a while ago, and maybe things had changed.

"I think it'll be okay. Brandon and Lydia will advocate for me, I think, keeping me on after Tamara returns. There is enough work. But kindness can only go so far. If I can't work at all, I'm no use to them."

"So you're sicker than a dog and yet you have to drag your carcass in there to treat kids with runny noses."

"Adults with runny noses. I don't do pediatrics. Many people do this—get cancer treatment and keep on working. I'm just going to be another one of them."

"I can drive you to work if you want. And pick you up."

She put her hand against my cheek. "Thank you, but no. I have to find out what I can do, how much this is going to affect me. If I need you to drive, I'll let you know, okay? But right now I need to do this myself."

I nodded. It is hard to desperately want to help someone and know all you can do is stand aside. I leaned in and kissed her and then watched her walk out the door.

And all I could do was walk out the door myself and go on with my life as best I could.

Somehow I ended up in front of my office without really being aware of driving there—it was a good thing that I worked in a quiet, mostly residential neighborhood, with roadways more forgiving of inattentive drivers.

I trudged up the stairs, feeling helpless and impotent, a bystander in a great drama, one with an uncertain end. As I hid my crying from Cordelia, I suspected she hid her fears from me—this was her first mention of insurance and how tenuous it might be for her to keep it.

My answering machine was blinking like a strip club on Bourbon Street. I could remotely check it, but hadn't bothered to do that yesterday.

Danny had called to let me know that Dudley had finally woken up and immediately lawyered up. He was still in the hospital, from which he would be transported to the jail as soon as he was well enough.

Joanne called to tell me essentially the same thing with an added warning to be careful; while Dudley wouldn't be knocking on my door anytime soon, it was possible he might ask someone else to do it for him. He was stupid enough to think that killing me might make his legal troubles go away.

Mr. Charles Williams had also called—*why* was I not surprised—and wanted to know if there was any update on the case. Oh, and would I be willing to speak to his nephew? He couldn't pay me anything, but he made really good gumbo and he'd bring me a batch.

Alex had called, just to see how I was doing. I was heartened to hear from her. She left a Baton Rouge number to call back. If she was worried about how I was doing, maybe it meant she was doing better herself.

Lydia had called, no message except to call her. I didn't recognize the number as the office one, so I guessed it was her cell phone. I could only hope that it was to tell me how wrong I was and that everything was some stupid mistake, a computer error or something. Cordelia needing them to keep her on for insurance made that almost necessary.

Then a call from someone named Rafe—I think—he mumbled, no message, just a number to call back. Probably a wrong number.

Several hang-ups. Wrong numbers or people who didn't like leaving messages.

E-mail was also a pile. The problem with catching up on responding to people is that a large number of them feel the need to respond back again, so then you're no longer caught up.

Vincent had written Deborah, a chatty little piece about offering to help if she needed any advice or suggestions. Interestingly it wasn't from his NBG e-mail, but from another account. Guess he didn't want to be caught poaching in the alpha wolf's turf.

Mrs. Fletcher McConkle—Donna—had asked her father the name of the bad contractor. It wasn't one of the names Prejean had used. Maybe it was an additional alias. And maybe just another sloppy contractor. She also passed on that the man they were working for told her that Dudley was misguided and had gotten in with the wrong crowd. Right—that so didn't sound like my kind of neighborhood—anyone rich enough to live close to me can't be bad.

But I didn't call anyone back. It seemed too hard to pick up the phone and pretend that I cared about whatever it was they were worried about.

Alex. Call Alex. I finally dialed her number. But no good deed goes unpunished. My call went straight to voice mail. I started to hang up, but instead left a message that she could call me if she had the chance.

Then I booted up a computer game and played for the next hour.

I had just been killed and was trying to decide whether to go back and start again when my character was still alive or give up and spend the next half hour debating on what to get for lunch when the phone rang.

I might not have the energy to make a call, but I could at least not be so slothful as to not answer one. I picked up the receiver.

"Michele Knight?" my caller asked in a voice that was a rough whiskey growl. I didn't recognize it.

"This is the Michele Knight Detective Agency," I answered, using a slightly higher nasal tone, as if there was an actual secretary here.

"Need to talk to Knight. She in?"

"May I say who's calling?"

"Rafe Gautier."

"Just a moment, I'll see if she's available." I put the phone down, took a sip of water, and pitched my voice lower as I answered, "This is Michele Knight. What can I do for you?"

"Detective business not going well?"

"I beg your pardon?"

"Moonlighting selling herbal shit. Or are you on a case?"

"Who are you and what do you want?"

"You were pretty good, didn't card you till I ran your license."

The pro at the NBG meeting. I felt stupid for letting him get my license plate and tracing me. "What's your interest?"

"What are you up to? If you say extra money, I won't believe you."

"You're a voice on the other end of a phone. No reason in hell for me to do anything other than hang up."

"Would it surprise you if I told you that Grant Walters was indicted on fraud about ten years ago?"

"Nope, no surprise. But he wasn't convicted, as there was no record."

"Enough money, good lawyers, he got off. He pissed off a lot of people up in Dallas. Interested in teaming up? We seem to be working on something similar."

"Sorry, I'm all booked up this week and next."

He ignored that. "Let's set up a meeting. Tomorrow morning? I'll even come to your office."

"How about that coffee shop right near the corner of Royal and Conti?"

"Across the street from the cop shop? Don't trust me?"

"Any reason I should?" I said affably enough, considering the situation.

"Nope, not a one. Tomorrow at ten."

I started to protest—not that I had anything else scheduled, but I wasn't going to give in to his calling the shots, but the phone was already buzzing in my ear. He'd hung up.

Of course, nothing said I had to show up.

But his call reminded me that life doesn't stop. I needed to call back the people who had called me and write those who had e-mailed. Maybe their concerns were less important than mine—and maybe they weren't. I only knew pieces of their lives. Certainly in the past I'd stumbled over someone who was staring at loss and they returned my call, went on as if their heart wasn't breaking. It was now my turn.

Joanne and Danny were also messages on voice mail. I assured them both I would be careful.

Mr. Charles Williams could wait. Maybe I'd get great insight into the case over coffee with Rafe tomorrow. I desperately wanted to delay—until infinity—any discussion of talking to his nephew.

I dialed Lydia's cell phone number. She answered on the third ring.

"This is Micky Knight returning your call."

She didn't answer for a moment, as if trying to remember who I was and why she called me.

I added, "So are you going to tell me I was wrong about the problems with the billing?"

She said, "Can we meet? I can't talk now."

"Yeah. When and where?" I almost hoped she'd say ten a.m. tomorrow so I'd have an excuse to avoid Rafe. He sounded like the kind of man who smoked.

"Tomorrow evening? Maybe around seven?"

"I can do that. Where?"

"I'm not sure. I'll text you. Please don't mention this to Cordelia."

She didn't wait for a reply.

I stared at my phone for a moment, puzzled. I couldn't come up with a good reason for Lydia to want to see me. If I was wrong, then I was wrong and she just had to tell me that. If I was right, she should be calling the police—or their insurance investigator, not me. My best guess was she found something not quite a smoking gun, but worrisome enough to concern her. She didn't know enough about private eyes to know we specialized just like doctors and fraud wasn't my specialty.

Or maybe she thought I was interesting and wanted to get to know me just in case I was single in the near future. I quashed that thought.

My social calendar for tomorrow was getting full—that just left me with today to get through.

I, as Debbie, replied to Vincent's e-mail, nicely stringing him along—what was the one thing he wished he'd known when he started out and what did he think made him so successful, before asking the same question I'd asked his boss—if someone was sick, cancer, what would he recommend to help?

Then I tackled the weighty lunch issue. After perusing all the takeout and delivery menus in the office, I went with the cheese and crackers I kept here. With an apple for the fruit and veggie serving.

After lunch I roused myself. Rafe making my license plate convinced me that I did need a cheap cell phone for Debbie to use. It was too risky to attempt to get away with mine—or if I could find one, a pay phone. No one used pay phones these days. Debbie might be down on her luck, but she wasn't cell phone–less down on her luck.

I wasn't up for the Metairie 'burbs, so I headed east to Chalmette. It had been inundated during Katrina, a working-class town down the river from the devastated Lower Ninth Ward. I was guessing enough people had come back that there had to be a few cell phone stores. It was one of those places that you drive to and it's different every time—new stores, something rebuilt, something torn down.

I was right. There were still gaping holes, empty parking lots, but a surprising number of new stores and businesses had opened. Including the kind of cheap electronics places I was looking for.

In less than an hour I was heading back to my office, with a new prepaid cheap plastic cell phone. Hot pink case because that was the kind of girl Debbie was.

Once back in my office I debated calling Grant Walters, aka alpha wolf, but decided to hold off for another day. I didn't want him to think I was too eager. Or too desperate. I suspected he didn't like desperate. And if I was lucky I might be able to find out a few more things about him at my coffee klatch with Rafe tomorrow.

I spent the rest of the afternoon searching online for food ideas for people struggling with nausea. Cordelia could not live on chicken soup alone. After jotting down a few recipes, I didn't even pretend that I could work. Instead I made another run to the grocery store to stock up on thinks like rice, broth, oatmeal, and small containers so she could eat in little portions. Several times during the day I had wanted to call her, but she was right, she had to do it on her own. I had to trust that she would call me if she needed me.

CHAPTER TWENTY-ONE

I took it as a good sign that I got home first. That meant she was still at work, which meant she was okay working.

Or had gotten so sick they'd hospitalized her.

No, someone would have called me. Especially as I'd already talked to Lydia. It wasn't likely that she'd ask me not to mention our meeting to Cordelia, but forget to tell me that Cordelia had collapsed and was rushed to the emergency room.

I started two pots of rice, one plain, bland white rice, the other a brown rice with a nice mix of rosemary, garlic, and chicken.

I even fed the cats early. They started to eat, then heard her car pull up and decided to pull the "this food is from the morning and we're starving" routine and stuck up their noses. "Don't bother," I admonished them. "She'll believe me before she believes you. Speech, it's a human thing."

I stayed in the kitchen, resisting my instinct to meet her at the door. As much as I could, I was determined to keep to our usual routines.

"Hey, you're home early," she called from the other room.

"Slow day. I wanted to be here for you." I turned around to look as her as entered the kitchen. Tired, dark circles under her eyes. "How was your day?"

"I managed to keep lunch down for fifteen minutes. All three crackers and half a cup of soup." She put her arms around me, resting her head on my shoulders. "I did okay as long as I didn't eat. I think it was the smell of the fried chicken that did me in. I don't think I can ever do grease again. Plus everyone was way too nice. Maybe that was what made me barf—the skinny little receptionist offering to carry a stack of charts, Brandon offering to write me any prescription I needed, three people offering to bring me back lunch, two bottles of water in the bathroom while I was vomiting. I really wish they'd stop reminding me that I have cancer." Then she lifted her head and said, "But I'm okay, mostly. Alex called. It looks like she and Joanne are breaking up."

"What?" I said. "She called me, too, but we just traded messages. Joanne left a message, too, but it was business." I decided that there was enough going on without revealing that Dudley was awake.

"She's taking an apartment in Baton Rouge, says that she just can't do the commute every day anymore."

"Joanne can't be happy about that."

"Call her tomorrow—Alex, Joanne, too, if you want. Someone at her office has an open apartment over their garage and offered it to her. Three hours in her car every day was exhausting."

"Can they afford it? Two living places?"

"I'm guessing it'll be tight—but it's a small place and she's getting a good deal."

"They'll never see each other."

"It wasn't like they were spending much quality time together. Alex didn't tell me they were breaking up, just that she'd be spending the week in Baton Rouge and Joanne didn't much like it. But that kind of tension has to wear on a relationship."

"Are we doing the dyke soap opera so you can avoid talking about yourself?" I asked.

She gave me a look that said, *Yes, but how dare you call me on it?* "No, I talked to Alex just a while ago so it was on my mind." She crossed to the stove and glanced into the pots. "You know I'm not...I told you the gist of things." She paused. "Am I scared? Yes. But I was scared in Charity with the winds howling and the desperate days following. And I was scared afterward—that nothing would be the same. Yeah, I'm scared now." She ran her fingers under her eyes. "And I'm profoundly grateful to come home to someone who cooks two batches of rice on the chance that I can eat..." and she started crying.

I put my arms around her, her head again resting on my shoulder. I hadn't meant to make her cry, just keep her from too deeply burying her feelings as she tried to protect me. "I considered three batches, but thought that might be overkill, plus a lot of dishwashing."

She didn't say anything, just tightened her grasp, holding me fiercely for a moment. She pulled away and announced, "I need to wash my face," and headed to the bathroom. She added from down the hallway, "I think I might even be hungry."

When she came back, she tried a couple of bites of the bland rice, then a small serving of the actually edible version. We talked about what she might like to eat, agreed to do a grocery run together in the next few days. It was in the open now, how embarrassed she was for me to have to clean the bathroom after her—until I reminded her of my food poisoning and the cleaning chores she did. We'd both been doing online research, so we compared notes. I showed her the recipes I'd downloaded, she added some she'd found. It was hard to talk about; the only thing harder was the silence.

She ate slowly, as if wanting to make sure everything would stay down before adding anything more. She finally said, "What about you? What are you working on?"

I told her about my case (still leaving out that Dudley was awake) including 'fessing up to the boxes of NBG in my trunk.

"What are you going to do with it?" she asked.

"The one thing I'm not going to do with it is sell it. Maybe once it's over, just give them away to anyone who wants them."

"Good. Promise me that you'll tell them the things I told you— little is proven and/or regulated. It could be bat shit."

"I will give them a full and complete bat shit warning." I took a breath and told her about the irregularities I'd stumbled over on the billing. As requested, I left out meeting with Lydia tomorrow.

After I'd finished, she didn't reply for a moment. "That can't be right. It's not easy to fake records. I don't know these people over years, but I can't pick any who I'd consider likely to do this. Do you want me to—"

"No, don't get involved. Don't let on that I've told you about this. If it's a mistake, it'll be fixed. If it's not a mistake, then it's something you want to stay as far away from as possible. If it's fraud, people go to jail for a long time for this kind of stuff."

She agreed, almost relieved to be told it wasn't her concern.

And from then it was a quiet night of reading and watching TV. She took the anti-nausea medication and managed to keep everything down. We went to bed early. I wasn't really sleepy, but wanted to be beside her as she slept.

In the morning, she ate dry toast and a banana with her coffee. I prepared a small container of rice and one of chicken soup for her lunch. She could eat one or both depending on how she felt. She seemed a little better, more rested.

Or maybe I was just getting accustomed to how she looked now.

Then we were both out the door and on our way.

I cheated and picked up an order of bacon and eggs on my way to work. I could be a loving, caring partner, but didn't think I could completely give up fried and grease, so I'd have to get it on the side.

Once at work, I considered calling the people I needed to call, but gave myself the excuse of the morning meeting. I didn't want to get into a conversation only to have to cut it short.

Assuming I'd actually go.

At the penultimate moment, I decided to go hear what he had to say. Plus I could sneak in a croissant.

Parking in the French Quarter is a challenge—as Vincent's tickets reminded me. I decided on the easy route, to pay for parking in one of the lots by the river. It was a business expense; if I couldn't write it off to a client, I could at least deduct it from my taxes.

I arrived a good five minutes late and he wasn't there. Annoying. I scanned the street. I was betting he was playing games; payback for him not spotting me as a private dick at the NBG sales pitch.

"You get another five minutes," I muttered to myself. I entered the coffee shop, selected an appropriate pastry as compensation, and found an out-of-the-way table that allowed me to scan the room.

Four and a half minutes later, he was looming over my table.

"You're late," I greeted him.

"You were late; I'm later," he said as he pulled up a chair. He was tall, broad shouldered, a little paunch, but that seemed more from age and good living than skimping at the gym. His hair was a reddish brown, no gray yet, but now in a sharp V at the hairline, showing his age in a way the color didn't. He had a raffish mustache, full and droopy. His eyes were a light hazel, focused and observant. He wore expensive jeans that were meant to seem casual, with a wine-colored crewneck sweater, also expensive, also looking informal, as if he was just another tourist.

But there was nothing relaxed about his eyes.

"You were watching? Just waiting to see how long I'd stay?"

"No, they were brewing my tea and doing it on tourist-on-vacation schedule. I stepped outside to wait. Must have wandered down the block." He placed a paper cup with a tea bag string hanging out of it on the table.

"So why are we here?" I gulped the last bite of my pastry.

"It's a beautiful day in a beautiful part of the world. No place I'd rather be."

"That includes only you. I have many places I'd rather be. And I live here, so I can come back at any time." I glanced at my watch.

"I'm looking into Grant Walters, which I suspect you might be as well. Otherwise, why be at that meeting?"

"I'm not looking into Grant Walters; whatever he's done, it doesn't involve my clients."

"What are you investigating?"

"You first." I took a sip of my coffee.

"As I hinted on the phone, Walters likes to make money, especially when it's other people's money that he can help himself to. He has a silver tongue and a ruthless eye on the bottom line."

"From what I can tell, Nature's Beautiful Gift is legit."

"Agreed. However, what you probably can't tell is that he's taken control of this region, promising great returns, and has a significant amount of the product out on credit. All the people under him are funneling the moola to him, and it doesn't go any further."

"At some point the company has to notice that."

"At some point, yes. Just before that point, Mr. Walters will be gone, with claims that things were stolen, he was cheated, he has no money, save for the big stash in the Cayman Islands that no one can touch."

"Interesting, but as I said, I'm not after Mr. Walters."

"So what are you after?"

"I'm looking into something called The Cure," I said.

"Ah, so you stumbled over that."

That got my attention. "What do you know about it?"

He took a sip of his tea. "Was that Danish any good?"

"It was quite tasty. And it was a scone. What do you know about The Cure?"

"That if you're interested in that, you're interested in Mr. Walters." He got up, heading to the counter.

I'm used to the boys playing their games. To be fair, most guys are pretty cool, even the obnoxiously straight ones, but there are a few who have to pay undue attention to my sex. I didn't know if Rafe Gautier was one or this was just his standard shtick. "Better dicks than you have tried and failed," I muttered. Sometimes a positive attitude can be the most obnoxious thing you can do.

He rejoined me.

"So what'd you get?" I asked.

"A cheese Danish."

Boring tourist choice. I launched into a laundry list of the various baked goods—beignets, shoe-soles, turtles, rum cakes—that can be procured in this town, with suggestions of where to get them. As I started in on pralines, he finally held up his hands.

"Touché. You play the sport well, no wonder I thought you a wide-eyed innocent at the NBG sell-a-thon. Now I'm starving."

I was good. I didn't even smile. "Tell me about The Cure."

"Walters has his hand in as many pies as he can. Nature's BG, as I call it, is legit, The Cure stuff not so much, but by carefully mixing the two of them, he can use the BGs to make the other stuff look better than it is."

"It's ephedra and cheap Mexican speed."

He looked at me. "Ah, interesting. I suspected, but haven't gotten a sample to run it by a lab."

"Limited resources or not willing to bother?"

"They don't openly sell The Cure. I haven't been able to get a sample yet."

"So, what do you want from this?"

"To tie Walters in such a big knot that he can't escape. He screwed over some rich people—and they'll never get their money back, but they can afford to pay for revenge. So my job is to track him down and catch him doing something that'll get him in big trouble. What do you want from this?"

"Small stuff. Someone is spending big bucks on the BGs, possibly The Cure, and her relations think she's being snookered. They wanted me to find anything I can to help get her away from them."

"Cards on the table. You got something I need and I'm backed by people who will pay for what I need. Walters isn't going to give me his used toilet paper. No way I can get close enough to him to do shit."

"You want me to do your heavy lifting," I said bluntly.

He didn't deny it. "I can make it worth your while."

"Nothing is worth my while if I get killed."

"He's a swindler, not a fighter."

"A lot of swindlers become fighters when they're cornered."

"True. But I like to think I'm smarter than he is. Between the two of us, we're a lot smarter. Think about it. You've got your case; if you stumble over anything that I might use, I would really appreciate it if you'd toss it my way. If you want to help, I will be there every step of the way; if he chooses to fight, he'll have to fight me." He put his business card on the table. I noticed it had several phone numbers, including a cell. "Now, where do I get those good pralines again?"

I took his card and gave him directions. Once he was out of sight, I hurried back to my car. If Grant Walters went down, Vincent was likely to tumble behind him, which would get Aunt Marion out of his grasp. In truth, the McConkle's weren't paying me enough to do that kind of work, but Rafe had hinted his clients could more than make up for it. It could be dangerous—criminals with a lot to lose aren't altruistic people—and on your garden variety day, I try to avoid danger. With Cordelia ill—in truth, struggling for her life—I wouldn't be much good to her with a broken leg or arm. Or worse.

But if Grant Walters was behind The Cure, he was, even if not directly, the person who killed Reginald Banks, promising him a cure and giving him cheap drugs. How many more were there? Desperate people with few choices being sold the promise of a miracle by the kind of slime willing to profit off other people's misery?

Like insurance companies who deny coverage because it saves them money? We needed what we didn't have—health care that put people's well-being before making money. But we didn't have it, and instead left gaping holes for the profiteers—legal and illegal—to wring the last cent out of the ill.

By the time I got back to my office, I knew I'd take Rafe up on his offer—after checking him out to make sure he was who he said he was and had the kind of backing he claimed to have. If Walters was selling The Cure, and playing NBG on both sides, working with Rafe would solve everything in a tidy packet—preventing another Reginald Banks, getting Aunt Marion to believe more in kale for colon regularity than a pill, and putting a bad man out of action. Plus making me enough money to make up for the pro bono work for Cordelia and the bargain-basement rate I was charging the McConkles.

The only thing it didn't neatly wrap up was the insurance mess at Cordelia's office.

Two out of three isn't bad.

As I put my key in the door, I heard my phone ringing. I managed to get to it just before my machine kicked in.

"No, we're not breaking up."

"Hi, Alex, good to hear from you," I said as I tried to catch my breath. I carried the phone with me back to the door to properly lock it.

"Good to talk to you. It seems my communication these days is leaving messages. Or being too tired to talk. I needed to get the topic du jour out of the way before I could ask the important question—how's Cordelia?"

"She's okay. So far. Nausea, but that was expected. Continuing to work."

"I know I'm stuck in Red Stick, I know there is not a lot I can do, but she has been my best friend for most of my life and I can't lose her. She won't request anything, but you might, so anything you need, anything I can do, ask. Please ask."

"I can't lose her either," I said softly. That was what Alex was good at, not letting the unspoken remain silent.

"We're not going to. That just has to be the way it is."

"So you've moving to Red Stick?" We hadn't really got that out of the way.

"Yes and no. I have a job here. I don't have one in NOLA. I can't drive back and forth every day. Some days I have late meetings, or I have extra stuff I need to do. Plus I'm beginning to have violent road rage fantasies. Killing everyone who tries to enter at Highland Park Road. One of my coworkers just finished renovating a small apartment over her garage and asked if I'd be interested. She's charging me five hundred a month, which is a deal these days. I can leave Monday morning and come back Friday night. It's not much difference from what we're doing now—I'm too tired by the time I get home to be company."

"Except that you're in bed next to Joanne every night."

"I know that's what she wants. And in a perfect world, it's what

I'd want as well. But right now with the commute and my job, I'm doing twelve to fifteen hour days every day. Joanne is angry because I'm not there and I'm angry because I'm so tired and stressed out and… that's not good."

"But you're not breaking up," I interjected.

Alex sighed. "I'm not trying to break up. I'm trying to hold on to my sanity and take care of myself. I…I'm not sure where it will lead. I hope that if I can be better, maybe we can be better. And if we can't… at least I'll be better."

"Oh, Alex, I'm sorry."

"Everything changed. You didn't do it, I didn't do it, Joanne didn't do it. But…it changed." She didn't pause long enough for me to respond. "Call me if CJ needs anything. Or if you do. Promise?"

"Promise."

"I have to run. Maybe we can get together this weekend?"

"Yeah," was all I got out before she said, "Good. Later. Bye."

I put the phone down and stared at it for a while. Everything was changing. Maybe it always did, sometimes at such a rushed pace it felt dizzying.

Right as I got up to get some water, the phone rang again. Today was my day to be in and answering the phone.

"Hey, I'm glad I got you." Cordelia.

"What's up?"

"There is a support group. I thought it might be helpful to go. It's for people who are…going through what I'm going through."

"That sounds like a good idea," I agreed, ever the helpful spouse.

"There's a meeting tonight, so I might be home late, nine or even ten. I wanted to let you know."

"So this is my fried food night?"

She gave a gentle laugh, "As long as you get rid of the smell. I'm sorry, that's unfair to you."

"If I decide to indulge, I don't need to bring it home. It's not a problem."

She thanked me and we rang off.

No, not a problem except that she now lived in the land of the ill and I was still on the other side of the divide—well, without the word "cancer" attached to who I was. It wasn't that she was going to a support group—of course that was all right—but there were now more and more places where I couldn't help her, not in the way others could.

Everything changes.

My cell phone made its weird little text message sound.

Lydia with our location for tonight's meeting. I wondered if she knew about the support group, maybe had even suggested it to Cordelia. Curious, her chosen location was in the parking lot of a drugstore up around UNO. I thought Cordelia had mentioned her living Uptown. Their office was around Touro, also Uptown, so this was far afield. Maybe she had a class at UNO and this was convenient. Or maybe she wanted to meet some place away from where anyone she knew was likely to see her.

Vincent had e-mailed me—Debbie—to say he could suggest a few things and would love to get together and see how he could help. *Ah, Vincent*, I sighed, *you're about to be collateral damage.*

I took out the hot pink cell phone and found the card Grant Walters had given me. Time to test the waters and see if I could be of any use to Rafe and his revenge plot.

Walters answered after three rings.

Perky Debbie said, "Mr. Walters? I mean Grant? This is Deborah Perkins. You signed me up to sell Nature's Beautiful Gift products last week?"

"Yes, Debbie, how are you?" The silver tongue, warm and inviting as if saying of course he remembered me well. "How are sales going?"

"Quite well," I lied. "I'm over halfway through the order, with several visits scheduled for the next few days. I've found it really helpful to not do a hard sell, but instead approach it as healthy living and Nature's Beautiful Gift being part of that."

"An important part."

"Oh, of course. But people like to think they control things, so I guide them so they're making the choices, not me selling them something. It's psychology—they think I'm trying to help them—which I am—so they want to return the favor by buying something."

"Very clever. I thought you'd do well. Would you like to restock soon?"

Silver tongue and ruthless eye on the bottom line. "Very soon, maybe after a few more sales. Right now I should sell out what I've got before getting more, but in the next month or two, once I'm going full steam, I'll be able to order a lot more."

"That's very good to hear."

"I'm so grateful to you, Grant, for this opportunity. I feel like this gives me a chance to not just struggle, but to do well." I had to remind myself to not take it too far over the top. He had an ego, but he wasn't stupid.

"I don't give people opportunities; they earn them."

"I know you're a busy man. I had mentioned to you that I have someone close to me who is very ill and wanted to know what would be the best for her. You said you might have some suggestions if I'd call you in a few days. If now's not a good time, I can call back later."

"I might have some suggestions. As you know, our government and big industry have control of health care. There are things they don't want you to know."

"Yes, I'm well aware of that. Nothing is ever cured, so their profits never stop."

"Exactly. It's a challenge and can be costly to take them on, to offer things that should be on every pharmacy shelf, but instead aren't allowed in the country."

"Yes, I understand. I can't let someone I care about undergo horrible treatment because that's what makes the most profit."

"Who is your family member?" he asked.

Damn, I was hoping to keep it vague. "My sister. She's older than I am and kind of raised me—my mother suffered from depression, so she wasn't always there. We've always been close. I've been taking her to her chemo appointments." I wasn't going to get into the lesbian issue—plus this was not Cordelia and I but Debbie and her sister. I needed the lie that would best work for this situation.

"What's wrong with her?"

No, he wasn't stupid. If it was true, I should be able to easily answer these questions. "Lymphoma. Stage three when they found it. It's one of the more aggressive forms, so they're doing heavy chemo. She's living on plain rice and dry toast."

"Who is her doctor?"

"Uh, let me remember." Cordelia called her Jenny. "Oh, now I have it, Jennifer Godwin. She's at...oh, what's that place Uptown? On Prytania."

"Ah, yes, I think I know where you're talking about. Listen, you have to make sure your sister knows what she's getting into. It could help her, help her greatly, but there are forces out there that would shut this down the second they found out about it. Let me see what I can do. In the meantime, let's keep you going with Nature's Beautiful Gift."

His meaning was clear. I had to prove myself and earn his trust.

He continued, "Why don't you come by this afternoon and get some more product? It's the only time I'll be around this week and I like a chance to meet personally with my associates."

This was the cliché "offer I couldn't refuse"—not if I wanted him to believe in perky Debbie and her fake sister.

"I'm a little short on cash—"

"Don't worry, just give me half of what you've made so far and I'll give you the same amount of inventory. Unless you want more?"

Rafe and his Dallas money buddies will cover this. At least I hoped they would. "I definitely think I could sell more—I'm meeting some of my old sorority sisters over the weekend, so if you trust me with more, I'd be glad to take it."

"How about double if you give me three-quarters of what you've made so far? I'll make it a no-interest loan for a month. Sell everything and pay me back in that time and it'll be yours for cost."

"Thank you, sir—I mean, Grant. This is a great deal and I appreciate it."

He gave me instructions to meet him at the same place in Metairie in the late afternoon.

Bathroom break.

My cell phone—mine, not Debbie's—starting jangling as I was zipping up.

Worried about Cordelia, I ran out of the bathroom and grabbed it.

"Mick!" It was Danny.

"What's up? What's wrong?" Would Danny be calling me about Cordelia? Her partner Elly was a nurse and might be with Cordelia.

"I'm afraid I have some bad news."

"What? Just tell me!"

"Dudley escaped. The oldest trick in the book—faked being barely able to move, got his guard to uncuff him so he could take a leak, then punched the guy, grabbed his gun, and took off running."

"That's all?" I asked, relief coursing through me.

"Isn't that enough? A man who tried to kill you has escaped and is armed."

"Can you hold a minute? Someone is knocking at my door. Oh, wait, they're breaking the door down."

"Get the fuck out of—bullshit. The phone would be on the floor."

"My bad, just a woodpecker outside."

"Mick, someone might be trying to kill you. You're taking this a bit lightly."

"I thought you might be calling about Cordelia," I said softly.

"Ah…yeah." It was all the explanation needed. "Go lock your downstairs door."

"It's already locked. As is my office door. And I'm carrying my gun. Anything else?"

"Don't take candy from strangers."

"Roger that. Any reason to think he's coming after me rather than trying to be at the Mexican border before dark?"

"No, just that he's loose, armed, and dangerous."

My office phone started ringing. I glanced at the caller ID. Joanne, presumably to tell me the same thing. "Joanne's calling," I told Danny.

"No jokes about people breaking down the door," Danny admonished me before hanging up.

"If you're calling about Dudley, I already know," I answered the phone.

"Bingo. Be on the alert. The good news for you is that he's not in great shape. Some busted ribs and other stuff, and once his pain meds wear off, he'll be very aware of it. He might come after you, but right now he's so doped up he probably couldn't shoot straight."

"Which means he might hit me given what a lousy shot he was sober."

Joanne ignored that. "He's due for another pain pill in about half an hour, so we're guessing that he'll be at one of his favorite drug haunts in about an hour."

"So what should I do in the meantime?"

"Doors locked, gun handy, steer clear of crack houses. Call me later in the day and I'll update you."

"All of the above. I'm sorry I didn't get a chance to call you back yesterday. How are you doing?"

"Fine," she said in a tone that let me know she wasn't and she wasn't going to talk about it. The phone was dead before I had a chance to say anything else.

I retrieved my gun and put it right in the middle of my desk. This would not be a good day for Mr. Charles Williams to visit, because I was inclined to shoot first and ask questions at a later date.

My stomach was growling. It was well past my usual lunchtime. I decided to venture out. It might be risking my life, but sometimes an oyster po-boy is worth it. Right now I was craving something fried. All our talk last night of how off-putting fried was for Cordelia had lodged the waft of hot grease in my brain. I put on my gun, found a light enough jacket so it didn't look too out of place in this weather, and went in search of something golden brown.

I was careful, checking the street from one of the stair landings, my hand on my gun as I opened the downstairs door.

But all was quiet, no cars, no trucks, no maniacs trying to kill me.

I ate at the restaurant, not wanting to bring the hot oil smell back to my office. Cordelia didn't go there often, but in case she did, I wanted it smelling of apples and arugula.

The trip back was just as uneventful and I was soon safely behind two locked doors.

I'd carried the hot pink cell phone with me, but it hadn't rung. The wait made me glad I wasn't really Debbie, caught between hope and desperation. Instead, I used the time to do due diligence and run a background check on Rafe Gautier. He was a private eye out of Dallas, part of a large organization. His picture matched the man I'd met. Basically, he checked out as much as I needed him to check out.

Time to call him—he was the only way I'd get a couple of thousand dollars anytime soon. I'd done some quick calculations. At twenty dollars apiece and selling over half of what she'd taken, Debbie would have taken in close to three thousand dollars. That meant handing Grant Walters over two thousand.

The games were over—Rafe answered on the second ring. I gave him a quick rundown of my phone call with Grant Walters. His response to the money was, "Not a problem."

"I need it by three thirty," I reminded him.

"Still not a problem." We agreed to meet in front of his hotel. He'd hand me an envelope and I wouldn't even need to get out of my car.

I passed the afternoon by checking e-mail, reading the news online, the weather, celebrity gossip. I'd made it to pork belly futures, by which time Dudley had to be well over the pain threshold and therefore presumably in search of drugs and not me.

At around 3, I prowled in my costume closet. Debbie couldn't wear pink every day—mostly because Micky Knight didn't own that much pink. I found a frilly aqua shirt and a knock-off version of designer jeans for her. In the bare nick of time, I remembered to shift all the putatively sold product out of my trunk and added it to the obstacle course that led to the back door of my building.

As promised, Rafe was standing a little down the block from the entrance to his hotel.

"Be careful out there," he told me as he leaned in to hand me a thick envelope. "It's a mix of bills, a couple of fifties just to keep it from being too bulky, but mostly twenties and tens."

"Just like someone would get from selling things at twenty bucks each." I tossed the envelope on the passenger seat and headed off.

Traffic was a snarl, early rush hour going out to the suburbs. I avoided the interstate for my sanity and the safety of others—if one more big SUV cut me off, the gun in my glove box might prove too tempting.

It was just a little after four when I got to the place in Metairie. I scanned the parking lot. It seemed pretty empty, only a few cars by the pizza place. Maybe Grant gave up on Debbie because she was a few minutes late. I didn't see any car that looked expensive enough for him.

I took the money out of the envelope and stuffed them into my purse, making sure the bills were in a different compartment from my gun.

Show time.

I hurriedly traipsed up the stairs, as if Debbie would be concerned about being late.

When I got to the second floor, the door was ajar, not welcome open like it had been the last time.

I rapped softly on the door. "Mr. Walters? I mean, Grant?" I pushed the door open a few more inches and stuck my head in.

"Ah, Debbie, I'm glad you could make it."

It was just the two of us. He was sitting at the far end of the room at the big table he had used before.

"Yes, sir—Grant. I'm happy to do it. So far everyone I've told about Nature's Beautiful Gift has been interested and willing to buy at least a bottle or two." Much as my feet wanted to stay near the door and freedom, I forced myself into an easy saunter across the room to him.

"Good, I'm glad to hear it."

I pulled up a chair so I was sitting opposite from him. Just far enough away he couldn't easily grab me.

I reached into my purse and pulled out the money. I wanted to keep this meeting focused on business. "This is all the money I've made so far," I said, as if wide-eyed, naïve Debbie would so willingly reveal everything.

He nodded, picking up a stack and proceeded to count it. I counted another stack and pile by pile we both went through and counted the entire amount.

"Two thousand, eight hundred and seventy-two dollars," he announced.

"Exactly what I got," I said, although I'd counted ten dollars more. I did not want to quibble and have to sit here and count again. It was Rafe's money anyway.

"So three quarters of that is two thousand, one hundred and fifty-four." He quickly separated that from the stack.

"Oh, well, easy come, easy go," I said, looking at the small amount left for me.

"The start-up phase is always hard," he assured me. "You're doing quite well. Several of the others are still struggling to sell their first bottle."

"I may not be great with math," I said, doing my best to actually giggle, "but I'm pretty good at talking to people."

"You are good at talking to people," he echoed. "I could see you wanted to succeed at that first meeting." He reached out and covered my hand with his. Then he gave me the kind of smile a man gives a woman to show he's interested.

Holy fuck balls, what now? I kept a smile plastered on my face. "Thank you, Grant. I hope I never disappoint you." I lifted my thumb slightly as if responding to his touch.

He again smiled at me.

I desperately tried to think of a lie that would require me to have to be on the other side of the city in fifteen minutes.

Then he glanced at his watch and his smile changed to annoyance. "I'm sorry, I have to be somewhere. It was great to see you. I hope you continue to sell very well and we can see each other again soon. I'll walk you out and give you your inventory."

"I'm sure you'll see me again soon," I told him. I hastily stuffed seven hundred and eighteen dollars in my purse and followed him out of the room.

He didn't bother locking the door.

When we got to the parking lot, the truck—driven by Vincent—was parked in front.

"Hello, Vincent," Grant greeted him. He handed Vincent a sheet of paper—my order. "Please fill this for Debbie."

"Hi, Vincent," I greeted him.

"Ah, hi, Debbie," he said, looking at me then at Grant.

I pulled my car around, facing my trunk to the back of the truck.

Vincent quickly tossed the boxes out of the truck. I started to grab them, but Grant insisted on helping me.

"Can't have a beautiful woman like you doing grubby work." He smiled at me.

When we were done, Grant put an arm around my shoulder in a possessive way and kissed me on the cheek.

I leaned into him, playing along. He wasn't really interested in Debbie, I had figured out. This show was mostly for Vincent, partly for the woman he assumed to be Debbie. Grant Walters, with his money, smooth talk, and distinguished looks, could easily get young blond women with perfect hair and teeth, breasts skillfully enhanced.

I didn't break mirrors, but I was over forty, wearing cheap knock-off clothes and, even as fake Debbie, at least one divorce past doing anything to get a man.

He only did it to see the hurt puppy dog look in Vincent's eyes—a reminder that no one could compete with the alpha wolf.

Grant got in the truck with Vincent, clearly his designated driver. I could almost see the satisfied smile he'd give to Vincent, all the little ways he'd play that he and Debbie had been doing more than counting money.

Moments like this make me glad I'm a lesbian. I waved cheerfully—my happiness genuine that Grant was as interested in having sex with me as I was with him—and drove away.

Rush hour driving prevented me from thinking about much on my way home.

I detoured by my office to change back into Micky Knight garb.

CHAPTER TWENTY-TWO

I still had to meet Lydia, so I decided to do what a good detective with a maniac trying to kill her should do—vary my hours. Cordelia wouldn't be home. The support group was near her office, so she was staying Uptown. I went home, fed the cats, and had an apple and some nuts for myself. My late lunch was still working its way through my digestive tract.

I left at a quarter to seven, heading up Elysian Fields toward the lake. At least the days were getting longer and it was still light out.

I got there right at seven, but didn't see Lydia. I parked on the far side of the lot, got out, then stood by my car fiddling with my cell phone. I had run through about every function except the ones I didn't know what they would do and had never tried because I was afraid they might cause the phone to go into the fetal position, when I saw her come out of the drugstore.

Like she'd come here to do shopping and just happened to meet me in the parking lot.

At a major intersection where anyone could drive by and see us. Amateur. Not that I intended to tell her that. I wasn't a double agent and she wasn't the KGB. In the unlikely event that anyone asked, we could say we ran into each other. She asked about Cordelia and I engaged her in a lengthy conversation about colon health.

She spotted me, did a passable—for someone driving by at a high rate of speed—acting job of being surprised to see someone she knew here. She trotted over to me, looking over her shoulder as she did.

"Hey, thanks for meeting me," she said, with another glance behind her.

"Let me watch behind you," I said. "It's more natural that way."

She blushed, actually blushed. "I'm not sure what I'm doing."

I agreed with that, but didn't express it. "So tell me, what made you want to see me?"

"I looked through some of the charts and there are... irregularities."

"Like what?"

"I mean, no one is perfect. We're in a hurry, we jot down something wrong. If you search everything you're going to find something."

"You didn't want to meet with me because someone mixed up a blood pressure reading."

"No, but now I feel stupid, like I'm adding two and two together and somehow came up with ten."

"Were other people billed for appointments they didn't make?"

"Maybe. I thought so, now I'm not so sure."

Denial. It's hard to think that someone you work with every day, chat with at the water cooler, eat lunch with, is a criminal, taking advantage of you and your patients. Lydia was obviously struggling.

"What did you see?"

"A few of the charts indicated appointments that weren't on the books. But maybe the chart is right and the appointment book is wrong. Maybe someone canceled the wrong appointment, so it disappeared."

"But the person still showed up and was seen?"

"If we messed up we would have seen them."

"If the appointment was erased, how would you know that you messed up and that the patient hadn't come on the wrong day? And how often could something like this happen?"

She again looked behind her, but this time it seemed more as a way to avoid the implications of my question than worry about being followed. She finally shook her head and replied, "I don't know. When I was there looking at them it seemed wrong, but now that I'm away, I keep thinking maybe I should have checked this, or looked there. I have to be wrong about this, I just have to be."

"It's hard to think that someone might be fudging the system. It's someone you know, isn't it? And that's even harder."

She looked down at the ground. "I have to be wrong. We're doctors, nurses, not the kind of people who would cheat the system."

"All kinds of people cheat. Including doctors and nurses. There are probably even a few bad nuns. Tell me what you found."

She again shook her head, clearly upset. "It's all so jumbled now; it doesn't seem to make sense. I'd need to show you."

"Then show me. Can we go there now?"

"No! The support group is meeting on the next floor and both Ron and Brandon are doing rounds late and might come back. It has to be at a time when no one will be around."

"You work there; you have a right to be there."

"But you don't."

"Cordelia does. I could say she left something and asked me to get it."

"And why wouldn't she come for it?"

"She was feeling too sick."

Lydia looked stricken—lost in her own dilemma, she'd forgotten about Cordelia. "Oh, I'm sorry, of course. But it'll be better if we don't run into anyone and we don't need to tell anyone any stories."

"It might be helpful to tell Cordelia."

"No!" She looked around, worried someone might have overheard her vehemence. "Not yet. I want to be sure before I involve anyone else."

"You might want to talk to an insurance person; that's not my specialty."

"Look, I'm trying to do the right thing. For everyone. If we're wrong, we could ruin someone's career, a medical education down the drain. I have to be sure I'm right before I let anyone else know besides you. And only you because you already know."

I tried not to let my exasperation show. This wasn't my case; no one was paying me here. *Except*, I reminded myself, *my being involved might shield Cordelia*. And that was a very important reason. "We can take it slow, but if someone is committing fraud, there are patients who aren't being seen. Reginald Banks had a denial-of-service letter from his insurance company claiming that he was being treated too often. Can you risk that happening to someone else?"

She looked miserable. "No, I can't. Let me check everyone's schedule tomorrow. Can I let you know?"

"Yes."

"And can you come up with a reason to not tell Cordelia?"

"I'll tell her I'm on a job. She doesn't need to know what it's about."

"I'm sorry," she said, as if she knew the impossible favor she was asking. "I'm not usually like this. But if I'm not wrong, then someone I thought I knew very well is a complete stranger." Improbably, she leaned in and hugged me, then quickly let go, embarrassed at her show of emotion. Without another word, she hurried across the parking lot, got in her car, and drove away.

My hand was on my car door when my phone rang, the hot pink one.

I answered it with a breathless, "Hello?"

"Hi, Debbie, sorry I had to rush away so abruptly."

Grant Walters.

"Not a problem. I know you're a busy man."

"You mentioned you might need some help for your sister. Are you still interested?"

"Yes, yes, sir, Grant. Very much so."

"I may be talking to someone I know in the next few days. It may take a while, though, for me to have anything for you. He has to talk to people as well."

"I'd appreciate whatever you can do for me."

"You're a special woman, Debbie. I like doing things for you."

The lies that rolled off his tongue.

"You're a very special man, Grant. I hope someday I can show my appreciation to you." And the lies that rolled off mine.

The call ended. He was a busy man, after all, little time to talk to even the special women.

I started my car and drove away.

When I got home, Cordelia wasn't there yet. In the past she had often worked late hours, but this was different. When she was away before, it was because she was the strong person taking care of others; now she was being taken care of.

Worrying won't help you or her, I told myself as I turned on lights against the coming dusk. It wouldn't do to continually obsess over her health. Taking advantage of her absence, I poured half an inch of Scotch into a glass, enjoying the burn of the alcohol as I swallowed the first sip. Then another.

On the fourth sip, I heard the sound of her car pull up outside. I hastily gulped the last of the alcohol, put the glass in the sink under the tap, and swished a handful of water through my mouth. I grabbed one of the sports drinks from the refrigerator and took several swallows.

I just turned off the tap as she came in the door. She found me at the sink, finishing up the few dishes from breakfast.

"How are you? How was the group?" I asked, my voice too jovial.

"It was good, I think. One older man tended to dominate. This is his second bout of cancer, so he considers himself an expert. How was your day?"

"It was okay," I said. In truth, filled with things I couldn't tell her. I was debating whether to mention Dudley or not. Joanne hadn't called with an update, but I was taking that as a good sign. She clearly didn't want to talk about Alex, but was honorable enough that if she thought I was in danger, she'd let me know. Since she was avoiding me, I was taking that to mean I wasn't in danger.

Much as I wanted to consult her about the medical records, while I hadn't exactly promised Lydia, I would hold off until we met and then decide what to tell Cordelia. So I was left with, "Mostly a lot of phone calls and paperwork. It's never like this on TV."

She flopped down in a kitchen chair. "I am so tired."

"You're fighting cancer with poison. Would probably make just about anyone tired."

She managed a wan smile. "I think I just need to go to bed." She watched me as I as I started drying the dishes and putting them away.

"Have you eaten? Do you want me to fix something?"

"They had food, so I ate there. Thanks. I need to rest right now."

"Do you have to go to work tomorrow?" She looked worn, as if she had aged since she left in the morning, her skin pale, the dark under her eyes pronounced.

"Yes, I have to," she said shortly. She looked pointedly at the glass I was putting on the shelf. "One of us has to hold it together." Almost immediately, she covered her face with her hands. "Shit, shit, shit. I'm sorry. I don't know what's happening to me."

I quashed my anger—having a drink of Scotch at home wasn't exactly falling apart—and knelt in front of her, resting a hand on her knee. I didn't say anything. I didn't know what to say.

"I'm sorry," she repeated. "I don't know where that came from."

"Maybe because you're going through something that I can't be much help with," I said softly.

"Don't say that. Don't even think that. I need you now more than I ever have. You can drink a bottle a day. Just don't leave me." She broke down crying.

I put my arms around her, reaching up from my kneeling position. "I'm not planning on leaving you." I admitted, "Alcohol is a crutch. I don't drink because I enjoy it, but to blur the edges, make life go away. I learned the hard way, it doesn't really help. But...some days I just can't be perfect."

"I have no right to judge you," she said, wiping her eyes.

"Yeah, you do. You live here, so when I screw up you bear the consequences."

She slid down to the floor—we were both kneeling and she held me tightly. "Right now you're getting the consequences. I'm sorry, I seem to be much more emotional than usual."

"Could it be the chemo?"

"It could be anything. And everything. The chemo, the cancer, the exhaustion." She put her head against my neck. "Maybe I'm angry because this isn't supposed to happen to me. I watched my diet, exercised. If you take care of sick people, then you shouldn't get sick."

"It's not fair."

"Life isn't fair. Most of the people in the group were older than I am, but a few were younger. Some of them have supportive family, some don't. I told them about cooking two dinners last night. Several of them asked if they could borrow you."

"I hope you said no."

"I only didn't say 'no fucking way' because I was in company." She lifted her head up. "My knees are hurting and I can't breathe."

I stood up and helped her up.

She grabbed a paper towel and hastily blew her nose. "The best thing about the support group is that it made me realize how lucky I am. I have good medical care, insurance, enough money that if it comes to it, I could afford COBRA for six months. And I have you to come home to." She looked at me and smiled a heartbreaking smile. "You're not dating your secretary."

"I don't have one."

She took my hand and continued, "Or asking for a divorce."

"We're not legally married."

"Or leaving the vomit for me to clean up or bringing home fried chicken when I can't cook even though you know I can't stand the smell. I have noticed and I need to do a better job of letting you know. The extra trip to the grocery store, the chicken soup in the freezer—home-made—cooking several different dinners and then packing them into small containers for me to easily grab. There are so many ways that you have told me you love me…" She paused to wipe away a stray tear.

"I'd better, you've put up with me all these years."

"And you've put up with me." She looped her arms around my waist and rested her cheek against mine. "I've always been in love with you and I've fallen more in love with you over these last few weeks. Maybe I could do this without you, but I wouldn't want to and I'm glad I don't have to."

"I even got an organic chicken for the soup." I tightened my arms around her and said, "I love you, too. And…the thought of losing you has made me realize how much. It's more than I have any words to say." I tried not to cry.

"Shh, it's okay," she said, reaching up to wipe away my tears. "Don't leave me and I will do my best not to leave you."

We spent several minutes silently holding each other. She broke it with, "I need to do a better job of handling my anger. I can't let it out at work or at my patients, so that kind of leaves you, and that's not fair."

"Politicians. There have to be enough idiot ones in just Louisiana alone for you to spend days screaming abuse at them."

We both laughed and she agreed it would be a much better strategy.

But she was still tired and we both went to bed. I left the rest of the dishes for the morning.

CHAPTER TWENTY-THREE

When we woke in the morning, I let Cordelia have the bathroom first—after all, she had people who expected her in by a certain time.

I made a breakfast of oatmeal, which I left plain. I cut up strawberries and a banana and rinsed some blueberries. She came out of the shower just as I was placing containers of honey and cinnamon by the steaming bowl of oatmeal.

"Wow, I thought I smelled something." She wrapped a still-damp arm around me and gave me a quick kiss as appreciation.

We ate together. I was pleased to see that she had a decent appetite.

After she left, I did my morning routine in the bathroom and was out the door.

The first thing I did after I got to the office was call Rafe to give him an update on what had happened with Grant Walters—and that I had his change. His voice mail answered. Probably too early in the morning for him.

Several other cases needed my attention. I was still chasing down heirs from the ninety-one-year-old who had died. She'd had five children, two who had passed away before her, so I had to find their progeny, which had spread to twelve people to locate who might get a few hundred dollars from the sale, since there were so many heirs. A hairy case, to be sure. A company that I did a lot of work for wanted me to track down an employee who had gone missing. He'd disappeared at the same time they discovered that over one hundred thousand dollars had been embezzled. They really wanted to talk to him.

The McConkles and even Rafe weren't paying me enough to ignore the other cases.

Rafe called back in the afternoon. I told him I thought Grant was playing cat and mouse with me. He had to be confident that Debbie was everything she said she was before he'd give her more.

"That's okay," Rafe said. "It'll give us time to be subtle about checking him out and we'll get a better idea of what's going on with him here."

"What if he bails?"

"He can't yet. Not enough money in the account for him. He'll need a couple of million at the least to disappear."

We left it at we'd call each other if anything happened.

I had to track Mr. Embezzler to sunny Phoenix and work with both the authorities there and the ones here. It took several trips out there for me to get enough evidence of a flashy lifestyle with no apparent means of support and enough of a stable location for the police to arrest him.

Just before the last one, I again went with Cordelia for her chemo treatment.

It hit her harder this time; she didn't make it home before the nausea hit her. She had to make use of the plastic bag in the last few blocks from home.

I offered to delay my trip, but she insisted I go. Elly, Danny's partner and a nurse, was off and would stay with her while I was gone.

"If I need someone to stay," she added. "I've had to throw up by myself before and managed to survive it."

I talked to her every night. Elly had stayed the first night after I was gone, but Cordelia insisted that she was fine, even going back to work the following day.

Phoenix is a nice place to visit, I thought, as I exited the airport to the waiting humidity, but there wasn't enough green for me. I was too accustomed to verdant New Orleans where every and anything could and did grow.

Just as I stowed my suitcase in my truck, my phone rang.

The one I got for Debbie.

"Hi, Debbie, how are you?"

It took me a moment to place the voice. How many men would call me without identifying themselves? Torbin, but I knew his voice and he wouldn't be calling on this phone.

Grant Walters.

"Hi, Grant, I'm fine. How are you?"

"I've been wondering how the sales are going? I thought I'd hear from you by now."

Damn, I'd gotten so busy with travel—and Cordelia—that I had neglected my budding career as a saleswoman for NBG. "I'm doing quite well. I meant to get in touch with you a few days ago, but…" But what? "But my sister hasn't been doing well and I had to go with her to the doctor."

"I was calling about that as well. I'd love to see you—and now you're selling well, I did want to follow up with that."

"I'm so scared for her," I said, letting real emotion into my voice for false purposes.

"Is she interested in this as well?" he asked.

"She's the one that asked me to search around for her. We feel the same way. If there is anything out there that can help, that can get us through this hell, we'll both do whatever it takes."

"Sadly, because of the danger and the efforts of concealment, it can't be as inexpensive as it might be otherwise."

"I understand. You have to cover your costs. I'm just glad that you're willing to take the risks to make this available."

"Thank you, but I'm not the one behind this. There are others involved and I do this to protect them. The first payment is five thousand dollars, and it usually requires three to five courses."

"Wow, that's expensive," I acted. "But worth it if it cures her cancer." His ruthlessness was tripping over his silver tongue. Of course, he assumed he had Debbie well hooked—a desperately ill sister, someone who believed in the conspiracy theory that cures were out there, just hidden, and someone developing a romantic interest in him—the perfect way to blind a person to reality. But Micky Knight easily saw through his denial of having anything to do with it and rattling off the costs like they were second nature.

"Yes, it is. But it barely covers their expenses. Some people sell jewelry, or cash in retirement plans—what good is retirement if you never live that long? Or they borrow from friends. It may be difficult, but surely your sister's life is worth it."

"Yes, of course. We'll get the money. I have some pictures from when we were young and stupid that I'll bet my husband wouldn't want his law partners or his new wife to see. I never thought I'd really use them, but this seems like a good enough reason."

"It's best if you can bring two or three payments. That way you don't have to meet so often and it cuts down on the risk to do as much as you can in one time."

"Of course, that makes perfect sense."

"How long until you have the money?"

"I can squeeze my ex pretty hard. Within the week. Maybe the next few days. Is that soon enough?"

"Yes, it certainly is. Give me a phone number where I can reach you and where there won't be someone else answering the phone or listening to messages."

I rattled off the cell number. "The phone stays in my purse. No one else touches it," I assured him.

"Good. I'll pass your number along, and you should hear from someone in the next few days. And when's a good time for you to restock your inventory? I'm going to be at our office tomorrow afternoon if you can do it then."

"I'm pretty sure I can, Grant. But let me see if I can rearrange some things."

"Or you can talk to Vincent. He's more available than I am."

More available in multiple meanings of the word.

"I'll make it. At four?"

"Four. I'll see you then."

The phone clicked off. He'd spent about five minutes with me and earned thousands of dollars. At least he thought so. I got up and paced around the office. Deborah Perkins, were she real, was simply a means to an end to him. He was willing to damage her and her sister, and I doubted she was more than just a sideline. The thousands he would bilk from her would be a night at the casino, not the houses and cars and flush bank account he was really after. The man chilled me, and I understood why Rafe's clients wanted revenge.

If I hadn't already decided to help him, this would have done it for me. But I wanted to calm down before I called Rafe. Right now I was too angry. Grant Walters had only a rotting hole where his soul should have been. Despite Rafe's assurances, he was dangerous. He covered himself well, clearly had layers between him and his deeds, but we planned to corner him, and with his back up against the wall, he was capable of anything. I needed to be calm and rational before I agreed to whatever Rafe was planning.

And out of the airport.

I drove home. The cats were happy to see me. Cordelia was still at work, but arrived just after I threw my dirty laundry in the washing machine.

She looked tired. I could clearly see the dark circles under her eyes.

But she smiled at me and gave me a long hug to show that she had missed me. To prove that she was better she suggested we go out to eat so I wouldn't have to cook anything after flying halfway across the country.

We agreed on a place in the Quarter about five blocks from where we live. I changed from my airplane clothes and she changed from her professional clothes—more laundry—to something more comfortable.

We walked there. I started slow, but she kept at our usual pace. I could tell she'd lost weight. Her clothes draped more loosely.

She captured my hand as we crossed Dauphine, holding it as we walked.

"I'm partly through the cycle," she said. "Probably why I feel better. It's far enough along."

"So you get to feel better just in time for the next chemo?"

"Pretty much," she said with a wry smile. "Enough to kill the cancer has to be enough to make me sick. But I think it's going well. Another few weeks and we'll do a CT scan and check."

A breeze came off the river, lifting her hair, still mostly auburn and thick. I reached up and smoothed it out of her eyes.

"Will you still love me when I'm bald?" she asked.

"You think that's going to happen?"

"Mostly likely. After about the third or fourth chemo, that's when it starts to happen. Already I'm noticing more hair after I shower or brush it."

"Your hair is gorgeous. But it's not the reason I love you. I will still love you if you're bald."

She squeezed my hand.

"Promise me we'll take advantage of the times when I'm feeling okay and do something like this."

That was a promise I could easily make.

We held hands until we were seated and needed to look at menus.

CHAPTER TWENTY-FOUR

D ebbie needed to be more pink than my wardrobe allowed. After going to my office and taking care of the basics— checking e-mail, phone messages, eating a breakfast croissant (I couldn't live on Cordelia's plain oatmeal alone)—and calling Rafe— voice mail—I headed for some secondhand stores to augment my wardrobe. I had to remind myself that Dudley was still on the loose—at least last time I'd been updated.

The fairies of pinkness were with me today. The first place I stopped had a decent pink short-sleeved sweater and, best luck of all, a hot pink jacket that I could wear over it and my gun.

After that for most of the morning I alternated between paperwork and goofing off by reading news stories online. It really is fascinating to discover that some people (usually male and inebriated) forget to put their pants on before they take a drive.

Just before I moved on to the big lunch debate, Rafe returned my call.

"Grant needs more NBG money," I told him, updating him on our conversation.

Again he replied, "Not a problem."

I didn't repeat that I'd need twice as much as Grant had given Debbie double her first amount.

"I've still got the crap in my trunk," I told him. "Want to help with storage?"

He agreed, said that we could meet in a convenient parking lot. He'd take the NBG out of my trunk and give me the money.

We agreed to meet at a large lot just over the parish line. It served several different stores. We were so agreeable.

I ate a quick lunch, then put on my new pink wardrobe and went to meet Rafe.

When I got there, I quickly spotted him, but drove around the parking lot just as if I was one of those obnoxious suburban ladies who is sure life owes her a parking spot so much closer to the store.

What I was really doing was checking it out. It wouldn't do to run into Vincent.

Or Dudley.

But Rafe was the only man waiting for me today.

I pulled up beside his big blue SUV.

As I got out I said, "You know this is the small end of what he's doing. A few thousand dollars is a lot of money to someone like Deborah, but nothing to him."

"That might not be a bad thing. He's not stupid, and the longer he's gotten away with it, the more he thinks he's always going to outsmart the people after him. He'll be paying less attention to the small end of the deal."

"He likes to play with people like Deborah, but this is the—just barely—legal end. If he's smart, he'll be a million miles away from peddling The Cure."

"Naw, he likes to watch."

"What? This isn't porn."

"It is to him. He's a sick enough bastard to like to watch people like Deborah get taken for the ride of their life."

"So what do we do now?"

"You get more of this NBG crap and wait for another phone call. I and my team keep on watching him. We take it from there."

He handed me the envelope. I again tossed it on the passenger seat. We loaded the still unsold—and likely to never be sold—NBG bottles from my truck into the back of his SUV.

Then it was time for another tête-à-tête with Grant.

As before, the parking lot was almost empty. I was a little early this time, so maybe he wasn't here yet.

I again took the money out of the envelope and did a quick and dirty count. Almost five thousand in cash. A big pile of paper. I stuffed it in my purse. If I'd actually sold as much as I claimed, I'd be making decent money.

I waited until a minute before four but no one else arrived. It was time to climb the stairs and see what waited for me. I could only hope that my guardian angel—or devil—would be kind enough to prevent Grant from thinking he actually had to have sex with me.

But when I got there the room was empty.

Maybe his game this time was to see how long Debbie would wait.

I glanced at my watch. I had to give him fifteen minutes at least.

But I didn't have to do it here in this empty room. There were no windows, the only natural light coming from the entrance; the only other illumination was from a wall sconce near the back. The room hadn't been high end to start with, and the shadows and dim light brought out the dingy.

I turned to go.

And almost crashed into Grant Walters.

He had been quiet, deliberately so.

"Grant!" I said. "I didn't hear you." I didn't need to act startled because I actually was.

"Sorry, soft-soled shoes. I didn't mean to sneak up on you."

Oh, yes, you did, I thought. Rubber soles alone aren't quiet enough to sneak up a flight of stairs and halfway across the room. Not on someone who was listening like I was.

"Oh, that's okay. I know you didn't," I answered. "I spent most of last night with my sister—she just had chemo and was feeling pretty sick—so I didn't get much sleep. At this point a truck could crash in front of me and I might not notice."

"I'm very sorry to hear that. I'm still waiting for my contacts to get back to me. I hope to hear something in the next week."

"I hope you hear something soon," I said. The sooner the better. I wanted no more one-on-one meetings with him.

"How are you doing on getting the money?" he asked. "That sounds crass, doesn't it? I don't mean to be. I don't want you left out. Often there are more people who want the treatment than we can give it to. I don't have much control—otherwise I'd see to it you're taken care of—they usually have to dispense it to those who bring the money first.

And they have to do that because the money is the only thing allowing them to continue." The silver tongue was in full flight.

"I understand, really I do. I sent some copies of the pictures to my ex, plus I hocked my engagement ring. At least he wasn't a cheap enough bastard to demand that back. I'm really working on selling, so even after I buy more, I think I'll clear about a few thousand. I'd do anything to help my sister."

"You're very dedicated," he said. "A lot of families wouldn't go as far as you have."

"She's a couple of years older than I am, practically raised me. My parents weren't…well, let's just say they weren't perfect. My sister at least made sure the ramen noodles got heated up."

"What's her name?"

Of course my sister had a name. I just needed to make it up. "Donna." Donna and Deborah, nice alliteration. To cover my slight hesitation, I said, "That's her official name. I usually call her Dough because that's how I pronounced it as a kid. The family calls her Park Place because that's where she always wanted to land in Monopoly." If I gave her three names maybe I'd remember one.

We were still standing facing each other. I hadn't moved farther into the room, mainly because I didn't want to have any more distance between me and the door. But Grant was blocking my way.

"She also really helped me through my divorce, gave me a place to stay right after and helped me get back on my feet. So I feel I owe her," I added. I didn't want to throw in too many details. They can trip you up, but I had to make him believe Deborah would scrape together the thousands of dollars required for her sister.

"She sounds like a special person. It must run in the family," he said and smiled at me.

"She is. I'm lucky to have her as a sister. But I know you're a busy man, Grant, and you didn't give me a chance just to listen to my problems." I turned from him and walked to the table.

No, his shoes weren't that quiet. I could hear his steps behind me now that he wasn't trying to be concealed.

I put the money on the table.

The piles of bills got his attention. I doubt he was even aware of what his expression revealed—money was his true interest, his one real passion. Everything—and everyone—else was just a means to an end.

This time I didn't even count, but let him. I was more interested in watching his expression as the bills slide through his hands.

"You're doing quite well," he said when he finished. "That's almost five thousand."

"It does include what was left over from the last time," I said. "I've been hustling. My sorority sisters have been buying like hotcakes. Guess we're all hitting the age when we have to be better about taking care of ourselves."

"Look, I'm going to do you a favor. Two thousand will cover the costs of a full order of product. I think you're ready to go for the high end of sales." He slid enough bills to cover that amount to his side of the table. "If you let me take another two—if you can spare it—I'll tell my contacts that I already have a down payment on your sister's treatment. If I vouch for you and show some money, it'll almost guarantee that you'll get something from the next shipment."

He kept his hand on the remaining bills.

I swallowed as if this was a hard decision for Debbie. That kind of money would mean something for her. Hell, it was a fair chunk of change for Micky Knight. "Okay," I said with another swallow, as if this was hard. "Thank you for doing this for me. For us."

"I'm doing this for you." He looked directly at me the perfect smile on his face. He kept his hand on the money. "I know this is hard. My mother died of breast cancer, so I can feel what you're going through."

I dabbed my eyes as if I was about to cry. He slid an additional two thousand dollars to his side of the table, leaving the smallest pile for Debbie.

"I'm sorry, I know this is hard for you," he said. The money now safely in his grasp, he put an arm around Debbie's shoulder.

I leaned my head into him, smelling his expensive aftershave.

Like him, I'd heard the footsteps on the outside stairs.

In best heroine fashion, I laid my hand against his manly chest.

Vincent came through the door.

Grant jumped up as if we were doing more than just a comforting arm around the shoulder. "I thought you were going to wait out in the parking lot," he growled.

Even in the dim light, I could see the red in Vincent's face.

"Sorry, I...uh...sorry. I knew you were in a hurry and didn't want to keep you…waiting," the poor puppy stammered out. "I'll wait downstairs." He hastily left the room.

I stood up. "Thank you, Grant. You've been very kind to me." Steeling myself, I leaned into him and kissed his cheek. "But I know you're also a very busy man, and I don't want to take advantage of your kindness."

He smiled at me, perhaps even a genuine smile at me not being a clinging type of woman who mired him down.

He scooped the money into his briefcase, then took my hand and led me down the stairs.

"I wish I weren't so busy," he said as we got to the parking lot.

"It's part of who you are. I don't want you to change."

I just want you in jail.

I smiled at Vincent as he loaded my little car with more of Nature's Beautiful Gift. Grant helped again, insisting that it wasn't something a woman like me should do.

I let them. It would save me a dry-cleaning bill for Debbie's pink wardrobe.

Grant again kissed me good-bye on the cheek, this time resting a hand on my waist and letting it slide toward my breast as if he had permission to touch there, only stopping as if suddenly remembering that we were in a parking lot.

Vincent was staring.

I got in my car and drove away as quickly as I could.

Back at my office the first thing I did was strip off the pink clothes and take a shower. The smell of Grant's expensive aftershave was causing me to gag.

CHAPTER TWENTY-FIVE

L ydia blew me off. *This week won't work,* she texted, the coward. *Maybe next week. I'll let you know.*

I met Rafe in another parking lot up on Carrolton, one that was still desolate. I claimed it was to update him, but it was mostly to dump the piles of NBG boxes on him. All the weight was affecting my gas mileage.

Grant was truly a busy man. I heard nothing from him.

"Maybe you should call him," Rafe called me to suggest, the first hint his Dallas clients weren't bottomless pits of money.

"He's playing with me, let him play a bit longer." I would be happy to never see Grant Walters again in my life. His encore might be having Vincent walk in on us actually doing it, and I wanted no part of that.

I had to spend a month in Alabama tracking down heirs. Okay, it was just a week, but because it was Alabama, it felt like a month.

Cordelia again had a needle in her arm and chemicals in her body. This time she made it home before throwing up.

In the evening, when I was taking the garbage out, Torbin came over carrying a big pot.

"Crawfish bisque," he said. "It's the best apology I could make."

It's a hard dish to make; you have to stuff the crawfish heads and cook for a while.

I put my arms around him and gave him a hug. I didn't take the pot.

"Thanks, but…this isn't the right time."

"You're turning down my crawfish bisque?"

"Right now, yeah. It was a chemo day. Cordelia can't do much more than a few spoonfuls of white rice. Even strong smells can set her off."

He put the pot down on the sidewalk. "Bad timing on my part. I've missed you—both of you."

"I missed you, too. Both of you. Only the timing is bad. Everything else…is okay."

"Andy's hand looks fine. I think he kind of likes the scar. He certainly uses it as an excuse not to chop veggies."

"Did you get the job?"

"No, they were nice, but it was between me and someone with fifty years of HIV experience and who speaks Spanish. I'll keep looking. Andy now has work with coverage, so we're much better off. Maybe it's time for drag queens to unionize."

"Maybe it is. I could hire you. You could work under my license, join one of the professional associations and get insurance through them. It costs, but it's a group rate."

"Drag queen detective. Has a nice ring to it. Let me cogitate on it."

"Cordelia has good days between when they actually pump the stuff in her. She can probably eat most anything that's not fried in about a week."

"I'll make it again," Torbin said as he picked up the pot.

"No, you won't. We're going to all the restaurants we've been meaning to go to. Join us."

He smiled at me. "Done. Let me pick the next one. You can't even know which one it is."

I gave him another hug and agreed, then went back inside to see if Cordelia was up for a little rice.

The next day, I took Rafe's advice and had Debbie call Grant. It went to his voice mail. By the end of the day he hadn't called back.

So much for special.

The day ended and it was time to go home to a quiet evening of cats in the lap, a roasted chicken—light on the pepper for Cordelia—for dinner and early to bed.

The next morning as I was fumbling to put my key into the lock at my office, my cell phone rang. I dropped the keys on the ground and left them there to answer my phone.

But it wasn't the phone now in my hand ringing. I quickly dug through my briefcase to get Debbie's phone, barely managing to answer before it went to voice mail.

Maybe I was special enough to get a call the next morning.

"This Debbie?" It was a woman's voice. Nope, still not special.

"Yes, yes, this is. Who is this?"

"It doesn't matter who I am. What matters is that I have information for you. Get ready to jot this down." She wasn't impolite, her voice sounded professionally warm. But she wasn't concerned where I was or what I was doing—I needed to write down the information right now.

"Let me find a pen," I said as scrabbled in my briefcase for a pen and scratch paper.

"Tonight at eight thirty."

"Got it," I said. I finally located a pen and grabbed the first blank piece of paper that came to hand. I hoped it wasn't my Entergy bill.

She gave me an address in New Orleans East, off Lake Forest Boulevard. "You're going to have to park on the street, the lot still has a chain link fence around it, but you can get through at one end," she instructed. "This is for your sister, right? She needs to be there and you need to bring the money. You have to pay up front before you see the doctor."

"Okay, we'll be there."

"You can come with her, but only she can go in, got that?"

"Yes, of course. Who are you? What's the doctor's name?"

She ignored my questions, repeated the address and reminded me to bring the money, and hung up.

If there weren't enough glaring warning lights, this was just another. No legit doctor would operate this way. I suspected it was either someone who lost his license for selling too many diet pills or, more likely, someone in a white coat who had a vague idea of how to take blood pressure. Theater is largely props and suspension of disbelief. Call someone a doctor, do a few doctor things. Someone badly needs this charade to be real, and they believe enough to hand over their life savings.

I scooped my keys off the sidewalk just as a large black truck cruised by.

His was wrecked.

He could have got a new one by now.

I jammed my hand into my briefcase for my gun.

The truck kept going and turned the corner.

I hurriedly stuck my key in the door, opened it, just as quickly locked it again when I was on the other side and ran up the stairs.

I called both Joanne and Danny to see if there was any update on Dudley. Neither was available. I left messages.

Then I called Rafe.

"Lights, action, camera," he said.

"Easy for you to say."

"True. Do you trust me enough for me to come to your office? Or should we meet somewhere in public for me to wire you?"

"You think they won't check for a wire?"

"I assume they will. This is why you'll be wearing a state-of-the-art one."

"Why don't we meet at your office?"

"Because it's in Dallas and we'd have to meet at my hotel room."

Given that choice, I started to tell him my address, but he cut me off.

"I'm out front right now." Of course he'd know where I worked. He was smart enough to add, "If now's not a good time, I can come back."

I had been debating whether or not to say I had a client and wasn't free. He just edged over not being blown off. "It's a fine time, come on up."

Of course, his coming up meant my going down to unlock the door.

"Not much to steal in here," he commented on the austere lobby—which was basically enough room to fit two people and the stairs and the junked-up hallway that led to the back door.

As we chugged up those very stairs, I explained about Dudley. It was a brief explanation as by about the third flight, talking becomes punctuated by obvious breathing.

"The cops really think he might come after you?" Rafe asked just as we were on the final flight.

"The cops don't know that he won't," I answered. I waited until I was unlocking my door to continue. "He's an addict. Probably meth, from the look of his mouth. He could be crazy enough to think that if he kills me, his legal problems will go away."

"So we should be watching out for this guy as well?"

I didn't want to be baby-sat. "The police probably already have him in custody." I explained about the wreck and his need for pain meds.

"Damn, I forgot to scan the news feed to check up on you."

Enough of this. "Okay, so what are we doing tonight?"

He pulled a thick envelope out of his briefcase. "Seven thousand," he said as he tossed it on my desk. "Tell them it was all you could scrape up. That you can have more next week. The more contact we have, the more we're likely to catch Grant Walters there."

He pulled out another envelope, not as thick. "Five hundred for you up front. You get another thousand after tonight. More if we need more of your time. Bonus of ten thousand if we catch Walters."

I put the envelope in a desk drawer. Then I showed him my wardrobe for tonight. The rhinestone jeans would make another appearance; Debbie was the kind of girl who had to wear clothes more than once. Plus the new pastel pink sweater and hot pink jacket.

"That should make it easy to spot you."

"I'm playing a character," I told him. "If it was me, I'd be in black leather."

"My kind of woman," he muttered while groping in his briefcase.

"Not if you knew me better," I muttered back.

He gave me a choice of wires. The better one was a small device that I could slip into a pocket, with a mic I could attach to a brooch. The other was a watch. I opted for the watch, remembering the woman on the phone had mentioned a doctor. I didn't want to risk having anything fall out of my pocket should I have to undergo a physical.

Which I sincerely hoped was not to be the case.

We wouldn't meet again. He asked me to call him when I was about to leave and they would discreetly tail me.

Then he was gone and I was left staring at a watch—ladies' style, no less, and two envelopes. I delayed lunch long enough to count the money—but it was as he said, seven thousand in one and five hundred in the other. I put the seven thousand in another envelope, one that would only have Debbie's fingerprints on it. It wasn't likely they would check, but better safe than wishing I'd done something as simple as change envelopes.

I again went the high-calorie route for lunch, popcorn shrimp salad, so at least I got some greens. I needed to get back into the habit of bringing my lunch and sticking closer to the turkey sandwiches side of the spectrum and not the fried side. Cordelia's eating habits—no, there was no habit here—what she could eat—was affecting mine. Like I had to make up for her bland rice and oatmeal.

I called Joanne, ostensibly to find out what was happening with Dudley, but only got her voice mail. Tried the same thing with Danny and got the same result.

The only person who seemed to want to talk to me was Lydia. I'd wondered what had happened to her. I was beginning to think she'd decided ignorance was bliss and blown me off. More likely, it was hard to suspect someone she knew well and she'd had to work through her ambivalence. And she only wanted to talk briefly. "Can we meet tomorrow night at nine?" she asked.

I thought she was being a little cloak and dagger—Friday evening anywhere work-ish would be deserted, but I agreed. She was worried, and some emotions aren't worth arguing with.

I left around four. To make up for going out again in the evening, I finished all the dishes and decided on pizza for dinner. I made two batches of dough so we could do two, one bland with spinach and mild cheese and the other artichoke hearts and sun-dried tomatoes with caramelized onions.

Cordelia, in perfect timing, got home just as I finished chopping the onions and garlic.

"You know you don't have to cook every night," she said as she joined me in the kitchen.

"I do on the nights when I have to go back out."

"What for?"

"Work. Helping with surveillance," I hedged.

But it was enough for her. She nodded and went upstairs to the bedroom to change.

After we ate—she had a small slice of each—she proclaimed that she was fine vegging in front of the TV and would probably be in bed before I got back. I kissed her good-bye and left a little before seven.

I went back to my office. I didn't want to have to explain my pink clothing, so opted to change there.

Carrying a gun wouldn't do. They would certainly check for that. It wouldn't protect me much in the glove box of my car except make me feel better. There was always the possibility that I'd run into Dudley either coming or going.

A little before eight, I called Rafe. Our conversation lasted about two seconds. Then I headed downstairs, carefully locked up behind me.

The last glimmer of light was leaving the day. They had set the time to make sure it was dark.

New Orleans East is, as it name implies, in the east. It hugs the lake and is on the other side of the Industrial Canal. Left largely untouched until the 1960s, it developed into a suburban style enclave, mostly single family homes with large yards. It was badly flooded during Katrina and is still struggling to come back. The two hospitals out here hadn't reopened. Many of the businesses, especially the large scale national chains that had anchored the malls, hadn't returned.

Now, driving there at night, the devastation felt sinister. The lights were back on, but so many places were vacant and dark, as if pieces of the city had been ripped away and only a black stain remained. Just as I had entered the freeway, a dark blue SUV closed in behind me and the driver waved. Then it faded into the traffic. Now either I had lost them, or Rafe and his crew was very good. I'd given him the address so they didn't need to tail me to get there. I would give them the benefit of a doubt and assume that they would be there.

Once I exited the interstate, there were only a few other vehicles around. I drove at a steady pace, as if I belonged here and wasn't searching for a location. I'd given myself plenty of time. The last thing I wanted to do in a situation like this was to hurry.

I had to remind myself that I might need to not be Debbie, but her ill sister. Being sisters, I assumed that they both liked pink. I tried to remember the name I'd given Walters. Donna. Now I was Donna Perkins. Wait, was that her married name? No, I decided, she'd gone back to her maiden name after the divorce. And Donna had never married, so she was still Perkins.

Keeping all this straight was enough to earn me the five hundred.

As I got close, I noted they had picked a desolate area—the better to come and go without anyone watching. Only the street lights and a few distant cars offered illumination. I wondered where Rafe and his crew were. Maybe I should have spent more time checking him out, even sicced the Grannies on him. He could be double-dealing, working with Grant Walters.

The dark was spooking me, creating vampires in every dark crevice. Rafe would lose his license and his business if he helped someone like Grant Walters.

I drove past the address I had been given. It was indeed enclosed with a chain link fence, the parking lot filled with weeds growing through the cracked asphalt. One end of the building had lights on the top floor; the rest was dark.

At the first corner, I took a right, traveling past the end of the building with the lights. Trying not to slow down too much, I tried to look into the windows, but they were covered, only a diffuse glow escaping. I continued around the block, losing sight of the building behind empty houses as I turned the next corner.

The next turn brought me to a small parking lot behind the building. There had been no cars visible from the front because they were back here. I counted four. I didn't want to stop and stare, that would be too obvious if someone spotted me—Donna Perkins might have overshot and gone around the block, but she wouldn't stop and mark down license plates. One car was the expected dark SUV—the choice of criminals. Two were nondescript sedans and one, improbably, was a high-end sports car, a Lotus or Lamborghini.

Somebody—my bet was on Grant Walters—was flaunting his wealth with an adolescent wet dream.

I turned again and this time parked in front. It was 8:25. Mine was the only car there. Assuming all the gang had parked in back—four of them, unless they were thrifty crooks and carpooled, that meant that I, aka Donna Perkins—was the only client. For a few thousand dollars this didn't seem worth their while.

Or they could be smart and schedule us far enough apart to make sure there was no overlap. It might not do to have someone with AIDS chat with the cancer patient and discover they were getting exactly the same treatment.

I sat in my car for a few minutes—I was early, after all—pondering all the things that might go wrong. *They want money, not murder,* I reminded myself. The only big danger was that Rafe Gautier had totally misled me. But there was no reason to go through this scheme if he was playing me. Other than as a ruse to get me to a desolate part of destroyed

New Orleans. But then I'd have to believe in cloak and dagger that made Lydia's paranoia seem perfectly sane by comparison.

I got out of the car, following the directions to find the opening in the chain link fence.

It was at the far corner, clearly a deliberate opening, but only large enough for one person to get through. Then a long, ill-lit walk across the broken, weed-choked asphalt. But as dim as the light was, I was easily visible to anyone watching. The dim light of the lot was blocked by the building's portico. I had to pause for a moment to give my eyes a chance to adjust to the deep blackness before I could see the faint outline of a door. I scanned the façade, but it was the only place that looked like an entry.

I tried to open the door, but it was locked. Okay, this was beginning to feel more cloak and dagger than I liked. This was a lot of high security for bilking desperate people out of their money. And I had to remember that I was one of those desperate people. What would a woman dying from cancer do?

The answer that came to me was be at home sitting and dozing in front of the TV. Then I reminded myself she wasn't dying.

Why had Reginald Banks come? What would bring a young man to a place as desolate as this? *Desperation,* Cordelia had said. Medical care offered him bills he couldn't pay for treatments that never cured his illness. This was the only way out of a life of illness, an early death. One last, desperate chance.

I knocked on the door.

Waited. Then was about to knock again when it was flung open, the sudden light blinding me.

"Where is your sister?" a male voice asked.

I couldn't place the voice, then my eyes adjusted and realized I was standing in front of Grant Walters.

"Oh, Mr. Walters. I mean Grant. I didn't expect to see you here." Didn't expect, didn't want. It was time to improvise; no way I could pretend to be Debbie's sister.

"Didn't they tell you to bring your sister?"

"Yes, sir, but she's having a rough day. She asked me to do this for her and I—"

"She has to come. The patient has to meet with the doctor. You can't do it for her." He smiled at me as if he realized that was what he was expected to do. I was special, after all. "I'm sorry, but she really has to come."

"I brought the money," I said, holding up the envelope.

He grabbed it out of my hands, glanced inside, then looked at me. "Come back and bring your sister. They'll take care of you then."

I reached for the envelope, but he held it beyond my grasp. "I can't leave the money, unless I get—"

Again he cut me off. "It guarantees that we'll reserve the treatment for you when you come back. At times we run out, the demand is so great. You've paid up front."

"But I already gave you money up front—"

"That was to help get you in. With this, you're guaranteed. Just bring your sister."

He started to shut the door. I put my hand against it. "But when? When can we come back? She's not doing well."

"Someone will call you," he said.

"But wait, what are you doing here? I thought you said you weren't involved?"

"I'm not. I'm here on an unrelated manner." He shoved the door closed, leaving me in the dark, my eyes burned by the light.

I stumbled back out, going slowly over the cratered asphalt as my eyes adjusted. "Damn, damn, damn," I muttered, staying enough in character. I was sure they were watching me. I could be an upset Debbie, but I couldn't be an upset Micky Knight.

I didn't look around to see if I could spot Rafe. Debbie wouldn't be looking for anyone. She was someone about to go back to her sister to tell her she no longer had the money and she didn't have the promised treatment. Someone would call to let them know when they could come again.

"Damn," I muttered again as I got in my car. But I wasn't Debbie, it wasn't my money, and no one was desperately hoping that this would save her life.

I drove away, in a hurry, as an agitated Debbie would. I headed back to my office, wanting to get out of this desolate neighborhood as quickly as possible.

As I was coming over the High Rise, the section of I-10 that crossed the Industrial Canal, the dark blue SUV came up behind me. I assumed that he'd follow me back, but he disappeared again into traffic.

Or maybe it was just a random SUV. There certainly are enough big, dark things prowling the roadways.

I parked in front of my office, but didn't get out of my car. I was guessing that if Rafe wanted to talk, he'd follow me here. By waiting for him, I could save myself three flights up and back. Plus make sure that Dudley hadn't decided on an unplanned visit.

I'd guessed right. It took only two minutes for the blue SUV and a battered and rusted silver sedan to pull in behind me. I was prudent enough to wait until they got out, Rafe and another man from the SUV and a woman from the small car.

"This is it? Just three of you?" I asked as I exited my car.

"Left the other two watching the building. Shall we go inside? Best not to be hanging out on the street."

I agreed and opened the door, having them follow me up the stairs.

"This how you keep in shape?" the woman asked as we mounted the third landing.

"Naw, I actually exercise to stay in shape," I said as I opened my office door.

The man was about Rafe's age, mid to late forties. The woman was young, in her twenties, and read as dyke to me—or maybe short hair, black jeans, black T-shirt and jacket were giving me a false impression.

"Joe," Rafe said nodding at the man, "And Gem," at the woman.

"The J/G team," I noted. "Well, I assume you got most of it from the wire. Why do you think Grant was there?"

"My guess? He's picked up feistiness in the fictitious Debbie—you. And he wants to ride her."

"Pretty sick," I said. "He is certainly playing a game. It's the same crap; why not just give it to me? Why make me produce a sick sister?"

"Because he can," Joe answered. "He's made his money, now he wants to play with people."

"'Flies to wanton boys,'" I quoted.

"Exactly," Rafe said. "You have to jump through his hoops, bring your sick and dying sister to him if you want the stuff."

"Except I don't have any sisters, let alone any who are ill."

We both glanced at Gem. Way too young and healthy.

"Let me think about it," Rafe said. "Run it by some legal eagles.

It might be enough that we have a good idea of what's going on there. Might be able to get someone to raid it."

"So what do I do?"

"Keep that cell phone with you. Let me know the minute they call. I'll figure out something from there." He pulled an envelope out of his pocket and tossed it in my direction.

I caught it and peeked inside. The rest of the money. "You don't need to pay me—it wasn't like we accomplished what we set out to do."

"You took the big risk. You get the bucks. Walters wants to play with you—Debbie. That just might be his undoing." He stood up. "We've had enough fun for tonight."

Joe and Gem nodded. I caught her looking at me. Not in the way a straight woman would look.

They trooped out of my office and I followed them down the stairs.

Rafe and Joe got in the SUV. Gem hung back.

Once their engine started she said, "I like older women," and looked me up and down.

I smiled. The ego boost was nice. "So do I. I have one at home waiting for me."

"Had to try," she said good-naturedly as she got in her junker car.

I watched just long enough for them to pull away from the curb, then went back upstairs. Yes, indeed workout by stair. I needed to get out of my pink attire. I took off the watch wire and placed it in my desk drawer, along with the envelope of money. I could deal with everything tomorrow. It was time to get home and not think about Debbie and her problems.

CHAPTER TWENTY-SIX

When I'd arrived home last night, Cordelia was already in bed asleep. She didn't rouse when I got in next to her. I had stared at her in the dim bedroom light. A clump of hair was beside her on the pillow. I gently scooped it up and put it in the trash. She still didn't rouse. Only her soft breathing let me know she was alive.

I again fixed her breakfast, but she only ate a little. She took some chicken soup with her for lunch, but that was all.

I left soon after she did. The cats stared at me, as if they couldn't understand my shifted hours. I was supposed to stay for another hour or two in the morning before I left. To make up, I gave them some treats.

Then I was at my office staring at the walls and trying to make sense of the various balls I was figuratively juggling.

The NBG investigation seemed at a dead end. I, or should I say we, had to produce a sick sister in the next day or two—someone who could reasonably be my sister, who could reasonably fake ill, and who had enough of a law enforcement/private eye background to pull it off. I had used some of the bare outlines of Cordelia's illness as the basis of the story, but there was no way I'd involve her. It couldn't be anyone actually sick, the physical demands would be too much. The only option on my end was to consider asking Joanne if she'd like to moonlight. Maybe borrow some forms from Cordelia to give her the appropriate paperwork. But even that I had to consider and consider again before suggesting it to Rafe. This wasn't Joanne's investigation—plus she was a cop and that meant she had to play by the rules. We did, too, but we have different referees to answer to.

Dudley seemed to have disappeared. Maybe rich daddy gave him a one-way ticket to Bangkok and told him to stay there for a few years. Or maybe Prejean didn't want to be involved in whatever Dudley might do, so he'd paid for the ticket. Probably Greyhound to L.A.

Then there was the mess with insurance paperwork at Cordelia's office. That one, at least, should be easily solved. I'd meet with Lydia tonight. She'd show me what she'd found. Unless I was way wrong, I'd tell her to go to the authorities. After that, no more promises to not tell Cordelia. She needed to know what she might be involved in.

My phone rang.

Mr. Charles Williams. "Hey, just wanted to check on how things are going? You missed out on a good pot of gumbo."

I didn't show my relief. I might be able to make a mild chicken gumbo Cordelia could eat, but other than that, gumbo would not be darkening our door anytime soon. "That's too bad. Guess I'll have to make do with my own. There's not much I can update you on about the McConkles' case at the moment," I said.

"That's too bad. But I got good news. My nephew called me. Pissant needed a job, so he was beating the bushes. Including calling his uncle."

"That is good news. He call you recently?"

"Just yesterday. Set him up working with Fletcher and his wife. They could use an extra hand now that they're so busy."

"That's great. Really good to hear." He had no idea how good. Clearly my suspicion about his nephew being Reginald Banks was wrong. I wondered what else I was wrong about.

"Yeah, so I'm hoping with him working for them and all, if you find more stuff that says that Nature's whatever is crap, then you can tell them and maybe they'll influence him. You oughta come by the work site some day. I'll do my gumbo even."

"You manage a pretty mean bribe, Mr. Williams. Once I have some more info, I'll set up a time to join them."

"Just gumbo, not a bribe. You really oughta check this place out. Six-car garage—his regular car is Porsche. My nephew couldn't stop talking about it last night."

"Too posh for my taste, but I'll let you know when I have more to report. Sorry, my other line is ringing." With that little white lie, I politely got him off the phone. I was happy about his nephew mainly because it spared me the mess of either avoiding his request or telling him his nephew was dead. Once Rafe came up with a resolution of how to handle Grant Walters, I'd have more to tell the McConkles. If they were willing to have Mr. Charles Williams there, fine by me.

Then, as if fate didn't want me lying, my phone rang again.

"Is this Michele Knight?" I didn't recognize the voice.

"Yes, this is."

"I'm Sylvia Wayne, Jennifer Godwin's nurse. She's Cordelia's doctor—"

"What's wrong?" I cut her off.

"She asked me to call you—"

"What's wrong?" I demanded.

"She fainted. She'd come in to see Dr. Godwin, to say how tired she was and then collapsed." She hurriedly added, "She's all right, alert and talking now. They admitted her just to check things out."

"Where is she?"

She rattled off a room number, clearly assuming I'd know they'd taken Cordelia to the hospital just across the street from the doctors' office.

I was out of the office so quickly, I was halfway there before wondering if I'd locked the downstairs door. Or the upstairs one. Everything was a blur and I couldn't remember. It didn't matter, I couldn't turn back.

She's okay, alert and talking, I had to remind myself to not break every traffic law on the books. But every slow car, every red traffic light was a trial.

I didn't even bother to look for parking on the street, just used the pay lot.

"Can I help you?" a blur in scrub greens asked me.

I had been almost running. "I'm here to see my—" then I wondered what word to use with this stranger. The truth, there was no time for anything else. "My partner, Cordelia James. She's in room five-eleven."

The stranger pointed me in the direction I had been heading. I barely remembered a thanks.

Then I was at the door and into her room.

She was sitting up, sipping orange juice. I thought there would be some sea change from this morning. But she looked as she had when she left, save for the setting, a bland, boring room, white sheets and blanket, muted green walls.

"Hey," I called softly.

She looked over at me. "I'm okay," she said as if apologizing. "You didn't need to rush down here. Probably my electrolytes are unbalanced, so I got faint. They're just checking me out."

It's just routine, no big deal, don't worry. Was she trying to convince me or herself?

I crossed to the side of her bed and took her free hand. "It's one of those boring, read-through-financial-records cases. It doesn't take much to distract me from those."

A nurse entered to take her vital signs and I retreated to the chair on the far side of the bed. After he left, she again apologized for the fuss, seemingly caught between wanting me here and feeling guilty for causing this disruption. I considered leaving. Maybe it would be better for her if I wasn't here, but I knew there was no way I could go back to my office and get anything done. As guilty as she felt, Cordelia seemed to like having me here, to have someone to take care of her, from helping her maneuver the IV pole to go to the bathroom to running out and getting ice chips.

They wanted to run tests, make sure she wasn't anemic. To be sure that her fainting was just being weakened from the chemo and eating so much less and pushing to maintain a normal life. She would probably be here over the weekend.

I was so preoccupied with Cordelia I almost forgot about agreeing to meet Lydia.

I was saved having to lie to her—or blow off Lydia—by her insisting that I go home. "I'm falling asleep and it's stupid for you to stay here and watch me snore. So, go home, please."

I assured her I'd be back bright and early in the morning and left, only a little late for my meeting.

It was just across the street and a little down the block. It was a dark night, the moon and stars obscured by clouds. The bright fluorescence of the hospital and the surrounding buildings cast little light into the shadows.

I entered via the parking garage, using the stairs instead of the elevator. Three flights up to the walkway from the garage to the building and another two flights to their office. Lydia wanted to be cloak and dagger, so I would honor her wishes—and make up for my fried lunches. No one was around, at least not anyone willing to climb stairs.

"I'm sorry I'm…" I said as I came into the lobby, but no one was there. I looked at my watch. Okay, I was fifteen minutes late. Maybe she had assumed that I wouldn't show because of Cordelia. I pulled out my phone to look at it. No call, no text message.

I waited five minutes, then texted her, *Hey, I'm here. Sorry, I was a little late. Are you still around?*

As if on cue, the elevator rumbled to life, startling in this quiet space. I listened to its slow assent. At the last minute, I ducked back into the stairwell. Lydia had to have been standing right by the elevator with her phone in her hand, otherwise there wasn't enough time for her to have read my text and be almost here.

Maybe the quiet was spooking me. Who else could it be except Lydia?

Someone too tall and too flat-chested to be her. I had only a brief glimpse through the crack in the door. Probably a man, but he was wearing a ball cap and the hood of a sweatshirt over it, and dark glasses. Whoever it was, he had keys. I heard him open the door and go into the office.

Perhaps Lydia was right to be cloak and dagger, I thought as I quietly crept down the stairs. While it wasn't yet hot here, a baseball cap and a hooded sweatshirt was overkill. Not to mention the dark glasses. That shrieked someone who didn't want to be recognized and was going out of his way to make sure the security cameras didn't get a good picture. Not the kind of thug I wanted to deal with.

I moved as quickly as I could, but I had to both be quiet and also move at a normal enough pace that if I ran into anyone I wouldn't seem suspicious. I had to pause at the landing by the bridge as I heard voices. I remained in the stairwell as they waited for the elevator on the other side of the door. People remember the unusual, and someone using the stairs might be enough for me to be noticed. The elevator finally came, they moved on, and no one was around to see me cross back to the parking garage. As I headed for my car, I pondered what had happened. There were plenty of doctors and nurses who were drug addicts and might be stopping by the office for a late-night fix. If the drugs came up missing, they wouldn't want their face on the cameras or to have been seen by the security guard. The stranger clearly had access—there had been no fumbling with the keys. That indicated someone who was a regular, not the boyfriend or girlfriend who had borrowed—willingly or not so—some staff member's keys and access codes. Besides drugs, people had affairs. With a wife/spouse/partner at home, a deserted office could be a rendezvous place.

Or maybe another private eye who had been hired to check out some hinky insurance reports.

All those explanations were possible. It was just coincidence that this person showed up at around the same time I was supposed to meet Lydia. Except I don't like coincidences that rile my intuition. My text message, the timing of the elevator, and that my instincts told me to hide, not wait for the person I was expecting to meet. Throw into that it seemed odd for Lydia not to be there and have made no effort to contact me.

When I'd got here in the middle of the day, the garage was pretty full, but now with the doctors' offices closed, it was empty. I'd parked on the next-to-top floor and there were few cars around. I looked at my phone. She hadn't replied to my text. *It's late*, I told myself, *time to get out of this empty area. I'll catch up with her later and we can sort it out.*

I got in my car. Before I pulled out I texted her number, *Hey, sorry we couldn't meet. When do you want to reschedule?* It bothered me that she hadn't replied. I wanted to see if something that needed an answer would get her attention. She had gone to a lot of trouble to set up this meeting.

I heard a vehicle start on another floor. Again my instincts kicked in and I slid down in my seat to make it look like no one was in my car. I kept my eyes on the rearview mirror, not even sure what I might see. I heard the rush of tires, someone going too fast for this space and a black SUV zoomed by in my mirror. It was speeding and my angle was too extreme for me to get more than that. Big, dark, I couldn't even tell what make it was.

My phone chimed with the text message sound. *Everything is okay. We don't need to meet*, from Lydia.

Now I was annoyed. If it was okay and no meeting was required, why hadn't she bothered to tell me that before I'd come here? She couldn't have known I was right across the street with Cordelia. If I hadn't gone on her wild goose chase, I'd be home by now.

"Fuck you," I muttered.

I heard another car start. I wondered if it was Lydia. Or just another odd coincidence. Cordelia had mentioned that she was driving some hybrid car—a blue Prius. I again slid down in my seat.

Again the car was going too fast, taking no account that anyone else might be pulling out. This time it was a blur of red, some fancy sports car. I waited until I could no longer hear the roar of its exhaust before sitting up and starting my car.

But instead of heading to the exit, I kept going up to the top floor. Why had those two cars been in such a hurry to get away? Probably because they wanted to get home in time for a TV show, but I was already here, my curiosity was piqued. This way I could have "closure" on my snooping. If the top floor was empty I could go home and not wonder about this ever again.

As my car nosed up around the last curve, it seemed that the TV show was the mostly likely reason. I didn't see any vehicles, no one was up there. But then in the far corner I saw there was one car. Probably someone else who had come like I had, when it was parked up, and ended up in the last spot.

It was a small car.

A blue car.

A blue Prius.

Phone. Gun. Flashlight. The gun in one hand, the flashlight in the other. The phone was relegated to my pocket.

It was still most likely that I was overreacting, tired. Just yesterday I'd seen two red Mini Clubmans parked next to each other. There had to be more than one blue Prius in the area. And even if this was Lydia's car, she might have had some emergency to deal with—either professionally or personally.

I looked carefully around before getting out of my car, but could see no one. I left the keys in the ignition, not even properly parking. Using the flashlight, I quickly scanned the parking lot, but the dark corners were empty save for a couple of soda cans and the contents of someone's ashtray.

Now I turned my light on the Prius. Someone was in the car.

I didn't move and neither did she.

No one in a big empty parking lot who has just had a bright light shined on them doesn't move. Unless they're setting a trap.

I edged closer. Still no movement.

A trap? Asleep? Dead?

I circled around from the back of the car to the driver's side, still keeping a good ten feet away.

Now I got a clear look at the person. Lydia. Slumped over the steering wheel.

"Lydia!"

She didn't answer.

"Lydia!" I called again. But now I was close enough to see the bullet hole in the back of her head and knew she would never answer.

I shoved my gun in my waistband, barely remembering to click the safety on, and grabbed my phone, hastily dialing 911.

I told the operator my location and my emergency. For now I kept it brief. I'd been at the hospital with someone, returned to the parking lot, and found someone slumped over in her car.

But it wasn't that simple, nowhere near that simple. The shot was a professional execution. One bullet to the brain. Her purse had been emptied on the seat next to her. I was betting that was to make it seem like a robbery. Low-life thugs can certainly shoot their robbery victims, but not with this accuracy and precision.

Given the location, the paramedics were here almost immediately.

In the two minutes it had taken them to arrive, I had seen all I needed to see. Lydia was clearly dead, her eyes open and glassy, a massive amount of blood soaked into her seat. She was probably dead the minute the trigger was pulled. Her skin was warm to the touch; if it had the faint beat of life, she could be just sleeping. She hadn't been dead long.

I moved away from them, properly parking my car on the far side, out of the way. I couldn't leave, not until the police got here, but I had no interest in watching the futile efforts of the EMTs.

Several police cars arrived, sirens and flashing lights. I wondered why they needed them to spiral up seven flights to the top of a parking garage. One patrol officer asked me two yes-or-no questions—had I found the body and would I stay until the detective arrived.

I replied yes to both and then was left to wait. More cars arrived.

I didn't recognize the detective who ambled over. But I did know his attitude—he seemed like he didn't want to be here, and because he didn't want to be here, he would make everyone else join him in his misery.

He didn't introduce himself. "You're damn lucky. This is why we tell people it's not good to be alone in dangerous places. This was a robbery gone wrong. You could have easily been dead in your car."

I'd been debating how much I wanted to let the police know. Selfishly, how involved I wanted to be. But also that this was turning into a complicated mess. Just my luck to have a police detective who clearly didn't like complicated messes when he was the one to catch the case. He seemed to have already latched onto the quick and easy explanation—a robbery gone sour.

"What the hell were you doing up here anyway?" he demanded, the first question he'd asked after his lecture.

"I was with my partner over in the hospital," I explained.

"Partner?" He squinted his eyes at me. "Business partner?"

"The person I live with."

"What's wrong with him?"

I didn't see how that had anything to do with this investigation. "Why do you need to know that?"

"I ask the questions here. You don't like it, we can go downtown."

Power mad bastard. "She has cancer," I said tersely.

"What, you queer?"

I stared at him. Most of the NOPD are pretty cool. They deal with Mardi Gras and Southern Decadence with aplomb, letting the leather boys pose with them for pictures. I get the one remaining homophobe. "I guess if you're going to ask questions like that we're going downtown. I need to stop by the internal affairs guys anyway."

He stared at me. Finally backed down, "What time did you find the body?"

I glanced at my watch. "An hour ago, around nine thirty."

"Can you be more exact?"

"Nine thirty-one."

"What did you do?"

"Called nine-one-one."

"Anything else?"

"Waited for the EMTs."

"When did they get here?"

"Nine thirty-three."

"You see anyone around here?"

"When I was getting in my car, two cars from up here came by. A dark SUV and a red sports car."

"You get a look at the people driving them?"

"No, they were going far faster than they should have been and I just glimpsed them in my rearview mirror."

"You weren't parked on this floor?"

"No, one level down."

"So what where you doing up here?"

"Got turned around and missed the exit."

"And just happened to notice a dead woman in the car?"

"She wasn't driving fast. I wondered about those two cars speeding out of here, so I looked carefully," I explained. It was as close to the truth as I felt I could get with him.

"Next time you might want to curb your curiosity. You almost walked into a bad robbery. These punks don't give a damn who they kill. They probably got twenty dollars from her." He started stalking away from me.

"Pretty good shots for punks."

He turned back. "What the fuck's that supposed to mean?"

"Shot at the base of the skull. Professional execution."

"You been watching too many crime shows." He turned away and kept going.

I could pull out my license to indicate I knew more than the average Josie parked in front of *Law & Order*. But Nameless Asshole didn't want a complicated case, and I would get the opposite of thanks if I pointed out the holes in his robbery gone wrong theory.

"Am I free to go?" I yelled.

He didn't bother answering.

I took that as a yes. They could stop me if they really didn't want me to leave.

They didn't. No one even glanced my way as I drove off.

CHAPTER TWENTY-SEVEN

I was beyond tired by the time I got home. It had been an emotionally exhausting day. I shut my brain off, helped by gulping half a glass of Scotch and fell into bed, only pausing long enough to toss off my clothes. My teeth could survive missing one brushing.

But the alarm clock woke me early—I had set it—and the events of yesterday loomed over me.

Cordelia was in the hospital. I needed to get up there and see her.

Lydia was dead.

Lydia hadn't sent the text.

I had the kind of hangover that doesn't come with alcohol. In retrospect, I should have just jumped through whatever hoops Nameless Asshole would have required for me to give him all the info. Lydia and I were supposed to meet last night to look at records and see if someone was cooking the books. She hadn't showed. She had been what I thought was paranoid about secrecy, worried that someone might find out she suspected. Someone wanted her silenced.

Someone had walked up to her car, put a gun against her skull, and pulled the trigger. It had probably happened so quickly, she had no time to react. If she was lucky, she had no time to think and realize she was about to get killed. It had been a cool, professional hit.

If she had died shortly before I found her, then it was likely that the two cars I saw had something to do with it. If she had been dead for a while, then maybe it was just coincidence that they left around the same time. She was parked in a dark area—or had the light been destroyed? I saw her because I was looking. Most people would have just gone to their cars and left.

A dark SUV and a red sports car. I had seen a dark SUV and a red car out in New Orleans East. No, it wasn't the same. The car out in the east had been a very high-end car. Even though I'd managed only a glimpse, this one was not nearly as fancy.

And how could these two cases be connected anyway?

But they could. Reginald Banks had been a patient with this group and he had taken The Cure. For the kind of money he was making, Grant Walters had to be doing more than NBG and selling The Cure. How about insurance fraud? That would be a moneymaker.

He would have the connections to bring the kind of professional who killed Lydia. He could even be that kind of killer. His eyes were hard and flat, as if people were only to be used or shoved out of his way.

The only thing that didn't make sense was the text. That was amateur. Someone panicking and hoping that a few words could make it all go away.

I grabbed my phone and replied, *Okay, cool. Glad things are okay. You have a great weekend.*

It was a long shot—the phone was probably in a landfill by now, but I wanted them to think their ruse had worked. Meth heads like Dudley were bad enough, I didn't need a pro after me as well.

I felt numb, surrounded by circling events that felt like they were spinning out of control.

I forced myself to eat a good breakfast, resisting the urge to add a Bloody Mary to it.

Cavalry. That's what I needed.

Really wanting that drink, I picked up the phone and dialed Joanne. She wouldn't be happy that I'd made a mess for her to clean up—withholding information from an asshole. But it was info the cops needed to have, otherwise Lydia would be another victim of a senseless robbery and no one would look any further.

"What?" she answered the phone.

I gave as brief an explanation as I could. The silence when I finished didn't bode well.

"What the fuck were you thinking?" Not giving me time to answer, she said, "Look, I'm in Baton Rouge, I'll deal with it Monday when I'm back in the office."

"But…"

"The woman is dead. Nothing is going to bring her back. You made a bad decision to not tell him everything. I'm not going to upend my life to make up for your bad decision. Didn't want to talk to that detective? I don't blame you—if it's who I'm thinking of, he is a major asshole. But you can do what other citizens do and call someone else. Nothing is stopping you from doing that."

"Okay. Got it," I said. She had a point, not one I wanted to concede.

"Look, I'm sorry. But…I just can't do it all, okay?"

"Yeah, I know." I did know—we were all stretched too thin—she could be here or with Alex in Baton Rouge. I had taken a case, then another case, and somehow stepped off the ledge and Cordelia had cancer. Pulled too tight and in too many directions.

"I'll see you Monday morning and we'll take care of it," she offered.

"Thanks. You didn't even need to answer the phone. I'll see you then." When we hung up I realized I didn't know if she was with Alex or had some other reason for being there. I hoped it was for Alex.

If you can't have the cavalry you wanted, you went with the cavalry that was available. I called Rafe. He didn't answer. Probably too early in the morning for him.

That left me staring at my hands, wondering what the hell to do next.

Go see Cordelia. Pretend that none of this is happening.

I stopped at a florist on the way there and got a big flower arrangement. Every hospital room needed something to brighten it up. I also went Uptown and ran through the grocery store. I got her some cut-up fresh fruit, a really good chocolate bar, and some magazines to read. Maybe I was being nice; or maybe I was being guilty at all the things I was withholding from her.

Temporarily, I reminded myself as I looked for parking on the street. It would be a long time before I'd park in the garage again. She would know soon enough that Lydia was dead, and I'd have to tell her my part in everything. But maybe it would wait until Monday. We could have a weekend with a calm surface.

"Hi, a stranger bringing gifts," I said as I entered her room.

She smiled at the flowers, at the same time saying, "You didn't need to do that." But her smile won the battle, especially when I produced the fruit and the chocolate.

She shook her head, but opened the wrapper and took a chunk.

"Chocolate on Saturday. Let's make it a rule from now on," she said. Then she prudently put the candy away and nibbled on the fruit.

We didn't talk much, mostly it was enough that I was here and could see her, how she was doing. Maybe I needed it, but she seemed better than yesterday. She pointed to the IV tube; it was making up for her lack of appetite.

The day was punctuated by nurses coming by to check her vital signs, our occasional talk.

Rafe called me back to say that he'd flown to Dallas on Friday evening to check on some things and was on an early morning flight tomorrow. We could connect then. I'd stepped out of the room to take his phone call.

As long as Cordelia didn't hear about Lydia, I wasn't going to mention it. She needed to focus on herself and getting better.

But I couldn't help thinking about Lydia and wondering what she had wanted to show me. What was hidden in those records across the street?

In the late afternoon, Cordelia's doctor came by. They were waiting on a few more tests, but she could probably go home tomorrow. I did another food run after that, getting her a fancy smoked turkey sandwich with avocado. Also a very good dark chocolate bar. And some fruit. Her appetite seemed to be better—maybe because it had been a while since the chemo, so I wanted her to eat while she could.

After supper—the one the hospital delivered—she told me to go home. But I stayed for another hour. Mostly to be with her. Partly because I was considering not going straight home.

"Do you want me to take your clothes home? Bring you clean stuff?" I offered as I was getting ready to leave.

"Would you? I'd appreciate that. Just take everything. That way I don't need to worry about carting home my purse and briefcase tomorrow."

"Not a problem." I smiled at her and kissed her good night.

The last place I wanted to go was back into that garage and office building. So why was I rooting through Cordelia's briefcase to get her keys and access card?

Because there had been something in those files worth killing to protect. It was likely they'd disposed of whatever it was yesterday. But they might have assumed that with Lydia out of the way, they had time. Maybe even with her out of the way and her death written off to a chance robbery, they were in the clear.

They wouldn't expect me to be able to get into the building at all and certainly not late on a Saturday night. The sooner I—or anyone, but I seemed to be the only one available—took a look, the more likely I'd find something.

Lydia had died. Cordelia, even inadvertently, was involved.

I'd be quick; I'd be careful. I put her stuff in my car, keeping the keys and swipe card. I also stuffed some latex gloves and a small flashlight in my pocket, put on my holster under my jacket, and took my gun out of my glove compartment. That and my phone, in the other pocket, were my protection.

I again entered through the garage, but this time went up the stairs and carefully scanned each floor looking for red sports cars and dark SUVs. I saw a number of the latter, but closer inspection revealed a toddler seat in one, a dog blanket in another, a rainbow flag on a third one. Of the ones that didn't so clearly eliminate themselves, they seemed the wrong shape or size; the one I'd seen was big and brutish.

I took the stairs back down to the bridge into the office building, listening carefully before opening the door. No one was around. From there I took the stairs up to the floor where the office was, again listening carefully before entering the elevator lobby. Again, no sound.

I held there for a minute, listening for any noise. First from the elevators, then with my ear against the office door, in case anyone was there. Still quiet, no sound.

I took a deep breath, then put the key in the lock. Cordelia hadn't mentioned an alarm, so I was hoping they relied on multiple keys and access points. Now was not the time to ask her.

I opened the door and stepped inside. It was dim, only a few lights left on. No alarm sounded. It was lame, but if someone caught me here, I'd claim Cordelia left her house keys here and needed them. Very lame.

I'd only been here once. I tried to remember the layout of the space. Latex glove time. My fingerprints would be on Cordelia's keys—she'd given them to me, after all. But nowhere else here.

On the first door I came to, I gently tried the knob. It opened to a sparse exam room. The next two were also unlocked and also exam rooms. Across the hall from them was a small reception cubby and, next to it, a waiting room.

I didn't want to linger, certainly couldn't stay here long enough to check every room. When she'd retrieved the charts, Lydia had turned to the left on her way to get them. I quickly bypassed the exam area and went back to the door to the conference room and used that as my point of reference.

From there the first door was a bathroom. But the next was locked, with a door swipe pad. I used Cordelia's. It was an office. A messy office, with piles of paper on the desk and the floor. Only the chair behind the desk wasn't covered. On it was placed a note—clearly the lone place that it would be noticed—*Dr. Hackler, Mr. Bernstein from your bank called. He needs an answer ASAP.*

Dr. Hackler? I searched my memory. Ron Hackler, the aloof one from Ole Miss. A bank calling. Did he need money? But his office was a mess. I would need a lot more time than I had and some idea of what it was I was looking for. In truth this was a fishing expedition, with some vague hope of turning up something.

I closed his door, making sure that it locked.

The next was also an office, but almost as opposite from Ron's as it could be. The desk was neat, only one small pile of journals in the far corner. This was clearly Brandon Kellogg's office. The walls were framed with his diplomas and certifications, several fishing trophies, and a picture of a blond woman, presumably his wife, and two equally blond boys. Nature was either generous or she'd paid for her bustline. And probably her perfect white teeth and blond hair. He was a doctor; he could afford a good-looking wife. Cordelia was also a doctor, so maybe I was misjudging him. Perhaps she was a cardiologist and he loved her for her brain.

But I was wasting time here. His taste in women wasn't my concern.

I exited his office, again carefully locked his door.

Third try was the charm. I'd found the file room. First line to cast was to look for the two names I knew—Reginald Banks and Eugenia aka Eugene Hopkins.

Reginald still had a file. I quickly glanced through it, most of the words a foreign language to me. But he was listed as deceased, on the day he died. I couldn't find any indication that his insurance company had declined treatment. I did find a sheet that read *pt. contacted, att. to reschedule, pt. will call later.* I flipped back to the sheet before. It was a list of notes from his last visit, another flip back and another visit. Then another flip to another visit. The notes from this one were identical to the notes in the first, as if every few visits, they could just be recycled. I checked through all the visit notes. They skipped in irregular patterns, but every third to fifth visit, the notes were almost identical, just the dates changed. I also noticed a crease on the top of the page, like a bent paper clip had held it. The crease carried through several pages. It wasn't on the page with the note, but then was on the page following. The note about trying to contact him had been added, slipped in between two other pages.

I placed the file back where I found it and searched for Eugenia's file. According to her file she was still in treatment, had been there last week. As I put her file back I realized how difficult it would be to sort this all out. If the records said someone was here, the only way to disprove that was to talk to each individual, one by one. And even then you'd need to speak to enough of them to prove that it wasn't just someone misremembering, but a pattern of concocted visits and insurance payments.

There's a reason I didn't go into insurance fraud, I thought. I randomly grabbed another file, wondering if anything would stand out—like the repeated notes in Reginald's files. After glancing through ten files, I did notice one thing: no patients left the practice—at least none of these ten. Especially in post-Katrina New Orleans, that alone was odd—people moved all the time. I'd switched most of my doctors since half of them hadn't come back and the other half had moved to either the north shore or out in the suburbs. For some it took me two or three tries to find someone I liked—and who took my insurance.

The eleventh file showed a glaring mistake—a chart note signed by Cordelia in what was clearly not her handwriting.

That was my fear, that whoever was doing this would be willing to implicate the innocent to cover his or her tracks.

There was a faint rumble in the background. The air-conditioning system? No, that had clicked on and off several times. The elevator?

I hastily shoved the file back in its place, then locked the file room. This was a multistory building with ten to fifteen offices on every floor. What were the odds that they were coming here?

Given that they killed people, ones I couldn't take a chance on.

I didn't dare risk going out of the office as I might run into them at the elevators. If these were the people who had killed Lydia, they weren't likely to fall for my lame excuse. I couldn't hide in any of the offices or the file room; those were the likely places they would go.

I wished I knew where Cordelia's office was. It would be safe there since I could be sure she wasn't coming to visit.

Except they might enter it to plant more phony incriminating evidence.

The exam rooms. I could only hope that they wouldn't check exam rooms—unless this was an affair and they were into the kinky stuff.

I headed for the first room, the one closest to the door. I had just got the door shut and taken one deep breath when I heard a key in the lock. Sometimes, I hate it when I'm right.

Maybe it was the cleaning crew.

But the person who entered was quiet and didn't turn on any lights. From the stealthy footfalls, it was just one person. I heard him—or her—shuffle by. It sounded like he went to the file room, but I couldn't be sure and I didn't dare look.

Now I had another quandary—did I stay here until this silent person left or did I try and get out? And if it was the latter, should I be quiet or just make a run for it?

I heard a sound like a copy machine. The machine had been just outside the file room, which was on a side hallway. It would be out of sightlines from here, and if I was lucky—and quiet—it would cover any sound I would make. There was a white lab coat hanging on the back of the door. I put it on. That, at least, would make it seem more like I belonged here. I caught a faint lingering perfume. Cordelia. Appropriate.

I cautiously cracked open the door. A weak light spilled from the conference room hallway. Edging out of the room, I pulled the door almost shut, but didn't want to risk the snick of the catch.

"Goddamn it," came from the hallway.

But it was followed by a frustrated kick against a machine. The gods of copy machines were on my side and had chosen this moment to jam it. Then I heard that faint rumble again. The elevator.

Taking a risk, I gambled that I had enough time to get out. Balancing haste and silence as best I could, I opened the main door and slid into the elevator lobby, pausing only long enough to close the door as quietly as I could. In an awkward tiptoe to keep the noise down, I hurried past the elevators to the stairs. I was just closing the door when I heard the whoosh of the elevator doors opening.

Two people arriving on this floor at this time of night? Too suspicious. Tempted as I was to crack the door, it was too risky. Whoever got off strode quickly to the office door. He—I was guessing it was he—made no attempt at quiet, jangling the keys as he shoved one into the lock.

I heard the door open and from inside a voice said, "Hey, we've got a problem. I think she moved the files."

Had I not put everything back correctly?

No time to ponder. I put my hip on the banister and slid down, skating around on the landing to do it again on the next set of stairs. And the next. Much as I wanted to run, I couldn't risk the tramp of feet on the stairs.

At the third floor, I cut across the bridge to the garage. I'd parked on the street, but I didn't want to be in that empty building with two possible killers. With Cordelia across the road, I had a good reason to be here in the garage, but not in the office building.

I scanned the floor, but they wouldn't park here. With its bridges to the office building and the hospital, this was the busiest floor. I ran up one flight of stairs and scanned the next floor. They probably parked at the top, so I ran up several flights, but police tape blocked the door, so I went down one.

There they were; the black SUV and the red sports car. They could be back at any time and they were guaranteed to come here. I couldn't see the license plates from where I was and I was loath to walk far enough away from the stairs to get to where I could see them. From this perch I could hear the rumble of the elevators next to the stairs or any footsteps. To get close enough to see the license plates would take me too far to hear them coming. I could at least get the make and model. A Cadillac Escapade and a Porsche Boxster. Not Bentleys, but not cheap cars either.

That was all I could do. I needed to get out of here. I again took the stairs, now breathing hard, but I didn't want to slow down. I'd be safe—or as safe as I was going to be only when I was out of this building, away from the possibility they might spot me.

When I got to the bottom floor of the garage, I took off the white coat before I left the stairwell. The white would only make it easier to spot me in the dark. I walked briskly away from the lights of the hospital, breaking into a trot in the darker spots.

My car was where I had left it all those hours ago, as if nothing had happened. I jumped in, immediately started the motor, and only managed to put on my seat belt at the first red light.

CHAPTER TWENTY-EIGHT

It was just as well Cordelia wasn't here. I slept with my gun on the nightstand. The safety was on in deference to cats who liked to knock things over, but that was my only prudent concession.

I slept little, every noise waking me. I wondered if I could make it through until Monday—and if I did, what help could Joanne actually give?

I had to tell Cordelia what was going on. I didn't think I could fake it through another day. The forgery of her signature meant that she was involved. Her knowledge of both that particular office and the medical field might be useful. If she was doing okay. I gave myself that little wiggle room.

This time I couldn't even make myself eat a decent breakfast. It was two cups of coffee and a granola bar that felt like chewing cardboard. If this was what emotions could do to you, I could understand how adding toxic chemicals would completely ruin any desire for food.

I barely remembered to take her old clothes out of the car and bring clean ones for her to wear.

It was a bright and sunny day, and that at least helped dispel the demons of the night. I was again at the hospital. Again forced to park in the garage that I never wanted to see again. But if I was picking up Cordelia, I could wheel her across the walkway from the hospital to the car, and that seemed the only practical way to do it.

When I got to her room, she was sitting on the side of the bed, talking to her doctor.

"My chariot out of here," she said, seeing me.

"Great, all the paperwork is signed. We've rescheduled you for Tuesday, to give you an extra day to rest. Remember to eat as often as you can, small meals four to five times a day, protein drinks to supplement."

The doctor left. I helped Cordelia change, mostly handing her things and the ever-challenging bra fastening. Halfway through, an administrative person arrived and had her fill out a sheaf of paperwork. She was decent, just lacking socks and shoes. By the time she was fully dressed and we had gathered up her things, including the half chocolate bar still left, an orderly with a wheelchair arrived. Cordelia started to protest she could walk, but recognized he was just doing his job and it would be easier to let him do it.

I got to carry the flowers and the chocolate.

After the logistics of getting her into the car and us out on the street she said, "I really am okay. It was about the best case it could be, not anemia, but I wasn't eating enough and was pushing too hard."

"Yeah, I know, I'm glad to hear that."

"Are the cats okay?"

"The cats? Yes, they're fine. Upset that they haven't been able to play us against one another for treats."

She was quiet for a moment. "What's going on? You seem distant. Is it Alex and Joanne?"

"No. Or not that I know of. Joanne is in Baton Rouge this weekend."

"With Alex?"

I had to admit, "I'm not sure. I assume so. We only had time for a brief conversation."

Again she was silent, as if hoping I would say more. When I didn't, she asked, "What is it you're not telling me? I know about Lydia."

"You do? How?"

"So you did know." Again a pause I didn't fill. "Ron came by last night, not long after you left, and he told me. Said the police thought it was some stupid, random robbery."

Interesting that Ron was also in the area. "Let's get home. This isn't about us, or our friends. It's a case I've been working on and it's gotten very complicated."

She sighed, but didn't ask again.

Thankfully for us both, New Orleans is not a spread-out city and the drive was only another fifteen minutes of silence or comments about the weather.

Once we were inside I asked, "Are you hungry?"

"Avoiding the conversation?" she said, but with a hint of a smile.

"No, just following doctor's orders."

"Tell me what's going on. I'll eat after."

I started at the beginning, Mr. Charles Williams, then the McConkles and their questions about Nature's Beautiful Gift. She listened carefully, occasionally asking questions, but mostly letting me talk. I ended with, "I don't think Lydia's death was a random robbery. She was shot execution style, close range at the base of the skull."

Cordelia said, "You think someone where I work is committing major insurance fraud? And that they would kill to cover it up?"

"I think it's enough of a possibility that I can't rule it out."

"So what do we do now?"

"I'll talk to Joanne tomorrow. We'll figure it out from there. Today, we stay in and I pamper you."

She smiled the smile that broke my heart. "Oh, Micky, you need to be safe. I can't lose you now." She reached out and touched my cheek, then as if that wasn't enough, wrapped her arms around me. She took me by the hand to the bedroom asking, "Slow and gentle?"

"Yes," I agreed though I was scared to touch her, worried how fragile she had become. But she took my hands, leading them where she wanted to go. "I can't lose this," she murmured in my ear.

No, we can't let go of this, I thought as I stroked her face, running my fingers down her neck to her breast. *I could lose her, could never have a moment like this again.* A searing thought.

We made love as if clocks didn't exist and time would never catch us. First, slow, lingering, stroking everywhere, then again, with passion, a frenzy of touch as if it could last a life time. And when we were done, we lay in each other's arms, knowing how precious and fragile this moment was.

My exhaustion from the last few days caught up with me and I fell asleep. I vaguely remembered Cordelia murmuring, "Get some rest," and easing out of bed.

I knew time had passed by the changed light.

"Honey, wake up," Cordelia was saying. "Someone named Rafe says he needs to speak to you."

"What?" I mumbled, then managed to sit up. "What's he doing calling here?"

"He called on your cell," she said. "It rang several times, so I finally answered it."

"Tell him I'll call him back in five minutes," I said as I swung out of bed. Talking to Rafe with a sleep-fogged brain was not a good option.

Splashing water on my face helped to revive me. I looked at my watch. Morning had slid into midafternoon.

When I rejoined Cordelia, I asked, "Have you eaten?"

"I finished the chocolate bar. Does that count?"

"No."

"Aren't you going to call your friend?" she asked.

"He's not a friend, he's another private investigator from Dallas," I said. Once I called him, I'd be back in the middle of this mess, trying to explain to another skeptical man why the muddle with the insurance could be linked to Grant Walters and The Cure. What was it based on really? A red car and a black truck? "Taking care of you is more important. You need to eat and I'm hungry."

"Taking care of me is fine. Using me as an excuse to avoid something, not so fine."

Ouch. "Okay, I'll call him. Your job is to decide what you want for lunch."

I picked up my cell phone and went to the bedroom, the better to blow him off.

"I'm back in town," he answered—caller ID. "We need to meet."

"How about tomorrow?"

"How about right now?"

"How about I'm home and about to eat lunch?" I countered.

"I'll bring pizza."

"No." I wasn't sure Cordelia could handle the smell of grease. "I'm not in the mood for pizza," I covered. "How about a couple of hours?"

"I know it's a cliché, but now or never. We got intel that indicates he'll be doing something big today or tomorrow."

"Bad timing for you to be out of town," I said.

"Was out of town to get this info."

"How'd you get it?"

"Don't ask and I won't tell."

Illegal wire tapping was my guess. "Can you give me an hour and can we meet at my office?"

"You that bad a housekeeper?"

"No, my partner is here"—Cordelia entered the room—"and I'd prefer to keep work separate from my home life."

"It's okay if they come here," she said. "I can't stay hidden forever."

I nodded as if agreeing with her.

"I can be a polite Southern gentleman," Rafe said. "We're right out front."

"You're pushy," I said as I got up and went to the front room. His dark blue SUV, the banged-up silver car, and a sedate sedan that said "I live in the suburbs and have two kids" were all out front.

My other cell phone rang. The pink one.

"Oh, fuck," I said. "He's calling Debbie." I hung up on Rafe.

Cordelia had joined me in the living room, curious and puzzled about this part of my life, a place she rarely saw.

I picked up the pink phone and put my finger to my lip, indicating she needed to be quiet.

Of course it wasn't him calling. It was the same woman, vaguely polite, relentlessly professional. "Shipments have been slow, sorry it took so long," she said in a voice that had no sorry in it. "You and your sister need to come in tonight. At nine p.m. at the same address." She rattled it off.

I had barely enough time to say, "Okay, we'll be there," before she hung up.

Of course, we wouldn't be there. There was no "we." Joanne was out of town, so not a possibility. I couldn't pass Danny off as my sister—plus she was a lawyer, not a cop or PI, and it was too risky for anyone without training. Maybe Rafe had come up with a solution.

He was on my porch, knocking on the door.

Cordelia looked at me and I gave her an exasperated nod. She opened the door.

Rafe brought Joe and Gem, plus another man and an older woman.

I told him, "If we put you in drag, you could be my sister."

He ignored my comment. "You remember Gem and Joe, right? This is Steve and Madeline."

"This is Cordelia," I said. I could be polite back.

"Come in," my partner said, shaking everyone's hand. Even the cats were friendly. No one was on my side. We arranged ourselves in our living room. I pulled a couple of chairs out of the kitchen.

"So, shall we order those pizzas? Or would you prefer something organic?" Rafe asked.

I tried to look at Cordelia without being obvious.

"Maybe we should—" I started.

At the same time, she said, "Go ahead. If I get nauseous, I can go to a different room."

Rafe looked at her. "Are you not feeling well?" he asked.

Does it show? I wondered. I glanced at her, trying to see her as a stranger would. Shallow skin, some of it loose, the dark circles under her eyes, her hair lank and thin, the lost patches making it look like she'd had a haircut from a psychopath.

Anyone who was a trained observer would know she wasn't well. I didn't want them staring at her, judging her.

But she was willing to face them. "I'm undergoing chemo," she stated simply. "Sometimes certain foods don't agree with me."

Rafe shot me a look.

"No," I said. "Just no."

He nodded and backed off. "Seven people, how many pizzas?"

They settled on three, one cheese, one veggie, and one with meat. Gem was relegated to the logistics.

"What's your info?" I asked.

"Maddeningly vague," he admitted. "'We do it tomorrow.' But it was late last night, so tomorrow as tomorrow or tomorrow as today? And 'it' is just about as vague as you can get."

"Best guess?" I asked.

"His pattern is to set up several enterprises and suck in as much money as he can. When it gets to the point that he needs to put some money out, he disappears, leaving his confederates paying the bills, at best."

"What's at worst?"

"Some have disappeared. On an island somewhere or at the

bottom of the sea is anyone's guess. A few witnesses had unfortunate accidents."

"Like a robbery gone wrong?" I asked.

He looked at me. "Why do you ask?"

I took a breath and said, "I think I have two cases colliding. One started out to find two medical patients who got lost in the system."

"As a favor to me," Cordelia interjected.

"One of them claimed she hadn't been seen recently—but her records indicted she had. The second...wasn't doing so well. When I knocked on his door, he was in bad shape and didn't live. He had bottles of both NBG and The Cure. A second client was worried that a relative was being taken advantage of by the NBG salesman and wanted me to get info to disprove it. Which is how we met"—with a nod at Rafe—"at the sales meeting.

"One of the cars at the place in the east—the dark SUV. I saw a similar vehicle very close to when Lydia was killed and again when I borrowed"—here an apologetic look at Cordelia—"a set of keys to check out the files. There was a red car, too, but it wasn't the same as the one in the east." I had to backtrack and explain Lydia—who she was and why she was killed.

"Who did you borrow the key from?" Cordelia asked, knowing the answer. She crossed her arms.

"Someone I hope will forgive me for my transgressions," I said. "We know Walters is involved with The Cure—he met Debbie there. He's involved with NBG. I had assumed that the second patient, the one who died, had just stumbled over The Cure. But what if he hadn't? What if whoever is committing the fraud is also steering patients there as well?"

"That's monstrous," Cordelia said. "No one in health care should do anything like that. No one...that..."

No one that I know and work with, I silently finished for her.

Rafe looked at the two of us.

I explained, "Cordelia is a doctor and was taken on by this group on a temporary basis to cover for someone on maternity leave."

"Medical providers aren't any more perfect than anyone else; they might justify insurance fraud as not really stealing, just working a dysfunctional system," Cordelia said. "But knowingly sending people to a sham cure? That could kill someone."

Indeed, it had. I didn't remind her of Reginald Banks. "It might not be a doctor. It could be anyone with enough cunning and willingness to take the risks," I said.

"Grant Walters is good at exploiting people," Rafe said. "Good at making them think what they're doing isn't so bad, or that they won't get caught."

"What do you know about Grant? Who does he know? How can he be connected? How long has he been here?"

The older woman opened a large satchel and took out a folder. She handed it to Rafe.

He opened the file. "Let's see, he moved here about a year ago, from the L.A. area where he was hunkering down after his games in Dallas. We lost him for a while; he seemed to move around a lot until he came here."

"How'd he get involved with NBG?" I asked.

"Legit, as far as we can tell," Rafe answered. "Applied for a franchise and was awarded this area."

Joe added, "As legit as he could be. We assume that he faked his background and references."

"He plunked a chunk of money on the bank when he came here," Rafe said. "A couple of hundred thousand. Plus buying his house in cash."

"Where's he live?" I asked.

Rafe read off an address. I couldn't place it, but it sounded familiar.

I jumped up, went to Cordelia's home office, and grabbed her laptop, turning it on as I walked back into the room.

The pizzas arrived as I was waiting for it to boot up. Cordelia did hostess duties, finding plates and napkins.

Grant lived out in Old Metairie, on a very well-to-do street. Right next door to Dudley Etherton Senior.

"Fuck!" I said so loudly everyone stopped eating to look at me.

Prejean had claimed that he hadn't sent Dudley after me. But he was such a slimeball I didn't believe him. Dudley had never gotten close enough to explain exactly which case he wanted me off. I had jumped to the conclusion it had to be related to Prejean. But Walters might have worried that a private eye looking into things could stumble over the fraud. Exactly as I had.

Everyone was looking at me, so I explained. Grant could have hired Dudley to go after me by chatting over the backyard fence.

"Holy fuckballs," Gem summed up for all of us.

"But that doesn't connect him to our practice," Cordelia pointed out.

"There is a connection," I said. "We just don't know who yet. Lydia got too close. That's why they killed her."

"Once we get Walters, that'll be uncovered. The big question is, does he know that Micky Knight is Debbie Perkins?" Rafe asked. He put down his plate to take the computer from me and look at the map himself.

"It's possible," I conceded. "All he had to do was look up my name and find a picture to go with it."

"But he shouldn't know much about you," Cordelia interjected. "I mean, I don't know that I referred to you as anything other than my partner Micky. We didn't officially hire you; there is no paperwork, they only contacted you through me."

"He knew enough to sic Dudley on me," I said.

"But he probably hasn't considered that a tough lesbian PI could also be pretty-in-pink Deborah Perkins. If he knew you were Debbie, he wouldn't be playing with you like he is," Rafe said. He handed back the laptop to me, then took a big bite of pizza as if that could help him think.

"Yeah, you'd be dead," Joe added, not even putting his slice down to say it.

Cordelia looked disconcerted. She put her pizza down. She had taken a small plain slice, but only managed a few bites.

"He tried with Dudley and didn't succeed," I said.

"Bet it never occurred to him that two private dicks could be on his tail," Rafe surmised. "He copped to me, but I'd bet my last beer that he didn't spot you. Plus he probably never figured that you might have a whole other case that could cross paths with him."

"Jeez, this is confusing," Gem said.

"Eyes on the prize," Rafe cut in. "If he's on to you, it's way risky tonight. If he's not, we can proceed as before."

"How?" I asked. "We're still minus a sister with cancer."

"That could be me," Cordelia said.

"No, absolutely not," I rejoined. *Damn*, I cursed myself, *I should have picked another disease.* I had conveniently used Cordelia, never expecting that my lie might turn into the truth.

"All I need to do is be who I am—a woman with cancer," she replied.

"No, you need to be someone who is trained in law enforcement and security. These men have proven themselves to be killers. It's too risky," I argued.

"Can we talk privately?" she asked me.

I nodded agreement and followed her back to the bedroom. She took her plate with her, leaving it by the sink, a clear indication that she wasn't going to eat any more.

The second the door closed, I said, "Look, Cordelia, we're trying to catch someone who will do anything not to be caught. We don't know for sure that he hasn't figured out that Debbie and her sister don't exist. This could be very risky."

"So you should go instead of me?"

"I carry a gun and I'm trained in how to use it. I'm also a brown belt in karate. And I've been in situations like this before."

She looked away, then down, finally said, "If something happens, it would be better if it happened to be me. You're healthy, you have—"

"No!" I cut in. "If...I have to, maybe I can bear it—eventually—if it's the brutal randomness of fate. But if you're hurt—or killed—because I got you involved, I'll never be able to live with that."

She put her arms around me. "I'm not going to work as a doctor... at least for a while. And...maybe never again. This might be my one last chance to save a few more lives. If I've got to have this ugly disease, please let me at least use it to save others."

"I can't; I'm too scared for you."

"Please," she whispered in my ear. "I need this. I need to be as alive and useful as I can be."

The die had been cast. She could do this despite me. Rafe would welcome her and nothing I could say would stop them. I desperately wanted to keep her safe, as if protecting her now could save her later.

"If you get killed, I'll never forgive you," I said, trying to hide the catch in my voice, trying to make this as okay as I could, a joke instead of a sob.

Her arms tightened around me. "I'll be okay," she murmured in my ear. "We'll catch some bad guys together."

"Would you carry a gun?" I asked.

"Micky, I don't know how to use one."

"You point it at the bad guys and pull the trigger."

"Plus they'd probably notice. I'll carry a purse with a nail file."

I kissed her hard, my arms tightly around her.

I abruptly let her go. "Let's do this." I couldn't think about everything that could go wrong. I couldn't think about that even if everything went right, she still might be gone.

She seemed to understand, squeezing my hand. "Yeah, let's do this."

We rejoined the others. They looked at us expectantly.

"So, do you think we can pass as sisters?" I said.

Rafe openly smiled.

Madeline, the older woman, spoke first. "Yes. You have an ease and intimacy with each other. It's noticeable when it's not there. You clearly know each other and have known each other for a while. Like sisters."

Rafe added, "Plus you're both tall, both have dark hair. The rest can be called genetic differences."

"AKA the milkman," Gem added.

Then it was just waiting until it was time to go.

Chapter Twenty-nine

Cordelia chose to rest, taking a nap. Rafe, his team and I went over the logistics. I would be Debbie and wear the watch wire—it might be suspicious if we both showed up with the same watch, and evidently they didn't make ladies' watches with wires in them in multiple styles.

I would also carry a gun. It would be night. The day was cloudy sliding into rain, perfect jacket weather. They hadn't patted me down before; I would have to hope they wouldn't this time. If they did, it might be a sign that they were on to me. I insisted if that seemed to be the case, we were out of there. We'd walk away if we could—if not, Rafe and his team would descend. They'd be listening to every word.

While Cordelia slept, I did a quick run to my office to get the watch and Debbie's wardrobe. It would have to be the rhinestone jeans yet again. With that, the pink T-shirt and a black jean jacket that was more my wardrobe than Debbie's.

Our goal was to see enough that we could bring in the cops. Cordelia, as a doctor, would be a credible witness that they were engaging in medical fraud. I told myself, *All she has to do is have them hand her The Cure. That ties them to medical fraud, including fraud that might have caused Reginald Banks to die.* If we could tie that to someone at her practice sending people there, that could be probable cause for searching the records, reopening Lydia's murder as something other than a robbery, and all the pieces would fall prettily into place.

If everything went well.

When Cordelia woke up, we had to choose her clothing. Lucky

for her, she had a more professionally female wardrobe than I did. She found a well-worn pair of gray slacks that were showing their age. I vetoed a blue shirt—it could bring out her blue eyes and we were supposed to be sisters. Instead she found an old elephant green one and a brown cardigan the cats loved to curl up in. As a final touch, she tied a dark green kerchief around her head to hide the chemo hair. It just missed matching her shirt, like she had tried to pair them, but didn't have the money or the fashion sense to pull it off.

Madeline left first, in the sedate sedan. She would be the least suspicious and could watch who entered the building. She would report back to Rafe.

He was smart, I had to admit. Older women can be invisible. Alpha males like Grant Walters often overlook those they have dismissed as being weaker and not worthy opponents. Like women—especially older women. Or sick women. He had treated Debbie as if he had nothing to fear from her—of course, I had played her that way.

Rafe, Joe, and Steve left. They would pick up another car so they could split up, with Steve in one car and Rafe and Joe in the SUV with the monitoring equipment. We decided that if they needed to talk to me, they'd call my cell phone—it might be safer than giving me the kind of equipment that Debbie would be unlikely to have. With the wire on, they'd hear everything I said.

Gem stayed behind in case we needed any help with the wires. I got the watch and Cordelia had a camera hidden in a big, frumpy brown bag that they provided for her. It had a hidden compartment. The camera eye was where the strap joined the purse, so she had to try to remember to keep that side facing front.

Then it was show time.

Gem left before us, saying we should give her about five minutes to get away.

I looked at Cordelia, desperately wanting to say, *No, we can't do this, let's call it off now.*

But she smiled at me. "Maybe this can be a new career for me." She looked at herself in the mirror, the frumpy clothes, the cheap (looking—I'm sure the camera rig cost a pretty penny) plastic bag. At a first glance I might not have recognized her. Seeing the look on my face, she said, "It'll be okay. At the moment, I'm not a sick person, and that means a lot to me."

I could only nod. I leaned down to pet Rook, the closest cat, took her hand, and headed for the door.

We took my car, since they might have seen me as Debbie in it.

The rain had started, a steady drizzle that slicked the streets and bent the lights into fractured diamonds.

If Cordelia was scared or nervous, she didn't show it. Perhaps she felt she couldn't, that I would take it as a sign not to do this.

Or maybe she meant what she said—for the moment she wasn't a sick person, and the chance to escape that small world was worth the risk.

We said little, mostly my mutterings about the traffic, but this late on a Sunday evening, it was fairly light.

Once we left the interstate, there were few cars. Those few dwindled until ours were the only headlights as we got closer.

"They picked the middle of nowhere, didn't they?" she commented.

"This used to be a busy commercial area. Maybe someday it will come back," I said. But now it was desolate, few lights shining, no traffic. All the better to conduct an illegal operation with no one around to see you.

I had deliberately taken an earlier exit from the freeway. I wanted to come from the back of the building, to get one last chance to scope it out.

"There it is, that big monolith ahead," I said.

"It looks dark. Maybe they're not here."

But then I saw a glow from the far third floor. They had the windows covered, so little light slipped out, to make the building seem empty and unoccupied. I pointed it out to her.

"They're making cancer patients walk to the third floor?"

"They're not nice people."

As I turned onto the street that ran in front of it, I scanned the area for Rafe. Jen's silver sedan was visible pulled into a driveway a block away. I couldn't see the others. Nor could I do more than a quick scan. Debbie wouldn't case the neighborhood. I'd have to trust that they were there.

I pulled in front and parked. It was 8:55. My cell phone rang. Unknown number. I answered it with a cautious "Hello?"

"Rafe. Just checking in. We're all in place. Maddie saw three cars arrive, a big black SUV, a red sports car, and a small truck. Plus one small sedan was here. We think there are probably about four people in there. One of the plates matches Grant's car, so be careful. Test your wire now."

"Beautiful night for a drive," I said, resisting the urge to talk to my watch.

"Perfect. You're loud and clear and we have a great shot of your glove compartment." He added, "Good luck. See you on the other side."

I put my phone away. I pulled Cordelia to me—I couldn't kiss her; we were sisters—and silently held her for a second. Everything we did now would be watched and heard.

"Let's roll," she said quietly.

We got out of the car. I hadn't brought an umbrella, so we had to ignore the rain. I led the way to the opening in the chain link fence, then took her elbow to guide her over the weed-strewn asphalt to the building, the wet slickness making it even more treacherous. I wanted to take off my jacket and hold it over her, but couldn't because of the gun.

We stood for a moment under the portico, shaking the water off and letting out eyes adjust.

As before, the door outline was almost invisible in the dark. I felt against the wall until my hand bumped against the frame. I hesitated for a second. This was the last moment to turn back. Then I knocked.

The door was thrust open, the light blinding.

"Hey, Debbie, I didn't expect to see you here," a male voice said.

I squinted at the light, searching my brain for the voice.

Vincent.

Grant Walters had sucked him into the criminal side. I wondered if he even knew.

"Hi, I didn't expect to see you here, either," I managed to get out. *Keep up the façade.* "This is my sister, CJ. I'm here with her. I mean Donna, that's her given name. CJ is just a nickname," I covered. The fourth nickname, the one I forgot to mention.

We came in from the rain. The lights were harsh fluorescents, hidden from the outside by windows covered with boards.

"Hi, CJ, pleased to meet you," he said, sticking out a hand.

Cordelia gave him a weak smile and gingerly put out her hand as if she was weak and movement was hard.

At least I hoped she was pretending. No, I reminded myself, she hadn't been like this walking here from the car.

"What are you doing here?" I asked him.

"Mr. Walters asked me to help. I was so excited to hear about this project." Vincent's puppy-dog eyes sparked.

"But why? This is…kind of irregular," I said.

"You're here, right? Because it's so important that we help people."

"Vinnie? Who are you talking to?" A woman entered through a door behind Vincent.

"This is Debbie and her sister, CJ. They're here for the nine p.m. appointment."

The woman gave us a quick once-over. She was probably in her late thirties or early forties. The lines had settled in her face from long-ago days in the sun, her hair streaked blond as if she missed those days. She seemed neither happy nor sad to be here, none of the excitement for working for a cause like Vincent. If anything, a weary resignation that this was where life had brought her. Her voice sounded vaguely like the woman who had called to set up this appointment. Walters would want to keep his operation lean.

"What's your diagnosis?" she demanded of Cordelia.

"Aggressive NHL, non-Hodgkin's lymphoma, stage three, involvement of lymph nodes in the neck and groin."

You're not a doctor, I said silently, *but a patient*. She didn't go on.

"Take off your head scarf," the woman ordered.

Tentatively, as if embarrassed, Cordelia removed it, bending slightly so the woman could clearly see her ragged, patchy hair.

"How are they treating you?" the woman asked.

Cordelia put her scarf back on before answering, "CHOP."

"Which is?"

"Some chemotherapy drugs: cyclophosphamide, hydroxydauno-rubicin, Oncovin, and prednisone." She caught herself and added, "I was stuck waiting for a long time, so I occupied myself with learning the names."

I let out the breath I was holding.

The woman's face was blank. She didn't have a clue what Cordelia was talking about.

But that seemed to do the trick. Cordelia had used enough medical jargon—plus the hair loss and sallow skin—to pass whatever test they used.

"Come with me," the woman said. I started to follow and she said, "Just her, not you."

"Why can't I come with her?" I asked, trying to keep the demand out of my voice.

"It's the way we do things. She comes alone or you leave together."

"It won't take long," Cordelia said, managing a wan smile for me.

"But I promised I would be with her the entire time," I said. I couldn't let her go off without me. And my gun and my wire.

"She has to come alone. We never allow family," the woman replied.

"It won't be too long," Vincent added. "I'll keep you company."

"I'll be okay," Cordelia said.

There was nothing I could do except watch as she trailed behind the woman.

The door thudded shut.

"It's good to see you again," Vincent said.

Shut the fuck up, I thought. I managed to say, "What happens now? Where are you taking C.J.?"

"She'll be checked out."

"Checked out by whom?"

"We have a doctor who works with us. Guess he wants to really save lives as well. He's a really nice guy."

"So, is that why this is important to you?"

"Government runs health care for a small bunch of people; the big drug companies, that sort of stuff. They know there are cures out there, but they don't want anyone else to know about them. But it's important to get those cures to the people."

"You're here to help people?" I prompted.

Vincent needed little encouragement. He was happy to talk about his latest fixation. "Yes, I was thrilled when Mr. Walters told me about this, that we could do more than just help with the little trickle they allow from places like Nature's Beautiful Gift. This is real, makes a real difference."

"How do you know it works?"

"Of course it works. The doctor explained it to me, but he used a bunch of technical terms and I didn't really understand."

"What kind of doctor is he?" I asked.

"Someone who truly wants to help people, not just make money. Hell, he could lose his license for doing this. He says it works and I trust him. Plus one of my friends used it. He wasn't doing so well, and he talked to me and it turned out his doctor is our doctor, so he got on it and the last I talked to him he said it made him feel great."

"What was wrong with him?" I didn't think I was going to like the answer.

"Sickle-cell anemia. It's a bitch—I mean, not nice—disease. We used to hang out all the time until he got too sick. Two days after he stared on The Cure, we met for a drink and he told me how much energy he had."

"How long ago was that?"

"About…a couple of months ago."

"How's he doing now?"

"Now? Fine, I guess."

"You haven't talked to him lately?"

"Nah, I figured old Reg was busy, probably had a new girlfriend."

"Can you do me a big favor? Can you call him and see how he's doing? I really want to be able to tell my sister how great this stuff is. He can say he's been on it for a few months and it's going great. It was hard to scrape together the money."

He glanced at his watch. It was about 9:15. "Um, sure. I'll do that right now."

I wondered what he would do when he discovered that no one answered.

Vincent moved to the far side of the room to make his call. As he started to dial, I pulled out my cell phone. I called the McConkles. I turned from Vincent, hoping that between his call and keeping my voice quiet, he wouldn't catch what I was doing.

Donna answered.

"Hi, sorry to bother you so late," I said, hoping I wouldn't have to identify myself. "I've stumbled over something and might have news for you soon. But that house you worked on? The one out in Old Metairie? What's the owner's name?"

On the far side of the room, I heard Vincent leaving a message, asking his friend to call him back as soon as possible.

"Just a sec," Donna said. I heard her calling to Fletcher, asking him my question.

She came back on the line. "Brandon Kellogg."

"Thanks." I hung up.

Brandon lived just across the street from Grant Walters. Fletcher had mentioned him owning lots of sports cars. Red, like the ones I had seen. He would know Cordelia was not a desperate believer in a miracle cure.

"I couldn't get hold of him," Vincent said.

I had to get to her.

"You won't. Reginald Banks is dead."

"What? What are you talking about?"

I might be able to convince him that he was being used, on the side of the killers, not the savers, but could see no way to do it quickly enough to save Cordelia. I had been so right when I'd tagged Vincent as collateral damage.

I kicked him as hard as I could in the balls.

He went down, surprise and pain mixed on his face.

"You are involved with criminals who kill people," I told him. Into my watch, I screamed, "Get in here now! The doctor knows who Cordelia is!"

I couldn't wait for Rafe. Rushing past the moaning Vincent, I shoved through the inner door and sprinted up the stairs. This was a large building and I had less than no time. The split second he laid eyes on her, Brandon would recognize Cordelia and know that Lydia's death hadn't diverted me from the case. They had killed Lydia, they would kill her.

The glowing light on the third floor. If that wasn't where they were, Cordelia was dead.

Second floor.

Third floor. As I shoved open the door on the landing, I pulled out my gun. The hall was dark, but at the far end, a dim light seeped under the door.

If I was lucky, Vincent didn't have a way to contact them and they wouldn't know I was almost outside their door. But I had little time to be quiet. I raced down the hallway, hoping that the rubber soles of my shoes would mask the sound.

Just as I got to the door it opened.

"Vincent, what's—" the woman started. "You! You can't be here."

I grabbed her by the shoulders and spun her out of the door, shoving her down the hallway. "The police are on their way. Get out," I told her.

I didn't look to see if she was leaving or not. She had been in a small reception area. Behind it were several other closed doors. "Third floor, lighted office," I said, holding my watch close enough that they had to hear. Rafe and his team couldn't waste time searching the building.

It had windows to the outside. I dashed for the door closest to the back and nearest the outer wall.

I thrust open the door to a scene of horror, a room with only one light, focused on a heavy wooden chair in the center.

Grant Walters had Cordelia pinned in that chair, his knee against her chest, his hands wrapped around her wrists.

Brandon Kellogg had put an IV into the vein on the back of her hand and was about to attach it to a vial of fluid.

He was saying, "You're going to die anyway. This will be easier."

I couldn't shoot; they were too close together.

Cordelia saw me first. She quickly looked away and started to struggle, to distract them.

"No!" I screamed, launching myself. I used my body as a weapon, flinging my torso at them, striking Grant's chin with the butt of my gun as I tackled him, pushing him off Cordelia and onto Brandon.

"What the fuck?" he yelled as he went down.

"You said you came alone," Brandon yelled over him. "What's she doing here?" Then as if remembering his partner in crime, he shouted, "It's the PI, the one I warned you about."

I was a fury, heedless of any pain or danger. I backhanded Brandon in the nose, then turned to Cordelia and ripped the IV out of her hand.

Brandon fell back, making a whimpering sound.

"Look out!" she screamed.

Grant was behind me, grabbing my arm, going for the gun. I dug the fingernails of my free arm into his hand. He howled in pain, but didn't let go.

Suddenly Brandon grabbed my other arm. "What do we do?" he asked. "What do we do now?" His nose was dribbling blood onto his expensive tie.

With Brandon on the other side of me, Grant again went for my gun. To keep it from him, I dropped it, then kicked it away. He couldn't get it, but I couldn't use it either.

Cordelia struggled up, gaining a hold on Brandon, using her weight to pull him away. But she didn't have the strength and stamina for a long fight.

Where the hell were Rafe and his crew?

Maybe they were in this with Grant and I was the only person who could save myself. And Cordelia.

She managed to get Brandon away, freeing one arm. I swung at Grant, but with him holding the one arm from behind, I had to punch him over my shoulder. I couldn't get a good angle and couldn't land a decent blow.

"You fucking bitch," he snarled. "I don't know who you are, but you're dead."

Brandon punched Cordelia, then threw her down. I heard the sound of her hitting the floor, falling away into the shadows.

I kicked at Grant, slamming my heel down on his instep.

To retaliate, he yanked my hair, jerking my head back. I tried to duck away from him, going with the direction of his pull, then twisting away. But he was expecting it and moved with me. Then he kicked me hard at the back of the knee, forcing me to bend, then sag down on my knees.

I struggled and turned, but he was a strong man and knew what he was doing. He wrapped an arm around my throat in a choke hold. Then he grabbed my wrist and slapped it on the armrest of the chair.

"Put the needle in her arm. We'll do them both," Grant said.

He was making it hard for me to breathe.

Brandon started to get an alcohol swipe.

"Fuck that! Hurry!" Grant barked.

No need to worry about infection if you're about to kill someone.

Brandon did as he was told, ripping a needle out of a pack. Just as he tried to stab me, I jerked my arm.

But it was no more than a pitifully small delay.

"Hold it steady," Brandon said.

Grant shoved down with brutal force, placing his knee in my back so my face as forced into the seat of the chair, my arm bent up at a painful angle. Only then did he let go of my throat, using both hands to hold my arm down.

"I'm sorry," Brandon said. "But this will be easier. You won't feel the pain as you die."

"I'm not about to die, you're murdering me," I growled at him.

He hesitated.

"Do it!" Grant yelled.

I felt a prick at the back of my hand.

Then a huge roar, as if the world was drowned out.

"What the hell!" Grant bellowed.

Something liquid dripped onto my arm.

Blood.

Brandon stumbled backward, his chest an oozing red mess.

I rolled away from Grant, turning the chair over. He tried to hold on, but I spun around just enough to grab him between the legs. I gripped tightly and twisted as hard as I could, yanking down as I turned my hand.

His yowl of pain was satisfying.

I rolled away from under him, kicking at his legs as I regained mine. He thudded heavily to the floor, still moaning in pain.

I jerked the needle out of my arm and plunged it into his, then pulled the clip off the line to the vial. It wasn't likely I'd hit a vein, but that might hold him if he recovered from the ball torture.

I looked around for Rafe. But he wasn't here.

Cordelia, just at the edge of the shadow, stood holding my gun.

She looked at Brandon, then at me, then down at her hand.

I rushed to her, taking the gun. I knew what I was doing; I hoped she wouldn't. I fired, aiming as the side wall. My fingerprints were now on the gun and powder residue on my hands.

As if coming out of a trance, she said, "I have to try to save him." She half walked, half stumbled to him, placing her hands on his chest, trying to stop the blood of the man who had tried to kill us both.

Rafe and his team ran in.

"Holy fuck," he said, on seeing the scene.

"Nothing holy here," I said and went to help Cordelia.

CHAPTER THIRTY

It had been a lifetime and only five minutes.

I got to that room on the third floor only five minutes before Rafe and his team arrived. Vincent had recovered enough to slow them down.

Dudley had been caught in Houston. Once Texas got finished with him, he'd be sent back here.

Fletcher and Donna got the result they wanted. Vincent spent a few days in jail, then got out on parole. They passed on the information from their aunt. He had told her he no longer believed in this stuff, a friend of his had died and he was now with his family's insurance company.

Mr. Charles Williams did indeed make a big pot of gumbo—quite good—and I gave him, his nephew, and the McConkles an edited version of what had happened. A version that had my hand on the gun.

Rafe made his clients in Dallas very happy. They displayed their happiness by paying him very well. A nice chunk trickled down to me. Rafe told me if I ever moved to Texas, I'd have a job. I told him I'd never move to Texas.

Grant Walters was in jail. He was a master at manipulation, looking at everyone he met as to how they could be useful to him. Like his neighbors. He quickly picked Dudley as a rebellious meth head. Brandon was already chiseling a little away on insurance fraud, small enough time that he might have gotten away with it for a very long while. But Grant had talked him into expanding, opening several clinics that existed in name only and ramping up the amount he was taking from the practice. Grant had even talked him into putting up the bulk of the investment for the Nature's Beautiful Gift franchise. Brandon was an amateur. Grant was a pro. Brandon was a busy doctor and didn't keep up with the various ways the insurance fraud was trickling down to his patients. When Cordelia had first suggested asking me to locate the missing patients, he didn't consider the possible consequences of having me around.

He diagnosed disease. I diagnosed crime.

Only after I'd found Reginald, involved the police and medical authorities, he panicked. He immediately called Grant, who arranged for Dudley to shut me down as quickly as possible. He had been lucky—and I had been unlucky—that Dudley was in need of a fix and was quickly on his way to my office.

He was there so soon after I'd found Reginald Banks I didn't consider there could be a link. Instead I assumed Prejean had sent him.

Grant had carefully involved Brandon with Dudley, introducing him at a backyard cookout. At least in Dudley's telling of the tale, Grant had been the leader, with Brandon willingly following along. Poor Dudley was just an addled meth addict trapped in their clutches.

Grant had picked Brandon as the one who would be left behind, with a pile of debt and a pile of bodies that couldn't easily be explained away as a robbery.

But he hadn't gotten away, and the police found everything they needed to tie him to fraud, extortion. And murder.

Brandon Kellogg was dead.

I told Cordelia that he had killed himself and she had nodded agreement. But I could tell she vehemently wished it hadn't been her finger on the trigger.

I was sitting in another dull green room, waiting for her as they did a CT scan to see if the treatment was working this time. She had given up trying to work full-time; now her life was lived in the walls of doctors' offices, medical tests, and drugs that left her exhausted, at times too weak to make it to the bathroom to vomit. She had good days, but they couldn't be counted on to last. The next chemo treatment left her too sick to do much. The nausea wore off only to be replaced with fatigue.

Those five minutes had cost her a lot. She claimed not, but a haunted look had crept into her eyes as if she had seen too much and for too long how brutal the world can be—a place where the only choice is who will die. Maybe it made her want to fight less hard. Or maybe it was just fate and a disease.

Spring, as it often does in New Orleans, had fled, turning to a searing summer.

Maybe it was hard to want to live when the sun burned so brightly.

The first time she went into the hospital, Torbin had come over, didn't even say anything, just held me. Far longer than five minutes.

Alex had come down from Baton Rouge. She and Joanne had officially broken up. Unofficially they were still enmeshed, still owned the house here together, in a limbo of which way to go. On the good days, I hoped they said they had broken up just to ease the expectations and avoid the explanations. On the bad days, it felt like everything was changing and changing more than I could bear.

Danny and Elly insisted on being there when I couldn't be there. Joanne came by when I wasn't there; we passed once in the halls. Alex came by as often as her schedule allowed, at times talking her way around the visiting hours rules when she came in late.

The medical practice had voted to keep Cordelia, but place her on leave. Brandon had been the one who voted against her; with him gone, the tie had been broken. That allowed her to retain her insurance. She had to pay for it, but at their group rate. Abrasive Ron turned out to be her champion. He told me, "I'm not a people person; I'm a lab guy and a numbers guy. But I'm a good doctor. She's a good doctor. It could happen to any of us."

Now she just needed to live.

"Michele Knight?" A nurse beckoned me.

I followed her down a long hallway. They all seemed long; they all seemed some pale shade of blue or green as if color was too much of a taunt to the sick and dying.

She ushered me into a doctor's office.

Cordelia was already there, dressing in the clothes that now hung on her. Her hair was gone, only a few stark white tufts remaining. She had taken to wearing a baseball cap backward like the teenaged boys do, but now she was bareheaded. The people in this building had seen too much to need to avert their eyes.

Jennifer Godwin, her doctor, entered. "Good news or bad news?" she said.

"Start with the bad," Cordelia answered.

"Your cancer is being stubborn. I know the side effects are hell for you. I'd like to try the bone marrow transplant and add that to R-CHOP."

Cordelia looked pensive. "When do you throw in the kitchen sink?" she asked sardonically. "Bone marrow and monoclonal antibodies? Jennifer, I'm tired, I don't know if..." She trailed off as if she no longer had the energy for words.

I took her hand, then knelt in front of her. "You have to. You just have to. Don't leave me, don't give up any chance." Her eyes were still the blue they had been when I first saw her.

A light that had been gone came back into them. Then she smiled at me, as if she suddenly wanted to be in a world where love was possible.

"Okay," she said. "Okay, we try everything."

About the Author

J.M. Redmann is the author of a mystery series featuring New Orleans private detective Michele "Micky" Knight. Her last book, *Water Mark*, won an Over the Rainbow award from the Gay, Lesbian, Bisexual and Transgendered Roundtable of the American Library Association and a ForeWord Gold First Place mystery award and was shortlisted for a Lambda Literary Award. Two of her earlier books, *The Intersection Of Law & Desire* and *Death Of A Daying Man*, have won Lambda Literary Awards; all but her first book have been nominated. *Law & Desire* was an Editor's Choice of the *San Francisco Chronicle* and a recommended holiday book by Maureen Corrigan of NPR's *Fresh Air*. *Law & Desire* and *Lost Daughters* were originally published by W.W. Norton. Redmann was a 2010 recipient of the Alice B. Readers Appreciation Award, gave the keynote address at the Golden Crown Literary Society Conference in 2009, in 2006 was inducted as a Literary Saint into the Saints and Sinners Hall of Fame, and in 2011 was an invited speaker to Vassar's 150th anniversary LGBTQ conference, Smashing History. Her books have been translated into Spanish, German, Dutch, Norwegian, and Hebrew, and one short story even made it into Korean. Her most recent project was co-editing with Greg Herren two anthologies, *Women of the Mean Streets: Lesbian Noir* and *Men of the Mean Streets: Gay Noir*. Redmann lives in an historic neighborhood in New Orleans, at the edge of the area that flooded.

Books Available From Bold Strokes Books

Burgundy Betrayal by Sheri Lewis Wohl. Park Ranger Kara Lynch has no idea she's a witch until dead bodies begin to pile up in her park, forcing her to turn to beautiful and sexy shape-shifter Camille Black Wolf for help in stopping a rogue werewolf. (978-1-60282-654-0)

LoveLife by Rachel Spangler. When Joey Lang unintentionally becomes a client of life coach Elaine Raitt, the relationship becomes complicated as they develop feelings that make them question their purpose in love and life. (978-1-60282-655-7)

The Fling by Rebekah Weatherspoon. When the ultimate fantasy of a one-night stand with her trainer, Oksana Gorinkov, suddenly turns into more, reality show producer Annie Collins opens her life to a new type of love she's never imagined. (978-1-60282-656-4)

Ill Will by J.M. Redmann. New Orleans PI Micky Knight must untangle a twisted web of healthcare fraud that leads to murder—and puts those closest to her most at risk. (978-1-60282-657-1)

Buccaneer Island by J.P. Beausejour. In the rough world of Caribbean piracy, a man is what he makes of himself—or what a stronger man makes of him. (978-1-60282-658-8)

Twelve O'Clock Tales by Felice Picano. The fourth collection of short fiction by legendary novelist and memoirist Felice Picano. Thirteen dark tales that will thrill and disturb, discomfort and titillate, enthrall and leave you wondering. (978-1-60282-659-5)

Words to Die By by William Holden. Sixteen answers to the question: What causes a mind to curdle? (978-1-60282-653-3)

Tyger, Tyger, Burning Bright by Justine Saracen. Love does not conquer all, but when all of Europe is on fire, it's better than going to hell alone. (978-1-60282-652-6)

Night Hunt by L.L. Raand. When dormant powers ignite, the wolf Were pack is thrown into violent upheaval, and Sylvan's pregnant mate is at the center of the turmoil. A Midnight Hunters novel. (978-1-60282-647-2)

Demons are Forever by Kim Baldwin and Xenia Alexiou. Elite Operative Landis "Chase" Coolidge enlists the help of high-class call girl Heather Snyder to track down a kidnapped colleague embroiled in a global black market organ-harvesting ring. (978-1-60282-648-9)

Runaway by Anne Laughlin. When Jan Roberts is hired to find a teenager who has run away to live with a group of antigovernment survivalists, she's forced to return to the life she escaped when she was a teenager herself. (978-1-60282-649-6)

Street Dreams by Tama Wise. Tyson Rua has more than his fair share of problems growing up in New Zealand—he's gay, he's falling in love, and he's run afoul of the local hip-hop crew leader just as he's trying to make it as a graffiti artist. (978-1-60282-650-2)

Women of the Dark Streets: Lesbian Paranormal by Radclyffe and Stacia Seaman, eds. Erotic tales of the supernatural—a world of vampires, werewolves, witches, ghosts, and demons—by the authors of Bold Strokes Books. (978-1-60282-651-9)

Derrick Steele: Private Dick—The Case of the Hollywood Hustlers by Zavo. Derrick Steele, a hard-drinking, lusty private detective, is being framed for the murder of a hustler in downtown Los Angeles. When his brother's friend Daniel McAllister joins the investigation, their growing attraction might prove to be more explosive than the case. (978-1-60282-596-3)

Nice Butt: Gay Anal Eroticism edited by Shane Allison. From toys to teasing, spanking to sporting, some of the best gay erotic scribes celebrate the hottest and most creative in new erotica. (978-1-60282-635-9)

Murder in the Irish Channel by Greg Herren. Chanse MacLeod investigates the disappearance of a female activist fighting the Archdiocese of New Orleans and a powerful real estate syndicate. (978-1-60282-584-0)